NEVER-ENDING TALES

Never-Ending Tales

STORIES FROM THE GOLDEN AGE OF JEWISH LITERATURE

EDITED BY JACK ZIPES

PRINCETON UNIVERSITY PRESS
PRINCETON & OXFORD

Published by Princeton University Press
41 William Street, Princeton, New Jersey 08540
99 Banbury Road, Oxford OX2 6JX

press.princeton.edu

GPSR Authorized Representative: Easy Access System Europe - Mustamäe tee 50, 10621 Tallinn, Estonia, gpsr.requests@easproject.com

ISBN 9780691263779
ISBN (e-book) 9780691263786

Library of Congress Control Number: 2025933668

British Library Cataloging-in-Publication Data is available

Editorial: Anne Savarese and Emma Wagh
Production Editorial: Sara Lerner
Jacket Design: Haley Jin Mee Chung
Production: Erin Suydam
Publicity: Tyler Hubbert and Carmen Jimenez
Copyeditor: Jennifer Harris

Jacket Credit: Courtesy of The Jewish Museum, New York / Art Resource, NY.

This book has been composed in Arno

Printed in the United States of America

10 9 8 7 6 5 4 3 2 1

In memory of my two friends and compatriots
Joachim Neugroschel and Dan Ben-Amos, who have created
great books of Jewish tales

Jews will be Jews while the world lasts, and they will become, through suffering, better Jews with more Jewish hearts.

—HELENA FRANK

CONTENTS

ACKNOWLEDGMENTS

As usual, Anne Savarese has guided me in my endeavors to answer various Jewish questions. Anne has been my guardian angel. Sara Lerner, too, has done wonders as production editor, while Jennifer Harris has been an exceptional copyeditor.

Finally, I want to thank my wife, Carol Dines, for supporting me throughout some difficult years.

INTRODUCTION

Never-Ending Jewish Tales and the Jewish Question

IN 1991 I PUBLISHED A BOOK WITH the title *The Operated Jew: Two Tales of Anti-Semitism*. In translating these tales from the original German—Oskar Panizza's "The Operated Jew" (1893) and Salomo Friedlaender's "The Operated Goy" (1922)—I hoped to create a discussion about anti-Semitism through two extraordinary and disturbing stories, written nearly thirty years apart, that explore the topic from very different perspectives. When I first published that book, I wanted to demonstrate how a dialectical "feud" between Oskar Panizza and Salomo Friedlaender concerning the Jewish Question might ignite debates and studies of Jewishness, or what it means to be a Jew, both in the past and today. At the time I had yet to discover the hundreds, if not thousands, of tales and essays from the late nineteenth and early twentieth centuries that dealt with the Jewish Question, a long-standing debate in European society about the status and treatment of Jews.

For Jewish and non-Jewish readers alike, this new anthology is my attempt to share and explain my views about Jewishness in European cultural history through a collection of tales, including a short novel, and two commentaries by Jewish writers published during the period from about 1870 through the 1930s. It combines familiar tales by well-known writers with lesser-known stories that deserve a wider audience, all of them examples of how Jews, whether religious or secular, found ways to survive and to find hope.

The Jewish Question, which first arose in Great Britain during the eighteenth century and spread throughout Europe in the nineteenth century, can be summarized as follows: After the so-called emancipation of Jews in Europe and elsewhere, should Jews be accepted as full citizens and allowed to live as they wish in different nation-states throughout the world, or should they be eliminated, or confined to monitored regions? Despite widespread emancipation in Great Britain and most of Europe, Jews were not recognized as equals or "native" citizens of the states they inhabited. As Ritchie Robertson writes in his important book *The "Jewish Question" in German Literature, 1749–1939: Emancipation and Its Discontents*:

> Emancipation (of Jews) culminated in 1871 with the bestowal of equal rights on all Jewish citizens of the newly formed German Empire (four years after similar legislation in Austria). And along with progress towards emancipation, the Jewish presence in German and Austrian culture became increasingly conspicuous, reaching a peak of brilliance and diversity in the Weimar Republic, before being annihilated or sent into exile by the National Socialist regime.[1]

By the end of the nineteenth century, fear and resentment of Jews in Europe became stronger the more emancipated Jews became. The formation of self-determined Jewish ghettos did not provide protection, nor did assimilation. Anti-Semitism became culturally acceptable in most European countries and in North America. Anti-Semitism was also common in books and other media, which often prompted anti-Semites to answer the Jewish Question with violence, branding Jews as blasphemous murderers, greedy bankers, and deceitful evildoers. In many countries, non-Jewish populations restricted where and how Jews could live; in others, they attempted to annihilate Jews in pogroms.

Anti-Semitism resulted not from the behavior of the Jews but the practices of elite groups and religious organizations in every society:

their behavior violated the rights not only of the Jews but also of their own people, while placing blame on the Jews.

Storytelling and the publishing of stories became a means through which Jews could share their problems among themselves. Through their behavior and their stories, they formed a resistance to the anti-Semites. At first, the tales Jews shared among themselves were told and printed mainly in Yiddish, Hebrew, or some other dialect. Yiddish literature in particular, as well as all kinds of Jewish art, blossomed and became flowers of possibility for most Jews, until the dark days of the 1930s. As Irving Howe and Eliezer Greenberg point out in their important collection, *A Treasury of Yiddish Stories*:

> Yiddish literature, like any other, has always had its schools, groups, and cliques, but there is hardly a Yiddish writer of any significance whose work is not imbued with this fundamental urge to portray Jewish life with the most uncompromising realism and yet to transcend the terms of portrayal. How could it be otherwise? Simply to survive, simply to face the next morning, Yiddish literature had to cling to the theme of historical realism. Beyond hope and despair lies the desperate *idea* of hope, and this is what sustained Yiddish writing.[2]

As Aesop long ago demonstrated in his fables, storytelling was not only subversive, but it also brought listeners together so they could create and maintain their own culture. To survive the Jewish Question, Jews had to learn to be imaginative and act on their own beliefs.

I propose that fairy tales, folk narratives, and fantasy enable us to grasp the dilemmas of Jews, who sought (and seek) to identify themselves by themselves, and yet also hope to become fully assimilated despite the hostile conditions of various nation-states.

In her book *Revisiting the Jewish Question*, Élisabeth Roudinesco traces the growth and spread of anti-Semitism from the medieval period to the present, suggesting that answers to the Jewish Question propose eradication as the only final solution:

> Up until the First World War, anti-Semitism spread throughout Europe in several variant forms: biological, hygienist, and racist in Germany, nationalist and Catholic in France. Its proponents set up leagues everywhere and founded a press specializing in denunciation and insult, aiming at a broad public in search of scapegoats. They published several pamphlets against the Enlightenment spirit and absorbed, to different degrees, the main components of Christian anti-Judaism, so as to integrate them into a political program that was oppositional, anti-liberal, monarchist, anti-Marxist, populist, xenophobic, anti-universalist, anti-modern, anti-emancipatory, and anti-progressive. Now, when the word "anti-Semitism" was used, it targeted exclusively the Jews—and not the other Semites, the Arabs in particular, who had previously been associated with the Jews.[3]

Hundreds of essays in academic journals and popular magazines have dealt with the Jewish Question as well, including Franklin Foer's 2024 article "The Golden Age of American Jews Is Ending: Anti-Semitism Threatens the American Experiment Itself."[4] Articles about the Jewish Question and anti-Semitism appear constantly in social media throughout the world. As I was doing research for this book, I came across a disturbing article, "Anti-Semitism: A Growing Contagion," which appeared in *The Week* in 2022 and begins this way:

> "The sheer amount of gross, blatant anti-Semitism on the right," said David French in *The Atlantic,* "has reached a level I never thought I'd see in the United States of America." Former President Trump recently chastised American Jews for not appreciating how much he did for Israel, and warned them "to get their act together . . . before it is too late."[5]

Even today, when Jews have their own nation-state, the Jewish Question has not disappeared, and Jews themselves rarely agree on its meaning.[6] Some argue that the Holocaust brought the question to an end: the foundation of the state of Israel in 1948 allowed self-emancipated Jews to take destiny into their own hands, in their "own" country. Yet in the twenty-first century, it seems that Israel has politically complicated the future for Jews and Jewish identity, for one could argue that the Jewish state has become like other racist and hypocritical nations. Now the Palestinians seem to occupy the role of the oppressed, while Israel appears to be the oppressor.[7] This is one of the sad paradoxes of post-Holocaust history. What is a Jew to do when roles are reversed? How can anti-Semitism be conquered in a world of misinformation? What is the cause of renewed, widespread anti-Semitism in the world? In these questions we see the legacy of the Jewish Question in contemporary life.

This anthology of Jewish stories is not intended to provide a resolution to the never-ending debate, but to demonstrate how Jewish folk tales and fantasy writing can help us comprehend how deeply the Jewish Question is entwined in cultural history. Sometimes it takes art to address and make sense out of the deplorable way Jews have been treated over centuries, and to remind us that the dangers of anti-Semitism have not subsided.

To demonstrate how Jewish tales tenaciously engender hope in the possibility of overcoming and dismissing anti-Semitism, I have collected twenty-eight tales, a short novel, and two essays, all originally published from the late nineteenth century through the 1930s. At the start of the tales, I have included new translations of Oskar Panizza's "The Operated Jew" (1893) and Salomo Friedlaender's "The Operated Goy" (1922), because they represent the conflict between anti-Semites and Jews, and the manner in which Jews were compelled to operate or not operate on themselves so that they could assimilate into the reigning Christian order. Following the tenaciously hopeful tales, I have included Hugo Bettauer's "The City without Jews," a satirical representation of the gentile Viennese, who answer the Jewish Question by ridding their city of the Jews and then finding themselves hapless and hopeless without them.

Two essays conclude the book: Theodor Herzl's "The Jewish Question" (1896) and Leo W. Schwarz's essay "The Essence of Survival" (1935). More than any critic in the nineteenth century, Herzl believed that the Jews' only hope to save themselves from annihilation was to establish their own independent nation-state, while Schwarz, a brilliant professor of Jewish studies, published numerous anthologies about the faith and quandaries of the Jews in the 1930s and 1940s.

All of the tales in the book were told or written by Jewish authors who dealt with their own "Jewish" questions about assimilation, conversion, secularization, religious dogmatism, pogroms, and more pogroms. Written largely for a Jewish readership, many of the narratives include ironic twists and self-deprecating humor. Yet they all stress the necessity of hope for the survival of the Jewish people and their diverse religious traditions.

Most of the tales in this collection cannot be considered "pure" fairy tales, but they all have certain magical commonalities that distinguish them as Jewish tales of hope. They all speak for little people who use their talents as best they can to overcome authoritarianism and fascism. Most of the stories include a miraculous transformation or turn of events when it appears that a particular Jew might be harmed or killed. Yet there is no violence, and the writers of these tales generally reflect the difficult conditions in shtetls, ghettos, and towns. Some of the tales were written or collected by familiar authors like Karl Emil Franzos, Israel Zangwill, I. L. Peretz, and Sholem Aleichem, and others by less well-known writers such as Hersh Dovid Nomberg, Helena Frank, and Gertrude Landa. I have organized the shorter tales chronologically so that readers can gain a sense of the changing times for Jews, and I have included tales told by ordinary people.

The Golem, the gargantuan savior, is a favorite character protecting Jews in two very similar tales by Peretz, "The Image" and "The Golem," and of course, magic is primary in several tales about rabbis, whose wisdom and patience are startling—especially in Peretz's "The Shabbes Goy" and "If Not Higher," Helena Frank's "The Clever Rabbi," A. S. Rabinovitz's "The Rabbi in Jail," Shmuel's Bastomski's "Rabbi Leyb Saves the Jews of Prague from Evil Decrees," and Rachel Seri's "The Ba'al Shem Tov and the Sorcerer." It should be noted that the rabbis use wisdom to accomplish transformations that enable their congregations to feel secure.

Pogroms were common during the period from 1890 to 1933, and Jews lived with the knowledge that they might be attacked night or day.

We are reminded of this in Karl Emil Franzos's "Two Saviors" and in Sholem Aleichem's "Two Anti-Semites." Jews always had to have their bags packed.

I have shaped this anthology around the Jewish Question and how it has penetrated the minds of people throughout the world for centuries. This is also why I have returned to the two tales "The Operated Jew" and "The Operated Goy," for they reflect, I believe, how bitter the conflict between Jews and gentiles of different persuasions was and still is today.

Panizza's tale "The Operated Jew" is filled with incidents that reflect extreme hatred and fear of Jews, who are both ridiculed and regarded with awe. To add to this ambiguity, Panizza criticizes Jews for wanting to be part of a philistine German society and argues that they would be better off by not giving up their particular faith and racial characteristics. In a most ingenious fashion, he conceives a fantastic constellation that allows him to reproduce all the worst stereotypes and attitudes about Jews while criticizing the deplorable development of instrumental rationality in the form of eugenics, the hypocrisy of church and state in Germany, and socialization in the form of physical alteration. It is chilling to see how Panizza, writing decades before the Holocaust, placed his finger on the sore spots of German–Jewish assimilation at the end of the nineteenth century and anticipated the virtual destruction of the Jewish faith.[8]

In a response to Panizza, about 1922, Friedlaender wrote "The Operated Goy," a satirical response to Panizza that demonstrates how a Jewish woman manages to captivate a rich gentile man and transform him into a Jew. It is important to clarify that Friedlaender did *not* intend to denigrate gentiles or celebrate Jews in his narrative. In fact, the story is intended to bring about cathartic laughter in his readers. Friedlaender has his anonymous Mynona tell a story in which a certain fictious Dr. Friedlaender attains the final laugh by minimizing racial differences and thus debunking nationalism and anti-Semitism. It is through laughter, then, that the author Friedlaender wants to undermine prejudice and violence, and this laughter is predicated to a great extent on self-mockery, for he also pokes fun at himself throughout the story.

It is this modest humor that one can find throughout the tales in the present collection. Instead of gathering similar tales published only in

Yiddish from the Pale Settlement, I have chosen diverse narratives. Some are ironic and bittersweet, but they all express the tension between Jews and gentiles without necessarily resolving conflicts. That is, they assert that assimilation is impossible, even in the short novel "The City without Jews."

My project has been strongly influenced by Caspar Battegay's book *Geschichte der Möglichkeit: Utopie, Diaspora, und die jüdische Frage* (The History of Possibility: Utopia, Diaspora, and the Jewish Question). Battegay maintains that "politics is the art of realizing the possible. However, art directs itself more to possibilities whose realization remain unforeseeable, possibilities which are directed *as* possibilities to a reflection of the political."[9] His book, a study of the utopian tendencies in numerous artworks from the late nineteenth century to the present, is intended to disclose the various possibilities of the Jewish Question through literature that can bring about change for the better.

Battegay notes that the period from approximately 1870 to 1945 is extremely important with regard to the conflicts caused by anti-Semitism and the Jewish Question, because so many possibilities for change were revealed in art, literature, philosophy, and politics. Battegay makes full use of Ernst Bloch's theories in *The Principle of Hope* and examines traces of possibility for change in both secular and anti-Semitic works.

This anthology intends to uncover the hope of various Jewish writers whose works contend with anti-Semitism. As Bloch, Battegay, and other scholars have reminded us, utopian possibilities from the past may still help us regain our sense of humanity.

Tales

The Operated Jew (1893)

Oskar Panizza

NOBODY WILL BLAME ME for wanting to erect a monument in honor of my friend Itzig Faitel Stern. At least, as long as this lies within my power. I almost fear that I lack such power, for Itzig Faitel Stern, my best friend at the university, was a phenomenon. It would take a linguist, a choreographer, an aesthete, an anatomist, a tailor, and a psychiatrist all in one to grasp and fully explain Faitel's entire appearance, what he said, how he walked, and what he did. Thus, it will not be surprising after what I have just said, when my sketch presents only bits and pieces. I must rely on my five senses, which, according to today's prevailing school of literature, should completely suffice for creating a work of art—without attempting to ask much about the why and how and without attempting to provide artificial motivation and superficial construction. If a comedy should originate instead of a work of art, then let the school of literature bear the responsibility. Itzig Faitel was a small, squat man. His right shoulder was slightly higher than his left, and he had a sharp protruding chicken breast upon which he always wore a wide heavy silk tie ornamented by a dull ruby and attached to a breastplate. The lapels on both sides of this tie ran top right to bottom left so that when Faitel moved along the curbstones, it appeared as though he were veering down the sidewalk to the other side or going in a diagonal direction. Faitel could not be convinced that the arrangement of his clothes came from the rhombic shift of his chest cage. This is why he complained terribly about Christian tailors. After all, the suits that he wore were always made from the finest worsted.

Itzig Faitel's countenance was most interesting. It is a shame that Lavater had not laid eyes upon it. An antelope's eye with a subdued, cherry-like glow swam in wide apertures of the smooth velvet, slightly yellow skin of his temple and cheeks. Itzig's nose assumed a form that was similar to that of the high priest who was the most prominent and striking figure of Kaulbach's painting *The Destruction of Jerusalem*. To be sure, the eyebrows had meshed, but Faitel Stern assured me that this meshing had become very popular. He even knew that people with such eyebrows had allegedly been drowned at one time. Yet, he countered this by assuring me that he never went near water. His lips were fleshy and overly creased; his teeth sparkled like pure crystal. A violet fatty tongue often thrust itself between them at the wrong time. Neither beard nor mustache adorned the chin and upper lip, for Faitel Stern was still very young. If I may also add that my friend's lower torso had bowlegs whose angular swing was not excessive, then I believe that I have sketched Itzig's figure to a certain degree. Later I'll talk about the curly, thick black locks of hair on his head. This, then, was the student Stern as still life. But who will help me—what clown, what imitator of dialects, what mime—in my endeavor to depict Itzig in motion as he spoke and acted?

Itzig told me that he came from a French family and was raised according to French tradition. He even spoke some French. Naturally, it was warped. It was his misfortune to have moved at a young age to the nearby Palatinate, where he sucked up the enunciated sounds of this region as though they were milk and honey. Of course, Faitel could speak high German, yet it was not his language but that of a dressy doll. When Faitel was in private company and did not have to feel embarrassed, he spoke the dialects of the Palatinate—and something more than that. Yet, before I get to this, let me make a few remarks about his way of walking and gesticulating.

When he walked, Itzig always raised both thighs almost to his midriff so that he bore some resemblance to a stork. At the same time, he lowered his head deeply into his breastplated tie and stared at the ground.

One had to assume that he could not gauge the strength needed for lifting his legs as he went head over heels. —Similar disturbances can be noted in people with spinal diseases. However, Itzig did not have a spinal disease, for he was young and in good condition. When I asked him one time why he walked so extravagantly, he said, "So I can moof ahead!" —Faitel also had trouble keeping his balance, and when he walked, there were often beads of sweat streaming from the curly locks of hair around his temple. The collar wrapped around my friend's neck was fastened tightly and firmly. I assume that this was due to the difficulty and work Itzig needed to keep his head pointed upright toward God's heavens. In its natural position, Itzig's head was always pointed toward earth, the chin drilled solidly into the silk breastplated tie.

Such was Itzig Faitel Stern as still life and in motion. But what were his gestures like? Of course, this depended on Faitel's mood, whether he was disposed or indisposed; whether he was pleasant or contrary. He was never highly emotional. His constitution prevented him from getting angry. But when he became zealous and had a good opportunity to wage an argument, then he reared up, raised a hand, pulled back his fleshy, volatile upper lip like a piece of leather so that the upper row of teeth became exposed, spread open both his hands like fans pointing upward with his upper body leaning backward, bobbed his head up and down against his breast a few times, and rhythmically uttered sounds like a trumpet. Up to this moment my friend may not have said a thing. But I always knew from the entire series of gestures and expressions in what direction Faitel's arguments would move. Faitel meowed, rattled, bleated, and also liked to produce sneezing sounds and at the right time so that one could infer even more from all this noise than mere words interjected here and there. If his position were dubious or even endangered, or if he wanted to convince his opponent about an impossible matter, then he threw his rotating upper body with pinched-in stomach away from the side of his opponent and toward himself as though he wanted to pull the concerned person over toward his entire corporeal mass of flesh. The burring sounds that accompanied this act were filled with zeal, grunts, and comfort. Anyone who chanced to see and hear all this for the first time would be astonished and overwhelmed. One would surrender in the debate, just in recognition of the zealous way in which he went about convincing the opponent. In realizing the effect he had, Faitel would often be driven to even greater heights.

Ultimately, he would become monstrous.

So much for his agitations.

But who will help me describe Itzig Faitel Stern's speech? What philologist or expert in dialects would dare analyze this mixture of Palatinate Semitic babble, French nasal noises, and some high German vocal sounds that he had fortuitously overheard and articulated with an open position of the mouth? I can't do this. So, I want to confine myself to presenting to the reader what I remember about Itzig Faitel's phrases according to the standard phonetic system. But before I do this, I must emphasize two points about Faitel's speech that are of particular grammatical interest. After this, I shall unfold the horrifying comedy, which Itzig Faitel Stern produced in Heidelberg, where we both studied, without interruption.

Among the numerous and hardly perceptible peculiarities of his manner of speech, Faitel had two in particular—what I shall call speech particles—that recurred time and again and struck me finally as syntactical components of some conceptual value. Faitel Stern said something like this when I questioned him about the immense luxury of his wardrobe and toilet articles: "Why shoodn't I buy for me a new coat, a bootiful hat-menera, fine wanished boots—menera, me, too, I shood bicome a fine gentilman after this. Deradang! Deradang!"

His upper body rocked back and forth. At the same time, there was a spreading of the hands at shoulder height in a slightly squat position; an ecstatic look with a glossy reflection; an exposure of both rows of teeth; a rich amount of saliva. The reader will have discovered two surprising words here, or rather an annexation, an appendage, and an interjection that cannot be found in any dictionary. "Menera," a kind of purring word, short–long, with the stress on the last syllable (anapest), was appended with substantives, which were endowed with a consonant. Then "menera" was frequently added, but with such dazzling speed that the stress remained on the substantive, allowing the annex to attach itself as a purring sound with four short syllables. Many times, it also seemed as if "menera" was only to serve as the connection to the next word if the latter began with a sound that caused difficulty for Faitel's tongue.

Therefore, it was only used when he talked rapidly or was in an excited mood. The two annexes lacked a declinatory character as is the case with some Negro languages. —The situation was completely different with the strongly nasal "Deradang!" This was an interjection, an exclamatory particle. It had its own word and concept. It was sing-song, babbled with saliva in the mouth. It closed the sentence and seemed to mean so much as "Well, I'm right, aren't I?" —"You see!" —"Who would have thought of that?" —"That takes care of that!"

Yes, dear reader, try as you might to pronounce "Deradang! Deradang!" you will never be able to do it with such a fatty guttural noise, such soft bawling, such a great amount of spit as Itzig Faitel Stern. Now, I no longer want to keep the reader in the dark as to how I became associated with this remarkable figure. Nor do I want to cloak my purposes in mystery and mislead the reader who might suppose that it was pity that moved me to make the close acquaintance with this dreadful piece of human flesh named Itzig Faitel Stern. There was certainly a great deal of what I would call medical or rather anthropological curiosity in this case. I was attracted to him in the same way I might be to a Negro whose goggle eyes, yellow connective optical membranes, crushed nose, mollusk lips and ivory teeth, and smell one perceives altogether in wonderment and whose feelings and most secret anthropological actions one wants to get to know as well! Perhaps there was also some pity here, but not much. I observed with astonishment how this monster took terrible pains to adapt to our circumstances, our way of walking, thinking, our gesticulations, the expressions of our intellectual tradition, our manner of speech. But there was a much stronger and more egotistical reason for me since I wanted to learn something about the Talmud, which was Faitel's religious book. All the remarkable rumors spread about this vast prayer book interested me a great deal.

To be sure, Itzig was not a Talmudic scholar, but he knew a great deal about the Talmud. He knew a lot of little customs, weaknesses, practices, and eccentricities, which could not be found in books and translations of the Talmud, and which had great anthropological value for me. Of course, many of the strangest rumors were spread about me by the students in Heidelberg, who showed little understanding as to why I had chosen to associate with Itzig Faitel Stern. Those rumors were mainly connected to Faitel's money, for Faitel Stern was enormously rich. At that time Heidelberg was a very small city, and the students played such a conspicuous role there that the appearance of Itzig Faitel Stern and everything in his orbit became the talk of the town. And, to put it more succinctly, Faitel Stern was a kind of Kaspar Hauser: here was a man, then, who emanated directly from the stingy, indiscriminate, stifling, dirty-diapered, griping, and grimacing bagatelle of his family upbringing, and as a result of a hasty decision, with his pockets full of money, was suddenly thrown onto the great pavement of life in a European city, and there he began to look around, ignorant, with blundering movements. Consequently, he was beheld with ridicule and astonishment. But the matter could not continue like this.

Soon after the beginning of our acquaintance, I made some suggestions to Faitel in regard to changing him and making him more modern, and I found that he was receptive to these remarks. Hopefully I have not forgotten to mention that we both studied medicine. The fact that Faitel chose this discipline as his field of study was, after all that we know about his appearance, certainly a propitious *testimonium intellectus*. "Faitel," I said to him one day, "you must change your way of walking. You are completely convoluted. And this is why you're mocked and ridiculed by everyone in the city!"

"So wot can I do? You tink dis don't make me depressed?" Faitel exclaimed and stamped his flat feet helplessly but with a great show of force on the floor. "I was walking dis way my life long. Mine fadder goes like dis too und hiss de alte Stern Solomon. Geeve me sum new legs. I should pay vat it costs!"

"Yes, pay!" I cried out. "That would be the right thing to do. But who could possibly straighten out your rickety bones?"

We agreed that we had to seek the advice of an orthopedist. However, the worthy representative of this discipline declared that Itzig was too old and that his bone structure had become too set. Yet, he recommended Professor Klotz, Heidelberg's famous anatomist, who might conduct a scientific examination of Itzig's skeletal framework. So, we visited this famous man, and he made all sorts of measurements on Itzig's naked body, had him walk back and forth, and finally clapped his hands over his head. Never in his life had he seen such a thing! Then he took out a well-known book, Meyer's *Statistics and Mechanics of Human Anatomy*, Leipzig, 1873. He had been commissioned to write the second edition, and he was displeased because he felt that he now had to revise the entire book after examining Itzig. At this point he asked whether it was certain that Itzig's parentage was human. Of course, this could be proven without a doubt.

"Then," Professor Klotz closed his remarks, "I may be forced to abandon all hope. It may be possible to restore the joints of the student Stern so that they all simulate human forms of motion. However," the famous anatomist hesitated, "the means and ways . . ."

"I'll pay wot you shood want," Faitel interjected quickly, possessed by a sudden presentiment. "I'll pay hit. I'll gung pay for mine new statue. So de Herr Professor, he'll hev de geld, a lot of geldera. Deradang! Deradang! (to be spoken with a long stress) I'll gonna payera! Deradang! Deradang!"

Spreading of the hands at shoulder length; bobbing of the head into the vest; rocking of the upper body like a pendulum; smiling positions of the mouth; upper row of teeth exposed; rich amount of saliva. Now hard times arrived for Faitel. Night and day, he hung in traction so that his scoliotic bones could be stretched by his own body weight. Or he was stuck in a cast built like a corset. The nape of his neck was shortened and tightened through a bloody operation to allow Faitel a view of the heavens. The bones that had been reassembled in a new harness had to be exercised and reformed week after week with the help of a gymnast. Faitel had to have private lessons since nobody wished to exercise with him. It was impossible for anyone to make use of these exercises for private purposes, nor did anyone want to see Faitel perform his neck-breaking exercises. Enormous sums of money wandered into the hands of the gymnasts, trainers, orthopedists, and those of Professor Klotz, who directed and supervised everything.

After three months the results were mediocre. Naturally the bowlegs remained the same during all these corrective attempts since there had been no possibility to place counterweights in a deeper position and stretch them out. Faitel's advisors were able to calm him down by explaining to him that such legs were also to be found among other classes of human beings such as bakers, and so on. But Faitel was indefatigable. Ever since his pointed chin stopped drilling into the breastplated tie, he had made the firm decision "to become such a fine gentilman just like a goymenera and to geeve up all fizonomie of Jewishness."

About that time a daring operation became known that was called *brisement force*. A crooked bone was intentionally broken and treated as an accidental breaking of the leg with the exception that the two pieces were healed in a straight direction. This method was employed in an operation on Faitel Stern's bowlegs. The consequences and incidental circumstances of this cure led to Faitel's being bedridden for many weeks at a time for each leg, with all kinds of pain and bandages and enormous costs for a process that at that time necessitated a doctor to come from Paris and perform everything according to the proper specifications.

Old Solomon Stern sent check after check, which was gladly honored by every businessman. Then there were weeks and weeks of attempts to walk with the freshly healed limbs of his body. And really, when Faitel Stern now went out for the first time, one could see that he had made great progress. He had become somewhat taller and resembled a respectable human being. Everything was and still remained stiff for a long time, but he could now pretend to be a normal human being. His face stood straight as a candle. His chin revealed itself now to be terribly long and pointed. His chicken breast was flattened out, and the lapels of his coat ran straight down. In order to prevent Faitel's customary bobbing of his upper body—which was always accompanied by his nasal gurgling "Deradang! Deradang!"—a barbed wire belt similar to a collar was placed around his hips on his bare skin (as they do with dogs) so that he was immediately spiked when he tended to move up and down or from side to side. Faitel Stern bore all this heroically and stood straight and tall like a pine tree. Yet, only now did the major problem arise.

It was clear that one could not introduce him in high society with his speech, of which we have already been given some samples, for it was the mode of expression of an oily, base, cowardly character. And though it was merely a question of changing his outward appearance, it was important to complete this change as soon as possible. Since it was hopeless to raise the level of his Palatinate-Yiddish to that of the related pure high German, an attempt was made to bring his former sing-song on the right track through its direct opposite. A private tutor was engaged, and Itzig was to repeat his clear nasal-sounding manner of speech like a schoolboy, sentence by sentence, so that he learned high German like a totally new, foreign language. Moreover, some students from Hanover were employed to provide company for Itzig in exchange for payment of tuition and diverse meals during one whole semester. This series of measures was the result of expert opinion gathered from the most famous linguist of that time in nearby Tübingen. In addition, a Heidelberg physiologist was brought in for consultation. These gentlemen proceeded from the following considerations: In our brain there is just one part for the speech faculties, and it is used either on the left or the right side. It is not impossible to make use of those faculties that have not been used to form a new speech aptitude, and this often takes place quite naturally—for example, after an illness. In such attempts, it is of utmost importance that one makes certain there is nothing in the formation of words and sounds of the new speech that recalls the old idiom—otherwise confusion will arise. As the Tübingen specialist expressed it, a new speech island had to be formed in Itzig. And now he was examined to determine which German dialect contained the least tonal affinity with Faitel's Palatinate-Yiddish.

At first, the specialists considered Pomeranian. But this was too difficult for Faitel. Finally, they agreed upon the Hanoverian dialect. My reader can well imagine that all these fine diagnostics cost a barrel of money, for these speech exercises were to continue for another entire semester. It is impossible for me to give the reader an account of all the garnishings, changes, injections, and quackeries to which Itzig Faitel Stern submitted himself. He experienced the most excruciating pain and showed great heroism so he could become the equivalent of an

Occidental human being. He continually watched for new things, studied secret Christian traits, copied distortions of the mouth, puffed cheeks, and gestures, and imagined himself to be part of the heroic Teutonic genre like some young stalwart, blond and naïve, who walked about smiling with great ignorance. Naturally, the tint—the wheat color of Faitel's skin—had to yield to a fine, pastel lead tint, which Itzig learned to exhibit in a superb way. I suspect—it's just a suspicion—that Faitel once nourished himself four weeks in a row on a drug about which I know nothing. It takes the form of a vegetable, and Faitel may have done this to attain the Caucasian color of skin in a natural way.

One relatively simple and harmless procedure that, nevertheless, had a gruesome effect concerned his hair. Right about that time, the English bleaches came into fashion. To be sure, since they were secret formulas, they were extremely expensive, but they did change each and every strand of dark hair into magnificent golden blond. The first English beauticians were traveling around Germany at that time, and one of them had settled down in rich Heidelberg, which was always frequented by people from high society. Faitel was one of the first ones to undergo the treatment. So Itzig's coal black curly locks, under which there had always been a suspiciously smelling sweat, were changed into the golden locks of a child. These locks were then straightened out into long Germanic strands by means of a painful process. In addition, Faitel was given a simple North German hairdo, and—finally—the dumb, awkward German lad was complete, a replica of the figure portrayed at times by Schwind in his paintings. He called himself Siegfried Freudenstern and had his matriculation forms and other papers changed.

Faitel was now an entirely new human being. The last treatments—he was very careful—had been completed during the university vacation period near the city and had changed him to such an extent that he was unrecognizable. It was suggested that he attend another university now, but he rejected this idea, mainly because he wanted to remain near Professor Klotz, who was still in charge of the entire psycho-physical operation. And, in fact, since the bleaching of his hair to gold, Faitel was no longer recognized in Heidelberg. He made his appearance there as the son of a Hanoverian landowner and moved in the finest circles of high society. He exercised the North German rasping sound with playful ease, and this scored an extraordinary success wherever he went. However, Faitel's ambition mounted even higher. —"Faiteles! Such a bootiful yid, such a fine yid! Such an elegant yid!" —This was the way Faitel frequently spoke to himself when he stood in front of a mirror, but only in his thoughts. —"So you tink now you're a Chreesten, wit no drop Jewishness? You tink you could go wearevver you want wot you shood take a seat wit de fine peeple wot everyone should tink: dat's one of us!"

Faitel knew that it had not yet come to this. Yes, whatever pomade, makeup, white buckram, some yards of worsted, cotton, and some varnish could accomplish with a human being, all this had been accomplished with Faitel. But what did everything look like inside? Did Faitel have a soul? This question was debated everywhere for months by all those people, educators, and doctors who had something to do with him. Of course, the soul necessary for expression of a few hypocritical sentences such as a marriage vow or for throwing a few silver coins to a poor devil at the right moment—Faitel possessed this soul just like everyone else. But Faitel had heard about the chaste, undefined Germanic soul, which shrouded the possessor like an aroma. This soul was the source of the possessor's rich treasures and formed the *shibboleth* of the Germanic nations, a soul that was immediately recognized by all who possessed one. Faitel wanted to have this soul. And, if he could not have genuine eau de cologne, then he wanted the imitation. At the very least, he wanted to appropriate this soul in all its expressions and daily manifestations. So, he was advised to go to England, where the purest effusion of this Germanic soul was to be found.

Language difficulties soon caused these plans to be dropped. A well-known educator felt that one could reach this higher goal on the basis of a general spiritual predisposition even with Faitel's present one. The famous Cambridge Professor Stokes had only recently published his *Psychological Researches,* in which he explained the primary spiritual predisposition of people like Faitel not as a *spiritual* possession but as a mechanical function or "rotation work," as he called it. This new theory led to the abandonment of all further attempts to cultivate Itzig Faitel's soul.

Once during these tests and examinations Itzig burst out with a question about the dwelling place of the soul. They had to explain to him that ever since Descartes had made the unsuccessful attempt to locate the abode of the soul in the pineal gland of the brain, nobody had tried to locate this spiritual power. Rather, attempts had been made to understand the soul from the combined effects of certain physical and spiritual functions. Since these functions were dependent in a particular manner on the quality of blood, it was possible to assert to a certain degree that the abode of the soul could be located in the blood and its changing condition. Right then Faitel conceived a plan for one of his most daring treatments. Some days after this discussion he was overheard talking joyously to his most intimate associates: "I gonna buy me sum Chreesten blud! I gonna buy me sum Chreesten blud!"

This was how he spoke, despite the fact that his advisors had strictly forbidden him to speak this way. My readers will shake their heads. But you must not forget that Itzig Faitel Stern was a medical student and knew all about the most recent developments in the field. And, furthermore, this is the place to remind you that at that time, when our story was taking place, blood transfusions became fashionable. The rich blood from a body filled to the lymphs was injected into a supine organism poor in blood by opening an exterior blood vessel in the arm. These operations were extremely dangerous and have already been abandoned today. Faitel was strongly advised not to proceed with this, but he would not be deterred.

Meanwhile, there were great difficulties to be overcome. Approximately six to eight hardy people had been found who were each to give a liter of blood in exchange for a great deal of money. Yet, when they heard that their blood was destined for a Jew, they withdrew their offer and spoke about the blood spilt on the Cross because of the Jews. They could not be convinced to change their minds. Only when seven strong women from the Black Forest, who had come to the country fair, were persuaded that it was time again to be bled could the major difficulty be settled. Faitel himself made the incision in an adjoining room, and since the amount of blood to be emptied had been exactly prescribed, he had the opened artery punctured in a warm bath until he became unconscious. He wanted to shed his

"Jewishness" and let everything run out that could run out. Eight liters of blood from the strong peasant women were then gradually and carefully injected into him during the course of the afternoon. After many days in a coma, Faitel survived this dangerous treatment unscathed.

However, he never allowed himself to be thoroughly questioned about its success and the psychological effect. It appeared that it had not been very great, for after a few weeks we found him again, making new attempts to gain possession of the German soul. Thus, he began reciting pathetic and sentimental passages by poets, especially in the social gatherings of the ladies' salons, and he astutely observed the position of the mouth, breath, twinkle of the eyes, gestures, and certain sighs that emanated so passionately and strenuously from German breasts satiated with feelings. To be sure, when the ladies from the aesthetic gatherings did not boost his ego enough, Faitel had actors come to Heidelberg from the nearby court in Darmstadt, heroes and lovers, and he learned Romeo soliloquies with them. To tell the truth, this was more successful than other experiments. Now Faitel could express statements with great adroitness in a discussion such as, "Oh, I must confess, when I reflect about this, when I consider this, everything seems gloomy to me, and my heart shudders."

These words would be accompanied by some brusque movements, both hands pressed on the left side of the breast. It was really a very clever way to pour out emotions. Of course, his eyes would rest lifelessly in their sockets like rotten cherries. Yet, he was able to deceive many people. He learned to inhale and exhale superbly. And one time he had the satisfaction of hearing from a student in the ladies' salons that Siegfried Freudenstern was a man with soul through and through. But Faitel still had a lot of other, old inherited habits, ways of thinking, comical manners, and eccentricities. On our frequent evening walks he liked to meditate and—I'm not sure whether he wanted to recapitulate his religious lessons or mock his former teachers—he would begin to talk with an altered, carping rabbi's voice examining himself in the following manner: "What doth Jehovah do at the beginning of the day?" —Then Faitel would answer himself in his own voice, but with a fresh witty accent: "He studieth the commandments!"

Again the first voice: "What doth the holy Lord do thereafter?"

Second voice: "Thereafter he sitteth and ruleth the entire world!"

"What doth Jehovah do after this?"

"Thereafter he sitteth and nourishes the entire world!"

"What doth he do then?"

"Then he sitteth and copulates the men and women!"

"How long doth the holy Lord copulate the men and women?"

"He copulateth the men and women for three hours!"

"What doth the holy Jehovah do then in the afternoon?"

"He doth nothing in the afternoon, Jehovah. He rests."

"What didst thou say? What doth thou mean? The holy Jehovah doth nothing? What doth he do? What doth Jehovah do in the afternoon? —Huh?"

Now it seemed that a remote squeaking voice of a young boy answered him from the last desk in the back of a classroom: "The holy Jehovah playeth with Leviathan in the afternoon!"

"Naturally," interjected the rabbi's voice, "he playeth with Leviathan!"

During these walks Faitel would be delighted and act like a wild little boy. When he went beyond the boundaries of the city, Faitel sometimes took out a white handkerchief, hung it around his neck, held the two tips in front and began to let loose with a barrage of song, rolling up and down the scales with a screeching gurgle that had a peculiar jubilant and cheerful character. I had never heard the words before, and he sung until his eyes popped and foam was on his lips. Then he almost threw up and meandered next to me along the way like a drunkard. When he came to his senses again, he remained silent and introspective, acted secretively, and appeared to be inundated by some unknown happiness. Naturally his advisors were not to know anything about this since they had forbidden all exercises, sounds, and gestures that might remind him of his former predisposition. Yet, I also suspected that Faitel, when he was alone, was still up to some mischief. During the day he was in the European corset, harnessed, supervised, under great surveillance. But in the evening, when he was no longer bound, when he took off the barbed belt and lay in bed, I'm sure he rocked as he formerly did, the pelvis moving back and forth, his hands spreading into the vest pockets, his tongue gurgling and bawling, "Deradang! Deradang!" And the entire Palatinate-Yiddish deluge could not be checked.

But Faitel still had other things that were even more ineradicable because, unlike movements, they were not controlled by one's will. Rather, they were lodged in his imagination. Now, in order to present a full picture, I am compelled to touch upon something distasteful: Faitel had a fear of the toilet. He believed in the old Hebrew spirits of the latrine and squalor who bothered people during their most urgent calls. These spirits could take possession of a person and could only be repulsed by certain prayers. However, since Faitel no longer knew these prayers nor could say any of them with conviction, his fear grew even greater. And only the fact that the spirits did not dare attack anyone in the presence of a third party enabled Faitel to dispose of such urgent business in peace—naturally, only after he always provided for the proper conditions.

Such was Faitel's new formation and transformation. Internally, there was much that had not been filled by new things, old functions that were still in operation. Externally, everything had been smoothed out, combed spic-and-span, thoroughly conditioned, and ready to go. All in all, Faitel and his tutors, advisors, and instructors should have been satisfied with what they had accomplished. Yet, Professor Klotz, whose concerned eye watched over his human work with growing interest from semester to semester, may have had mixed feelings when he congratulated himself. Either he felt like a circus director, who had finally tamed a difficult horse for the ring, or he felt like the sublime Creator, who had managed to blow life into a cold lump of clay. After all, hadn't Klotz also blown new life into a distorted bag of broken bones?

Only one thing was still missing, for it was also important to reproduce this human race, which it had cost so much to achieve. The new breed was to be grafted with the finest Occidental sprig. A blonde Germanic lass had to help preserve the results that had been garnered through fabulous efforts. This was the way it sounded in theory. In practice, this meant that the poor but beautiful flaxen-haired daughter of a civil servant, Othilia Schnack, was to become engaged to the enormously rich son of a landowner, Siegfried Freudenstern. This was what was agreed upon, and it met with Faitel's approval. Indeed, Old Solomon Stern, who sat quietly in his village of Patzendorf in the Palatinate, bought some property near Hanover to serve as the next residence for the young couple. The Hanover students, who had already acted superbly as speech instructors at one time, were to provide the necessary introductions to families in the city and district of Hanover when the time came. Some shaky mortgages on the parental homes of these young men in question were scheduled for foreclosure by Old Solomon sitting in Patzendorf in case they did not cooperate. An exceedingly fabulous trousseau was ordered from the best retailers of Heidelberg in case the wedding ties were indeed to be knotted. In turn, this put extra pressure on the business circles in this university city. One talked so much about the engagement it finally meant that the knots had to be tied. Or, this engagement could not be allowed to be dissolved, as though there had already been one at all. The young lady in question, Othilia, had light, starry eyes and was an open, lovely creature, but she had a strong woman's intuition. She did not feel entirely comfortable in the presence of the golden blond youth who purred as he spoke. She sensed something eerie but could not confirm her suspicion. Her father, a fearful man, who had worked himself up from a scribe to a middle-grade official through good behavior and honesty, was very anxious. He always obeyed, never said no, walked with tiny steps as though trotting, carried his chin and neck hidden in an unstarched, open-collared shirt, and as soon as he noticed that something like a family meeting was to take place, he grabbed his hat and cane and went for a walk. Her mother, a big-breasted, ponderous housekeeper who could be charming every now and then, but most of the time was energetic and industrious, was for the marriage. She already possessed earrings with gems as large as pigeon eggs as a gift from Faitel Stern. This clever woman was suspicious of the entire affair only because the Heidelberg professors, especially the professors of medicine, took such a lively interest in bringing about the marriage. Naturally, the hotel owners, wine merchants, clothiers, embroiderers, bakers, jewelers, printers, negotiators, coachmen, and porters were for the marriage. The

Protestant clergy—Othilia was Protestant—also gave a nod of approval to the entire project.

The fact that nobody had met any of Faitel's relatives caused some consternation in the Schnack family. However, word had it that the parents were well advanced in years. And the long journey from Hanover! If only a brother, or better yet, a sister of the groom could have appeared on the scene! But the cawing nest back in Patzendorf naturally took care not to utter a peep. Faitel was now in his sixth semester. His knowledge and good performances were praised. Still, it caused some sensation when it became known that Professor Klotz had appointed the young student from Hanover as his assistant right after he had been granted his degree. This appointment required the confirmation of the ministry in Karlsruhe. It came. Consequently, fuel was now added in Karlsruhe to the flaming rumor about the rich marriage that was going to take place in Heidelberg. The reigning sovereign could not help but hear all this talk. And one day the director of Schnack's office informed the man with a melting smile that someone had talked about his daughter's forthcoming marriage—in Karlsruhe—at the court. Now the peak had been reached! The old scribe kept quiet and held his head stiff behind his tie. His two dry lips tipped with a black-stubbed Kaiser moustache could not even gasp for breath until the tall, haggard director with long coattails disappeared from sight. Then old Schnack threw the feather pen on his desk, spraying some ink in the process, grabbed his hat and cane, and rushed home coughing along the way. "At the court! At the court!"

Now there was no stopping it. Poor Othilia, who shuddered upon hearing this, sobbed, threw herself into the arms of her mother, and declared that she would obey. Her mother immediately sent a message to the newly appointed assistant Dr. Freudenstern, and the wedding day was scheduled.

Now, my dear reader, I should like to have a word with you. Did you ever hear of people wearing a coat in the winter with its collar and lapels topped with fur to make others believe that the entire coat is lined this way? A trivial thing! A small weakness! Do you also wear a coat like this? Oh, then throw it away if you're a man. Otherwise, the fur will trip your tongue one day when you're most in need of a breath of air. (However, if you're a woman, you may wear it.) But that little bit of fur, there's so much talk about it, isn't that true? —Good! —Still, haven't you seen people, my dear reader, who wear such furs around their souls in order to conceal their porous and shabby constitution? And then they act as though they had a noble soul clad in the finest of fabrics. Oh, what a shame! Oh, the squalor and pity of it all! What if some well-behaved, open soul still clad in its confirmation suit, now somewhat snug, were to have trouble or to be deceived! —Perhaps you yourself, my reader, possess such wrappings for your soul? Oh, then throw this book in a corner if you're a man and spew everything out! This is not for you. Only a woman may lie and cloak herself in false wrappings. Perhaps, my dear reader, you have seen animals talking among themselves. Two pigeons or two roosters, two dogs or even two foxes? Do you think they understand each other? Certainly!

Certainly! Each knows what the other wants in a flash. But two people? When they stretch their heads toward one another, sniff and peep at each other, and then begin their facial magic tricks, blinking, ogling, rubbing, chewing thin air, and whimpering "fiddlesticks" and "the devil!"—what are they doing? Do they actually understand each other? Impossible! They don't want to. They can't and are not allowed to. The lie prevents them from doing this. Oh, horse manure and stinky resin, you are gems in comparison to what comes out of people's mouths! When Prometheus finally had permission from God to make human beings, it occurred only on the express humiliating condition that they had to have one quality that made them much lower than animals. Prometheus, who was only in a rush to see his artwork finished, agreed to this. It was the lie. Oh, base contract that allowed us all to be born under the same sign of the lie! And were you perhaps the cause for that lying tower of Babel forcing people to separate because they no longer understand each other in spite of the coughing and gesticulating? And, even if the German nations were the last to be created, received the least repercussions from all this because so much of the lying substance had already been used up by the previous Asiatic and Latin races, there is still enough there. —Oh, reader, if you can, spit out this dirt like rotten slime, and show your lips, your tongue, and your teeth just as they are! —And now listen to the conclusion of Faitel's comedy.

In the Inn of the White Lamb, which was on the Martergasse in Heidelberg, the large hall was filled with a radiant group of people who had witnessed the wedding ceremony of Othilia Schnack with Siegfried Freudenstern. It had been a long time since something like this had been seen in this university city. I'm not certain whether the civil ceremony had been preceded by a church wedding. Most likely. The papers testifying that Freudenstern was Protestant had been acquired from a Hanover pastor with a sympathetic ear. This I know. Nothing had been missing except for the birth certificate. Yet, many communities in the Lüneberger Heide near Hanover had expressed their joy and readiness to add a name to their birth register, especially the name of such a citizen as Herr Dr. Freudenstern, who immediately donated five thousand guilders to one community for the restoration of the church door.

Even the reader must make an extra effort, now that we have come to the end of this affair, to dismiss "Faitel" from his mind. It is only Freudenstern who is presently the hero of the story! A tall young man with strands of blond hair stands before us, or rather is talking at this moment seated at the table with Professor Klotz, while dessert is about to be served. Of course, the formation of the teeth, the padded lips, the nasal pitch in Faitel's face had to remain absolutely fixed to prevent a monster from becoming visible. And whoever had an eye for such things could recognize the sensual, fleshy, and jutting Sphinx-like face in Freudenstern's profile. However, first of all, not everyone has an eye for such things. Second, one does not always look at someone's profile. Third, during a wedding celebration one hardly sees unpleasant things. Fourth, it was still debatable whether the Egyptian Sphinx-face was of Semitic nature. Fifth, Klotz had dropped a remark most elegantly during one of his private seminars on anthropology, in which he was giving students information about the determination of skull measurements, that Freudenstern's cranium formation was one of the purest specimens among all the examples known to him, and that it corresponded closest to the head formation of the Hermunduren, who had been the earliest historically known inhabitants of Germany.

Just then, the pudding was brought out. The friendly innkeeper of the White Lamb went around the table of feasting guests in a sweat and counted and counted, for he was to be paid one ducat per person excluding the wine. The menu did not entirely meet his taste and did not suit, so he believed, the reputation of a first-class inn like the White Lamb. As owner of the establishment, he had demanded a pure French menu. The predominantly German character of the wedding banquet was the result of Klotz's express orders. Yes, even sauerkraut was served, and in his desperation the innkeeper tried to offset this German vulgarity by giving it the French appellation *choucroute*. There were selected morsels of pork, and fatty sparkling rinds gleamed from all the trays entrenched as *entremets* in the middle of the table for the entire evening. Freudenstern sat between the bride, who was pale as wax, and Klotz. Across from them were the Schnacks. The flabby skin of old man Schnack's face seemed to pull back, frightened by the wasteful quantities of food piled up in front of him, and he looked with astonishment through his large silver-framed monocle at these people who were well-versed in consummation. A stand-up collar with a shining white tie held in the correct position his long neck with the dug-out larynx. A medal sparkled on his tidy, black double-breasted jacket. It had arrived the evening before from Karlsruhe. Moreover, Schnack was addressed repeatedly as "Herr Councillor of the Chancellery." Frau Schnack, with her *embonpoint* covered by elegant gray silk, shook her head energetically back and forth. The gems as large as pigeon eggs waddled on her ears. There was a cloud of fetid medicine over this part of the table. —Dessert was still being served.

Now, dear reader, prepare yourself! Something extraordinary appears to be in the making. A sultry atmosphere was forming in the room, like one you feel when a storm is about to break. A great deal of wine had been drunk. Moreover, Faitel, who had been congratulated by everyone, had to make toasts time and again. I don't know whether Faitel could hold a great deal of alcohol. The customs of his race indicate moderation. On the other hand, it is known that if you inundate the brain with spirits, they may not only generate critical explosions in the psychological and motor sensories of humans but also open up parts of the brain, or rather, zones of memory, which, without the influx of the combustible substance, would normally remain quiet for a long time, perhaps for eternity. As I said, I don't know whether Faitel was accustomed to drinking. What I do know is that Faitel had discarded the barbed belt, the preservative of his correct posture, for the first time right before this celebration. Nobody can reprimand him for this, since the discarding was symbolic. Faitel had entered Christian society for good on this day. Furthermore, the smart female reader will comprehend that a wedding day is followed by a wedding night, which consists of a wedding disrobement, so that this strange ornamental object had to be removed from the eyes of the tearful bride.

But now the time has finally come to inform the reader that Faitel had been sitting rigid and motionless for about ten minutes and gaping directly under the table. His face turned crimson at times and then white as chalk. He seemed to be occupied with entirely different thoughts that expanded and entranced him without his help. But not without the help of many glasses of cliquot that he hurriedly gulped down and that the concerned innkeeper quickly filled one after the other since the wine was not included in the cover price.

Faitel raised his right hand from time to time and made a gesture with his index finger as though he wanted to say "Psst! Psst!" so he could hear his inner voice better, for there was still a great tumult, clanging of plates, and chatter in the room. Nobody had an inkling about the wondrous experiment that the avenging angel was in the process of preparing. Faitel appeared to add to this in a very systematic and purposeful way by pouring down champagne as one shoots oil onto a flame that is at the point of extinction. When it seemed that the illumination that glowed within him was about to fizzle, he slowly brought his upper body against the table, stretched out his right hand without regarding it, grabbed the filled glass, drank it down, and then raised his finger as though he wanted to say: "Listen, is it coming?" —And it came.

The contents of this frenetic chain of thoughts seemed to be more cheerful and dynamic, for Faitel slapped himself with the flat of his hands on his thighs a few times, making a loud smack, and he laughed and giggled to himself. Those people who had a good ear could already hear now a few "Deradangs! Deradangs!" But the guests were not at all aware, as the reader is, about the meaning of "Deradang!" And the joking, laughing, and toasting of drinks drowned out the first warning sounds to a great extent. Klotz was involved in a lively discussion with his neighbor on the left. Only the bride on the right observed these early symptoms of delirium with composure and curiosity. Faitel's chin drilled itself deeper and deeper into his breast in its rigid position so that it finally assumed that crippled-looking compulsive formation familiar to the reader from the early part of the story. The people closest to Faitel, among them Frau Schnack, who was quick to understand what was happening, were now forced to take notice of him.

However, they seemed to want to attribute everything to a peculiar mood that had come over him. —"Waiterera! . . ." Faitel screamed suddenly with a rasping, vibrating voice. "Waiterera! —Champagnerera! —So *nu*, wot's de metter? —So vy shoodn't I hev notink to drink? —I vant you shood know dat I'm a human bing jost as good for sumtink as any ov you!"

Now everyone's attention in the room was immediately drawn to him. Even the waiters carrying the large piles of dishes came to a stop and stared at the middle of the rows of tables where a bloodthirsty, swelling, crimson visage spewed saliva from flabby drooping lips, and gushing eyes glared at them. Everyone seemed to be under a magic spell, and nobody knew what to do. Even Klotz lost his composure and looked with horror at the Jew next to him. Faitel's glass had been filled once again by the innkeeper, who stood behind him. While terrified and sympathetic forces focused on him from all directions, Faitel himself began to speak with a squeaky and entirely different tone of voice. "What doth he do in the next three hours, the holy Jehovah? —Deradang! Der a dang!"

With one quick swoop, his thumbs were in the pockets of his wedding vest. Now he bobbed back and forth and gave an infatuated look at the heavens. —Again with a changed voice giving the answer: "He sitteth and copulateth the men and women!" Again the first voice: "How long doth the holy Lord copulate the men and women?" the same *positur*; lascivious movements back and forth on the chair; jumping up and down, gurgling, clicking of the tongue. —The voice answering: "Three hours long doth he copulate the men and women!"

First voice: "What doth he do in the afternoon, the holy Jehovah? Deradang! Deradang!" —Answer: "He doth nothing, Jehovah. He taketh a rest!" First voice: "What didst thou say? What doth thou mean? The holy Jehovah doth nothing? What doth he do? What doth Jehovah do in the afternoon? Huh?" —A young boy's voice from the distance: "The holy Jehovah playeth with Leviathan in the afternoon!" —The first voice interjects triumphantly: "Naturally! He playeth with Leviathan!"

At this moment Faitel jumped from his chair, began clicking his tongue, gurgling, and tottering back and forth while making disgusting, lascivious, and bestial canine movements with his rear end. "Deradang! Deradang!"

He jumped around the room. "I done bought for me Chreesten blud! Waiterera, vere iss mine copulated Chreesten bride? Mine bridera! Geeve me mine bridera! I vant you shood know that I'm jost a Chreesten human bing like you all. Not von drop of Jewish blud! —Wot misery! Vere is mine bridera?"

Everyone scattered. The terrifying visage drove the young ladies from the room. Those people who remained behind watched with horror as Faitel's blond strands of hair began to curl during the last few scenes. Then the curly locks turned from red to dirty brown to blue-black. The entire glowing and sweaty head with tight gaunt features was once again covered with curly locks. Meanwhile, it appeared that Faitel had peculiar difficulties and struggled with his exalted movements. His arms and legs, which had been stretched and bent in numerous operations, could no longer perform the recently learned movements, nor the old ones. Moreover, the paralyzing effect of the alcohol made itself quickly felt. To be sure, Klotz had cried for ice packs, but it was in vain. Everyone saw that this was a catastrophe that could no longer be prevented. The beautiful Othilia sought refuge in the arms of her mother. Everyone looked with dread at the crazy circular movements of the Jew. The ignominious end, which is the fate of all drunkards, befell Faitel, too. A terrible smell spread in the room, forcing those people who were still hesitating at the exit, to flee while holding their noses. Only Klotz remained behind. And finally, when even the feet of the drunkard were too tired to continue their movements, Klotz's work of art lay before him crumpled and quivering, a convoluted Asiatic image in wedding dress, a counterfeit of human flesh, Itzig Faitel Stern.

The Operated Goy (1922)

Mynona (Salomo Friedlaender)

THE COUNT VON REHSOK'S FAMILY was accustomed to boasting a great deal about the indisputable purity of a racial bloodline that had been documented for centuries. It could be proven that a Rehsok had already distinguished himself in a stunning way during Titus's destruction of Jerusalem. Ever since then, the struggle against the Jewish plague, which had threatened to wipe out the frail Aryans, had been joined by each and every respectable count in the Rehsok line as though it were his privilege. In fact, the Rehsoks supplied parliament with the most eloquent leaders of the anti-Semitic movement, and they especially inveighed against the Jewish-Aryan mix-breeds, who had succeeded in marrying into the Prussian aristocracy and even in poisoning the milieu of the king with the pestilential stench of their misbegotten blood. Every Aryan child knows what a Jew looks like. Indeed, every domestic pet can sniff out a Jew. If one carefully abstracted certain elements from each Jewish and each Oriental type, then one would be left with the type representative of the counts of Rehsok: they did not wear corkscrew locks; rather, their hair was soft and wavy, almost silvery blond. Their white foreheads dropped steeply like walls of granite instead of sinking and slanting toward the rear. They were suspicious of so-called eagle noses, for their noses were unbelievably straight. They all had thin lips, Prussian chins, proud necks, and fabulously slender builds, and their legs, which in their innocence did not know either X or O, stood simultaneously on aristocratic and pan-Germanic feet and took strides as though descending from Mount Olympus. Above all, they did not have narrow eyes with a dark brown glow but open, true blue ones that glistened like pure ice, and the power of their imperious look was enhanced exceedingly by the monocle.

Now, at the proper time Count Kreuzwendedich Rehsok traveled to Bonn in order to be with his noble relatives, the Borussians, and to spend a couple of semesters studying at the university before following the traditional path of a military career. Upon his departure his parents, siblings, aunts, and uncles kept warning him, for God's sake, not to throw his life away on a worthless woman: "Keep your blood pure! There are now enormously rich Semitic daughters who are keen on our kind. Sometimes they're not exactly bad looking—on the contrary. But it would be a disgrace to our noble heritage if one of us were to keep just one of them as a mistress."

As if such warnings were at all necessary for Kreuzwendedich! He was so much above and beyond this that he had promised his father he would order all his articles and utensils only from strict anti-Semitic manufacturers if at all possible. Whatever was around him, whatever he touched had to be completely cleansed of Jewishness and remain that way. For instance, he had a Bible produced in which all the Hebrew names were translated into German. Consequently, the wise Solomon was called the wise Friedrich. Incidentally, his favorite literature was not the Bible but Nordic mythology. His noble head was filled with Odin and his entourage. His future wife was to be called Frigga; his children, *in spe*, Balder, Braga, Hermod, Thor, and Tyr. He had given the name Audumbla to a cow in his father's barn and called his little castle Muspelheim. His servant responded to the giant's name Bor and was, in truth, a giant in stature. Moreover, Kreuzwendedich kept two trained ravens and called them Hugin and Munin. As was the case with all such lordly men, Count Rehsok also had a latent aversion toward Christianity, "that Jewish offshoot of an Indian tribe."

This, then, was the Count Kreuzwendedich Rehsok, who went to Bonn, where he mixed only with a few Borussians from the high aristocracy, remained silent most of the time, and if he talked, only in the style of a telegram. The giant Bor needed just half a word to guess what he meant. "Take walk! Clean street! Signal before! Swastika! Detour!" In good grammatical German this meant: Bor was to accompany him on a walk, and if anyone or anything Jewish showed up, he was to give him a signal so that he could make a detour around the Jewish schools or synagogues. And Bor was to stick a swastika on the arm of his coat. This was the way the cavalier strutted through the streets with the customary white student cap on his blond parted hair, his monocle on his eye, followed by his livery servant in a set distance. As soon as anything Hebrew showed itself, the servant made a shrill sound with a silver whistle. Of course, it would be superfluous to remark that the Count's Great Dane was carefully trained to bite any Jew who came too close. In addition, the raven Hugin could correctly chirp the well-known Borkum anti-Semitic hymn.

In the meantime, word got around about the young count's behavior, which was an immense delight to the Germanic families of the city. Even the quarrelsome Jewish children learned about it so that it was unavoidable that certain extraordinarily delicate ears would also hear about it. Indeed, Rebecca Gold-Isaac, a languishing odalisque with eyes like almonds, ebony hair, ivory skin, et cetera, et cetera, became tremendously upset because the count had become the talk of the town. "I'm going to buy me this pompous turkey," she decided for herself, "even if I have to marry him out of revenge."

Her papa was practically a billionaire. Therefore, it was immensely easy to transform Rebecca Gold-Isaac into the Baroness Freia-Rotraut von Isagold and to bestow upon her head a bronze wig like something painted by Titian. And yet, despite it all, she still had difficulty crossing the path that the count took on his walks with Bor whistling, the Great Dane snapping, and the fluttering raven, which Bor handled like a falcon, piping the customary hymn. So imperturbably sure of their purpose were they that their instincts functioned here perfectly despite her disguise. However, one time they were just a split second too late. And this split second was just enough for a veritable Count Rehsok. But patience, we are getting ahead of our story. . . .

Dazzled by the beauty of the young woman born Gold-Isaac, Bor almost forgot to whistle, and consequently the raven and the Great Dane almost forgot their duty so that Kreuzwendedich was able to take in the young Jewish woman for half a moment with eyes that were no less dazzled than Bor's. "Parbleu!"

He was startled. "Impossible! Especially since nothing smells. *Foetor judaicus* is otherwise infallible."

"Whoever can't smell should feel," retorted Freia-Rotraut, and lifted a riding whip. Together, Count Rehsok and Bor seized her by the arm. Her cheeks became feverishly crimson, and with a ravishingly beautiful and scornful Medusa look, she said, "Shame on you!" And she spit her contempt into the count's face, jumped into her carriage that came rolling up to fetch her, and drove away.

This incident, too, became the talk of the town. The Borussians threw mud at Gold-Isaac in front of his palatial mansion. However, love (preferably called Eros by people with a finer education) is capricious and likes to unite opposing forces (cf. the Montagues and Capulets). As far as purity of race was concerned, the house of Gold-Isaac was the Jewish counterpart to the family of Count Rehsok: ditto, ever since the destruction of Jerusalem, and ever since the dispersion of the Jewish people in many different countries, the family had never become contaminated by alien blood.

To be sure, this fact was passed on more by word of mouth than documents. Whatever the case may be, Count Rehsok had suffered a psychological trauma after gazing upon the beautiful Rebecca or rather Freia-Rotraut, for he had not been spared, and he could not get rid of this trauma because he did not clearly grasp what it was. And it was the same with Rotraut—a half a moment had been enough. Fascinated by his inimical strangeness, she felt hate, vanity, and fury mixed with love. She yearned ardently to overcome everything—that is, she yearned for complete assimilation and incorporation of the enemy.

She strengthened her resolve to marry him and thus intended to triumph over him and his clan. Just one look was like lightning and had revealed to her how much power she had over him. Still under the influence of her spit, Kreuzwendedich, enchanted by her, was in a trance. To be sure, he knew nothing about his feelings. His "high consciousness" was highly anti-Semitic enough to abhor Rebecca in an honest and unsuspecting way.

Nonetheless, she felt and knew perfectly well that she had to become the Countess Rehsok. Nor would she settle for anything less, and if she failed, she would have no other choice but to plunge into the crater of self-despisement. Who knows, then, whether what people call love is nothing more than the reinforcement of one's very own self-confidence? The weak feminine sex desires this reinforcement passionately, while the strong masculine sex enjoys the power of its self-possession doubly or three times to the full through the generous sensual pleasure of concession.

What a problem! Bringing about the reconciliation between the Montagues with the Capulets was child's play in comparison. Freia-Rotraut knew with utmost certainty that she would not be happy until Count Rehsok's offspring sprouted from her Jewish womb. The young count had strange feelings. He lacked something, but he did not like to recall what it was. He did not want to admit to himself that he was lost to the beautiful Jewess. For better or worse, Rebecca had to take the initiative. So, she revealed everything to her parents.

Mother Gold-Isaac, named Hagar, waddled about and wrung her hands studded with rings. Back and forth she went through three grand parlors, continually crying out, to be sure, in the purest high German: "*Veh is mir*, dear God! My child is *meshugga*!"

Papa Gold-Isaac, whose first name was coincidentally Isaac, dealt in *Realpolitik*, and as he sat in his easy chair, half-lying and twiddling his thumbs, he posed phlegmatic questions: "What a situation! It had to be the Rehsoks! If you had asked me, they're all *nebbechs* and rich to boot. I can't buy them for you. There's nothing I can do here. Good, my child, even though my heart is breaking on account of your poor mother—don't sob, Hagar dear—I won't stand in your way. If he has himself circumcised with everything that goes with it, caftan, *payess*, *tallith* tassels, Rebecca, you can have as many counts as you want. I can buy practically the whole city of Gotha. And, if I have to, I'll get you Rehsok—only he must let himself be circumcised. If not, we'll give you our good Jewish curse so that your womb will wither!"

Rotraut was horrified. Unfortunately, Isaac-Gold belonged to the sect of Birnbaumianers, who believe that the only real Jew is the East European Jew. The cultivated West European Jew, for example, the catholicizing Martin Buber, was already considered a decadent Jew. Freia was faced with a terribly difficult task. What could she do? Something occurred to her. She sensed with the sharpest feminine intuition that she had captured Kreuzwendedich's heart. Wasn't it precisely the radical despising of Jews that could serve as the most unlikely means to produce the opposite? Couldn't it generate the quickest turnabout to the other extreme?

Anti-Semitism is perhaps even more Jewish than Judaism. After all, whoever hates and despises predisposes himself in all secrecy, slowly but surely, for the most intimate ties of blood, indeed, for an identification with the object of his negation. If she could make the young count aware of all this, then she could be sure of him. Of course, the count would first have to feel how necessary it was to be psychoanalyzed. Rebecca bribed Rehsok's servant Bor much more with her charm than with money and sought contact with feudal aristocrats, who, in turn, influenced the young Rehsok gently but firmly in her interest until the count himself suddenly appeared in the office of the famous Dr. Freud, where the young man displayed some puzzling psychological inhibitions. In response, the authentic destroyer of subterfuges robbed Count Rehsok's psyche of its protective cover in such a sure-handed anatomical way that the count sank with a terrible cry into the arms of his servant who had rushed over to catch him. Then he collected himself, and with inherited bravery, indeed, with a certain boldness, he looked at his fate in the form of the marvelously beautiful Rebecca Gold-Isaac straight in the eye. At first, all this took place only in his imagination, but soon it was also to be in person.

Now he was prepared to surrender body and soul. Rotraut began to dominate him completely and he acquiesced, gnashing his teeth but also with delight. When he made his first visit to the palatial mansion of Gold-Isaac without ravens, Great Dane, and servant, the Borussians held him in ill-repute and sent their first office-bearers to the count's father, who most solemnly called for a family meeting. However, not only did Kreuzwendedich not appear, but the news also spread that he had become secretly engaged to Rotraut. As a result, the Rehsok clan announced that he was banned and excommunicated. However, he had already reached such a strong mutual understanding with Rotraut that he did not give the slightest care about the banishment. On the contrary, he breathed a sigh of relief. Yet, now that she had got him this far, Rotraut began to reject him. Consequently, he insisted on knowing the reason for her recent withdrawal since he wanted to marry her in a respectable manner.

"First become a Jew, completely Jewish, a Jew to the point of excess, with caftan, phylactery, and long locks of hair. You don't love me with all your heart unless you become utterly Jewish deep in the marrow of your Aryan bones, a Jew and nothing but a Jew. You in particular owe this to us as atonement."

After delivering this ultimatum, Rotraut refused to see him anymore and thereby drove him to commit a most exalted act that arose from his crazed love for her. He began studying Hebrew and had numerous rabbis initiate him into Jewish teachings, prayers, commandments, and customs. He visited many synagogues and other places of worship. Finally, he let himself be officially converted to Judaism and also underwent the fatal cut of the knife that every male Jewish baby, without being asked, tolerates without giving it a thought. Now he was given permission to appear before Rotraut, but he found her unmoved when he, his monocle covering the tears on his eyelashes, entered her blue parlor.

"A monocle? —Please, Moses—he was now called Moishe Mogandovidwendedich—drop the monocle! Your Jewish soul hasn't really taken complete hold of the infernal Rehsok body yet! This goyim posture is an insult to the memory of my forefathers. Is that love? Do you think I could stand with you like that under the *chuppa*? Do you think I want to be wed to such a bridegroom looking the way you still look? Until the former Rehsok really looks like a Jewish man, like in the paintings of Steinhardt, Segal, or Chagall, you can forget all about marrying me!"

After saying this, she showed him a picture of two warped young men, whereupon the man, who had now become the actual Moishe, crushed the monocle with one of the heels of his shoes that still clanked a little like a spur.

"You demand the impossible, Rebecca!"

"March!" Rebecca pointed with her index finger. "Go to Professor Friedlaender! He's expecting you and has already been paid to boot!"

Friedlaender was one of the most famous orthopedists around. However, he was now confronted with the perverse task, in a certain way to do the reverse, that is, to act as a caco-orthopedist. He was to transform an aristocratic, valiant figure of Germanic stock into the Jewish intellectual type. The static principle of Rehsok's feudal body was to be convulsed into the Jewish one.

So, first, the doctor used the most radical electrical instruments to eliminate the hair from the count's blond head, covered it with a wig of strict Galiziana coiffure, and dyed the eyebrows black. The doctor devoted special attention to the nose, which he endowed with an artificial hump and made the tip curl over. Thereafter, he performed one of his most famous spinal atrophies. The count's bones were broken at their joints and then carefully brought to heal in the shape of an egg. It was in this condition testifying to his change that Count Moishe had himself photographed and used the photograph to present himself to Rebecca and her *mishpocheh* in effigy for the time being. Then he disappeared, with brand new flat feet, to Romania to learn Yiddish from the wonder rabbis there as well as all the gestures that go along with it. He talked with arms, legs, and tongue, a man after Jehovah's own heart. In a letter written in Hebrew he announced to his fiancée's parents that he would soon be making the bridegroom's official visit.

The family cordiality at his reception could not have been more splendid. The marriage date was moved ahead. In order to obtain the inalienable portion of the disinherited Moishe's inheritance, Papa Gold-Isaac mobilized his attorneys, who reached an agreement with the Rehsok family whereby Count Moishe had to discard his aristocratic name. And, what a horror!

On this occasion, while they were having a great deal of trouble finding a Jewish name for the count, some jokester discovered that the family name of Count Rehsok was kosher spelled backward.

Thus, under pious laughter Count Kreuzwendedich Rehsok now became and embodied the real stockbroker Moishe Kosher. Rebecca's triumph was boundless, and she made sure that the entire world, especially the people who counted, learned about it. This grotesque affair reached the highest echelons. Indeed, nobody spoke about anything else at the court and in high society.

At the next family gathering of the Rehsok clan, astonishment and rage got the upper hand. They planned to disturb if not hinder the wedding celebration. Nor were they ashamed to stir up the Borussians, who had taken Bor and the two ravens into their employ after they had been discharged by Kosher. At the wedding table in Gold-Isaac's mansion, the close relatives were seated alongside the president of the Jewish congregation. The house organ played music by Mendelssohn and Bruch. After a dozen or so rabbis had blessed the young couple in the synagogue, they all held celebration speeches almost at the same time. Moishe Kosher handed Rebecca (it was just the time of Passover) a round *matzoh* to bite, and Rebecca herself was just about to take a bite when suddenly the giant Bor stormed into the large room and trampled the waiters. He was disguised or rather undisguised as one-eyed Odin, and on his shoulders were the ravens Hugin and Munin, who smartly croaked the Borkum anti-Semitic hymn.

All at once the organ became silent. "God of my fathers!" Moishe Kosher exclaimed, not so incorrectly, and he stood up on his crooked legs, the *tallith* strangely wrapped around his thighs. Now all the Borussians stormed inside, and there was hand-to-hand combat. The women and girls fled to the gallery and screamed with all their might. Rebecca, always sober, alerted the police by telephone. Gold-Isaac made his way to Odin and stuffed his pockets full with hundred-mark bills. "This is for you, my man, and more, if you drive these thugs out of here."

The two ravens flapped their wings and took off from Bor's shoulders like bats from hell zooming toward the tables.

"May God bless whoever has only one eye!" screamed Gold-Isaac. "He's king among the blind goyim."

Bor, nicely financed, helped the Jewish congregation drive the Borussians out of the room, where they fell into the hands of the police. Once they were charged, they had to pay dearly for their actions.

Now Mr. and Mrs. Moishe Kosher are living today as committed Zionists in a country villa near Jerusalem. To be sure their offspring are not called Balder, Braga, Hermond, Tor, and Tyr. Instead, they have more melodic and honest names: Shlaume, Shmul, Feigelche, Pressel, and Yankef.

The Rehsok clan has vainly sought to the present day to change its name and must consequently put up with the fact that, when something is not completely kosher, people in their circles say that it is not completely "rehsok."

Since then, anti-Semitism has noticeably slackened. Certain orthopedists are feared and resisted by people who are still proud of the purity of their race. Nevertheless, Professor Friedlaender has enjoyed an enormous increase of clientele. He has an institute that rents out masks, but it does not rent out mere costumes. Rather, it produces skin and hair, bones and muscle as disguises.

A former emperor from the West recently had himself transformed into a Negro in order to escape the Bolshevist rabble. Tsar Nicholas, who had disappeared, is living today as a harmless rabbi in Moishe Kosher's vicinity, and they are on familiar footing with each other. One no longer bases everything dogmatically on racial differences. Racial blood has stopped being considered a special kind of vital juice. Meanwhile, Professor Friedlaender gathers it in bottles and continues to transfer it undauntedly from one vessel into another.

Two Saviors (1877)

Karl Emil Franzos

WHOEVER HAS EVER VISITED Barnov will have certainly come across old Hanna, the mother of the head of the Jewish congregation, and I am sure that these visitors undoubtedly enjoyed her sensitive and gracious ways. As for those people who have never been there, it is almost impossible to describe how lovely and smart this old lady was. Everyone in this town called her "Babele," or grandma, and not just her own grandchildren, for she provided anyone who came to her with help and advice. She was tireless throughout her entire, long, and blessed life. Even those people who did not need her money or advice immediately looked to spend an hour or so listening to a tantalizing story. Indeed, she was just as highly regarded and loved as storyteller as she was helper. Whoever walked by the old synagogue, the Jewish "castle" on a sabbath afternoon during the summer about three o'clock could see how many people used to listen to her with rapt attention and at the same time how much she earned it. The wise old woman sat on the small steps in the shade, and fifty or so men and women sat close together in silence so that they wouldn't miss a word that old Hanna spoke.

And what were her tales about? I'll tell you right away: stories about the lives of people in the congregation that she had heard or witnessed. It would be most difficult to describe how she told these tales. If I, nevertheless, attempt to do this and retell one of her stories. I have one that especially prompts this venture—it is a story that she used to tell most frequently, and I myself heard it so often that I believe that I am capable of retelling it in high German just as I heard it many years ago.

"Who is great?" Grandma Hanna would often begin her storytelling. "And who is small? Who is strong, and who is weak?" Our poor short-sighted human eyes can rarely determine this. We all believe that the rich and powerful person is powerful and great, and the poor and frail person is weak and small. However, the truth is different. Wealth does not determine things. Nor the strength in one's arms. Rather it is the strong will and the good heart! And sometimes, my dear people, sometimes God lets us clearly recognize this. And we, the people of Barnov know something about this that's worth telling! Our congregation has experienced misery and distress two times, as well as trouble and mortal danger, and two times there have been saviors among us who have stood up and protected us from need and transformed wretched wailing into gratitude and a prayer. And who were these saviors? Do you think it was the strongest and wealthiest among us? Listen to what I have to tell you exactly as it happened.

If you walk across the marketplace, then you will see a thick, large wooden block emerging from the ground. It is right in front of the Dominican cloister. You can also see that it is brittle and weather-beaten, and they should have gotten rid of it long ago if it weren't for the fact that it is a remembrance of a terrible and oppressive time. I'm sure that you don't know anything about this older time—and you can be happy about that! I don't want to take away your happiness. The story I want to tell you is about a beautiful deed from this hateful period. You will be glad when I tell you more about this, for it was a heroic deed—so bright, so proud, and one that had never been accomplished on this earth. A simple Jewish woman accomplished this deed. Her name was Leah, and she was the wife of the rich and pious Samuel—the name was later changed to Beermann when the Prussian imperial rule arrived and changed all our family names to German names. In those days, when this story took place, we didn't have names like that. You must understand that all this took place more than a hundred years ago, and we lived under the rule of the Polish eagle.

Oh, the Polish reign took the form of a furious and grim predator, a single-headed white eagle! When its feathers were still unscathed, its eyes clear, and its claws tight and sharp, it was a noble, proud animal that raised and improved everything and magnanimously protected everything that fled beneath its wings. And, fortunately for us, we lived for three long centuries in light and freedom. However, as the eagle became old and weak and the other predators around him tore out a feather, one after the other, he became cowardly, insidious, and mean. And since he didn't dare to use his beak against the invaders, he began to torment the defenseless Jews. The power of the Polish kings was soon mocked and along with that, all the letters of freedom that they had given to us. The aristocrats became our masters, and they tormented us and did whatever they wanted with our possessions. Oh, it was an unspeakable oppression!

At that time, our tiny town already belonged to the noble lineage of the Bortynskis, who later were awarded the title of count by the good emperor Joseph. It was during this time that the young Joseph Bortynski took possession of the estate. He was a quiet, pious, and modest mensch and had been raised in a cloister. He did not act like the other young aristocrats. He hated wine, cardplaying, and women. He himself took charge of the estate's business and prayed four times daily. He treated his subjects justly and fondly. Of course, we did not benefit from any of this. He treated us harshly and cruelly—even when his heart wanted to touch and move him. His teacher knew how to hinder this. This man was his chaplain and had a great influence on him. I can't remember his name, but we always used to call him the vicious dark lord.

During this time we Jews were very anxious and tried to stay invisible. Even those Jews who were criminals sought to keep out of sight and didn't commit any crimes.

"You have crucified my God," the count said to Samuel one day and then angrily added, "Woe to you if I discover anyone among you who commits a sin. I'll set your nest on fire. Just like your own God did with Sodom and Gomorrah!"

You can imagine how we all felt.

Well, in the spring of the year 1773, Easter stood before the door, and a rumor was spread that the empress in Vienna wanted to take over the entire territory that the Poles had possessed. Moreover, her scribes were to replace the Poles. In the meantime, however, we did not see any change.

During this time the caretaker Samuel and his wife Leah lived in the same old house that is still standing on the marketplace. They were both highly respected in the community—Samuel because of his wealth, his intelligence, and devoutness, and his beautiful young wife because of her gentleness and charity. Unfortunately, they happened to be in great distress during this Easter: their only child, a little boy, one and a half years old, had suddenly died a few days earlier, and his parents could scarcely overcome the pain that they suffered. So one Sunday they sat late into the evening next to one another in sadness and grief. The next day the Easter celebration was to begin. They had worked and scrubbed the floors that entire day, cleaning the house, and Leah felt exhausted. All at once there was a knocking on the door that frightened her. Samuel went to the window, opened it, and looked outside. An old peasant woman with a bundle on her back stood at the gate, and she pitifully whimpered and groaned and asked whether she could spend the night there. She was too weak to return to the village.

"This is not a tavern," Samuel responded bluntly, and he slammed the window shut.

"The poor woman," Leah intervened. "Do you think we should turn her away like that?"

"This is a bad time," Samuel answered. "I don't want to put up with strangers in my house."

"But she is sick and weak," Leah pleaded, and since the old woman kept begging and moaning outside, Samuel yielded and let her enter into the house. Since the servants were already asleep, Leah led the late-night guest into a room on the ground floor, brought her some food and drink, and then left her with a friendly goodnight gesture.

The next morning the old woman said goodbye very early and expressed her thanks and gave her blessings a thousand times. Leah had a great deal to do to prepare for the holiday, and only toward late afternoon did she manage to have time to enter the room on the ground floor. She wanted to make sure that all the rooms were clean and that there were no rotten breadcrumbs before the holiday events began. When she entered the room where the old woman had slept, she saw that everything was in order except for a terrible stench. Even when Leah opened a window, the smell would not go away, and she could not determine the source of the abominable smell. She searched in all the corners of the room, and finally looked beneath the bed. Immediately, her blood curdled, and her hair stood on end out of horror. Indeed, the naked, emaciated corpse of a child, with broad wounds on his neck and chest, lay beneath the bed. With lightning speed Leah realized that the old woman had deceived them, and she fought with all the energy she possessed to prevent herself from fainting. The wicked woman had dragged the corpse into their home so that the old, terrible myth about Jews slaughtering Christian children during Easter would once again be revived and enable the Christians to take vengeance. With lightning speed she also recognized the terrible consequences and remembered the words that the count had spoken to her husband. The poor woman almost collapsed from the force of these awful thoughts.

"Oh, it was me, me alone, who has exposed our home and community to misery, torture, and death!" she cried and felt guilty because she had wanted and allowed the old woman to enter the house. And as she sat there, scared to death, she heard wild calls and screams and moaning bursting from the street. In between there was a clanging of weapons.

"They're already coming," she whispered, and just then, a thought flashed through her mind. It was so weird and atrocious that it perhaps had never before come to the mind of a woman. But it was also noble and heroic as only a woman could have imagined.

"I'm guilty," she heard within herself, "and I must pay for what I did."

Now she stood up and pressed her lips together and overcame the horror she felt. Then she grabbed hold of the child's corpse, wrapped him in a sheet, and put him on her lap.

She listened . . . and the minutes ran by very slowly. Then she heard the young count outside speaking roughly with her husband and his assistant.

"The old woman heard the death rattle very clearly. I won't leave one stone unturned until I find the corpse."

As the men drew near the room, she stood up and moved over to the open window. The roof slanted steeply, and beneath the window a stone courtyard spread out. Suddenly, the door was ripped open, and the count entered with the two caretakers and his guards behind him. To their surprise Leah dashed toward them, pointed to the corpse, and tossed it through the window so that it fell upon the stones in the courtyard and was smashed to smithereens.

"I am a murderer," she screamed at the count. "Yes, yes. Arrest me! Tie me up! Kill me! I have killed my own child. I won't deny it!"

The men stood dumbfounded. Then there were wild cries, screaming, and questions. Samuel, who was a strong and smart man, fainted. The other Jews quickly understood the situation and understood what Leah was doing and played along with her white lie. This was the only way that she saw that she could save herself from her doom. Leah gave her testimony and stuck to it. The count was dubious and gave her a sharp look. However, Leah comfortably withstood the count's look.

"Listen, woman," he said. "If what you have said is true, you will suffer the most terrible martyr's death than any person has ever suffered before. If other people have slaughtered the child to drink his blood at some feast, then you and your husband will not be punished. I'll only punish the others. I swear that I'll find the truth!! And now—you must decide!"

Leah did not sway a second from her testimony.

"It was my child!" she responded.

Now the count led Leah alone to the jail. He grasped just how improbable her story was. But he didn't believe that any Jew was capable of such magnanimity. "If what she said was a lie," he thought, "how could this woman be moved to sacrifice herself?"

The investigation was unable to bring the truth to light. All the Jewish witnesses incriminated Leah. One reported that Leah beat her child, and another witness said that Leah threatened to kill her child. You could see how terrified they were of being implicated. The only Christian witness was the dark man's housekeeper. She had disguised herself as a peasant woman and had come to the house of Samuel and Leah to destroy the entire community. And she had heard the child cough in the night, so she said. This was her only statement because if she had said more, she would have exposed herself. Her testimony supported Leah's white lie. The dark man himself seemed not to care much about the investigation. He was only afraid that his own crimes might accidentally be exposed.

The count's judges sentenced Leah to be taken to the marketplace and broken on the wheel. The block of wood over there was set up for this purpose. However, Leah did not die on this place of execution. Actually, she reached an advanced age and died peacefully in her house some forty years later, surrounded by her children and grandchildren. The imperial military government arrived and replaced the Poles in the summer of the year that all this had happened, and an auditor took over all the painfully embarrassing cases. The desperate Samuel told him the truth, and thankfully, the auditor sent her home free.

The block of wood is still standing there today. It sends a reminder about those dark times but also about a bright heroic deed. Indeed, it was a *woman* who had accomplished this deed. A so-called weak woman had saved the community.

And then, seventy years later, my friends, seventy years later, we had the same troubles and were terribly frightened. And who do you think saved us? This time it wasn't a woman, but a tiny, jittery man whose name will cause you all to laugh if I mention it. I can see that you are already smirking. Well, yes, it was Little Mendele. Now I know that he is somewhat barmy and whirrs merrily about the place. Yet, the stories about him are sumptuous, and he himself is very comical, the gray-haired man with the shape and character of a child. He doesn't walk along the streets. Rather, he hops. He doesn't articulate his words, he sings them. And it seems that the only reason he has hands is to use them to drum on tables or to beat time on them. Personally, I prefer a jolly person rather than someone who is always depressed. This is not Mendele Abendstern, for he is a good and great singer, and we can be proud that he is our cantor. Of course, sometimes he warbles a beautifully moving prayer as though it were a waltz and shifts one foot to another as if he were a dancer in the theater. However, all this doesn't disturb our prayers and devotion. We have become accustomed to Little Mendele for over forty years, and if anyone is justly irritated by him, that person should not hold it against him. Rather this person must take into consideration how Little Mendele can also be very serious and how he as a poor cantor did a great service for the whole town one time through his singing. In fact, he did more than all the wise and wealthy men with their counsel and money. And now I'm going to tell you how this came about.

You know now that the Jew is just as good as any other human being. And when a nobleman or a peasant hits or oppresses you, you only have to go into the house where the large eagle is hanging above the door, and the imperial district judge Mr. Negrusz will protect your rights. But before that great year, when the emperor guaranteed equal rights to all people, things were different. The landlord had a fixed mandate and could determine what was just or not just. Of course, this mandate was unjust. Oh, my dear friends, believe me. Those were difficult years. The landlord owned the entire land; he owned the people; he owned the core in their bones, and even the air that people breathed and the water they drank. Our landlord, the Count Bortynski, lived mostly in Paris and did not care very much about his property. His administrator was in charge of everything, and so we always had to pray that he would be a good man. Otherwise we would not be able to live in peace and quiet. At first, our prayers were heard by God, and the fat administrator Herr Stephan Grudza arrived, and we Jews could not have asked for a better man. Of course, he was drunk from morning until nightfall. So he was always cheerful, and if he was cheerful, he did not enjoy making other people sad. Then one time, as he was enjoying the midday meal a bit too much, he had a heart attack right after the meal. When he was buried, there was a good deal of sadness among the members of our community. Why? Well, simply because this Herr Grudza was really a good and kind man. So, then we were all worried that his replacement might not be as cheerful and kind.

Our sadness was unfortunately based very much on past experience. The new administrator was Friedrich Wollmann and was German. Usually the Germans tended to be milder toward us Jews than the Poles, but he was an exception. He was a tall, emaciated man with black hair and dark flashing eyes. His face was grim and sad—always, always. He never smiled. He knew a great deal about managing a large property, and he understood people extremely well. For instance, there was no one as good as he was at making the murderers and thieves confess their crimes. With regard to taxes, it was impossible for anyone to cheat and steal a single penny. Unfortunately, he hated us Jews with ferocity and caused us a great deal of suffering every day. He tripled our taxes. He forced our son Saline to join the army. He disturbed our celebrations and parties, and if we had some dealings and disputes with the Christian workers, he always took the side of the Christians. Our word was worth nothing, and the Christians were always right. Moreover he was also strict with the peasants and held them back and controlled them mercilessly. He completed the management of the property more perfectly than anyone could remember. In doing this there was always a certain justice. Yet, as soon as anything concerned the Jews, he had no understanding for us, and we had no rights.

"Why did he torture us this way?" you might ask. Nobody knew why, but the Jews suspected why it was so. They knew that at one time his name had been Froim Wollmann, and that he was a baptized Jew from Poland. He converted to Christianity because he fell in love with a Christian girl and wanted to marry her. However, the Jews in his hometown had persecuted him out of anger and indignation. In fact, they slandered him so much that the parents of the girl would not let him marry her. I am not certain who it was who brought this news to us, but when one looked at his face, it was indeed likely that he had experienced something traumatic, especially when one saw how badly he behaved toward us Jews. Consequently we experienced many sad days at that time, and Wollmann oppressed us whether we were to blame for what happened to him or not. Even if there really was some reason for the way he was, there was no escaping his power. And this was the way everything was in the autumn before the great year.

Among us Jews, it is not particularly comfortable to be a soldier, and in Russia it was even worse than death, and if a Jewish child was slated to be recruited by the army, then he was lost forever by God, his parents, and himself. It's no wonder then if the Jews in Russia did all they could and spent money to liberate him. Or it's no wonder that if a young Jew was unlucky to be recruited, he endeavored to flee. Many Jews were captured, and it was better for them that they had never been born. Yet, many Jews did manage to escape over the border to Moldau or to us. There was an incident like this during our time. A Jewish soldier—he was from Berdiczov—came to us over the boundary at Husiatynn and was brought to Barnov. The congregation did what they could for him, and a rich, mild-mannered man, Chaim Grünstein, the father-in-law of Moses Freudenthal, hired him as a stable boy.

Of course, the Russian government searched for the fugitive, and all of our overseers were commanded to look for the soldier. Our manager also received such an order. Immediately he ordered all the heads of the synagogue community to come to him, and he questioned them thoroughly. At first, they were frightened, but then they got a grip on themselves and denied knowing anything about the fugitive soldier. It was just the day before the day of atonement. How could they appear before God if they had betrayed the soldier on the evening of the day of atonement? This is why they remained steadfast even if our manager threatened them and was enraged

When he saw that they had nothing to say about the fugitive or did not want to say anything, he let them go and said grimly, "Woe to you if this young soldier is in Barnov! You don't know how tough I can be, but wait—by God, wait, just wait and you'll find out!"

So the men left, and needless to say, how sad, scared, and depressed the people in the town were when they heard the news. The young man, who was at the center of this dilemma, was a good and diligent mensch. It was impossible to let him down. If he were to stay in Barnov, it would be very dangerous, for Wollmann would find him sooner or later. Nothing could be hidden from him. If they were to send him away without a passport, without identification papers, his pursuers would find him several miles from Barnov. The people gave him all sorts of advice. Finally, by chance, Chaim Grünstein happened to come by. He had a relative who was a farmer in the region of Marmaros in Hungary. They decided to send the fugitive soldier there that very night right after the day of atonement under the cover of darkness. This was the safest way to escape his persecutors. Everyone agreed, and they ate their large meal with great relief. It was to strengthen them before they began the fast on the day of atonement. Then dusk arrived, and the many, many candles were set aflame, and the entire congregation rushed to the synagogue with heavy and contrite hearts, full of humility and remorse. Indeed, these are the difficult hours, when we beg our great judge of judges so that He will be merciful and forgive our sins. The women wore white dresses, while the men dressed in white mourning outfits. Chaim Grünstein and his family also went there to bow before God. The poor young Russian was among them. He was scared to death, and his entire body trembled.

When everyone had assembled and the service was about to begin, Little Mendele put his hand flat on his throat to utter the first sounds of the "Kol-Nidra," nimbly and jittery. Then there was some noise at the door, and the count's guards blocked the exit, and in walked Herr Wollmann, slowly down the aisle past the seats right next to Little Mendele, who began to quiver and moved aside. The head of the congregation humbly approached him.

"I know that this young fugitive is here among you," Wollmann declared. "Do you want to surrender him now?"

Everyone in the congregation remained silent.

"Well now," the manager continued. "Well, well. Then I shall have him arrested when you leave the synagogue. Not only shall I have him arrested. You will never forget this evening. I can assure you of this! Now don't let me disturb you. Keep on praying. I have time. I want to listen."

There was dead silence in the room. There was only some noise upstairs in the women's room. It was the shrill cry of panic and fear. Everyone was horrified and paralyzed. Then they pulled themselves together, stood up, and raised their eyes toward God. Shortly after, they returned to their seats in silence.

Little Mendele had not stopped trembling. Then he straightened himself out and began singing the "Kol-Nidra" again. This time it was in that age-old simple way that nobody can forget once he or she has heard it. Little Mendele's voice quivered and was uncertain at first. But then it became stronger and stronger. It sounded heart-rending and clear and full throughout the room and soared over the heads of the praying people and up to God. A miraculous solemnity came over the people. As Little Mendele sang, he was no longer a little warbling man, rather a powerful priest, who raised his voice to God for his people.

He thought of the former glory and then the many centuries of disgrace and persecution, and you could hear in his voice how ruthlessly Jews were hounded all over the earth, the most impoverished among the poor, the most unfortunate among the unfortunate. And how the persecution had still not come to an end and how new persecutors continued to oppress us, and how as usual new swords dig into our flesh. All of our suffering resounded in his voice, our unspeakable suffering, our innumerable tears. And there was still something else that sounded in his voice—our pride, our confidence, our faith in God. Oh, it is impossible to describe how Little Mendele sang in this difficult hour—every person there had to weep, weep, weep, and yet, also had to lift their heads with pride.

The women wept very loudly when he came to an end. The men sobbed. Meanwhile Little Mendele buried his face in his hands and broke down. Wollmann had been looking at Mendele's face while he sang the "Thora-Lade," and then turned away when the prayer ended. He was terribly pale. His knees trembled. The strong man could hardly sit erect. His eyes flickered with tears. Then Wollmann stood up and tottered by Little Mendele, and with his head lowered he managed to walk down the aisle to the exit. Once there he signaled the guards to follow him—nobody knew exactly what had come over him. Many suspected what had happened, but nobody talked about this.

On the day after this event, Wollmann summoned Chaim Grünstein to his office and gave him a passport that was blank. The only thing he said to Grünstein was: "You may be able to use this."

From this time onward, Wollmann treated us more mildly. But not long after this things began to change. In spring of the Great Year, the peasants whom Wollmann had tormented killed him.

Well, now, my friends, this is the story about our saviors. Think once more about the question—who is great and who is small, who is weak and who is powerful?

The Shabbes Goy (1894)

I. L. Peretz

THE RABBI OF CHELM, in ragged fur cap and tattered satin robe, was a tiny Jew with a prominent Adam's apple and laughing gray eyes in a shriveled face. . . . Between one Talmudic problem and the next, the cheerful, gray-headed rabbi gets up, surveys with confidence the open Gemara through glasses on the tip of his nose, his shawl popping out of his chest, and, as his rightful share of worldly pleasures, takes up the wooden snuffbox.

A softhearted person, a being contented with his lot, he smiles at the snuffbox and taps on the cover, drumming lightly with his small fingers as though asking: Is there a little something there?

And when the snuffbox replies softly, "There is a bit left, there is!" he opens it leisurely, takes a crumb of a morsel between his fingertips and brings it to his nostrils, presses gently to the right, gently to the left—and then again. His eyes brighten, his heart gladdens, he strolls about the House of Judgment almost dancing, and he gives praise to the world's Creator in sing-song: "Ay, ay, Gottenyu, dear God, what a sweet world you have created!"

"What splendid creatures walk about in your dear world! Jews, and—to be exact—others. Ay, people made of gold, of velvet, of satin. . . ."

Suddenly, someone drops in: "Rebbe, help!"

He is alarmed.

"What happened to you, Yankele? Yankele!"

He recognizes him. The rabbi knows everyone in Chelm, for he has been godfather to almost all. And when he sees Yankele's bloodied mouth: "Oy, Yankele, who wronged you so, Yankele?"

Yankele is already seated on the bench in front of the table of justice holding on to his cheeks with bloodstained hands and rocking away without stopping, from left to right, this way and that.

"Oy, Yankele, who wronged you so, Yankele?"

"Oy, oy, the Shabbes goy, Rebbe."

The rabbi of Chelm stares in amazement. "In the middle of the week, how do you come to the Shabbes goy, Yankele?"

"A destined thing, Rebbe Leyb. I'm walking as usual in the marketplace. Just walking. And do you think, Rebbe Leyb, that I have the Shabbes goy in mind? I have nothing else to think about but the Shabbes goy? A Jew thinks about making a living, that's what he thinks about. Soon I'll be going home with empty hands—and I don't stop worrying. What will my wife have to say? That shrew of mine . . . but you know her well, Rebbe Leyb! So, he comes toward me, the Shabbes goy, and I look and see he's eating pumpkin seeds . . . and with such skill! He throws a handful right into his mouth—a single crack and already he's spitting out the shells, to the right and to the left. So, I stop and observe this great dexterity.

"He becomes friendly, like an equal, and says, 'Yankele, come on, open your mouth, Yankele!'

"Well, seeing that a goy pleads, I open my mouth supposing, Rebbenyu, dear Rebbe, that he wants to throw some nuts into it. I open wide . . . so he takes his fist, and—bang!—right into my mouth!"

At this, Yankele starts crying afresh: "Oy, the murderer, the murderer. . . ."

But this does not please the rabbi of Chelm at all. He draws nearer and reproaches him: "That I don't like, Yankele. How can you say such a thing, just so, about one of God's creatures—murderer?"

"But take a look, he knocked out three of my teeth," sobs Yankele, and shows him the teeth. The rabbi looks closely, shakes his head and says incredulously, "Tell me the truth, Yankele, are these *your* teeth?"

"Whose then, Rebbe? Here, Rebbe, look!"

The rabbi looks and marvels.

And Yankele opens his mouth wide to show him the holes. "Wonder of wonders," says the rabbi after a pause, "that a Jew should have such teeth. . . ."

"What kind of teeth, then, should a Jew have?" asks Yankele, by this time alarmed.

"Here, look!" answers the rabbi and shows him the old "furniture" in his aged mouth. "Some have no teeth at all—in any case, not *such* teeth! After all, I wasn't born yesterday. Never have I seen such teeth in a Jew's mouth!"

And the rabbi proceeds to ponder two questions at once: How does a Jew come to have such large, strong teeth? As to the Shabbes goy, what impels him to knock out strange teeth?

He ponders and ponders, and then jumps up. "Aha! That is to say, solved!

"It's all very clear, Yankele! The one depends upon the other. Just like that, you say 'murderer.' About one of God's creatures, *murderer*? There's no such thing. If there were murderers in the world, would God permit the world to exist? So, what then? But since you are relating an incident that happened, after all, and I believe you, and I see with my own eyes the knocked-out teeth, I must conclude, you understand, thus . . ."

He pauses to catch his breath and expounds: "The guilt, Yankele, in reality belongs to your teeth!"

Yankele leaps up to his full height. "How is it possible, Rebbe—my *teeth*? And the goy?"

"Wholly innocent he is not, Yankele, that's not what I'm saying! The basic fault, however, lies in the teeth; that is to say, not *your* teeth. . . ."

"What do you mean?"

"Listen with attention, Yankele! By nature, the goy is an amiable creature. He was eating pumpkin seeds, he saw you, he really wanted to be hospitable and give you some, so, 'Open your mouth!' he says, and wants to throw nuts into it—after all, they're fond of doing favors and little tricks. But when you, Yankele, obeyed and he saw such fine teeth—that is to say, *his teeth in your mouth*—you understand, a goy, and his teeth in your mouth, so naturally he becomes excited. And since he's a goy, what else can he do when he gets excited? So, he hits out with his fist.

"Do as I tell you, Yankele," the rabbi concludes. "Don't make a fuss about it. Go home to your wife and tell her I told you, that I explicitly told you, she should make you a mouthwash out of figs. . . ."

As Yankele submissively departs, the rabbi calls after him: "And the next time a goy tells you to open your mouth, open just a little bit, not more than a bit—a crack! He doesn't have to see anything, that a Jew has teeth. . . ."

The rabbi of Chelm returns to his books, studies with gusto, and derives much joy from the holy Torah—and from time to time helps himself to a pinch of worldly paradise from the wooden snuffbox. His heart expands with joy!

"Oy, a dear world, a sweet world. . . ." And he glances again through the ancient, moldy pane of the House of Judgment's narrow window into the marketplace.

"Such precious people. Gottenyu, silky, satiny . . ." But he does not finish his praises, for here comes Yankele again. A full month has not yet elapsed.

The rabbi stares in wonder. "What I dreamed last night, just the other night. . . . What happened this time, Yankele?"

"The Shabbes goy, Rebbe! The Shabbes goy again!" yells Yankele, and collapses on the bench.

Benignly the rabbi scolds him, "What a pest you are, Yankele! Still bothering with the Shabbes goy? A murderer, God forbid, he's not, but what do you need him for?"

"He stole up on me from behind," explains Yankele, "*from behind*, Rebbe Leyb! I'm walking through the alley, I'm on my way home. I'm carrying a loaf of bread for my family, I bought a loaf of bread for my wife and little ones, his Dear Name destined a loaf for me! Under my arm I'm carrying it when suddenly, from behind, a blow on my head. I fall down, I faint, I've scarcely come to, and I see the Shabbes goy walking away with a full mouth, chewing—and the loaf of bread lies at my feet, bitten off. Here, look, Rebbenyu. Oy, my head, my head!"

He shows the rabbi the loaf and grabs his head.

The rabbi examines the bread and says, "The head is a triviality; from a blow, God forbid, one doesn't perish! But consider, Yankele, who was in the right? Here, take a look—*teeth*! A goy, as you see, has teeth! Do you see? One bite, and half a loaf gone at once! *I* couldn't do it!"

"Yes, Rebbe," admits Yankele, "but what's to be done with the murderer? All Chelm is in danger!"

"And don't think, Yankele"—the rabbi turns to him—"that I'm not suffering on account of this. I know what half a loaf of bread means to a person like you, with so many mouths in your house to feed, I know what it means. Alas, there won't be enough to go around. If it depended on me, and I tell you this in confidence, I would positively request that the community compensate you for half a loaf. Why not? True, the community is poor, but still, a Jew has suffered a loss from *everybody's* Shabbes goy. And half a loaf is not merely blowing—the community wouldn't be impoverished—but you know yourself, Yankele, that I have no say."

Yankele starts screaming, "So that's how it is? It means only one thing—there is no judge and there is no justice in this world—the murderer goes about scot-free!"

"'Murderer,'" replies the rabbi serenely, "is not necessarily the proper word. I explained that to you once before; if it were so, the world would not be permitted to exist. There are no murderers!"

"So, what then?"

"The guilt, I tell you, Yankele, lies in the bread. In the holy books it is written, 'A man sins because of bread.' You know the small print yourself. 'A man sins on account of a crumb of bread.' And all the books say that there are times when a Jew transgresses the commandment 'Thou shalt not covet'—sometimes even 'Thou shalt not steal.' A goy, to make a distinction, may transgress 'Thou shalt not steal'—sometimes even 'Thou shalt not kill.' But this too, however, not by nature. It's all the fault of the bread. You have no idea, Yankele, of the evil impulse that lies hidden in bread. Basically—now tell me your opinion frankly, Yankele—why should it exasperate the Shabbes goy when he sees that Yankele walks about on the street, feeds his little ones, and praises God? Hah? But when he sees *bread*, that Yankele is carrying a loaf of bread! Yes, Yankele—I see you comprehend me now. Chew it well!"

And the rabbi goes over to him, puts his arm about Yankele's shoulder, and says with great compassion, "You know what, Yankele? After all, you know that I am a humble person, by nature a humble person, and I don't like to do such things. However, I will do it for you, for your sake. I will pray to God especially for half a loaf on your account."

"Thanks, Rebbenyu!" Yankele jumps up overjoyed and starts to leave the hut.

But the rabbi detains him. "Listen carefully, Yankele. Don't ever carry bread exposed and uncovered that his Dear Name has destined for you! It is forbidden to tempt the evil impulse. You have a coat—cover it!"

A pacified Yankele takes leave of the rabbi and, after a short while, returns for the third time with a cry for help; again, the Shabbes goy.

"It is now beyond comprehension," says the rabbi, "that in the course of a single season a Jew should meet with the Shabbes goy three times—and three times get beaten up! It doesn't stand to reason.

"There's something more to this than meets the eye!" he says, wrinkling his forehead, and proceeding to cross-examine. "Did you show him the teeth?"

"God forbid, Rebbe! Since you told me not to!"

"Did you keep the bread uncovered?"

"What bread, when bread, Rebbe?"

Ah, if he'd only had bread, he would not have come to this pass. He was on his way home without bread . . . his wife had met him with the poker . . . so he ran away, she ran after him . . . he ran beyond the town to the bathhouse . . . a Jewish wife doesn't run outside the town . . . finally he reaches safety on the slope behind the bath, where the Shabbes goy is reclining on the grass. He jumps up and wants to kill Yankele. With his bare fists he'll kill him dead, he says, and punches away. He could barely tear himself away. . . .

"Do you know what, Yankele?" the rabbi says softly after a contemplative pause. "You will forgive me, but I don't believe you."

Yankele pulls off his coat. "Rebbe, I wish you pieces of gold as big as the blue marks I have."

And he wants to disrobe completely, but this the rabbi does not permit.

"Little fool, that's not what I mean," says the rabbi. "It's not the least bit necessary to undress. I'm only acting in harmony with my conviction. I can't possibly believe that the Shabbes goy, one of God's creatures after all, should, just like that, without a reason, be a murderer. The concept lacks reality. Tell me, Yankele, does it make sense—a murderer? Could you be a murderer?"

"No!"

"Nor I," says the rabbi.

He falls into a trance and says, "Solved!" and he breaks into a smile. "You know what, Yankele? Listen carefully to what I have to say!"

And he stands up, the better to savor each of his words.

"I tell you, Yankele, in the rear of the bath must be the place where Cain, as it says in the holy Torah, killed his brother Abel. The place itself, more or less, is capable of murder, but particularly is it a dangerous spot for 'an offspring of Noah' who cannot by nature control himself."

Yankele opens mouth and ears. "Ah!"

"What do you say?" smiles the rabbi. "It makes sense? Apparently, that's how it is! And I maintain that the goy doesn't even know he is guilty.

"So, listen to me, Yankele, and forget about the whole thing! If you wish, call an apothecary; if not, apply cold compresses yourself.

"And on the Sabbath—it's true I don't mix in community matters, but still in times of danger—on the Sabbath, God willing, I will announce in the synagogue and in the study house that everyone should avoid going to the rear of the bath.

"And perhaps the council will decide to move the entire bath into town, into the marketplace. Why not? Wouldn't it be better? But that's already outside my sphere. A good day to you, Yankele."

Hardly a month had gone by when Yankele showed up again.

He had no teeth to exhibit, he hadn't been to the rear of the bath, but he did have broken bones. The Shabbes goy had come upon him behind the synagogue.

This time the rabbi had to admit: "What a bandit! Indeed, quite a bandit!" And "A peril for all of Chelm. . . . For me personally, no. I hardly ever step outside the door of my house. . . . Why should I? But, the rest of Chelm!

"Why," he queries, "how are you in greater danger than any other Chelmer? Your name is Yankele, another is called Groinem. It has nothing to do with the name. And I don't even know if the Shabbes goy is acquainted with people's names—how that one is called, whose candlesticks he is taking down. . . .

"We must," he sighs, "call a meeting right away, yes. . . . And do you know for what purpose? Can you guess my fear, Yankele?" "What, Rebbe?"

"On Yom Kippur, when the goy comes into the synagogue to light the candles before the final prayer, he can destroy all of Chelm. He can at that moment, God forbid, wipe out the entire community at once!"

And with the rabbi of Chelm it's this way: when he comes to a decision, he acts without delay.

On the Sabbath, in all the houses of prayer, large signs with glaring letters are already hanging: "A MEETING WILL BE HELD! THE WHOLE TOWN IS IN DANGER!"

Danger? The notables gather, the ordinary citizens come running, they sit packed together, cheek by jowl.

"Now tell us everything; what's it about, Rebbe Leyb?"

"Let Yankele say," says he.

So Yankele tells his story. Then the rabbi tells how the supposition was revealed to him, but that, nevertheless, Yankele is in the right throughout.

"A murderer," yells Yankele, "a murderer!"

"So what's to be done, Rebbenyu?"

The rabbi does not keep them in suspense and speaks as follows. "Were I," he says, "to have a say in the community, if I were to be asked in all sincerity, this is what I would say: In the first place, and before anything else—to satisfy the Divine Name—in fact, right away, tomorrow before dawn, Yankele should go away, someplace else, because on him the Shabbes goy has a claim already—more than a claim—a *fixation*.

"Now, in order to appease his resentment, and with the object of redeeming the entire community from dire peril, let us give the Shabbes goy a raise: a larger portion of the Sabbath loaf and *two* drinks of brandy instead of one. And what else? Perhaps he'll have compassion!"

You're laughing?

Still, there's a little of the rabbi of Chelm in each of us.

Translated by Etta Blum.

The Conciliator of Christendom (1898)

Israel Zangwill

I

The Red Beadle shook his head. "There is nothing but Nature," he said obstinately, as his hot iron polished the boot between his knees. He was called the Red Beadle because, though his irreligious opinions had long since lost him his synagogue appointment and driven him back to his old work of boot making, his beard was still ruddy.

"Yes, but who made Nature?" retorted his new employer, his strange, scholarly face aglow with argument, and the flame of the lamp suspended over his bench by strings from the ceiling. The other clickers and riveters of the Spitalfields workshop, in their shocked interest in the problem of the origin of Nature, ceased for an instant breathing in the odors of burnt grease, cobbler's wax, and a coke fire replenished with scraps of leather.

"Nature makes herself," answered the Red Beadle. It was his declaration of faith—or of war. Possibly it was the familiarity with divine things that synagogue beadledom involves that had bred his contempt for them. At any rate, he was not now to be coerced by Zussmann Herz, even though he was fully alive to the fact that Zussmann's unique book-lined workshop was the only one that had opened to him, when the more pious shoemakers of the Ghetto had professed to be "full up." He was, indeed, surprised to find Zussmann, a believer in the supernatural, having heard whispers that the man was as great an "Epicurean" as himself. Had not Zussmann—ay, and his wigless wife, Hulda, too—been seen emerging from the mighty Church that stood in frowsy majesty amid its tall, neglected box-like tombs, and was to the Ghetto merely a topographical point and the chronometric standard? And yet, here was Zussmann, an assiduous attendant at the synagogue of the first floor—nay, a scholar so conversant with Hebrew, not to mention European lore, that the Red Beadle felt himself a man-of-the-earth, only retaining his superiority by remembering that learning did not always mean logic.

"Nature makes herself!" Zussmann now retorted, with a tolerant smile. "You might as well say this boot made itself! The theory of evolution only puts the mystery further back, and already in the Talmud we find—"

"*Nature* made the boot," interrupted the Red Beadle. "Nature made you, and you made the boot. But nobody made Nature."

"But what is Nature?" cried Zussmann. "The garment of God, as Goethe says. Call Him Noumenon with Kant or Thought and Extension with Spinoza—I care not."

The Red Beadle was awed into temporary silence by these unknown names and ideas, expressed, moreover, in German words foreign to his limited vocabulary of Yiddish.

The room in which Zussmann thought and worked was one of two that he rented from the Christian corn-factor, who owned the tall house—a stout Cockney who spent his life book-keeping in a little office on wheels, but whom the specimens of oats and dog-biscuits in his window invested with an air of roseate rurality. This personage drew a little income from the population of his house, whose staircases exhibited strata of children of different social developments, and to which the synagogue on the first floor added a large floating population. Zussmann's attendance there was not the only thing in him that astonished the Red Beadle. There was also a gentle deference of manner, not usual with masters, or with pious persons. His consideration for his employees amounted, in the Beadle's eyes, to maladministration, and the grave loss he sustained through one of his hands selling off a crate of finished goods and flying to America was deservedly due to confidence in another pious person.

II

Despite the Red Beadle's rationalism, which, basing itself on the facts of life, was not to be crushed by high-flown German words, the master-shoemaker showed him marked favor and often invited him to stay on to supper. Although the Beadle felt this was but the due recognition of one intellect by another, if an inferior intellect, he was at times irrationally grateful for the privilege of a place in which to spend his evenings. For the Ghetto had cut him—there could be no doubt of that. The worshippers in his old synagogue, which he had once dominated as Beadle, now passed him by with sour looks—"even a dog is not treated this way," the Beadle told himself, tugging miserably at his red beard.

"It is not as if I were a Meshummad—a convert to Christianity." Some hereditary instinct admitted that as a just excuse for execration. "I can't make friends with the Christians, and so I am cut off from both."

When after a thunderstorm two of the hands resigned their places at Zussmann's benches on the avowed ground that atheism attracts lightning, Zussmann's loyalty to the freethinker converted the Beadle's gratitude from fitfulness to a steady glow.

And, other considerations apart, those were enjoyable suppers after the toil and grime of the day. Beadle especially admired Zussmann's hands when the black grease had been washed off them, the fingers were so long and tapering. Why had his own fingers been made so stumpy and square-tipped? Since Nature made herself, why was she so uneven a worker? Nay, why could she not have given him white teeth like Zussmann's wife? Not that these were ostentatious—you thought more of the sweetness of the smile of which they were part. Still, as Nature's irregularity was particularly manifest in his own teeth, he could not help the reflection.

If Red Beadle had not been a widower, the unfeigned success of the Herz union might have turned his own thoughts to that happy state. As it was, the sight of their happiness occasionally shot through his breast renewed pangs of vain longing for his Leah, whose death from cancer had completed his conception of Nature. Lucky Zussmann, to have found so sympathetic a partner in a pretty female! For Hulda shared Zussmann's dreams, and was even copying out his great work for the press, for business was brisk, and he would soon have saved up enough money to print it. The great work, in the secret of which Red Beadle came to participate, was written in Hebrew, and the elegant curves and strokes would have done honor to a scribe. Beadle himself could not understand it, knowing only the formal alphabet such as it appears in book and scrolls, but the first peep at it, which the proud Zussmann permitted him, removed his last disrespect for the intellect of his master without, however, removing the mystery of that intellect's aberrations.

"But you dream with the eyes open," he said, when the theme of the work was explained to him.

"How so?" asked Hulda gently, with that wonderful smile of hers.

"Reconcile the Jews and the Christians! *Meshuggas*—madness." He laughed bitterly. "Do you forget what we went through in Poland? And even here in free England, can you walk in the street without every little *shegetz* calling after you and asking, Who killed Christ?"

"Yes, but in my husband's book he explains that it was not the Jews who killed Christ, but Herod and Pilate."

"As it says in Corinthians," broke in Zussmann eagerly: "We speak the wisdom of God in a mystery, which none of the princes of this world knew, for had they known it, they would not have crucified the Lord of Glory."

"So," said Red Beadle, visibly impressed.

"Assuredly," affirmed Hulda. "But, as Zussmann explains here, they threw the guilt upon the Jews, who were too afraid of the Romans to deny it."

Beadle pondered all this.

"Once the Christians understand that," said Zussmann, pursuing his advantage, "they will stretch out the hand to us."

Beadle had a flash. "But how will the Christians read you? No Christian understands Hebrew."

Zussmann was taken momentarily aback. "But it is not so much for the Christians," he explained. "It is for the Jews—that they should stretch out the hand to the Christians."

Red Beadle stared at him in shocked silent amaze. "Still greater madness!" he gasped at length. "They will treat you worse than they treat me."

"Not when they read my book."

"Just when they read your book."

Hulda was smiling serenely. "They can do nothing to my husband; he is his own master, God be thanked! No one can turn him away."

"They can insult him."

Zussmann shook his head gently. "No one can insult me!" he said simply. "When a dog barks at me, I pity it because it does not know I love it. Now draw to the table. The pickled herring smells good."

But Red Beadle was unconvinced. "Besides, why should we make up with the Christians—the stupid people?" he asked, as he received his steaming coffee cup from Frau Herz.

"It is a question of the future of the world," said Zussmann gravely, as he shared the herring, which had already been cut into many thin slices by the vendor and pickler. "This antagonism is a perversion of the principles of both religions. Shall we allow it to continue forever?"

"It will continue till they both understand that Nature makes herself," said Red Beadle.

"It will continue till they both understand my husband's book," corrected Hulda.

"Not while Jews live among Christians. Even here they say we take the bread out of the mouths of the Christian shoemakers. If we had our own country now—"

"Hush!" said Zussmann. "Do you share that materialistic dream? Our realm is spiritual. Nationality—the world stinks with it! Germany for the Germans, Russia for the Russians. Foreigners to the devil—pah! Egomania posing as patriotism. Human brotherhood is what we stand for. Have you forgotten how the Midrash explains the verse in the Song of Solomon? I charge you, Oh ye daughters of Jerusalem, by the roes and by the hinds of the field, that ye stir not up, nor awake my love till he please?"

Red Beadle, who had never read a line of the Midrash, did not deny that he had forgotten the explanation, but persisted. "And even if we didn't kill Christ, what good will it do to tell the Jews so? It will only make them angry."

"Why so?" asked Zussmann, puzzled.

"They will be annoyed to have been punished for nothing."

"But they have not been punished for nothing!" cried Zussmann, setting down his fork in excitement. "They have denied their greatest son. For, as He said in Matthew, I come to fulfill the Law of Moses. Did not all the Prophets, His predecessors, cry out likewise against mere form and sacrifice? Did not the teachers in Israel who followed Him likewise insist on a pure heart and a sinless soul? Jesus must be restored to His true place in the glorious chain of Hebrew Prophets. As I explain in my chapter on the Philosophy of Religion, which I have founded on Immanuel Kant, the groundwork of Reason is—"

But here Red Beadle, whose coffee had with difficulty got itself sucked into the right channel, gasped—"You have put that into your book?"

The wife touched the manuscript with reverent pride. "It all stands here," she said.

"What! Quotations from the New Testament?"

"From our Jewish Apostles!" said Zussmann. "Naturally, on every page!"

"Then God help you!" said Red Beadle.

III

The Brotherhood of the Peoples was published. Though the bill was far heavier than the Hebrew printer's estimate—there being all sorts of mysterious charges for corrections, which took away the last penny of their savings, Hulda and her husband were happy. They had sown the seed, and waited in serene faith the ingathering, the reconciliation of Israel with the Gentiles.

The book, which was in paper covers, was published for one shilling; five hundred copies had been struck off for the edition. After six months the account stood thus: Sales, eighty-four copies; press notices, two in the jargon papers (printed in the same office as his book and thus amenable to backstairs influence). The Jewish papers written in English, which loomed before Zussmann's vision as world-shaking, did not even mention its publication. Perhaps it would have been better if the jargon papers had been equally silent, for, though less than one hundred copies of *The Brotherhood of the Peoples* were in circulation, the book was in everybody's mouth—like a piece of pork to be spat out again shudderingly. Red Beadle's instinct had been only too sound. The Ghetto, accustomed by this time to insidious attacks on its spiritual citadel, feared writers even bringing Hebrew. Despite the Oriental sandal that the cunning shoemaker had fashioned, his fellow-Jews saw the cloven hoof. They were not to be deceived by the specious sanctity that Darwin and Schopenhauer—probably bishops of the Established Church—borrowed from their Hebrew lettering. Why, that was the very trick of the Satans, who sprinkled the sacred tongue freely about handbills inviting souls that sought for light to come and find it in the Whitechapel Road between three and seven. It had been abandoned as hopeless even by the thin-nosed gentlewomen who had begun by painting a Hebrew designation over their bureau of beneficence. But the fact that the Ghetto was perspicacious did not mitigate the author's treachery to his race and faith. Zussmann was given violently to understand that his presence in the little synagogue would lead to disturbances in the service. "The Jew needs no house of prayer," he said; "his life is a prayer, his workshop a temple."

His workmen deserted him one by one as vacancies occurred elsewhere.

"We will get Christians," he said.

But the work itself began to fail. He was dependent upon a large firm whose head was Parnass of a North London congregation, and when one of Zussmann's workers, anxious to set up for himself, went to him with the tale, the contract was transferred to him, and Zussmann's security deposit returned. But far heavier than all these blows was Hulda's sudden illness, and though the returned trust-money came in handy to defray the expense of doctors, the outlook was not cheerful.

"I will become a handworker myself," said Zussmann cheerfully. "The annoyance of my brethren will pass away when they really understand my ideas. In the meantime it is working in them, for even to hate an idea is to meditate upon it."

Red Beadle grunted angrily. He could hear Hulda coughing in the next room, and that hurt his chest. But it was summer now, and quite a considerable strip of blue sky could be seen from the window, and the mote-laden sun rays that streamed into their home encouraged Hulda to grow better. She was soon up and about again, but the doctor said her system was thoroughly upset, and she ought to have sea air. But that, of course, was impossible now. Hulda herself declared there was much better air to be got higher up, in the garret, which was fortunately "to let."

It is true there was only one room there. Still, it was much cheaper. Red Beadle's heart was heavier than the furniture as he helped to carry things upstairs. But the unsympathetic couple did not share his gloom. They jested and laughed, as light of heart as the excited children on the staircases who assisted at the function.

"My idea has raised me nearer heaven," said Zussmann. That night, after Red Beadle had screwed up the four-poster, he allowed himself to be persuaded to stay for supper. He had given up the habit as soon as Zussmann's finances began to fail. By way of house-warming, Hulda had ordered in baked potatoes and liver from the cook-shop, and there were also three tepid slices of plum pudding.

"Plum pudding!" cried Zussmann in delight, as his nostrils scented the dainty. "What a good omen for my ideas!!"

"How do you see this as an omen?" inquired Red Beadle.

"Isn't plum pudding associated with Christmas, with peace on earth?"

Hulda's eyes flashed. "Yes, it is a sign—the Brotherhood of the Peoples! The Jew will be the peace-messenger of the world."

Red Beadle ate on skeptically. He had studied *The Brotherhood of the Peoples* to the great improvement of his Hebrew but with little edification. He had even studied it in Hulda's original manuscript, which he had borrowed and never intended to return. But still he could not share his friends' belief in the perfectibility of mankind. Perhaps, if they had known how he had tippled away his savings after his wife's death, they might have thought less well of humanity and its potentialities of perfection. After all, Huldas were too rare to make the world sober, much less fraternal. And, charming as they were, honesty demanded one should not curry favor with them by fostering their delusions.

"What put such an idea into your head, Zussmann?" he cried unsympathetically, while Zussmann answered naïvely, as if to a question: "I have had the idea from a boy. I remember sitting stocking-footed on the floor of the synagogue in Poland during the Fast of Ab, wondering why we should weep so much over the destruction of Jerusalem, which scattered us among the nations as fertilizing seeds. How else should the mission of Israel be fulfilled. I remember"—and here he smiled pensively—"I was awakened from my daydream by a *Patsch* [smack] in the face from my poor old father, who was angry because I wasn't saying the prayers."

"There will be always somebody to give you that *Patsch*," said Red Beadle gloomily. "But in what way is Israel dispersed? It seems to me our life is everywhere as hidden from the nations as if we were all together in Palestine."

"You touch a great truth! Oh, if I could only write in English! But though I read it almost as easily as the German, I can write it as little. You know how one has to learn German in Poland—by stealth—the Christians jealous on one hand, the Jews suspicions on the other. I could not risk the Christians laughing at my bad German—that would hurt my idea. And English is a language like the Vale of Siddim—full of pits."

"We ought to have it translated," said Hulda. "Not only for the Christians, but for the rich Jews, who are more liberal-minded than those who live in our quarter."

"But we cannot afford to pay for the translating now," said Zussmann.

"Nonsense! One has always a jewel left," said Hulda.

Zussmann's eyes grew wet. "Yes," he said, drawing her to his breast, "one has always a jewel left."

"More *meshuggas*!" cried Red Beadle huskily. "Much the English Jews care about ideas! Did they even acknowledge your book in their journals? But probably they couldn't read it," he added with a laugh. "A fat lot of Hebrew little Sampson knows! You know little Sampson—he came to report the boot-strike for *The Flag of Judah.* I got into conversation with him—a rank pork-gorger. He believes with me that nature makes herself."

But Zussmann was scarcely eating, much less listening.

"You have given me a new scheme, Hulda," he said, with exaltation. "I will send my book to the leading English Jews—yes, especially to the ministers. They will see my idea. They will spread it abroad. They will convert first the Jews and then the Christians."

"Yes, but they will present it as their own idea," said Hulda.

"And what of it? He who has faith in an idea, it remains his idea. How great for me to have had the idea first! Isn't that enough to thank God for? If only my idea gets spread in English! English! Have you ever thought what that means, Hulda? The language of the future! Already the language of the greatest nations, and the most on the lips of men everywhere—in a century it will cover the world." He murmured in Hebrew, uplifting his eyes to the rain-streaked sloping ceiling. "And on that day God shall be One and His name One."

"Your supper is getting cold," said Hulda gently.

He began to wield his knife and fork as if he were hypnotized by her suggestion, but his vision was inward.

IV

Fifty copies of *The Brotherhood of the Peoples* went off by post the next day to the clergy and gentry of the larger Jewry. In the course of the next fortnight, seventeen of the recipients acknowledged the receipt with formal thanks, four sent the shilling mentioned on the cover, and one sent five shillings. This last contribution depressed Zussmann more than all the others.

"Does he take me for a *Schnorrer*?" he said, almost angrily, as he returned the postal order. He did not foresee the day when, a *Schnorrer,* indeed, he would have taken five shillings from anybody who could afford it. But he had no prophetic intuition of that long, slow progression of penurious days that was to crush his spirit. Though he managed for a time to secure enough work to keep himself and Red Beadle going, his rain was only delayed. Little by little his apparatus was sold off, his benches and polishing-irons vanished from the garret, only one indispensable set remaining, and master and man had to look for work elsewhere. Red Beadle dropped out of the ménage and was reduced to semi-starvation. Zussmann and Hulda, by the gradual disposition of their bits of jewelry and their Sabbath garments, held out a little longer, and Hulda also got some sewing of children's undergarments. But with the return of winter, Hulda's illness returned, and then the beloved books began to leave bare the nakedness of the plastered walls. At first, Hulda, refusing to be visited by doctors who charged, struggled bravely through rain and fog to a free dispensary, where she was jostled by a crowd of head-shawled Polish crones, and where a harassed Christian physician, tired of jargon-speaking Jewesses, bawled and bullied. But at last Hulda grew too ill to stir out, and Zussmann, still unemployed, was driven to look about him for help. Charities enough there were in the Ghetto, but to charity, as to work, one requires an apprenticeship. He knew vaguely that there were people who had the luck to be ill and to get broths and jellies. To others, also, a board of guardian angels doled out payments, though someone had once told him you had scant chance unless you were a Dutchman. But the inexperienced in begging are naturally not so successful as those always at it. 'Twas vain for Zussmann to kick his heels among the dismal crowd in the corridor, the whisper of his misdeeds had been before him, borne by some competitor in the fierce struggle for assistance. What! Help a hypocrite to sit on the twin stools of Christendom and Judaism, fed by the bounty of both! In this dark hour he was approached by the thin-nosed gentlewomen, who had got wind of his book and who scented souls. Zussmann wavered. Why, indeed, should he refuse their assistance? He knew their self-sacrificing days, their genuine joy in salvation. On their generosities he was far better posted than on Jewish—the lurid legend of these Mephistophelian matrons included blankets, clothes, port wine, and all the delicacies of the season. He admitted that Hulda had indeed been brought low, and permitted them to call. Then he went home to cut dry bread for the bedridden, emaciated creature who had once been beautiful, and to comfort her—for it was Friday evening—by reading the Sabbath prayers; winding up, "A virtuous woman who can find? For her price is far above rubies."

On the forenoon of the next day arrived a basket, permeating the air with delicious odors of exquisite edibles. Zussmann received it with delight from the boy who bore it. "God bless them!" he said. "A chicken—grapes—wine. Look, Hulda!"

Hulda raised herself in bed; her eyes sparkled, a flush of color returned to the wan cheeks.

"Where do these come from?" she asked.

Zussmann hesitated. Then he told her they were the harbingers of a visit from the good sisters. Immediately, the flush in her cheek deepened to scarlet.

"My poor Zussmann!" she cried reproachfully. "Give them back—give them back at once! Call the boy!"

"Why?" stammered Zussmann.

"Call after the boy!" she repeated imperatively. "Good God! If the ladies were to be seen coming up here, it would be all over with your idea. And on the Sabbath, too. People already look upon you as a tool of the missionaries. Quick! Quick!"

His heart aching with mingled love and pain, he picked up the basket and hurried after the boy. Hulda sank back on her pillow with a sigh of relief.

"Dear heart!" she thought, as she took advantage of his absence to cough freely. "For me he does what he would starve rather than do for himself. A nice thing to imperil his idea—the dream of his life! When the Jews see he makes no profit by it, they will begin to consider it. If he did not have the burden of me who would not be tempted. He could go out more and find work farther afield. This must end—I must die or be on my feet again soon."

Zussmann came back, empty-handed and heavy-hearted. "Kiss me, my own life!" she cried. "I shall be better soon."

He bent down and touched her hot, dry lips. "Now I see," she whispered, "why God did not send us children. We thought it was an affliction, but lo! It is that your idea shall not be hindered."

"The English rabbis have not yet drawn attention to it," said Zussmann huskily.

"All the better," replied Hulda. "One day it will be translated into English—I know it, I feel it here." She touched her chest, and the action made her cough.

Going out later for a little fresh air, at Hulda's insistence, he was stopped in the broad hall on which the stairs debouched by Cohen, the ground-floor tenant, a black-bearded Russian Jew, pompous in Sabbath broadcloth.

"What's the matter with my milk?" abruptly asked Cohen, who supplied the local trade besides selling retail. "You might have complained, instead of taking your custom out of the house. Believe me, I don't make a treasure heap out of it. One has to be up at Euston to meet the trains in the middle of the night, and the competition is so cut-throat that one has to sell at eighteen pence a barn gallon. And on Sabbath one earns nothing at all. And then the analyst comes poking his nose into the milk."

"You see—my wife—my wife—is ill," stammered Zussmann. "So she doesn't drink it."

"Hum!" said Cohen. "Well, *you* might oblige me then. I have so much left over every day, it makes my reputation turn quite sour. Do, do me a favor and let me send you up a can of the leavings every night. For nothing, of course. Would I talk business on the Sabbath? I don't like to be seen pouring it away. It would pay me to pay you a penny a pint," he wound up emphatically.

Zussmann accepted unsuspiciously, grateful to providence for enabling him to benefit at once himself and his neighbor. He carried a can upstairs now and explained the situation to the shrewder Hulda, who, however, said nothing but, "You see the idea commences to work. When the book first came out, didn't he—though he sells secretly to the trade on Sabbath mornings—call you an Epicurean?"

"Worse," said Zussmann joyously, with a flash of recollection.

He went out again, lightened and exalted. "Yes, the idea works," he said, as he came out into the gray street. "The Brotherhood of the Peoples will come, not in my time, but it will come." And he murmured again the Hebrew aspiration: "In that day shall God be One and His name One."

"Whoa, where's your—eyes?"

Awakened by the yell, he just got out of the way of a huge Flemish dray-horse dragging a brewer's cart. Three ragged Irish urchins, who had been buffeting each other with whirling hats knotted into the ends of dingy handkerchiefs, relaxed their enmities in a common rush for the projecting ladder behind the dray and collided with Zussmann on the way. A one-legged, misery-eyed hunchback offered him penny diaries. He shook his head in impotent pity, and continued pondering.

"In time God will make the crooked straight," he thought.

Jews with tall black hats and badly made frockcoats slouched along, their shoulders bent. Wives stood at the open doors of the old houses, some in Sabbath finery, same flaunting irreligiously their everyday shabbiness, without troubling even to arrange their one dress differently, as a pious rabbi recommended. They looked used-up and haggard, all these mothers in Israel. But there were dark-eyed damsels still gay and fresh, with artistic bodices of violet and green picked out with gold arabesque.

He turned a corner and came into a narrow street that throbbed with the joyous melody of a piano-organ. His heart leapt up. The roadway bubbled with Jewish children, mainly girls, footing it gleefully in the graying light, inventing complex steps with a grace and an abandon that lit their eyes with sparkles and painted deeper flushes on their olive cheeks. A bounding little bowlegged girl seemed unconscious of her deformity; her toes met each other as though in merry dexterity.

Zussmann's eyes were full of tears. "Dance on, dance on," he murmured. "God shall indeed make the crooked straight."

Fixed to one side of the piano-organ on the level of the handle he saw a little box, in which lay, as in a cradle, what looked like a monkey, then like a doll, but on closer inspection turned into a tiny live child, flaxen-haired, staring with wide gray eyes from under a blue cap, and sucking at a milk-bottle with preternatural placidity, regardless of the music throbbing through its resting place.

"Even so shall humanity live," thought Zussmann, "peaceful as a babe, cradled in music. God hath sent me a sign."

He returned home, comforted, and told Hulda of the sign.

"Was it an Italian child?" she asked.

"An English child," he answered. "Fair-eyed and fair-haired."

"Then it is a sign that through the English tongue shall the idea move the world. Your book will be translated into English—I shall live to see it."

V

A few afternoons later Red Beadle, his patched garments pathetically spruced up, came to see his friends, moved by the news of Hulda's illness. There was no ruddiness in his face, the lips of which were pressed together in defiance of a cruel and credulous world. That Nature in making herself should have produced creatures who attributed their creation elsewhere, and who refused to allow her one acknowledger to make boots, was indeed a proof, albeit vexatious, of her blind workings. When he saw what she had done to Hulda and to Zussmann, his lips were pressed tighter, but as much to keep back a sob as to express extra resentment.

On parting he could not help saying to Zussmann, who accompanied him to the dark, spider-webbed landing, "Your God has forgotten you."

"Do you mean that men have forgotten Him?" replied Zussmann. "If we now live in poverty, my suffering is in the scheme of things. Do you not remember what the Almighty says to Eleazar ben Pedos, in the Talmud, when the rabbi complains of poverty? 'Wilt thou be satisfied if I overthrow the universe, so that perhaps thou mayest be created again in a time of plenty?' No, no, my friend, we must trust the scheme."

"But the fools enjoy prosperity," said Red Beadle.

"It is only a fool who would enjoy prosperity," replied Zussmann. "If the righteous sometimes suffer and the wicked sometimes flourish, that is just the very condition of virtue. What! Would you have righteousness always pay and wickedness always fail? Where then would be the virtue in virtue? It would be more a branch of commerce. Have you forgotten what the Chassid said of the man who foreknew in his lifetime that for him there was to be no heaven? 'What a unique and enviable chance that man had of doing right without fear of reward!'"

Red Beadle, as usual, acquiesced in the idea that he had forgotten these quotations from the Hebrew, but to acquiesce in their teachings was another matter. "A man who had no hope of heaven would be a fool not to enjoy himself," he said doggedly, and went downstairs, his heart almost bursting. He went straight to his old synagogue, where he knew a *Hesped* or funeral service for a famous *Maggid* [preacher] was to be held. He could scarcely get in, so dense was the throng. Not a few eyes, wet with tears, were turned angrily on him as on a mocker come to gloat, but he hastened to weep too, which was easy when he thought of Hulda coughing in her bed in the garret. So violently did he weep that the *Gabbai* [treasurer]—one of the most pious master-bootmakers—gave him the "Peace" salutation after the service.

"I did not expect to see you weeping," said he.

"Alas!" answered Red Beadle. "It is not only for the fallen Prince in Israel that I weep, it is my own transgressions that are brought home to me by his sudden end. How often have I heard him thunder and lighten from this very pulpit!"

He heaved a deep sigh at his own hypocrisy, and the *Gabbai* sighed in response. "Even from the grave the *Tsaddile* [saint] works well," said the pious master-bootmaker. "May my latter end be like his!"

"Mine, too!" suspired Red Beadle. "How blessed am I not to have been cut off in my sin, denying the Maker of Nature!" They walked along the street together.

The next morning, at the lunch hour, a breathless Beadle, with a red beard and a very red face, knocked joyously at the door of the Herz garret.

"I have found work again," he explained.

"*Mazeltov*!" Zussmann gave him the Hebrew congratulation, but softly, with finger on lip, to indicate Hulda was asleep. "With whom?"

"Harris the *Gabbai*."

"Harris! What, despite your opinions?"

Red Beadle looked away.

"So it seems!"

"Thank God!" said Hulda. "The idea works."

Both men turned to the bed, startled to see her sitting up with a rapt smile.

"How so?" said Red Beadle uneasily. "I am not a Goy befriended by a *Gabbai*."

"No, but it is the brotherhood of humanity."

"Bother the brotherhood of humanity, Frau Herz!" said Red Beadle gruffly. He glanced around the denuded room. "The important thing is that you will now be able to have a few delicacies."

Hulda opened her eyes wide.

"Who else? What I earn is for all of us."

"God bless you!" said Zussmann, "but you have enough to do to keep yourself."

"Indeed he has!" said Hulda. "We couldn't dream of taking a farthing!" But her eyes were wet.

"I insist!" said Red Beadle.

She thanked him sweetly, but held firm.

"I will advance the money on loan till Zussmann gets work."

Zussmann wavered, his eyes beseeching her, but she was inflexible.

Red Beadle lost his temper. "And this is what you call the brotherhood of humanity!"

"He is right, Hulda. Why should we not take from one another? Pride perverts brotherhood."

"Dear husband," said Hulda, "it is not pride to refuse to rob the poor. Besides, what delicacies do I need? Is not this a land flowing with milk?"

"You take Cohen's milk and refuse my honey!" shouted Red Beadle unappeased.

"Give me of the honey of your tongue and I shall not refuse it," said Hulda, with that wonderful smile of hers that showed the white teeth Nature had made; the smile that, as always, melted Beadle's mood. That smile could repair all the ravages of disease and give back her memoried face.

After Beadle had been at work a day or two in the *Gabbai*'s workshop, he broached the matter of a fellow-penitent, one Zussmann Herz, with no work and a bedridden wife.

"That *Meshummad* [apostate]," cried the *Gabbai*, "He deserves all that God has sent him."

Undaunted, Red Beadle demonstrated that the man could not be of the missionary camp, else had he not been left to starve, one converted Jew being worth a thousand pounds of fresh subscriptions. Moreover, he, Red Beadle, had now convinced the man of his spiritual errors, and *The Brotherhood of the Peoples* was no longer on sale. Also, being unable to leave his wife's bedside, Zussmann would do the work at home below the union rates prevalent in public. So, trade being brisk, the *Gabbai* relented and bargained, and Red Beadle sped to his friend's abode and flew up the four flights of stairs.

"Good news!" he cried. "The *Gabbai* wants another hand, and he is ready to take you."

"Me?" Zussmann was paralyzed with joy and surprise.

"Now will you deny that the idea works?" cried Hulda, her face flushed and her eyes glittering. And she fell a-coughing.

"You are right, Hulda; you are always right," cried Zussmann, in responsive radiance. "Thank God! Thank God!"

"God forgive me," muttered Red Beadle.

"Go at once, Zussmann," said Hulda. "I shall do very well here. This news has given me strength. I shall be up in a day or two."

"No, no, Zussmann," said Beadle hurriedly. "There is no need to leave your wife. I have arranged it all. The *Gabbai* does not want you to come there or to speak to him, because, though the idea works in him, the other 'hands' are not yet so large-minded: I am to bring you the orders, and I shall come here to fetch them."

The set of tools to which Zussmann clung in desperate hope made the plan both feasible and pleasant. And so Red Beadle's visits resumed their ancient frequency even as his Sabbath clothes resumed their ancient gloss, and every weekend he paid over Zussmann's wages to him—full union rate.

But Hulda, although she now accepted illogically Red Beadle's honey in various shapes, did not appear to progress as much as the idea, or as the new book that she stimulated Zussmann to start for its further propagation.

VI

One Friday evening of December, when miry snow underfoot and grayish fog all around combined to make Spitalfields a malarious marsh, Red Beadle, coming in with the week's wages, found to his horror a doctor hovering over Hulda's bed like the shadow of death. From the look that Zussmann gave him he saw a sudden change for the worse had set in. The cold of the weather seemed to strike right to his heart. He took the sufferer's limp, chill hand.

"How goes it?" he said cheerily.

"A trifle weak. But I shall be better soon."

He turned away. Zussmann whispered to him that the doctor who had been called in that morning had found the crisis so threatening that he was to come again in the evening. Red Beadle, grown very white, accompanied the doctor downstairs, and learned that with care the patient might pull through.

Beadle felt like tearing out his red beard.

"And to think that I have not yet arranged the matter!" he thought distractedly.

He ran through the gray bleak night to the office of *The Flag of Judah*, but as he was crossing the threshold he remembered that it was the eve of the Sabbath, and that neither little Sampson nor anybody else would be there. But little Sampson was there, working busily.

"Hullo! Come in," he said, astonished.

Red Beadle had already struck up a drinking acquaintanceship with the little journalist, in view of the great negotiation he was plotting. Not in vain did the proverbial wisdom of the Ghetto bid one beware of the red-haired.

"I won't keep you five minutes," apologized little Sampson. "But, you see, Christmas comes next week, and the compositors won't work. So I have to invent the news in advance."

Presently little Sampson, lighting an unhallowed cigarette by way of Sabbath lamp, and slinging on his shabby cloak, went with Red Beadle to a restaurant, where he ordered "forbidden" food for himself and drinks for both. Red Beadle felt his way so cautiously and cunningly that the negotiation was unduly prolonged. After an hour or two, however, all was settled. For five pounds, paid in five monthly installments, little Sampson would translate *The Brotherhood of the Peoples* into English, provided Beadle would tell him what the Hebrew meant. This Beadle, from his loving study of Hulda's manuscript, was now prepared for. Little Sampson also promised to run the translation through *The Flag of Judah*. Thus Beadle could buy the plates cheap for book purposes, with only the extra cost of printing such passages, if any, as were too dangerous for *The Flag of Judah*. This unexpected generosity, coupled with the new audience it offered the idea, enchanted Red Beadle. He did not see that the journalist was getting gratuitous "copy," he saw only the bliss of Hulda and Zussmann, and in some strange exaltation, compact of whisky and affection, he shared in their vision of the miraculous spread of the idea, once it had got into the dominant language of the world.

In his gratitude to little Sampson he plied him with fresh whisky; in his excitement he drew the paper-covered book from his pocket, and insisted that the journalist must translate the first page then and there, as a hansel. By the time it was done, it was near eleven o'clock. Vaguely Red Beadle felt that it was too late to return to Zussmann's that night. Besides, he was liking little Sampson very much. They did not separate till the restaurant closed at midnight.

Quite drunk, Red Beadle staggered toward Zussmann's house. He held the page of the translation tightly in his hand. The Hebrew original he had forgotten on the restaurant table, but he knew in some troubled nightmare way that Zussmann and Hulda must see that paper at once, that he had been charged to deliver it safely, and must die sooner than disobey.

The fog had lifted, but the heaps of snow were a terrible hindrance to his erratic progression. The cold air and the shock of a fall lessened his inebriety, but the imperative impulse of his imaginary mission still hypnotized him. It was past one before he reached the tall house. He did not think it at all curious that the great outer portals should be open; nor, though he saw the milk-cart at the door, and noted Cohen's uncomfortable look, did he remember that he had discovered the milk-purveyor nocturnally infringing the Sabbath. He stumbled up the stairs and knocked at the garret door, through the chinks of which light streamed. The thought of Hulda smote him almost sober. Zussmann's face, when the door opened, restored him completely to his senses. It was years older.

"She is not dead?" the visitor whispered hoarsely.

"She is dying, I fear—she cannot rouse herself." Zussmann's voice broke into a sob.

"But she must not die—I bring great news—*The Flag of Judah* has read your book—it will translate it into English—it will print it in its own paper—and then it will make a book of it for you. See, here is the beginning!"

"Into English!" breathed Zussmann, taking the little journalist's scrawl. His whole face grew crimson, his eyes shone as with madness. "Hulda! Hulda!" he cried, "the idea works! God be thanked! English! Through the world! Hulda! Hulda!"

He was bending over her, raising her head.

She opened her eyes.

"Hulda! The idea wins. The book is coming out in English. The great English paper will print it. In that day God shall be One and His name One. Do you understand?"

Her lips twitched faintly, but only her eyes spoke with the light of love and joy. His own look met hers, and for a moment husband and wife were one in a spiritual ecstasy. Then the light in Hulda's eyes went out, and the two men were left in darkness. Red Beadle turned away and left Zussmann to his dead wife and, with scalding tears running down his cheek, pulled up the cotton window blind and gazed out unseeing into the night.

Soon his vision cleared, and he found himself watching the milk-cart drive off, and, following it toward the frowsy avenue of Brick Lane, he beheld what seemed to be a drunken fight in progress. He saw a policeman, gesticulating females, the nondescript nocturnal crowd of the sleepless city. The old dull hopelessness came over him. "Nature makes herself," he murmured in despairing resignation. Suddenly he became aware that Zussmann was beside him, looking up at the stars.

The Story about the Sorcerer (1902)

Leo Wiener

ONCE A RICH MAN who had no children went to consult a wonder rebbe.[1] The rebbe said, "You were born with either of two fates: you can be rich, or you can have children. It's up to you. If you have children, you'll have to be poor. Choose."

The man replied, "I prefer to have a child."

The rebbe said, "Go back home. In nine months, your wife will give birth to a son."

A few months after he returned home, all the man's goods were destroyed in a fire, and he became poor. And in nine months, his wife gave birth to a son.

The family struggled for thirteen years to keep their home together. Then, seeing that nothing could be done about their poverty in that town, the father and son decided to beg their way in the wide world. They went from town to town until finally they arrived at the city of Odessa.

In Odessa, they went to the House of Beggars, where all the poor folk seemed to be delighted by something. The father asked them, "What makes you all so happy?"

"Don't you know?" they said. "There's a rich man in town who makes a banquet for poor folk once a week. If you like, you can come too."

So, the father and son went to the banquet and had plenty to eat and drink, the best of everything. At one point a coach drawn by four beautiful horses drove up. A sorcerer stepped out and began to astonish the guests by turning himself into a horse, then an elephant, then a lion, then a cat. He kept the company entertained until two o'clock in the morning.

When the father was ready to leave, the son said, "I won't move from this place until you apprentice me to the sorcerer." The father first reasoned with him, but the son was stubborn. "Apprentice me to the sorcerer," he said.

So, the father ran after the sorcerer's coach and lay down in front of the horses. "Sire," he said, "my son won't move from his place unless he can become your apprentice."

And the sorcerer drew up a contract agreeing to teach the boy sorcery for three years. "When the time is up," said the sorcerer, "you can come and get him."

Three years later the father arrived at the sorcerer's house. The path to the door was guarded by wild animals, but he loved his son so much that he walked bravely past them. In the house he found his son sitting with the sorcerer and the sorcerer's daughter.

The sorcerer recognized the father at once. "You've come for your son," he said. "Well, you may have him only after you have passed a test. I will turn my daughter and your son into doves, and if you can tell me which of them is your son, you can have him. If you fail, he stays with me forever."

The father was very angry and ran from the house, ran and ran until he came to a forest where he lay down and wept bitterly. Then he fell into exhausted sleep. He dreamed that somebody was poking him, and he awoke to see a gray old man standing by his side. "Why were you crying, my friend?" the old man asked.

The father told him all that had happened. "I sacrificed everything I owned for a child," he concluded, "and now I'll lose him forever if I fix on the wrong dove."

The old man said, "Leave the forest and you'll come to a field of rye. Pluck several stalks and take them with you to the sorcerers. Tell them that you're ready for the test, and when he presents the doves to you, throw the kernels of rye in front of them. Watch carefully: The dove that gobbles up the rye is the sorcerer's daughter. The bird who is your son will eat slowly because he is yearning to be with you."

The father did as he had been told, and everything happened as the gray old man said.

After the father had chosen the dove who was his son, the sorcerer said, "Yes, you've picked out your son. But you can't have him unless you sign a contract that he will perform no magic in my lifetime."

The father agreed to the contract, and he and his son went on their way. Then the son said, "Father, you're very poor. Let me turn myself into a horse so you can take me to market and sell me. You're certain to get a good price. But when you've sold me, be sure to take my bridle off; otherwise I'll be a horse forever. When you've taken off the bridle, I'll turn into a dove and fly after you. And when I spot you, I'll fly down and turn into a human again."

So, the son turned himself into a horse and his father led him to a market. A great many dealers were interested in the horse. But the sorcerer was also there and saw what was going on. Disguising himself, he went up to the father and asked, "How much do you want for your horse?"

"A thousand rubles," said the father.

"Let me try him out to see if he's worth it," said the sorcerer.

"Go ahead," said the father.

The sorcerer jumped on the horse and said, "You'll see your son about as soon as you can see your own ears. You signed a contract and you've broken it." With that he lashed the horse and rode away.

When the sorcerer arrived home, he kept the animal in his stable. He beat it and watered it, but gave it no food. Then one day the rich man in Odessa sent for him again to perform tricks at another banquet for the poor. Before leaving, the sorcerer told his daughter to give the horse ten lashes and some water every day.

Yet the next morning when the daughter entered the stable, she was moved by the horse's beauty. She caressed his head and removed his bridle. As soon as he was free of the bridle, the horse turned into a human and she recognized him at once. "Give me some water," he said. And when she went to get the water, the boy turned himself into a dove and flew away.

The sorcerer on the way to Odessa saw the dove in flight above him. At once he understood what had happened and he turned himself into a hawk and flew in pursuit, upon which the dove turned himself into a ring and dropped into the sea. The hawk transformed itself into a duck with a copper bill and searched for the ring in the sea. The ring, meanwhile, moved toward the shore, little by little, until it washed up on a beach. There it was spotted by the king's daughter, who had come to bathe. The duck, seeing her put the ring on her finger, flapped his wings and said to himself, "I'll not be able to get him now, but just wait, I'll use all my powers to get him back."

Once she was at home, the king's daughter felt the ring squeezing her finger. So, she tugged and tugged at it until it fell to the ground where it turned into a young man.

"Don't be frightened," he said to her. "I'm human, and I'm a sorcerer. But a more powerful sorcerer is coming who means to kill me. He'll promise you mountains of gold for me, but it's only a trick. When he tries to take me, I'll turn into a ring again. Put the ring on your finger, and if he tries to grab it from you, throw it to the ground and it will turn into a pea. Then he'll become a hen and try to eat me. But if you put your foot on the pea, it will turn into a polecat and wring the hen's neck."

And that's what happened. And they threw the hen's carcass into the street. The boy went back to the sorcerer's daughter and married her, and they are alive and well to this day. Now the boy rides to Odessa instead of the sorcerer and performs tricks for the poor folk.

The boy's father lives with them and is happy and has no need to go begging any more.

If Not Higher (1906)

I. L. Peretz

AND THE REBBE OF NEMIROV, every Friday morning, as slices of time disappeared, melted into thin air! He was not to be found anywhere, neither in the synagogue nor in the two houses of study, or worshipping in Home Minyan, and most certainly not at home. His door stood open, people went in and out as they pleased—no one ever stole anything from the Rebbe—but there was not a soul in the house.

Where can the Rebbe be?

Where *should* he be, if not in heaven?

Is it likely a Rebbe should have no affairs on hand with the Solemn Days so near?

Jews (no evil eye!) need a livelihood, peace, health, successful matchmakings, they wish to be good and pious, and their sins are great. Satan, with his thousand eyes, spies out the world from one end to the other, and he sees, and accuses, and tells tales—and who should help if not the Rebbe? So thought the people.

Once, however, there came a Lithuanian—and he laughed! You know the Lithuanian Jews—they rather devise books of devotion, but stuff themselves with the Talmud and the codes. Well, the Lithuanian points out a special bit of the Gemoreh—and hopes it is plain enough: even Moses our Teacher could not ascend into heaven, but remained suspended thirty inches below it—and who, I ask you, is going to argue with a Lithuanian?

What becomes of the Rebbe?

"I don't know, and I don't care," says he, shrugging his shoulders, and all the while (what it is to be a Lithuanian!) determined to find out.

The very same evening, soon after prayers, the Lithuanian steals into the Rebbe's room, lays himself down under the Rebbe's bed, and lies low. He intends to stay there all night to find out where the Rebbe goes, and what he does at Sliches-time. Another in his place would have dozed and slept the time away. Not so a Lithuanian—he learned a whole treatise of the Talmud by heart!

Day has not broken when he hears the call to prayer.

The Rebbe has been awake some time. The Lithuanian has heard him sighing and groaning for a whole hour. Whoever has heard the groaning of the Nemirover Rebbe knows what sorrow for All-Israel, what distress of mind, found voice in every groan. The soul that heard was dissolved in grief. But the heart of a Lithuanian is of cast-iron. The Lithuanian hears and lies still. The Rebbe lies still, too—the Rebbe, long life to him, *upon* the bed and the Lithuanian *under* the bed!

After that the Lithuanian hears the beds in the house squeak—the people jump out of them—a Jewish word is spoken now and again—water is poured on the fingers—a door is opened here and there. Then the people leave the house, and once more it is quiet and dark, only a very little moonlight comes in, through the shutter.

He confessed afterward, did the Lithuanian, that when he found himself alone with the Rebbe, terror took hold of him. He grew cold all over, and the roots of his ear-locks pricked his temples like needles. An excellent joke, to be left alone with the Rebbe right before dawn.

But a Lithuanian is dogged. He quivers and quakes like a fish—but he does not budge. At last, the Rebbe, long life to him, rises in his turn. First he does what beseems a Jew. Then he goes to the wardrobe and takes out a packet—which proves to the dress of a peasant: linen trousers, high boots, a pelisse, a wide felt hat, and a long and broad leather belt studded with brass nails. The Rebbe puts them on. Out of the pockets of the pelisse dangles the end of a thick cord, a peasant's cord.

On his way out, the Rebbe steps aside into the kitchen, stoops, takes a hatchet from under a bed, puts it into his belt, and leaves the house. The Lithuanian trembles, hut he persists.

A fearful Solemn-Day hush broods over the dark streets, broken not unfrequently by a cry of supplication from some little Minyan, or the moan of some sick person behind a window.

The Rebbe keeps to the street side, and walks in the shadow of the houses. He glides from one to the other, the Lithuanian after him. And the Lithuanian hears the sound of his own heartbeats mingle with the heavy footfall of the Rebbe; but he follows on, and together they emerge from the town.

Behind the town stands a little wood. The Rebbe, long life to him, enters it. He walks on thirty or forty paces, and then he stops beside a small tree. And the Lithuanian, with amazement, sees the Rebbe take his hatchet and strike the tree. He sees the Rebbe strike blow after blow, and he hears the tree creak and snap. And the little tree falls, and the Rebbe splits it up into logs, and the logs into splinters. Then he makes a bundle, binds it round with the cord, throws it on his shoulder, replaces the hatchet in his belt, leaves the wood, and goes back into the town.

In one of the back streets, he stops beside a poor, tumble-down little house, and taps at the window.

"Who is there?" cries a frightened voice within. The Lithuanian knows it to be the voice of a Jewess, a sick Jewess.

"I," answers the Rebbe in the peasant tongue.

"Who is I?" inquires the voice further. And the Rebbe answers again in the Little-Russian speech: "Vassil."

"Which Vassil? and what do you want, Vassil?"

"I have wood to sell," says the sham peasant, "very cheap, for next to nothing."

And without further ado he goes in. The Lithuanian steals in behind him, and sees, in the gray light of dawn, a poor room with poor, broken furniture. In the bed lies a sick Jewess huddled up in rags, who says bitterly:

"Wood to sell—and where am I, a poor widow, to get the money from to buy it?"

"I will give you a six-groschen worth on credit."

"And how am I ever to repay you?" groans the poor woman.

"Foolish creature!" the Rebbe upbraids her. "See here, you are a poor sick Jewess, and I am willing to trust you with the little bundle of wood. I believe that in time you will repay me. And you, you have such a great and mighty God, and you do not trust Him! Not even to the amount of a miserable six-groschen for a little bundle of wood."

"And who is to light the stove?" groans the widow. "Do I look like getting up to do it? Right now my son is away at work!"

"I will also light the stove for you," said the Rebbe.

And the Rebbe repeated the first part of Sliches, groaning as he laid the wood in the stove. Then, when the stove was now ignited and the wood crackled cheerily, he repeated, more gaily, the second part of Sliches. He repeated the third part when the fire had burnt itself out, and he shut the stove doors. . . .

The Lithuanian who saw all this remained with the Rebbe, as one of his followers. And later, when anyone told how the Rebbe early every morning at Sliches-time raised himself and flew up into heaven, the Lithuanian, instead of laughing, added quietly: "If not higher."

The Image (1906)

I. L. Peretz

GREAT PEOPLE HAVE BEEN KNOWN TO do great wonders; witness the time when they attacked the Ghetto in Prague and were about to assault the women, roast the children, and beat the remainder to death. When all means of defense were exhausted, the Maharal laid down the Gemoreh, stepped out into the street, went up to the first mud-heap outside the door of a schoolmaster, and made a clay image.

He blew into its nostril, and it began to move. Then he whispered a name into its ear, and away went the image out of the Ghetto, and the Maharal sat down again to read his book. The image fell upon our enemies who were besieging the Ghetto, and threshed them as it were with flails—they fell before him as thick as flies.

Prague was filled with corpses—they say the destruction lasted all Wednesday and Thursday; Friday, at noon, the image was still at it.

"Rabbi," exclaimed Kohol, "the image is making a clean sweep of the city! There will be no one left to light the fires on Sabbath or to take down the lamps!"

A second time the Maharal shut his book. Then, he took his stand at the desk and began to chant the psalm, "A Song of the Sabbath Day," whereupon the image ceased working, came back to the Ghetto, entered the synagogue, and approached the Maharal.

Once again, the Maharal whispered into its ear, its eyes closed, the breath left it, and it became once more a clay image.

And to this day the image lies aloft in the Prague synagogue, covered up with cobwebs that stretch across from wall to wall, and spread over the whole arcade, so that the image shall not be seen, above all, not by the pregnant women of the "women's court." And the cobwebs may not be touched. Whoever touches them, dies!

No man, not the oldest there, recollects having seen the image; but the Chacham Zebl, the Maharal's grandson, sometimes wonders, whether, for instance, such an image might not be included in one of the ten men required to form a congregation?

The image, you see, is not forgotten—the image is still there. But the name with which to give it life in the day of need has fallen as it were into the deep seas! And the cobwebs increase and increase, and one may not touch them.

What is to be done?

The Golem (1908)

I. L. Peretz

GREAT MEN WERE once capable of great miracles.

When the Ghetto of Prague was being attacked, and they were about to rape the women, roast the children, and slaughter the rest; when it seemed that the end had finally come, the great Rabbi Loeb put aside his *Gemarah*, went into the street, stopped before a heap of clay in front of the teacher's house, and molded a clay image. He breathed into the nose of the *golem*—and it began to stir. Then, he whispered the Name into its ear, and our *golem* left the ghetto. The rabbi returned to the House of Prayer, and the *golem* fell upon our enemies, threshing them as with flails. Men fell on all sides.

Prague was filled with corpses. It lasted, so they say, through Wednesday and Thursday. Now it is already Friday, and the clock strikes twelve. But the *golem* is still busy at its work.

"Rabbi!" cries the head of the ghetto. "The *golem* is slaughtering all of Prague! There will not be a gentile left to light the Sabbath candles or take down the Sabbath lamps."

Once again, the rabbi left his study. He went to the altar and began singing the psalm "A Song of the Sabbath."

The *golem* stopped its slaughter. It returned to the ghetto, entered the House of Prayer, and waited for the rabbi. And again the rabbi whispered into its ear. The eyes of the *golem* closed, the soul that had dwelt in it flew out, and it was once more a *golem* of clay.

To this day, the *golem* lies hidden in the attic of the Prague synagogue, covered with cobwebs that extend from wall to wall. No living creature may look at it, particularly women in pregnancy. No one may touch the cobwebs, for whoever touches them dies. Even the oldest people no longer remember the *golem*, though the wise man Zvi, the grandson of the great Rabbi Loeb, ponders the problem: may such a *golem* be included in a congregation of worshippers or not?

The *golem*, you see, has not been forgotten. It is still here! But the Name by which it be called to life in a day of need, the Name has disappeared. And the cobwebs grow and grow, and no one may touch them. What are we to do?

The Wedding That Came without Its Band (1909)

Sholem Aleichem

"I DO BELIEVE THAT I promised to tell you about another of our Slowpoke's miracles, thanks to which, don't you know, we were saved from a horrible fate. If you'd like to hear about it, why don't you stretch out on this seat, and I'll lie down on that one. That way we'll both be more comfortable."

So said my friend, the merchant from Heysen, as we were traveling one day on the narrow-gauge train called Slowpoke Express. And since this time, too, we were all by ourselves in the car, which was rather hot, we took off our jackets, unbuttoned our vests, and made ourselves right at home. I let him tell his story in his jovial, unhurried manner, making a few mental notes as he did so that I could write it down later in his own words.

"Once upon a time . . . it happened a while ago, back in the days of the Constitution, when we Jews were getting the glad hand. Actually, though, we in Heysen were never afraid of a pogrom. Shall I tell you why not? For the simple reason that there was no one to do the job. Of course, I don't mean to suggest that if you looked hard enough, you couldn't have found a few public-spirited citizens who would have welcomed the chance to dust off a Jew or two, that is, to break all our bones—the proof of it being, don't you know, that when the glad tidings began to arrive from other places, some of our local patriots dashed off a secret message to whomever they thought it might concern: seeing as how, they wrote, it was time to stand up and be counted in Heysen, too, where there was a dearth of volunteers, could they please be sent reinforcements in a hurry. . . . And don't you know that twenty-four hours hadn't gone by when word reached us Jews, and again in strictest secrecy, that the reinforcements were already on their way. Where were they coming from? From Zlunerinka, and from Kazatin, and from Razdyelne, and from Popelne, and from a few other places that were equally famous for their roughnecks. How, you ask, did we get wind of such a top secret? The answer, don't you know, is that we had a hidden agent, a fellow called Noyach Tonkonog. Who was this Tonkonog? I'll try to describe him for you, because being a traveler in these parts, you may run into him some day.

"Noyach Tonkonog is a Jew who grew more up than out. And since God gave him a pair of long legs, he learned to put them to good use. He's always on the run and hardly ever at home. He's got a thousand irons in the fire, most of them not his own. His own business, that is, is a printshop. And because it's the only one in Heysen, he rubs elbows with government officials, and with our local gentry, and with all kinds of people in high places.

"It was Noyach who broke the good news to us. That is, he personally spread it around town by whispering in everyone's ear, 'This is strictly for your private consumption, because I'd never tell anyone else. . . .' Before long the word had traveled like wildfire that hooligans were being brought in to attack the Jews. We even knew the exact hour of the attack and the direction it would come from—it was all planned like a military operation. Well, there was great gloom in Heysen, don't you know! And it was the poor who panicked the most. That's not what you'd normally expect, is it? After all, it makes more sense for a rich Jew to be scared to death of such a thing, because he's liable to be cleaned out of house and home. If you own nothing to begin with, on the other hand, why worry? What's there to lose? Still, you should have seen them drop everything, grab their children, and run pell-mell for cover. . . . Just where, you ask, does a Jew hide in Heysen? Either in the cellar of a friendly Russian, or in the attic of the town notary, or wherever the owner puts you in his factory. And in fact, everyone managed to find a place. There was only one Jew who didn't bother, and you're looking at him right now. I'm not trying to boast, mind you, but you'll *see* if you think about it that I had logic on my side. In the first place, what good does it do to be afraid of a pogrom? You either live through it or you don't. . . . And second, even assuming that I'm no braver than the next man, and that, when push comes to shove, I'd like to be someplace safe myself, where, I ask you, is safe? Whose word do I have that, in all the excitement, the same friendly Russian, or town notary, or factory owner isn't going to . . . do you follow me? And besides, how can you just go and abandon a whole town? It's no trick to skedaddle—the whole point is to stay and do something! . . . Of course, you may object, that's easy to say, but what exactly can a Jew do? Well, I'll tell you what: a Jew can find—a string to pull. I suppose there's someone with the right sort of influence where you come from, too. In Heysen he's called Nachman Kassoy, a contractor with a round beard, a silk vest, and a big house all his own. And because he builds roads, he was on good terms with the prefect of the district, who even used to have him over for tea. This prefect, don't you know, was quite a decent goy. In fact, he was a prince of a goy! Why do I say that? Because he had his price, if you paid it through Nachman Kassoy. That is, he was perfectly willing to accept gifts from anyone (why be rude, after all?), but he liked getting them from Nachman best of all. There's something about a contractor, don't you know. . . .

"In short, I fixed things via Nachman, drew up a list of donors, and managed to raise the funds and a tidy little sum it was too, don't you know, because you couldn't cross a prefect's palm in such a matter without giving it some good scratch . . . in return for which, he did his best to reassure us that we could sleep calmly that night because nothing would happen to us at all. Fair enough, no? The only trouble was that we still had our secret agent, whose reports went from bad to worse; the latest of them, which he of course passed on in such strict confidence that it was all over town in no time flat, was that he, Noyach Tonkonog, had personally seen a telegram that he very much wished he hadn't. What was in it? Just one word, but a most unpleasant one: *Yedyem*, it said—here we come! Back to our prefect we ran. 'Your Excellency, it looks bad!' 'How come?' 'There's a telegram.' 'From whom?' 'The same people.' 'What's in it?' *Yedyem!* You should have heard him laugh. 'You're bigger fools than I thought,' he said. 'Why, just yesterday I ordered a company of Cossacks from Tulczyn for your protection. . . .' Well, that put some spunk in us, don't you know: a Jew only needs to see a Cossack to feel so courageous that he's ready to take on the whole world! It was nothing to sneeze at, a bodyguard like that. . . .

"In short, there was just one question: who would arrive first, the Cossacks from Tulczyn or the roughnecks from Zhmerinka? It stood to reason that the roughnecks would, since they were traveling by train while the Cossacks were on horseback. But we had our hopes pinned on our Slowpoke: God was great, and the only miracle we asked of Him was to make the train a few hours late, which it usually was anyway, in fact, nearly every day. . . . Yet for once, don't you know, as though out of spite, the Slowpoke was right on time: it pulled in and out of each station like clockwork. You can imagine how it made our blood run cold to hear from our secret agent that another yedyemegram had arrived from Krishtopovka, the last station before Heysen—and this time, for good measure, the *yedyem* had a *yahoo* after it. . . . Naturally, we went right to the prefect with the news, threw ourselves at his feet, and begged him not to count on the Cossacks from Tulczyn and, if only for appearances' sake, to send a detachment of police to the station so that the hooligans shouldn't think the only law was that of the jungle. His Excellency didn't let us down. In fact, he quite rose to the occasion. What do I mean by that? I mean, he put on his full-dress uniform with all its medals and went off to the station with the entire police force to meet the train.

"But our local patriots, don't you know, weren't caught napping either. They had also put on their best clothes and their medals, taken along a pair of priests for good luck, and gone off to meet the train at the station—where, in fact, they asked the prefect what he was doing there, which was the exact same question he asked them. A few words were exchanged, and the prefect made it clear that they were wasting their time. As long as he was in charge, he said, there would be no pogroms in Heysen. He read them the riot act, but they just grinned back at him and even had the cheek to answer, 'We'll soon see who's in charge around here.' . . . Just then a whistle was heard. It made our hearts skip a beat. We were all waiting for it to blow again, followed by a loud 'Yahoo!'—and what that 'Yahoo!' meant, don't you know, we already knew from other towns. . . . Would you like to hear the end of it, though? There was a second whistle, all right, but there never was any 'Yahoo.' Why not? It could only have happened on our Slowpoke. Listen to this.

"The driver pulled into the Heysen station, climbed out of the engine full of prunes, and headed straight for the buffet as usual. 'Just a minute, old man,' he was asked. 'Where's the rest of the train?' 'What rest of the train?' he said. 'Do you mean to say you didn't notice,' he was asked, 'that your engine wasn't pulling any cars?' That driver, he just stared at them and said: 'What do I care about cars? That's the crew's job.' 'But where's the crew?' he was asked. 'How should I know?' he answered. 'The conductor whistles that he's ready, I whistle back that I am too, and off I go. I don't have eyes in the back of my head to see what's following behind me. . . .' So he said, the driver—there was nothing wrong with his logic. In a word, it was pointless to argue: the Slowpoke had arrived without its passengers like a wedding without its band. . . .

"As we found out later, that train was carrying a merry gang of young bucks, the pick of the crop, each man-jack of them, and in full battle gear too, with clubs, and tar, and what-have-you. They were in a gay old mood, don't you know, and the vodka flowed like water, and when they reached their last station, that is to say, Krishtopovka, they had themselves such a blast that the entire train crew got drunk too, the conductor and the stoker and even the policeman—in consequence of which, one little detail was forgotten: to hitch up the locomotive again. And so, right on schedule, the driver took off in it for Heysen while the rest of the Slowpoke, don't you know, remained standing on the tracks in Krishtopovka! Better yet, nobody—neither the roughnecks, nor the other passengers, nor even the train crew—noticed what had happened. They were all so busy emptying glasses and killing bottles that the first they knew about it was when the stationmaster happened to look out the window and see the cars standing by themselves. Did he raise Cain! And when the rest of the station found out, all hell broke loose: the pogromchiks blamed the train crew, and the train crew blamed the pogromchiks, and they went at it hot and heavy until they realized that there was nothing to do but shoulder their arms and tote them all the way to Heysen. What other choice did they have? And that's exactly what they did: they rallied round the flag and hotfooted it to Heysen, where they arrived safe and sound, don't you know, singing and yahooing for God and country. Shall I tell you something, though? They got there a little too late. The streets were already patrolled by mounted Cossacks from Tulczyn, who clearly had the whip hand—and I do mean whips! It didn't take those hooligans half an hour to clear out of town down to the last man. They vanished, don't you know, like a pack of hungry mice, or like snow on a hot summer's day.

"Well now, suppose you tell me: shouldn't our Slowpoke be plated with gold, or at least written up in the papers?"

Two Anti-Semites (ca. 1909–1910)

Sholem Aleichem

MAX BERLLIANT IS A lost cause. He travels from Lodz to Moscow and from Moscow to Lodz several times a year. He knows all the buffets, all the stations along the way, is hand in glove with all the conductors, and has visited all the remote provinces—even ones where Jews are only allowed to stay twenty-four hours. He has sweated at all the border crossings, put up with all kinds of humiliations, and more than once, has been aggravated—has eaten his heart, in fact—and all because of the Jews. Not because the Jews as a people exist, but because he himself—don't shout, whisper it—is also a Jew. And not even so much because he's a Jew, as because—if you'll forgive me for saying so—he looks so Jewish. That's what comes of creating man in God's image! And what an image! Max's eyes are dark and shining, his hair the same. It's real Semitic hair. He speaks Russian like a cripple, and, God help us, with a Yiddish sing-song. And on top of everything he's got a nose! A nose to end all noses.

As if that weren't enough, our hero is unlucky in his occupation. He's a traveling salesman, and it's part of his job to be friendly. He has to talk a lot, and in his business it's important that he should not just talk, but that he should be heard, and not just be heard, but above all, be seen. In short, he's a sorry creature.

True, our hero did avenge himself on his beard. Beardless now, and decked out like a bride, he curls his whiskers, files his nails, wears a tie as glorious as what the Lord God himself might have worn had he ever worn a tie. Max has accustomed himself to the food in railway restaurants, but he continually vents his bitterness on the pigs of world. If even half the curses he heaps on the species were to come true he would be happy. But what's the use of being fussy? Might as well be hung for a sheep as for a lamb. So, Max took his life in his hands and began to eat lobster.

Why do I say that he took his life in his hands? May our worst enemies know as much about their noses as Max Berlliant knows about eating lobsters. Should he cut them with a knife or stab them with a fork? Or should he eat them whole, just as they come?

Despite all these glorious achievements, Max Berlliant can't hide his Jewishness—not from us, the Jews, nor from them, the Gentiles. You can pick him out like a counterfeit coin in a handful of change, and in a crowd of Abels, he stands out like a Cain. At every twist and turn he is reminded who he is and what he is. In short, he's a sorry creature.

If Max Berlliant was unhappy up to the time of Kishinev, after Kishinev no one could touch him for misery. To harbor deep in your heart a great sorrow, and what's worse to be ashamed of it, is a special kind of hell. Max was as ashamed of what had happened in Kishinev as if he was personally responsible for it, almost as if Kishinev was part of himself. And as luck would have it, right after the incidents in Kishinev, his firm sent him into the very districts where it had all happened: Bessarabia.[1]

That's when a new hell opened up under his feet. He had heard a thousand horror stories about Kishinev in his hometown. Wasn't it enough that his heart had flooded with grief and filled with blood when he was told about the atrocities in Kishinev, atrocities such as never had been known or heard before? Will he ever forget the day they offered up special prayers in the synagogues for the slaughtered of Kishinev? Or how, on that day, the old men wept and the women fainted?

It must surely have happened to you while sitting on a train that you passed the place where some great catastrophe has occurred. You know in your heart that you are safe because lightning doesn't strike twice in the same spot. Yet, you can't help remembering that, not so long ago, trains were derailed at this very point, and carloads of people spilled over the embankment. You can't help knowing that here people were thrown out headfirst, while over there bones were crushed, blood flowed, brains were splattered. You can't help feeling glad that you're alive; it's only human to take secret pleasure in it.

Max knew he was bound to meet people in these parts eager to talk about the pogroms. He would have to listen to the wails and groans of those who had lost their near and dear, and he would also be forced to endure the righteous exhortations and malicious remarks of the Gentiles. So the closer they came to Bessarabia, the more he tried to find some way of escape, some way to hide from his own soul.

As they approached the region, Max thought of staying behind when the other passengers got off. Then he changed his mind and jumped down onto the platform with the others when the train stopped. He made his way to the buffet as if he hadn't a care in the world. He ordered a drink, followed it up with some tasty tidbits forbidden to Jews, washed it all down with a beer, lit a cigar, and went up to the counter where they sell books and newspapers. There his glance fell on a certain ugly anti-Semitic newspaper called *The Bessarabian*, published by a certain ugly anti-Semite called Krushevan. And here in the very region where this fine newspaper was conceived, hatched, and born, it lay innocently—almost anonymously—all by itself on the counter. Not a soul was buying it, nobody even gave it a second look.

The local Jews don't buy it because it's so scurrilous, and the Gentiles don't buy it because they are sick and tired of it. So, there it lies, nice and neat on the counter, put there to remind the world that somewhere on the face of this earth lives a certain Krushevan, a man who neither rests nor sleeps in his tireless search for new ways to warn the world against that dread disease: Judaism.

Max Berlliant is the only one to buy a copy of *The Bessarabian*. And why is that? Maybe because of the same urge that drives him to eat lobster. Or maybe he wants to see for himself what that dog of dogs has to say about Jews? It's a proven fact that the readers of anti-Semitic newspapers are mostly Jews. That means us, little brothers, with all due respect. . . . And though the publishers of such newspapers know it, they act on the principle that even, if the Jew is *treyf*, his money is *kosher*. . . .

Accordingly, our Max buys himself a copy of *The Bessarabian*, brings it back to the train, stretches out on the seat, and covers himself with the newspaper the way you cover yourself with a blanket. And while he is thus busying himself, a thought flies through his head: "What, for instance, would a Jew think if he came across a man stretched out on the seat covered with a copy of *The Bessarabian*? Surely it would never occur to him that the man under the newspaper might be a Jew. . . . What an idea, what a great way to get rid of Jews and at the same time keep a seat all to myself."

So reasoned our hero. And in order to make sure that no mother's son should find out who was lying there, he covered his face with the newspaper; he hid his nose, also his eyes and hair, and indeed the whole physiognomy of the one made in God's own image. He pictured to himself how in the middle of the night an old Jew, weighed down with packs and bundles, creeps onto the train, looks around for a seat, sees someone lying there covered with *The Bessarabian,* figures that he must be a squire at least, but a bad lot in any case, and probably an anti-Semite—possibly even Krushevan himself. So the old Jew with his packs and bundles spits three times and goes away, while he, Max, remains lying there in lonely splendor, lording it over the whole seat. "Oh, oh, as I live and breathe, what a great joke!"

So much did this plan please our Max as he lay under his *Bessarabian* that he burst into laughter. After all, when you have eaten, washed it down with beer, smoked a cigar, and toward evening stretched out on a seat all to yourself—you have something to crow about. . . .

Hush now, let's have quiet. Our hero, Max Berlliant, the traveling salesman, whose route stretches from Lodz to Moscow and from Moscow to Lodz, is lying on a seat covered with the latest issue of *The Bessarabian.* He has just dozed off, so let's not disturb him.

Let's admit it, Berlliant is smart. But this time fate outsmarted him. Everything happened almost as he imagined. Someone did come onto the train—a burly fellow with two suitcases, and someone did notice him as he lay there covered with his *Bessarabian.* But instead of spitting three times and going away, the newcomer stood there studying him, this queer anti-Semite with the Semitic nose (for, during his sleep the newspaper had slipped off Max's face to reveal his nose, his stigma).

Our new arrival stands there, smiling. After placing his suitcase on the seat opposite Max, he steps out on the platform and returns with a fresh issue of *The Bessarabian.* Out of his suitcase he takes a pillow, a blanket, a pair of slippers, a bottle of eau de cologne, and makes himself comfortable. Then, stretching out on the seat opposite, he covers himself with the newspaper in exactly the same way as our Max Berlliant. He lies there smoking, looking at Max and smiling. He closes first one eye, then the other, and finally dozes off.

So let's leave our two *Bessarabians* sound asleep, seat to seat. In the meantime we'll introduce the reader to our new character: who he is and what he is.

He is a general. Not a general in the army and not a governor-general, but a general inspector, an agent for a company. His real name is Chaim Nyemchick, but he signs himself Albert, and everyone calls him Patti.

I admit it sounds a bit crazy. How from a Chaim you get an Albert is understandable. After all, among us Jews doesn't a Vevel become a Vladimir, an Israel become an Isadore, and an Avrom an Avukem? But how does a Chaim get to be a Patti? To answer this, we'll have to employ logic, study linguistics, and use common sense.

Our first move is to get rid of the "ch" in Chaim. Then we say goodbye to the "i" and the "m," leaving only the "a" by itself. So all we have to do now is to add on an "l" and a "b" and an "e" and an "r" and a "t." Now doesn't that add up to Albert? And from Albert it's just a step to Alberti, and from Alberti we get first Berti, then Betti, and finally—how could we miss?—Patti! *Sic transit gloria mundi.* In other words, this is how to make a turkey out of a duck.

Our character is called Patti Nyemchick, and he's a general inspector, who travels the world the same as Max Berlliant. But his nature is entirely different. He's lively, active, and expressive. And in spite of the fact that his name is Patti and he's a general inspector, he's a Jew like other Jews, and he loves Jews. He also enjoys entertaining people with stories and telling Jewish jokes.

Patti Nyemchick is known far and wide as a raconteur, but he has one fault: whatever the anecdote, he'll swear by all that's holy that his story is true and that it actually happened. The trouble is he keeps changing the locale of his stories and forgetting what he said last time. It's also rumored that Patti, this inspector general, skims over prayers, bluffs his way through difficult Hebrew passages, exaggerates—or as they say in our parts, he's a liar.

So, having come into the train and having noted how our Max Berlliant is stretched out on the seat under an issue of the notorious *Bessarabian*, and having recognized from his nose that Max could in no way be a relation, either close or distant, to Krushevan and his fancy anti-Semitic rag, Patti's first thought is: "This'll make a great story; this'll have them rolling in the aisles."

That's the reason why Patti slipped out, provided himself with a copy of *The Bessarabian*, and lay down opposite our Max. Wondering what would come of it, he dozed off.

Now let's leave Patti the general inspector under *The Bessarabian* copy two, and return to Max the traveling salesman under *The Bessarabian* copy one.

Max Berlliant had a bad night. It must have been the things he ate at the station, because his sleep was troubled. He dreamed that he wasn't Max Berlliant at all, but Krushevan, the editor of *The Bessarabian*—and that he was riding, not on a train, but bareback on a wild boar, while a lobster, boiled and red, kept waving its claws at him, and all the while cries and echoes of "Ki-shi-nev" sounded from afar.

Now a little breeze seems to whistle in Max's ears. He hears the sound of rustling leaves and women's dresses and wants to open his eyes and can't. When he tries to touch his nose, he finds he hasn't got one; his nose is gone—disappeared without a trace. And in the place where his nose used to be is a copy of *The Bessarabian*, and he can't remember where he is. He tries to move and can't. He knows he's dreaming but he can't wake up, he can't get hold of himself. He simply cannot.

He lies there stunned and suffering, in utter confusion. He feels his strength leaving and summons up his last bit of willpower. Finally, he manages to squeeze out a groan, so low that he's the only one who hears it. He opens one eye a little, just a tiny little bit, and sees a ray of light. In the light he sees the figure of a man lying stretched out on the seat opposite him, also alone, and like him, taking up the whole seat. And that man is also covered with a copy of the same issue of *The Bessarabian*.

Our Max is amazed and bewildered. It seems to him that it's himself who is stretched out on the seat opposite, and he can't understand the logic of how he, Max, can possibly be lying there. How can a man see his own reflection without a mirror? Every single hair on his head stands on end, one at a time.

Gradually our Max begins to collect his thoughts and understand that the man on the seat opposite is not himself, Max, but someone else altogether. He wonders: "Where did the fellow come from and why is he lying on the seat opposite? And why is he covered with a copy of *The Bessarabian*?"

Max doesn't have the patience to wait for morning. He's in a hurry to answer the riddle, and right away. So, he starts stirring, rattling his newspaper until he hears that the person on the seat opposite is also stirring and rattling his newspaper. He keeps still for a minute, then takes a quick look and sees the other fellow regarding him with a half-smile. Our two *Bessarabian* customers are lying there across from each other, staring but not talking. Although each anti-Semite is dying to know who the other one is, they hide their curiosity and keep mum.

Then Patti has an idea and starts to whistle the tune of that well-known Yiddish folk song:

A little fire
burns cosily
in the old wood stove . . .

Our Max takes up the tune and whistles out the next line:

And the room is hot . . .

Then slowly, slowly both anti-Semites sit up, throw off the *Bessarabians*, and together they burst into the familiar refrain. This time they don't whistle it, but sing the words with loud abandon:

The rebbe sits
with little children
and recites with them
the Hebrew alphabet . . .

Translated by Miriam Waddington.

Happiness (1909)

Hersh Dovid Nomberg

IN THE ENDLESS UNIVERSE, through the tremendous cosmos, an angel was flying. He hadn't folded his wings for many, many years. And he had been flying and flying nonstop for many, many years. Here a sun and there a star and there an errant comet, and the angel halted and asked: "Can you tell me, please: where is Earth located?" And no sooner had he heard the reply, "I don't know," than he flew away. Every minute was precious, every second.

Many, many years ago, the angel had heard about the plight of the unhappy people on Earth, their harsh and bitter lives—and his angelic heart filled with pity. He threw himself down before the Throne of Glory and begged God to grant happiness to human beings, and God answered his prayer and he promptly handed happiness to the angel, who was to bring it to the unhappy people on Earth.

And this angel descended from Seventh Heaven, and he has been wandering ever since, among suns, stars, and comets, and he is looking for Earth.

His right hand is clutching happiness, and his white wings stir lightly in the thin ether. A thousand years have worn by, he has flown through millions of solar systems—but no one knows the location of Earth with its unhappy people.

Sometimes a tear rolls down from the angel's eye. Ah! Who can say whether his radiant wings are carrying him away from Earth?

But still—he *is* an angel after all.

His tear rolls down—not on his long wandering, but on poor humans who thirst and strive for happiness, which he, the angel, carries in his right hand. "Can you please tell me the location of Earth with its unhappy people?"

"No."

And the angel then flies on, inspired by his ideals.

Meanwhile the world grows old and new. People change, and ideals and religions change—and unhappiness rules everywhere!

"Where do we find happiness?!" the unhappy humans sigh.

Once, an old stargazer, an astronomer, peered up at a wandering comet. For a long time, he kept his eye glued to his telescope, following the comet wherever it turned. He didn't stop even when eating or sleeping. He would then have his young son replace him, and—he no sooner finished eating than he returned to his telescope.

The comet was very angry:

"What does that old wizard want from me? What's he after? Am I a thief? Is that why he stalks me?"

The comet got even angrier.

Suddenly, the angel caught up with the comet and asked him in his sad and gentle voice:

"Mr. Comet, do you happen to know the location of Earth with its unhappy people?"

"People on Earth?" the comet angrily replied. "Those are only old wizards and young killers. . . ."

"Ah, poor people," the angel sighed. "All because of their great unhappiness—alas! No, Mr. Comet, you mustn't get angry, hatred is a sin!"

And the happiness in his right hand shone and gleamed so strongly that even the comet's eyes, upon seeing it, grew radiant, and his dismal, misanthropic soul grew lighter.

"Where is Earth?"

With a long, thick beam, the comet pointed at the location of Earth. "Ah, how far from Heaven has Earth wandered!" the angel sighed softly. "And all because of great unhappiness."

And the angel then continued his journey.

Meanwhile, on Earth, the astronomer noticed the angel, and, through the telescope, he saw something glowing in the angel's right hand. And just like a prophet prophesizing for a long time that an angel is flying with happiness, the stargazer assumed that the angel was now bringing happiness to human beings. . . .

And the newspapers then brought the news to the entire world.

"An angel is flying with happiness . . ." people said wherever there were human tongues.

All stargazers focused their telescopes and clearly saw the angel coming closer and closer to Earth.

They started calculating and they calculated that the angel would reach Earth on such and such day, at such and such an hour, at such and such a minute, and on such and such a degree.

And the scheduled day arrived, and people from all over the world gathered at the scheduled place.

The crowd became very dense. People started crushing, fighting, punching. . . . They even began stabbing and killing one another.

Rivers of human blood were flowing there, and the moaning and yammering of the dying rose all the way up to the sky. . . .

From far away, the angel saw people shoving and pressing one another. And with his final bit of strength, the angel started shouting from on high:

"Stop fighting! I've got happiness for everyone!"

But they didn't hear him. When the angel flew nearer to Earth, when his radiant eyes saw the slashed-up victims, when his ears heard the moaning and groaning, a tear rolled down and fell upon happiness.

From then on, radiant happiness has been stained.

People say that the angel, who was worn and weary because of his long journey and because of what he saw on Earth, fainted dead away, and happiness dropped from his right hand.

The Rebbe of Apte and Tsar Nicholas (1912)

S. Ansky (Shloyme-Zanvl Rapoport)

NICHOLAS I WAS A bitter enemy not so much of Jews but of Judaism. All his life, he looked for ways of rooting out the Jewish religion and getting Jews—God help us—to convert to Christianity. That was why he planned to issue three anti-Jewish edicts. First of all, he ordered the burning of the Talmud and all the other sacred Jewish books. Secondly, Jews would no longer be permitted to celebrate the Sabbath. And thirdly, Jews had to cut off their beards and sidelocks and wear short garments. The tsar penned all three edicts with his own hands, but he had not as yet sealed the documents with his imperial seal.

That same night, the rebbe of Apte dreamed about the terrible misfortune that was being inflicted on Jews.

The next morning, the rebbe assembled all his Hasids. But instead of telling them about his dream, he asked his followers for the date and time of their births. It turned out that one man had been born on the same day and at the same hour as Nicholas I. The rebbe then ordered that they make royal garments—just like the kind worn by the tsar (though of plain cloth, to keep down the cost, and, according to Jewish law, without mixing wool and linen). The rebbe also asked them to make an imperial crown of paper, get hold of a big sword, build an imperial throne, and place the throne on the platform in the synagogue. Next, the rebbe wrote out the texts of Nicholas's edicts on three sheets of paper.

When everything was completed, the rebbe summoned the man who was born on the same day and at the same hour, and told the Hasid to don the "imperial" garments, gird his loins with the sword, and sit down on the throne, which was flanked by two Hasids dressed as Russian soldiers and clutching naked swords. Next to the throne there was a table, on which the rebbe placed the three documents. As for the other Hasids, the rebbe told them that no matter what they saw or heard, they were strictly prohibited from uttering a word or making a gesture. Otherwise they would be in great danger.

When everything was ready, and the Hasid in imperial garments was sitting on the throne, the Rebbe of Apte, wearing his Sabbath smock, entered the synagogue, halted at a distance from the throne, bowed deeply to the pseudo-tsar, and, coming closer, he shouted: "Long live our emperor, Tsar Nicholas I! May his glory be enhanced!"

He then signaled to his followers to do the same, and they all shouted: "Long live our emperor, Tsar Nicholas I! May his glory be enhanced!"

The pseudo-tsar glared at the rebbe and angrily snapped: "Who are you?" The rebbe bowed even deeper and answered with great servility: "Your Majesty! I am your servant, Yeshue Heshel, the Rebbe of Apte."

Upon hearing those words, the pseudo-tsar jumped up and, with savage wrath, he screamed: "You slimy worm! You filthy, disgusting yid! How dare you approach my imperial throne!"

When the other Hasids heard their friend cursing their rebbe, they were terror-stricken and they started pulling his coattails. But the pseudo-sentries flanking the imperial throne pounced on them, brandishing their naked swords, and they would have injured the Hasids if they hadn't scurried away and hidden in the corners.

The rebbe bowed again and replied: "Your Majesty! I dare to approach your imperial throne because a whole nation has sent me to kneel at your feet." The pseudo-tsar shouted: "Talk!"

And the rebbe began: "Your Majesty! My prayer is for my soul, and my request is for my people. You have penned a decree to burn our

Talmud and all our sacred books. By doing so, you will hurl Jews into an abyss of fear and sorrow. Take pity on us and rip up the decree!"

The pseudo-tsar furiously hollered: "I am determined to root out the Jewish faith—and I will do so!"

The rebbe retorted: "You will *not* do so! Before you, powerful kings, rulers over the entire world, lifted their hands against the Jewish faith. But they failed to vanquish it. Instead, they aroused the wrath of the Almighty and they were severely punished."

Spreading out both arms, the rebbe tearfully added: "Your Majesty! Almighty God has entrusted you with the sheep of the House of Jacob, and you will have to answer to Him for them! Just look at the fear and sorrow of the people of Israel! Its temple is in ruins, its land was stolen by foreigners, and now it roams the world abandoned and driven among the nations. It has no leaders and protectors of its own. All that remains of its former grandeur is its holy Torah, which is dearer to a Jew than life itself. If you now reach out and deprive him of his holy Torah, then remember, Your Majesty, what the prophet Nathan told King David about the spiteful rich man who took a pauper's only sheep. . . ."

The pseudo-tsar sat there, silent and with his head drooping. Suddenly he raised his head and spoke: "You are right, old man! I will destroy the order!"

And he took the first order from the table and ripped it to shreds.

The rebbe took one step closer to the imperial throne, bowed deeply, and said with great servility: "Your Majesty! Once you have imbued yourself with grace toward the people of Israel, and you have allowed the Jews to keep their holy books, do not interfere with their carrying out their commandment. You have written an order prohibiting the Jews from celebrating the Sabbath. Yet the fourth commandment of our Decalogue states: 'Remember the Sabbath day to keep it holy.'"

The pseudo-tsar glared angrily at the rebbe, but held his tongue. He took the second order and ripped it to shreds.

Now the rebbe took one more step toward the imperial throne and he said: "Your Majesty! You also penned a decree ordering Jews to cut off their beards and sidelocks and wear short garments. Show your deep grace and rip up this order too!"

The rebbe hadn't even finished speaking when the pseudo-tsar yelled furiously: "I'm fed up with your requests—you dirty, insolent yid!"

And leaping up from his imperial throne, he pounced on the rebbe, slapped him twice, then grabbed his smock and threw the rebbe out into the street. Meanwhile the crown came tumbling off the pseudo-tsar's head. The instant it fell, the pseudo-tsar halted in the middle of the synagogue like a man who doesn't understand what's happened to him. The other Hasids pounced on him and started cursing him for lifting his hand against the rebbe. But the man swore that he remembered nothing, and upon hearing that he had cursed and struck the rebbe, he burst into bitter tears.

Now the rebbe, with a bloody face, came back into the synagogue. He went over to the pseudo-tsar, placed his hand on the man's back, and said cheerfully: "Don't cry and don't grieve, my son! The two of us have pulled off a difficult piece of work. Too bad the crown fell off too soon."

During the time that the Rebbe of Apte had been standing in front of the pseudo-tsar, the real Nicholas I had been sitting on his imperial throne, reading the three orders and preparing to place his seal upon them. As he sat there, his mind teemed with everything the Rebbe of Apte had said to the pseudo-tsar, and Nicholas decided not to issue the first two orders; instead, he ripped them up. But then he placed his seal on the third edict. And when the order was issued, and Jews were forced to cut off their beards and sidelocks and wear short garments, Jews wept and fasted and created a sensation. But no one realized that two more horrible edicts had almost been issued, and that they had been annulled thanks to the Rebbe of Apte.

Later on, when the rebbe was talking about Nicholas I, he said: "He's nowhere as bad as I thought."

The Penitent: A Tale (1912)

S. Ansky (Shloyme-Zanvl Rapoport)

ONCE THERE WAS A JEW, a peddler, and he trudged through the villages, with his pack of merchandise on his back: needles, ribbons, corals, and other little things. On this income, he barely managed to support himself, his wife, and his child.

Now one winter's day, the peddler was wearing only a light jacket with a thin belt and carrying his goods on his back. It was snowing heavily, and the wind was blasting so hard in his face that he could scarcely catch his breath. He was also dog-tired and barely able to drag his legs out of the fallen snow. The peddler therefore thanked the Good Lord upon reaching a small forest and sitting down to rest under a tree. As he sat there a bit screened against the wind, the peddler felt his exhaustion. His eyelids drooped and he dozed off, forgetting that it was extremely dangerous to sleep in a frost. You run the risk—Heaven forbid!—of freezing to death. Nevertheless, the peddler dozed off, with his goods on his back and his head against the tree, and he had wonderful dreams. He dreamed that he had found a treasure and was counting the ducats—and meanwhile he was freezing more and more. And he would have simply frozen to death, counting the ducats in his dream, and then leaving this world.

But then a peasant woman and her boy, the two of them wrapped in a fur and a kilim, came driving through. When they spotted the Jew lying there, they pitied him and they started reviving him. They rubbed him with snow until his complexion changed, and he emitted a soft sigh. Next, they put him into their sleigh and headed back to their village. Once there, they doused the coach with cold water from the village well, stripped the Jew buck-naked, and put him in the coach. They rubbed him all over with the cold water until he heated up, turned red, and started gradually coming to. Next, they wrapped him in coarse cloth and laid him on the warm oven so he might catch up on his sleep.

The Jew awoke at dawn. The daylight had just begun seeping through the tiny window. The roosters were crowing in the garret. When the Jew found himself lying on an unfamiliar oven in a hot room, he was dumbfounded! Upon stepping into the room, he saw a holy icon with a flickering wick hanging in the corner. A bed stood by the wall, and a peasant woman was sleeping in it. Her hair was disheveled, and she wore a tiny cross on her throat. And a peasant boy was lying and snoring on a bench by the oven.

Unable to grasp all this, the Jew thought to himself: "A dream!" Relying on God's mercy, the Jew shut his eyes again and went back to sleep. When the Jew awoke once more, he saw that the peasant woman had already gotten up. She slipped into a petticoat and went over to have a look at the oven where the peddler was lying. He shut his eyes yet again. He was still certain that it was all a dream. And when he reopened his eyes, he saw that the woman had washed and was now kneeling at the image in the corner, murmuring softly with raised eyes, and then crossing herself.

The Jew rubbed his eyes; he now sensed he wasn't sleeping and he tried to move a limb, but he couldn't. All his limbs were aching, but he understood that he wasn't dreaming, he had suffered some kind of accident and was now lying sick—may you be spared! But he couldn't recall when and where he had fallen ill or how he had gotten here.

Meanwhile, the woman had stood up and turned around. And when she saw that the peddler was awake, she amiably smiled up at him on the oven and said "Good morning" in Polish. But he was afraid to respond. Perhaps he had been kidnapped—God forbid! When she saw that he was scared, she calmed him in her language, and she told him everything that had happened to him and how he had gotten here. Upon hearing this, the Jew became miserable—poor man! When she saw his reaction, the peasant woman asked him why he felt so sad.

He said to her: "Why shouldn't I feel sad? I'm a long way from home and I'm sick."

The peasant woman comforted him. Then she lit a fire, warmed up some milk in a glazed pot, and handed him a clean glass. He refused to take it, however. So, she said that a sick man must drink. He mulled for a minute, then took the glass of milk. Next, she woke up the boy. She told him to go and water the cow, then she went back to the fire. She set two huge pots of water to boil bran for the cow and the pigs. The boy stood in the middle of the room and got dressed. He looked up at the Jew and he smiled. The Jew now realized that the boy enjoyed the fact that he and his mother were keeping the Jew alive. Tears started running down the Jew's cheeks. The peasant woman came over to him again and asked him once more whether the oven was too hot for him to lie there. She then brought him a bundle of straw and prepared a bed for him in front of the oven. The Jew lay there for a while, and she waited on him loyally, serving him all sorts of food and drink that a Jew can consume in a Gentile home.

Meanwhile, at home, the Jew's wife and child were waiting for him. And the people in the shtetl were already saying that he had frozen to death out in the fields or been devoured by hungry wolves. Supposedly, the snow had buried him, and his body or at least his bones wouldn't be found until Passover, in the springtime, after the snow had melted. Day after day wore by, and the Jew was living in good health, in the home of the peasant woman. They had grown so used to each other that he was gradually forgetting all about his home and his family.

One night, when the small window was frosted over and the room was silent, the Jew was lying on his bed in front of the oven, and the peasant woman was sitting on the long wooden bench. Holding a spindle, she spun flax near a pine splinter that was burning in the fireplace. When the Jew looked at the frozen pane, he shuddered from top to bottom and he thought to himself: "Who knows where I'd be buried in snow now if they hadn't helped me!" His heart wept, and he sighed. The peasant woman heard him. Looking up from her spinning, she saw that his face was transformed. She felt very sorry for him, and she asked: "What's wrong, my dear Jew? Why are you sighing so deeply, and why have your features changed so much?"

He replied: "I can't help sighing—my life is so full of misery!"

She comforted him: "Look, you're still very young. Why do you allow yourself to be so miserable? Tell me what you're missing, and how I can help you?"

"I'm not asking anything of you. I couldn't possibly repay you for everything you've done for me."

"No, my dear Jew!" she answered him. "I've done nothing at all for you. And since you live in such great poverty at home, why don't you stay with me? You'll lack for nothing. I've got a whole farm—a field, wheat in my stable, a garden, beehives, and some cattle. All I'm missing is a man to run the farm. So, if you like, you can run the farm and you'll lack nothing."

When the Jew heard this, he flushed, cast down his eyes, and held his tongue. She gazed at him with loving warmth in her eyes, like a sister peering at her lone brother. Then she silently stood up, took his hand, and looked into his eyes. She wanted to ask him why he was so embarrassed, but she felt his hand trembling in hers, so she let go. Since she had a kind heart, she didn't wish to make him unhappy. She snuffed the pine splinter in the fireplace and went to bed.

The Jew was unable to get a wink of sleep that night. He silently prayed to God, asking Him to stand by him in his temptation. But then he glanced in her direction and saw that she was sleeping in her bed. And the flickering of the wick under the icon cast light on her face and her exposed upper body. All at once, lust overcame him. And when she got up in the morning, she knew that the Jew would stay with her and be agreeable to everything. And at Easter, when the Catholic priest made the rounds of the villages to sanctify their bread, the Jew and the peasant woman went along with him. They stepped into a church, where the Jew converted to Catholicism and married her.

Years passed, and the baptized man forgot that he had once been a Jew. One day, a cow had wandered off into the forest, and he went looking for her. He trudged and trudged, wearing a sheepskin and a four-cornered hat, clutching a whip and whistling a ditty. As he trudged, he penetrated deeper and deeper into the forest, amid dense trees—and he still couldn't find the missing cow. Eventually, however, he spotted the tail end of a kaftan sticking out from under a pile of moss. Raking it with one foot, he discovered a corpse, a murdered Jew, whom the Jewish community was traditionally liable to bury. The man was terror-stricken. He covered the corpse and dashed away. But after taking a few steps, he heard the corpse say: "Why are you deserting me? You're a Jew, aren't you?"

Thinking he was imagining it all, the convert hurried on. But he was haunted by that voice, which became all the louder and more tearful: "Please don't abandon me! My wife will remain a grass widow. According to Jewish custom, I ought to be buried by the Jewish community."

The convert shuddered and he turned back and sat down by the corpse. He sat there, all alone, in the depths of the forest, gazing at the corpse, despondent and wistful. His heart poured over and, out of dread or yearning, he remembered the melody of "The Thirteen Divine Attributes" [Exodus 34, 6–7], which include God's mercy, and he crooned the words to the melody of "Majesty, Dread and Terror"—a prayer sung around the Days of Awe.

But then the carpenter of the forest came driving by. He was going to celebrate a circumcision in his home and he was bringing the kosher butcher to perform the task. Now when they heard the sobbing voice, they went over to see what was wrong. First, they put the corpse into their wagon, but they no longer recognized the convert. So, they asked him how he knew that a Jew mustn't abandon a Jewish corpse. However, he didn't answer and turned away with tears in his eyes. The two Jews then drove to the shtetl to bury the corpse, and the convert went his own way. While trudging home, he removed the cross from his throat and threw it into the grain field.

From then on, he felt a deep longing to usher in the Sabbath on Friday evening. He stopped going to the tavern with the crowd of peasants. Instead, he sat outside his door, peering across the field and yearning quietly. And at times, unbeknown to his wife, he stole out of his home and hurried two miles to the carpenter's cottage. Before reaching it, he lay down in the grass and, from far away, silent and despondent, gazed into the window, where the Sabbath candles were burning. The carpenter and his wife and children, with shiny faces and in their Sabbath garb, sat around the radiant table, joyfully singing hymns and praising God. The next day, on the Sabbath, the convert spent the entire day in his garden, lying all alone, under the beehives, and very fidgety.

Whenever he now drove into the forest to gather wood, he would be overcome with heartache. He then tossed away the ax, sat down under a tree, and began reciting psalms in a weeping voice. And he kept reciting until past nightfall. It was only when the stars appeared that he loaded up his wood and drove home so quietly that no one found out.

One day, after harvesting his grain, cutting his hay a second time, and attending to his beehives, the convert joined a few of his neighbors—all of them Gentiles. Together they loaded their hay into several wagons and drove off to sell it in the town. When they arrived, the convert saw that the marketplace and the surrounding streets were deserted. Not a living creature could be found. The doors of homes and stores were nailed shut, while the booth in the center of the market and the tables bearing pork and baked goods were empty. The whole shtetl was forsaken as if it had died.

However, a loud din came from the side where the synagogue was located. So, the convert left the hay and dashed over to the synagogue. Through the open doors, he spotted burning candles, and Jews in smocks and prayer shawls were swaying to and fro, praying to God. A few women, who had come late after caring for a sick child or nursing a baby, hurried by in their stockings and white garments and, fearful and frightened, they dashed into the women's section. Then a greater clamor was heard—thousands and thousands of voices at the same time. And the convert shuddered like a tiny bird in a tempest, he was overcome with the terror of the Day of Atonement. Then he hurried back to his wagon and lay down underneath it. And his heart wept dreadfully and his entire body shook.

The peasants asked him whether they ought to go home, but he didn't reply. They figured he had gone crazy, and they went off to the

Christian baker, while the convert remained alone under his wagon. At the synagogue, the sobbing and the weeping grew louder and the clamor spread across the entire marketplace. And when it came time to recite the Prayer of Validation for the awesome Day of Judgment, the convert began shaking, and a deluge of tears came pouring from his eyes. He wept deplorably and he poignantly crooned the melody of that Prayer of Validation. And so, the convert lay under his wagon the entire day, all alone, his face down. He was dressed in his sheepskin, his fur cap, and his dusty boots, and he lamented so powerfully that the very stones melted.

Toward evening, when the sun was setting and the day was fading, the worshippers in the synagogue began chanting "Ne'ilah," the final prayer on the Day of Atonement. The convert wept even more ardently—and suddenly he shrieked, stood up, and dashed to the synagogue. There he threw himself on the threshold and he shouted:

> "Jews, sons of mercy, I want to repent, I want to become a Jew again!"

And before the worshippers could reach him, he gave up the ghost.

The Clever Rabbi (1912)

Helena Frank

THE POWER OF MAN'S IMAGINATION, said my Grandmother, is very great. Hereby hangs a tale, which, to our sorrow, is a true one, and as clear as daylight. Listen attentively, my dear child, it will interest you very much.

Not far from this town of ours lived an old Count, who believed that Jews require blood at Passover, Christian blood, too, for their Passover cakes. The Count, in his brandy distillery, had a Jewish overseer, a very honest, respectable fellow. The Count loved him for his honesty, and was very kind to him, and the Jew, although he was a simple man and no scholar, was well-disposed, and served the Count with heart and soul. He would have gone through fire and water at the Count's bidding, for it is in the nature of a Jew to be faithful and to love good men.

The Count often discussed business matters with him, and took pleasure in hearing about the customs and observances of the Jews. One day the Count said to him, "Tell me the truth, do you love me with your whole heart?"

"Yes," replied the Jew, "I love you as myself."

"Not true!" said the Count. "I shall prove to you that you hate me even unto death."

"Stop!" cried the Jew. "Why does my lord say such terrible things?"

The Count smiled and answered: "Let me tell you! I know quite well that Jews must have Christian blood for their Passover feast. Now, what would you do if I were the only Christian you could find? You would have to kill me, because the Rabbis have said so. Indeed, I can scarcely hold you to blame, since, according to your false notions, the Divine command is precious, even when it tells us to commit murder. I should be no more to you than was Isaac to Abraham, when, at God's command, Abraham was about to slay his only son. Know, however, that the God of Abraham is a God of mercy and lovingkindness, while the God the Rabbis have created is full of hatred toward Christians. How, then, can you say that you love me?"

The Jew clapped his hands to his head, he tore his hair in his distress and felt no pain, and with a broken heart he answered the Count, and said: "How long will you Christians suffer this stain on your pure hearts? How long will you disgrace yourselves? Does not my lord know that this is a great lie? I, as a believing Jew, and many besides me, as believing Jews—we ourselves, I say, with our own hands, grind the corn, we keep the flour from getting damp or wet with anything, for if only a little dew drops onto it, it is prohibited for us as though it had yeast.

"Till the day on which the cakes are baked, we keep the flour as the apple of our eye. And when the flour is baked, and we are eating the cakes, even then we are not sure of swallowing it, because if our gums should begin to bleed, we have to spit the piece out. And in face of all these stringent regulations against eating the blood of even beasts and birds, some people say that Jews require human blood for their Passover cakes, and swear to it as a fact! What does my lord suppose we are likely to think of such people? We know that they swear falsely—and a false oath is of all things the worst."

The Count was touched to the heart by these words, and these two men, being both upright and without guile, believed one the other. The Count believed the Jew, that is, he believed that the Jew did not know the truth of the matter, because he was poor and untaught, while the Rabbis all the time most certainly used blood at Passover, only they kept it a secret from the people. And he said as much to the Jew, who, in his turn, believed the Count, because he knew him to be an honorable man.

And so, it was that he began to have his doubts, and when the Count, on different occasions, repeated the same words, the Jew said to himself, that perhaps after all it was partly true, that there must be something in it—the Count would never tell him a lie!

And he carried the thought about with him for some time.

The Jew found increasing favor in his master's eyes. The Count lent him money to trade with, and God prospered the Jew in everything he undertook. Thanks to the Count, he grew rich.

The Jew had a kind heart, and was much given to good works, as is the way with Jews. He was very charitable, and succored all the poor in the neighboring town. And he assisted the Rabbis and the pious in all the places round about, and earned for himself a great and beautiful name, for he was known to all as "the benefactor."

The Rabbis gave him the honor due to a pious and influential Jew, who is a wealthy man and charitable into the bargain. But the Jew was thinking: "Now the Rabbis will let me into the secret that is theirs, and that they share with those only who are at once pious and rich, that great and pious Jews must have blood for Passover."

For a long time, he lived in hope, but the Rabbis told him nothing, the subject was not once mentioned. But the Jew felt sure that the Count would never have lied to him, and he gave more liberally than before, thinking, "Perhaps after all it was too little."

He assisted the Rabbi of the nearest town for a whole year, so that the Rabbi opened his eyes in astonishment. He gave him more than half of what is sufficient for a livelihood. When it was near Passover, the Jew drove into the little town to visit the Rabbi, who received him with open arms, and gave him honor as unto the most powerful and wealthy benefactor. And all the representative men of the community paid him their respects.

Thought the Jew, "Now they will tell me of the commandment that it is not given to every Jew to observe."

As the Rabbi, however, told him nothing, the Jew remained, to remind the Rabbi, as it were, of his duty.

"Rabbi," said the Jew, "I have something very particular to say to you! Let us go into a room where we two shall be alone."

So, the Rabbi went with him into an empty room, shut the door, and said:

"Dear friend, what is your wish? Do not be abashed, but speak freely, and tell me what I can do for you."

"Dear Rabbi, I am, you must know, already acquainted with the fact that Jews require blood at Passover. I know also that it is a secret belonging only to the Rabbis, to very pious Jews, and to the wealthy who give much alms. And I, who am, as you know, a very charitable and good Jew, wish also to comply, if only once in my life, with this great observance.

"You need not be alarmed, dear Rabbi! I will never betray the secret, but will make you happy forever, if you will enable me to fulfill so great a command.

"If, however, you deny its existence, and declare that Jews do not require blood, from that moment I become your bitter enemy.

"And why should I be treated worse than any other pious Jew? I, too, want to try to perform the great commandment that God gave in secret. I am not learned in the Law, but a great and wealthy Jew, and one given to good works, that am I in very truth!"

You can fancy—said my Grandmother—the Rabbi's horror on hearing such words from a Jew, a simple countryman. They pierced him to the quick, like sharp arrows. He saw that the Jew believed in all sincerity that his coreligionists used blood at Passover. How was he to uproot out of such a simple heart the weeds sown there by evil men?

The Rabbi saw that words would just then be useless. A beautiful thought came to him, and he said: "So be it, dear friend! Come into the synagogue tomorrow at this time, and I will grant your request. But till then you must fast, and you must not sleep all night, but watch in prayer, for this is a very grave and dreadful thing."

The Jew went away full of gladness, and did as the Rabbi had told him. Next day, at the appointed time, he came again, wan with hunger and lack of sleep.

The Rabbi took the key to the synagogue, and they went in there together. In the synagogue all was quiet.

The Rabbi put on a prayer-scarf and a robe, lighted some black candles, threw off his shoes, took the Jew by the hand, and led him up to the ark.

The Rabbi opened the ark, took out a scroll of the Law, and said: "You know that for us Jews the scroll of the Law is the most sacred of all things, and that the list of denunciations occurs in it twice.

"I swear to you by the scroll of the Law: If any Jew, whosoever he be, requires blood at Passover, may all the curses contained in the two lists of denunciations be on my head, and on the head of my whole family!"

The Jew was greatly startled. He knew that the Rabbi had never before sworn an oath, and now, for his sake, he had sworn an oath so dreadful!

The Jew wept much, and said: "Dear Rabbi, I have sinned before God and before you. I pray you, pardon me and give me a hard penance, as hard as you please. I will perform it willingly, and may God forgive me likewise!"

The Rabbi comforted him, and told no one what had happened, he only told a few very near relations, just to show them how people can be talked into believing the greatest foolishness and the most wicked lies.

May God—said my Grandmother—open the eyes of all who accuse us falsely, that they may see how useless it is to trump up against us things that never were seen or heard.

Jews will be Jews while the world lasts, and they will become, through suffering, better Jews with more Jewish hearts.

The Rabbi in Jail (1914)

A. S. Rabinovitz

WHEN THE LARGE AND HEAVY jail door closed clanging and creaking behind Rabbi Schneor Salmen, and the rusty lock fell into its place, it had already turned night. The mechanical noise of the door lock hit his ear, and he heard the echo of the steps slowly retreating. It was dark in the cell. The dim light in the corner beneath the skylight was not able to brighten the gloomy darkness. The inmates stood out as if they were formless shadows. Only here and there could one discern the face of a predator with greedy and burning eyes in which hunger lurked. These were hard criminals in this cell, and it was not the first time that they had been caught in a trap for having sinned, and they were already familiar with the strict punishing judge.

"Well, look here. Even a Jew!" yelled Timoscha the sinister criminal as soon as he caught sight of the rabbi.

This shout was followed by ugly laughter from the throats of the prisoners, and their sound did not stop ringing. It faltered and froze, and Rabbi Salmen did not hear or see any of this. He had sunk into a deep sadness because of the disgrace of his brothers who had handed him over and placed him under the power of people with a different faith. What was going to happen to him? How could he possibly expect a fair trial from these strangers when they whose ancestors stood on Mount Sinai trampled on justice with their feet.

The prisoners, who were at first gripped and overcome by the sacred figure of the rabbi, regained their courage when they saw how traumatized he was. The beast and brute in them awakened, and they began doing all kinds of malicious things. They rummaged through his clothes and robbed whatever they found. Meanwhile, he let them do whatever they wished, for how bad could their actions be in comparison with those of his brothers.

It was about this time that a burning pain had taken hold of the world and wrapped it in dismal mourning. Even the Rabbi Levi Yitzchok of Berditchev, who, as was well known, served the Lord, "out of joy," was gripped by dark worries. The dismal sadness swallowed him in a terrible flood in which his soul was trapped like Jonas in the stomach of the whale. The hour of the Mariv-Evening Prayers had already arrived, but he could not open his mouth. This was how strong the mourning had taken possession of him.

A direct line in the cosmos was broken, the world seemed lifeless. . . . And time flew. It was almost midnight. . . .

He started to pray. It didn't work. The words got stuck in his throat. . . . He gathered himself together—it didn't work.

He felt that it wasn't a simple matter. He suspected one of the great rabbis was in trouble. This is why he wasn't cheerful.

However, if a rabbi was in trouble, it wasn't due to his own fatality. Rather, it was due to the destiny of the community, because misfortune will soon strike. For instance, in the case of Rabbi Levi Yitzchok of Berditchev, he sat there, distressed and sweltering, with a sunken head. His dark thoughts and sadness concerned his congregation.

Then, he suddenly gathered himself together for an attack against Heaven (even though he rarely protested, he did so when it was important to stand up for saving the Jews), and he yelled:

"Lords of all the worlds, what are you actually planning for your rabbis? You have planted a tiny number of them in the world and placed the entire burden of making the world a better place that they can only reach through prayers. How are they to fulfill their mission when you yourself hinder their praying? How are they to do battle when you rob them of their swords and arrows. What do you actually plan to do with your rabbis? You long for their prayers. Well then, help them so that they can pray. The salvation of the pious comes from God, their refuge in the hour of need. He helps, he saves, he protects them from evil, or he is their salvation."

The rabbi screamed this verse from the Bible with a strong thunderous voice. And the members of the congregation noticed that the walls had fallen. The fog dissipated. Darkness disappeared. A flood of light began streaming and filled everything with the scent of balsam.

The elders of the congregation said that they had never in their lives heard such a prayer. It broke the gate to Heaven.

Our rabbi Schneor Salmen noticed that there was now a complete change in his voice. He woke from his brooding, and he regretted that he had growled at his people even for a brief moment and that he might have been responsible for someone being punished.

"Doesn't the immortal God determine what happens in the world? Won't he oversee what has happened? He is the cause of all causes, and whatever he does turns itself to good. So, why am I grieving so much about my arrest? Is this thick wall really a separating wall between me and the Lord who fills out everything? If I raise myself to Heaven, I shall meet you. When I sink into the grave, you are there. When I flee to the sunrise, to the end of the ocean, you are there. Even there your just ways embrace me. All the world is full of your glory. There is not the slightest place without you. There is not one place where a soaring in you, in your light would not be thinkable."

A miracle happened. The goys who were in the jail changed their relationship with the rabbi. In fact, even more, they changed the way they related to each other. There was no more talk about fleeing the prison. They did not raise their hands to hit each other. Even Timoscha, the fearful roughneck, did not use his muscles to disturb their relations. To the amazement of all the prisoners, he often laid for hours on his cot without speaking a word and tamed his wild and passionate thoughts through meditating. In fact, he even returned the money that he had stolen from the rabbi.

The rabbi refused at first and asked why? But Timoscha screamed: "Take back the money, or I'll murder you!"

So, the rabbi smiled and took the money back to his cell. Meanwhile Timoscha returned to his bed. Now the rabbi became more and more accustomed to the prisoners, and the prisoners to the souls of Simon den Jochai, of Ari, of Rabbi Bal-Schem, or other holy saints with regard to the creation of the world and the secret of the throne.

At times the rabbi completely forgot where he was, and since he forgot where he was, he sang the four stanzas of the well-known little song to himself, and he seemed to climb an invisible ladder up to heaven where he wandered cheerfully all about. The prisoners in the cell sat there without making a sound and listened.

And when he lit the candles on the first night of Chanukah and shouted out the prayer with great joy, the prisoners felt an ecstatic joy so that they sang along with him as the chorus. They extended their hands and formed a ring around the rabbi and danced. The guard stormed angrily into the cell, stood somewhat puzzled for a second, and then unconsciously joined the circle, and danced with the prisoners.

Now the jail became more and more cheerful and exciting. On the wings of the song, which wrested these fragments of humane existence, the entire house raised itself in holy regions up to the peak, to which even a congregation in the Schma-Prayers could not reach. Here was the situation: It saw the maid mocking the sea more than Ezechiel saw in the ecstasy of his prophesy.

Sometimes Timoscha happened to watch the rabbi in a strange way whenever the rabbi said his prayers. He felt small, almost as if he were nothing when he observed this stupendous figure, and it irritated him that the holy man could tame and control his wild passions. And how did he do this? He did it simply with a gaze, with his clear blue eyes. Despite all this, Timoscha loved the rabbi. He felt that his soul was strongly intertwined to that of the pious man. Many times he felt jealous of him, but soon he would repress his beastly instincts and would be completely devoted to the rabbi. But right after this he would be overcome by an unspeakable love for the Jew, and he felt the need to lie flat on the ground and to speak to him. However, he didn't know what to say or ask.

One day as the rabbi was steeped in prayer before the wall of the jail, silent as if he had been hit by a chisel and unaware of his surroundings, a young prisoner with a mocking attitude pushed Timoscha. In response Timoscha hit him so hard that the inmate almost departed this life. Later, Timoscha went to the rabbi and said: "Tell me holy man, why did God create such a measly man like me! What use am I? Why must I pollute the world through my existence? Tell me why, oh rabbi!"

The rabbi listened with great seriousness just as he used to hear all those who came to him seeking his advice. He was not startled at all by Timoscha's question. Not at all. In fact he had expected it, and he replied softly: "It is good, Timoscha, that you are questioning God's ways. But first you must cleanse your soul, for whoever wades in filth will not be able to understand what I am going to say."

"Cleanse my soul, you said!" Timoscha screamed. "That's totally impossible!"

"You only believe it's impossible," the rabbi calmed him down. "However, the truth about this is different. The soul of a human being, even the worst criminal's soul, is much greater than the human being can know. It is a divine spark that can never be completely extinguished."

"I don't understand what you are saying," Timoscha replied with a resigned voice. "I only know that I am a beast, a miserable and unfortunate beast, and I want to get rid of my soul. I want to become a Jew. I believe that God exists only in Israel and you are God's man. So, I'm beginning to understand, and do you know why? At the beginning, I hated you. I was jealous of your cleanliness, your faith in God. My measly self was furious about your holy glory. I wanted to murder you, but I couldn't do it. Now, however, I belong completely to you. I'd like to embrace you and kiss you. However, my lips are not worthy enough to do this. My touch could desecrate you. Therefore, I want to kiss the earth upon which you walk. I want to serve you and sacrifice my love to you. . . . If you want to be free, then I'll free you from the walls of this jail in a stormy night. I'll strangle the guards . . . beat them all to death."

Timoscha had to pause as he was delivering his speech, for the director of the jail entered to count the prisoners. To the regret of the inmates, the rabbi was led to another cell. This one had more room than the first one. His congregation had managed to arrange this for him. As the rabbi was leaving the cell, Timoscha called to him: "May you go in peace, holy man. I'll never forget you. And please never forget me and pray for my sinful soul."

The next day Timoscha broke out of the prison.

And later, in a small Lithuanian city, he converted to Judaism and was given the name of the arch-father Abraham. He hadn't learned very much nor understood much. He did not know the Jewish customs all that well. However, he believed deeply in Judaism. In fact, he traveled long stretches and converted numerous people in their villages to Judaism. They were the predecessors of the converted who are well-known in Russia.

King for Three Days (1919)

Gertrude Landa

GODFREY DE BOUILLON WAS A famous warrior, a daring general and bold leader of men, who gained victories in several countries. And so, in the year 1095, when the first Crusade was arranged, he was entrusted with the command of one of the armies and led it across Europe in the historic march to the Holy Land. Like many a great soldier of his period, Godfrey was a cruel man, and, above all, he hated the Jews.

"In this, our Holy War," he said to his men, "we shall slay all the children of Israel wherever we shall encounter them. I shall not rest content until I have exterminated the Jews."

True to his inhuman oath, Godfrey and his soldiers massacred large numbers of Jews. They did this without pity or mercy, saying: "We are performing a sacred duty, for we have the blessings of the priests on our enterprise."

Godfrey felt sure he would be victorious, but he also wanted to obtain the blessing of a rabbi. It was a curious desire, but in those days such things were not considered at all strange, and so Godfrey de Bouillon sent for the learned Rabbi Solomon ben Isaac, better known by his world-famous name of Rashi.

Rashi, one of the wisest sages of the Jews, came to Godfrey, and the two men stood facing each other.

"You have heard of my undertaking to capture Jerusalem," said Godfrey, haughtily. "I demand your blessing on my venture."

"Blessings are not in the gift of man; they are bestowed by Heaven—on worthy objects," answered Rashi.

"Don't you dare trifle with words," retorted the warrior, "or they may cost you dear. A holy man can invoke a blessing."

But Rashi was not afraid. He was becoming an old man then, but he was as brave as the swaggering soldier, and he faced Godfrey unflinchingly.

"I can make no claim on the God of Israel on behalf of one who has sworn to destroy all the descendants of His chosen people," he said.

"So, ho!" exclaimed Godfrey, "you defy me."

But he stopped his angry words abruptly. He had no wish to quarrel with any holy man, for that might make him nervous. And nervousness, then, was misunderstood as superstition. Besides, the rabbi might curse him.

"If you will not bless," he said, "perhaps you will deign to raise the veil of the future for me. You wise men of the Jews are seers and can foretell events—so they say. A hundred thousand chariots filled with soldiers brave, determined, and strong are at my command. Tell me, shall I succeed, or fail?"

"You will do both." Rashi replied.

"What do you mean by this?" demanded Godfrey, angrily.

"I mean that Jerusalem will fall to you. So it is ordained, and you will become its king."

"Ha, ha! So you deem it wisest to pronounce a blessing after all," interrupted Godfrey. "I am content."

"I have not spoken everything," said the rabbi, gravely. "You will rule three days, and no more."

Godfrey turned pale.

"Shall I return?" he asked, slowly.

"Not with your multitude of chariots. Your vast army will have dwindled to three horses and three men when you reach this city."

"Enough," cried Godfrey. "If you think you can scare me with these ominous words, you fail in your intent. And hearken, Rabbi of the Jews, your words shall be remembered. Should they prove incorrect in the minutest detail—if I am King of Jerusalem for four days, or return with four horsemen—you will pay the penalty of a false prophet and shall be burned at the stake. Do you understand? You shall be put to death."

"I understand well," returned Rashi, quite unmoved, "it is a sentence that you and your kind love to pronounce with or without the sanction of those whom you call your holy men. It is not I who fears, Godfrey de Bouillon. I do not seek to peer into the future to assure my own safety."

With these words they parted, the rabbi returning to his prayers and to his studies, which have enriched the learning of the Jews, while Godfrey proceeded to lay a trail of innocent Jewish blood along the banks of the Rhine in his march to Palestine.

History has documented the events of the Crusade. Godfrey, after many battles, laid siege to the Holy City, captured it, and drove the Jews into one of the synagogues and burned them alive. Eight days afterward, his soldiers raised him on their shields and proclaimed him king.

Godfrey was delighted, but two days later he thought the matter over carefully and decided that he could not always live in Jerusalem. So next day he called together his captains and said: "You have done me great honor. But I must return to Europe, and it would be more befitting that I should be styled Duke of Jerusalem and Guardian of the Holy City than its sovereign."

That night, however, he suddenly remembered the prediction of Rashi. "For three days I have been King of Jerusalem," he muttered. "The rabbi of the Jews spoke truth."

He could not help wondering whether the rest of the prophecy would be fulfilled, and he became moody. He was joyful when he gained a victory, but soon the disasters came, and he was plunged into despondency. The reverses affected the buoyancy of his troops, disease decimated their ranks, and desertions further depleted their numbers. Slowly but surely his mighty army dwindled away to a mere handful of dissatisfied men and decrepit horses.

It was a ragged and wretched procession that he led back across Europe, and daily his retinue grew smaller. Men and horses dropped from sheer fatigue helpless by the wayside, and were left there to die, with the hungry vultures perched on trees, patiently waiting for the last flicker of life to depart before they set to work to pick the bones of all flesh.

Godfrey de Bouillon had gained his victory, but at what cost? Thousands of men, women, and children had been murdered, thousands of his soldiers had fallen in battle, and now hundreds of others had dropped out of the ranks to end their last hours on the ghastly road that led from Jerusalem back to western Europe. Do you wonder that Godfrey was unhappy, and that he thought every moment about the words of Rashi?

Finally, he reached the city of Worms where Rashi dwelt. With him were four men, mounted on horses.

"It is well," he said, with as much cheerfulness as he could muster, as he surveyed the remnants of his once proud army. "The rabbi has failed."

Godfrey ordered his men fall into line behind him, and he proudly rode through the gate of the city. As he did so, he heard a cry of alarm. He turned hastily and saw a huge rock falling from the city's gate. It dropped on the soldier riding just behind him, killing both man and horse.

"You have spoken truth. If only I had taken heed of your words!" he said to the rabbi. "I am a broken man. You will assuredly achieve great fame in Israel."

And so it has come to pass. Should you, by chance, ever visit the city of Brussels, the capital of Belgium, do not fail to look at the statue of Godfrey de Bouillon, with his sword proudly raised. It stands in the Place Royale but a few minutes' walk from the synagogue. Should you ever be in the ancient city of Worms that stands on the Rhine, do as other visitors, Jews and Gentiles—enter the synagogue that was built many centuries ago, and you will see the room where Rashi studied and the stone seat on which he sat. And not far from the synagogue you will see the ancient gate of the city, named in honor of Rabbi Solomon ben Isaac, the Rashi Gate. Perhaps it is the very one under which Godfrey de Bouillon passed into the city with his three mounted companions, just as the legend tells.

The Pope's Game of Chess (1919)

Gertrude Landa

NEARLY A THOUSAND YEARS AGO in the town of Mayence, on the bank of the Rhine, there dwelt a pious Jew of the name of Simon ben Isaac. Of a most charitable disposition, learned and ever ready to assist the poor with money and wise counsel, he was reverenced by all, and it was believed he was a direct descendant of King David. Everybody was proud to do him honor.

Simon ben Isaac had one little son, a bright boy of the name of Elkanan, who he intended should be trained as a rabbi. Little Elkanan was very diligent in his studies and gave early promise of developing into an exceptionally clever student. Even the servants in the household loved him for his keen intelligence. One of them, indeed, was unduly interested in him. She was the Sabbath-fire woman who only came into the house on the Sabbath day to attend to the fires, because, as you know, the Jewish servants could not perform this duty. The Sabbath-fire woman was a devoted Catholic, and she spoke of Elkanan to a priest. The latter was considerably impressed.

"What a pity," he remarked, "that so talented a boy should be a Jew. If he were a Christian, now," he added, winningly, "he could enter the Holy Church and become famous."

The Sabbath-fire woman knew exactly what the priest meant. "Do you think he could rise to be a bishop?" she asked.

"He might rise even higher—to be the Pope himself," replied the priest.

"It would be a great thing to give a bishop to the Church, would it not?" said the woman.

"It is a great thing to give anyone to the Church of Rome," the priest assured her.

Then they spoke in whispers. The woman appeared a little troubled, but the priest promised her that all would be well, that she would be rewarded, and that nobody would dare to accuse her of doing anything wrong. Convinced that she was performing a righteous action, she agreed to do what the priest suggested.

Accordingly, the following Friday night when the household of Simon ben Isaac was wrapped in slumber, she crept stealthily and silently into the boy's bedroom. Taking him gently in her arms, she stole silently out of the house and carried him to the priest who was waiting. Elkanan was well wrapped up in blankets, and so cautiously did the woman move that he did not waken. The priest didn't say a word. He just nodded to the woman, and then placed Elkanan in a carriage that he had in waiting. Elkanan slept peacefully, totally unaware of his adventure, and when he opened his eyes he thought he must be dreaming. He was not in his own room, but a much smaller one that seemed to be jolting and moving, like a carriage, and opposite to him was a priest.

"Where am I?" he asked in alarm.

"Lie still, Andreas," was the reply.

"But my name is not Andreas," he answered. "That is not a Jewish name. I am Elkanan, the son of Simon."

To his amazement, however, the priest looked at him pityingly and shook his head.

"You have had a nasty accident," he said, "and it has affected your head. You must not speak."

Not another word would he say in response to all the boy's insistent queries. He simply ignored Elkanan, who puzzled his head over the matter until he really began to feel ill and to wonder whether he was Elkanan after all. Exhausted, he fell asleep again, and next time he awoke he was lying on a bed in a bare room. A bell was tolling, and he heard a chanting chorus. By his side stood a priest. Elkanan looked at the priest like one dazed. Before he could utter a word, the priest said: "Rise, Andreas, and follow me."

The boy had no alternative but to obey. To his horror he was taken into a chapel and forced to kneel. The priests sprinkled water on him. He did not understand what the service meant, and when it was over, he began to cry for his father and mother. For days nobody took the slightest notice of his continual questionings until a priest, with a harsh, cruel face, spoke to him severely one day.

"I perceive, Andreas," he said, "you have a stubborn spirit, but it will be curbed. Your father and mother are dead—all the world is dead to you. You have strange notions in your head, and we will rid you of them."

Elkanan cried so much on hearing these terrible words that he became seriously ill. He did not know how long he was kept in bed, but when he recovered, he found himself a prisoner in a monastery, where all the priests called him Andreas. They were kind to him, and in time he began to doubt himself whether he was Elkanan, the son of Simon, the pious Jew of Mayence. To put an end to the unrest in his mind, he devoted himself earnestly to his lessons. His tutors never had so brilliant a pupil, nor so intelligent a companion. He was a remarkable chess player.

"Where did you learn?" they asked him.

"My father, Simon ben Isaac, of Mayence, taught me," he replied, with a sob in his voice.

"It is well," they replied, having received their instructions what to say in answer to such remarks, "you are blessed from Heaven, Andreas. Not only do you absorb learning in the hours of daylight, but angels and dead sages visit you in your sleep and impart knowledge to you."

He could obtain no more satisfactory words from his tutors, and in time he made no mention whatever of the past, and his tutors and companions refrained from touching upon the subject either. Once or twice he thought of endeavoring to escape, but he soon discovered his plan was impossible. He was never allowed to be alone for a moment; he was virtually a prisoner, although everyone began to do him honor because of his amazing knowledge and learning.

In due time, he became a priest and a tutor and was even called to Rome, where he was promoted and became a cardinal. He wore a red cap and cloak; people kneeled to him and sought his blessing, and everyone spoke about him as the wisest, kindliest, and most scholarly man in the church. He had not spoken of his boyhood for years, but he never ceased to think of those happy days. And although he tried hard, he could not believe that it was all a dream. Whenever he played a game of chess, which was his one pastime, he seemed to see himself in his old room at Mayence, and he sighed. His fellow priests wondered why he did this, and he laughingly told them it was because he had no idea how to lose a game.

Then a great event happened. The Pope died, and Andreas was elected his successor. He was placed on a throne, and a crown was put upon his head. So, now he was called Holy Father. The power of life and death over millions of people in many countries was vested in him; kings, princes, and nobles visited him in his magnificent palace to do him homage, and his fame spread far and wide. But he himself grew more thoughtful and silent and sought only to exercise his great powers for the people's good.

This, however, did not altogether please some of his counselors.

"The Church needs money," they told him. "We must squeeze it out of the Jews."

But Andreas steadfastly refused to countenance any persecutions. Many edicts were placed before him for his signature, giving permission to bishops in certain districts to threaten the Jews unless they paid huge sums of money in tribute, but Andreas declined to assent to any one of them.

One day a document was submitted to him from the archbishop of the Rhine district, craving permission to drive the Jews from the city of Mayence. The Pope's face hardened when he read the iniquitous letter. He gave instant orders that the archbishop should be summoned to Rome, and to the utter amazement of his cardinals, he also commanded them to bring before him three leading Jews from Mayence, to state their case.

"It shall not be said," he declared, "that the Pope issued a decree of punishment without giving the condemned people an opportunity of defending themselves."

When the news reached Mayence, there was great wailing and sorrow among the Jews, for, alas! bitter experience had taught them to expect no mercy from Rome. Delegates were selected, and when they arrived at the Vatican, they were asked for their names. These were given and communicated to the Pope.

"The delegates of the Jews of the city of Mayence," announced a secretary, "humbly crave audience of Your Holiness."

"Their names?" demanded the Pope.

"Simon ben Isaac, Abraham ben Moses, and Issachar, the priest."

"Let them enter," said the Pope, in a quiet, firm voice. He had heard but one name; his plan had proved successful, for he had counted upon Simon being one of the chosen delegates. The three men entered the audience chamber and stood expectant before the Pope. His Holiness appeared to be lost in deep thought. Suddenly he aroused himself from his reverie and looked keenly at the aged leader of the party.

"Simon of Mayence, stand forth," he said, "and give voice to your plea. We give you attention."

The old man approached a few paces nearer, and in simple but eloquent language, pleaded that the Jews should be permitted to remain unmolested in Mayence in which city their community had been established a long time ago.

"Your prayer," said the Pope, when he had finished, "will have full consideration, and my answer will be made known to you without delay. Now, tell me, Simon of Mayence, something about yourself and your co-delegates. Who are you in the city?"

Simon gave the information.

"Have you come here alone?" asked the Pope. "Or have you been escorted by members of your families—your sons?"

The Pope's voice was scarcely steady, but none noticed.

"I don't have a son," said Simon, with a weary sigh.

"Haven't you ever been blessed with offspring?"

Simon looked sharply at the Pope before answering. Then, with bowed head and broken voice, he said: "God blessed me with one son, but he was stolen from me in childhood. That has been the sorrow of my life."

The old man's voice was choked with sobs.

"I have heard," said the Pope, after a while, "that you are a famous chess player. I, too, am credited with some skill in the game. I would like to try my skill against yours. Hearken! If you prove the victor in the game, then I shall grant your appeal."

"I consent," said the old man, proudly. "It is many years since I have sustained defeat."

It was arranged to have the game be played that evening. Naturally, the strange contest aroused the keenest interest. The game was followed closely by the papal secretaries and the Jewish delegates. It was a wonderful trial of subtle play. The two players seemed about evenly matched. First one and then the other made a daring move that appeared to place his opponent in difficulties, but each time disaster was ingeniously evaded. A draw seemed the likeliest result until, suddenly, the Pope made a brilliant move that startled the onlookers. It was considered impossible now for Simon to avoid defeat.

No one was more astounded at the Pope's move than the old Jew. He rose tremblingly from his chair, gazed with piercing eyes into the face of the Pope and said huskily, "Where did you learn that move? I taught it to only one other person."

"Who?" asked the Pope, eagerly.

"I will tell you alone," said Simon.

The Pope made a signal, and the others left the room in great surprise.

Then Simon exclaimed excitedly, "Unless you are the devil himself, you can only be my long-lost son, Elkanan."

"Father!" cried the Pope, and the old man clasped him in his arms.

When the others reentered the room, the Pope said quietly, "We have decided to call the game a draw, and in thankfulness for the rare pleasure of a game of chess with so skilled a player as Simon of Mayence, I grant the prayer of the delegates of that city. It is my will that the Jews shall live in peace."

Shortly afterward, a new Pope was elected. Various rumors gained currency. One was that Andreas had thrown himself into the flames; another that he had mysteriously disappeared. And at the same time a stranger arrived in Mayence and was welcomed by Simon joyfully as his son, Elkanan.

The Enemies (ca. 1920)

Paul Schlesinger

IT SO HAPPENED THAT, during the World War, two mortally wounded Jews were brought into a hospital, both within the same hour. One was a German—the other was a Frenchman. Their beds adjoined each other. For a long time they lay tossing about, wracked by fever and pain. The Jewish chaplain fluttered from one to another, trying desperately to get them to accept each other as Jews. Before he left them, he said:

"I cannot possibly spend any more time with you. Therefore I beg of you—talk to each other. Both of you are Jews, even though one is French and the other is German. Surely, as Jews you both share the same whole-hearted devotion to your fatherlands and to your parents, you are tormented by the same longing for your wives and children at home, by the same anxieties, and the same suffering, and soon both of you will stand before the same God. There certainly must be some virtues as well as vices that you both have in common. Therefore, I must plead with you—unburden your hearts to each other."

The Rabbi went away. The two Jews lay silent for a long time. The Frenchman, who began to feel somewhat better, moved his parched lips: "What have we got to say to each other anyway?"

The German did not answer.

"No doubt you are right for not talking to me. But I believe I am justified in wanting to talk to you. Therefore I say: 'A curse on you Germans for attacking us! A curse on your Hun Kaiser who has ravished Belgium, whose soldiers murder little children and rape women! A curse on all of you!'"

After saying this, the Frenchman sank wearily back on his pillow. Then the German replied:

"You sound like one of your newspapers. Could I expect you to be otherwise? I never had any great love for our Kaiser, nor for what he said and did. I also never really believed very much in what our newspapers wrote. But if I have to believe any of them, I certainly choose to believe our German newspapers more than yours. If I have to obey and sacrifice myself for anybody, then I certainly prefer to do it for the Kaiser rather than for any one of you. For after all, he is a German. His language is my language, his virtue is my virtue, and his guilt is my guilt, and for it alone I am prepared to atone."

So the two wounded men fell silent again. Night fell, and when the dawn broke, it found them both in a weaker condition. Once again the Frenchman began to speak:

"What do you fat Germans know about our crystal dear ideas? I know that I am dying now, but even in this hour they still flash clear in my mind. I experience the forked lightning of the soul. It illuminates the whole world, which is thus made endurable, civilized, and free!"

"I too am dying," murmured the German. "The twilight envelops me. I am getting lost in the mist. I feel so much alone! But I will return home now. I will be home soon. It is quiet and warm there. I do not want to think anymore—only to continue feeling—to feel like a German."

The Rabbi, who just entered, overheard these last words, and he said to them:

"Why do you persist in quarreling in this last hour? Can't you find something kind to say to each other? You are both Jews."

At this the Frenchman said:

"Don't Christians murder one another?"

And the German, his voice already sounding lifeless, added:

"They have drummed into our heads for too long a time already that brotherly love is an achievement of the Gospels. . . ."

Several hours later, one followed the other into the slumber from which they would never awaken.

A young blond medical assistant who had been listening to the discussion of the two dying men approached the Rabbi and said:

"Please explain to me . . ."

"What?"

"The Jewish riddle."

The Rabbi turned away from the dead, and followed by the doctor, left the barracks and went out into the fresh air.

"To be a Jew means to live another life not your own. To begin in another, to be fulfilled by another until completely possessed. At times it seems to me as if we were not at all ourselves. No sooner does the Gentile smell something than we begin smelling it too. Just look at the landscape about us, at the vegetation, the animals, the people and the city and surely you will become strangely enchanted by it all. Now who do you think experiences this landscape better and more thoroughly—the native who since childhood has lived in it, who perhaps knows no other, or the one who in passing derives pleasure from it in the sudden recognition of a newly experienced charm? His own charms are hardly revealed to the native. Woe to him if they were! He lives according to the genius of his climate. What he experiences and creates takes place in the style and the tradition of this climate. Because the commonplace and the insignificant are at work within him, therefore the unusual and the great must emerge, opening up new sources of self-development. The alien, on the other hand cannot react the same way. He can only have impressions of this world that is so alien to him, he can only describe it, translate it, write about it, sing of it.

"We Jews are everlasting strangers everywhere. There has never been a people in the world that has produced in ratio to its population so many musicians, actors, artists, writers as have the Jews. And yet there has never been a people in the world, having such a large number of musicians, actors, artists, and writers that has produced so little for itself. When we Jews sing about other peoples and other lands, we sing with a painful devotion, a deeper fervor, and a more dusky passion than when we sing about our own. Indeed, it appears as if all things achieve their fullest expression and their greatest charm through our efforts. The entire world concedes this and therefore cannot dispense with us."

"And how do you think it will be when the Jews return to Palestine?"

The Rabbi smiled and said:

"Boring, my dear doctor."

The Convert (ca. 1920)

Dovid Bergelson

THERE WERE RUMORS THAT Moyshe-Leyb Yanashov's daughter, the convert, was back in the country, with her husband, the justice of the peace. The rumors had begun right after Passover.

A Jewish beggar was walking from one village to the next. He was as pensive as his day of poverty after the charitable week of Passover: He couldn't tell whether his begging would bring in anything. And on the road, which was hidden in the green depths of tilled fields, he suddenly saw a wagon coming his way, heaped with furniture as tall as a house, tables and chairs with their legs jutting out toward the lofty blue sky of early summer, and rocking so slowly as if to tell that they were being brought from far away . . . off to the justice of the peace . . . straight to the justice of the peace.

And then here they were, the convert, and her husband, the justice of the peace. More than two weeks had passed since they had moved into the small manor house in the neighboring administrative village. Near the kitchen door, they kept a large number of turkeys, chickens, and geese; they never socialized with anyone and they commanded respect.

Now the spreading orchards in the village were in blossom. Trees were standing about like white brides, wistful, mournful, the air could not produce the slightest breeze to stir their branches, and, just before twilight, a Jewish merchant came driving through the village in his own coach. His coachman sat in front, urging on the horses. The merchant gazed over at the justice's attractive manor and saw the convert with her longish, beautiful, slightly weary face, which looked stubborn and was still demanding something from the entire county. There, among the different fowls, she wore summer clothes. She asked the coachman something as he came driving up, then she walked far over to the fenced-in courtyard, which was full of the lowing of the calf, a yelling from the kitchen, and the smell of a milch cow, and there was silence all around. From the remote end of the village came the brief tolling of the church bell, the bass. It was urging the Jew on. It was calling to a tardy Christian wagon in some green valley far away, and kept repeating incessantly:

"It's almost over, it's almost over, the strange, quiet Christian holiday."

People were saying that the young justice of the peace was kind and decent to everyone. He would always find a way of getting two hostile peasants to reach a compromise, or of gently reprimanding a drunk. Close to sundown, he would stroll through the village, handing out candy and laughing at the peasant children, who were sitting in dirty shirts with their bare buttocks in the middle of the road measuring the dust with their fists.

"Gophers!" he shouted to them.

The children concealed their embarrassed faces in their sleeves. But then they ran after him until the distant riverbank. There they stopped and watched him escaping from them as he sat down in his new white boat and skillfully rowed toward the overgrown neck of the river:

"Gophers!"

Fiery golden threads were running under his oars. So, many sunny suns were threaded, and the pieces sank into the depths of the river. The justice reached the peasants who were squaring logs for the old, decayed bridge. The air smelled of fresh oak, of chips, wet spices, and a silent summer evening. Soon a frog would be sticking out its head and croaking at the pale moon; a stork would be standing on one foot, clapping out a bony story to the thickening evening; and the justice would be sitting near the peasants for a long time, talking about the overgrown meadow. In his opinion, they were ultimately going to draw the river water over there and make the sluices stronger and deeper.

The convert with her earnest, longish face was even more of a recluse than in her youth, and she would never drive to the village. She loved her husband. Perhaps that was why she would often put on the white knitted dress that revealed her full, clear throat and made her look broader at her waist and her breasts. At dusk, when he went off to the village, she would walk by herself outside near the fence, and she looked so patient, as if constantly thinking about his having the right to go away for a long while. . . .

She couldn't say anything to him about it. . . .

Her voice was sad and wistful. Whenever she spoke, you couldn't tell which was sadder, her black eyes, her longish face, or her voice. And her voice was nearly always scolding her husband at lunch:

"Kolye, you're not eating!"

Some Jews once overheard her when they were called as witnesses in regard to a fistfight between peasants and were waiting for the justice at lunchtime, out in the hall. Her voice seemed maternal, protective. The Jews felt so strange, as if just noticing once more that they had been sitting without hats for a long time; they smiled and winked at one another:

"Looks like she really loves the goy, huh?"

And sometimes, from the inner rooms, a strange, tidy little creature came running out, a wee four-year-old, whose eyes were even bigger and blacker than his mother's, his small mouth was chewing, and he had a dimple in his left cheek. Each time, he would stop at the door and give the Jews such a curious look of surprise, as if they, the whole community, all Jews from near and far, were related to him on his mother's side. One of the smiling Jews even began teasing him with his finger, motioned to him with his wrinkled forehead, his nose, and his entire smiling face, and he mumbled in Yiddish: "Come here, you little bugger, come here. . . ."

But the little creature was frightened by these motions. He heard his mother's voice from the inner rooms and hurried back with a thumping heart, pounding his feet loudly and running quickly as if terror-stricken.

They're Leaving . . . (ca. 1925)

Simeon Yushkevitch

FOR THE FIRST TIME since the funeral of her daughter Manitchka, who had been killed in a pogrom, Khova appeared in the little grocery store. . . . How hard it was for her to be walking out of doors! For it was here that. . . . Yes, it was here that it had happened. . . . No, she must not think about it. It seemed to her that from all windows, curious eyes were leveled at her and, restraining her tears and thinking that God had vainly punished her with such a terrible humiliation, she glided through the open gate. . . .

"There are less of us now," she began, greeting the woman shopkeeper. "Well, such was God's will. And when God wills that. . . . Well, here I've come to you again! Yes, yes, I know how much I owe you. . . . But . . . my fool will pay. Don't be afraid."

The shopkeeper Hella, a gaunt woman with wild eyes, drew her thin bloodless lips taut. . . . What then? Hadn't the hooligans pillaged her shop? Hadn't they gotten away with everything that had been here on the shelves? After all, had she a million rubles' worth of goods on her shelves?

"Don't waste your breath to tell me," said Khova timidly. "Why waste words? But you're new in our street, and you don't know. . . . How does the broker live? By credit! And my fool hasn't paid rent for two months now, yet our landlord won't chuck us out into the street. He knows. If

God wills it, the broker will suddenly earn a hundred rubles. . . . And so you see, my dear, everything has to do with credit, all life turns around credit."

"I understand," Hella replied after a silence, "but where am I to get things for everybody? What am I going to do now with my little shop? There was a time my husband used to bring home each week four rubles, sometimes five. But you know as well as I that they've made a cripple of him. . . . They've broken both his hands—his right and his left. . . . What's he to do now? Try sewing with his feet?"

"My dear, my dear . . ." Khova implored. "I'll pay you soon."

Both began to talk in whispers of the horrors of the massacre, and both, frightened by their own words, broke into sobs.

"We all ought to leave this place," Hella persisted. "No matter what they say to me, I know one thing: they'll wipe out all of us. Sometime a night will come, such a night, and from house to house the murderers with axes in their hands will come, and they'll take all of us, as many of us as there are here, and they'll kill us. And I say to my old man: 'Let's leave! . . . Let's sell our little shop, and let them be accursed!'"

Two more women customers came in and, recognizing Khova, began to talk to her about poor Manitchka. Then suddenly—it is hard to tell how—they passed on to the subject of the fate of the Jews.

"They're all getting ready to leave," said the eldest in a harsh voice. "Now do you think I intend to remain here long? I have a son. . . . I have a good son. . . . A little while longer, and he'll take me to live with him . . . over there! Thank God for that, thank God!"

"And I have a son-in-law," said the second woman. . . . "Over there he has a fruit shop, and I'll help to sell fruit in his shop. . . . Yes, that's what I'm going to do—I'll save him a pretty penny. . . ."

As if stupefied, Khova started for home. Everywhere one and the same thing. . . . Fears and talk of flight. Indeed, why should they remain here? Wasn't one sacrifice—poor Manitchka—enough? She suddenly looked up at the sky, as if Manitchka's soul lured her there, and with pent-up emotion and grief she thought:

"You are now well off, my dear, my poor dear—but what's yet to become of us? . . ."

She found visitors at home: the broker Leyzer and Weitz. Cohan, her fool Cohan, was walking up and down the room and flourishing his arms.

"Come, come in!" he shouted in a distraught voice. "Listen to Leyzer. . . . Just hear what he says!"

Khova loved Leyzer for his sobriety as well as for his ability to talk roundly and beautifully even about trifles. He was tall, portly, and had the appearance of a merchant. He had big hands, broad shoulders, a large nose, and all this pleased her no little. He was not a bit like her Cohan, who was small, like a chick, with a slender little voice. . . .

"I listen to you as I listen to my own father," she said softly, as she seated herself and put the potatoes and the flour on the table. "Why didn't you bring Rose along with you?"

"Look-a-here," Cohan interrupted, and at the same time buttoned up his waistcoat, "Semka doesn't allow him to talk. You speak to him, Khova. He's been going on like this for some time."

"Semka," sternly pronounced Khova, but suddenly, on second thought, she took the youngster in her arms. "All right, put your head against your mother's breast. . . . Is this better? Now, keep quiet, keep quiet. . . . Listen to what Uncle says."

"If you're asking about my Rose," said Leyzer, when quiet was resumed, "then I must tell you that she couldn't come. Are you satisfied with that, Khova? No, I see you aren't. Then let me tell you that she isn't quite well."

"Go on with what you were saying," Cohan burst out, as with a single movement of his fingers he undid all the buttons of his waistcoat. "Why, you were beginning to say something about Russia."

"Yes, it's interesting," said Weitz in a deep bass voice; he sat in a corner, a dark, gloomy man.

"We'll come to Russia in good time," Leyzer quieted them and slouched down in his chair in such a way as to half recline in it. "I must finish about Rose first. . . . Stones! What are stones? Are they also a kind of disease? But when they happen to be in the liver, they become a problem. It comes to this: the stones creep their way into the liver. Well! And we've crept into this world!"

He noticed that he interested them all, and gradually he grew more heated. He gave the impression that he was playing with words as a cat with a mouse.

"Listen then! Either my Rose eats delicate food, because delicate food contains no stones? Then that leaves nothing more to be said. What then? Well, then, Rose's heart has begun to thump loudly in her breast. Let it be so! And why not, I ask you? Doesn't your heart thump hard? Or, thank God, we have no pogroms? And if you'll be such fools as to ask me, aren't my Rose's feet healthy, then I'll answer you that you know better than I how my Rose feels. Her feet are all swollen. . . . Why? That's what I can't understand. A human being must walk. Why then should the feet swell? Or must a human being lie—why give him feet? The question comes down to a couple of words: Yes, or no."

"I don't see what there is to feel cheerful about?" said Khova gloomily.

"And if I tell you," answered Leyzer satirically, "that whether I'm cheerful or not cheerful, that such good will come pouring down upon us? . . . All stones will become cured, all hearts will cease to thump hard, and our petty Jewish sorrow will rot away."

"That's well put," again responded Weitz, flourishing his fists high.

"I'll put it better than that," Leyzer brusquely interrupted him. "In this place our petty Jewish sorrow will never get cured, and that's why we ought to run away from here."

"Go on, go on, dear Leyzer," began Cohan, panting with agitation, and with the quickness of lightning he buttoned and unbuttoned his waistcoat.

"Yes, do go on!" put in Khova. "One can learn something from you. You're not a bit like my fool here. When he talks, I get nervous. . . . He doesn't speak clearly, not at all simply, but . . . in a way that frightens you."

"Let it be as you say," answered Cohan wearily. "But I do bring you money when I earn it, don't I? Am a good husband, eh? . . . I don't drink, and I don't play cards. As for running away from here, like everyone else, with everyone else, can't I do that? Maybe I could be the first to run away, if need be."

"You'd best keep quiet," cried Khova with evident suffering, shutting her ears with her hands. "Why should you be talking? Leyzer, it means we must all run away? Speak the truth. Everyone says, they're going to leave. . . . It's what you think that I want to know!"

"Aha!" Leyzer cried. "That tempts everyone: there and here! Who are we?" —Rapidly he began to bend his fingers, beginning with the tiniest—"Oh, you poor, you helpless, you accursed, you hungry and . . . the earth! That's five things to bear in mind. But let's proceed. . . . Millions of children, millions of illnesses, millions of worries, millions of pogroms and . . . Russia! That's another five things to bear in mind. But multiply five thousand times five and it won't be all? Aha! Above everything . . . there is Russia. What does Russia mean? Russia means a land in which they cut Jews' throats. Don't torment my poor head with the question: Why? What? Is it a civilized nation? A gentle nation? Tartars, Tartars, and Tartars! . . . No, no—no, don't tell us fairy tales, that because they've begun to cut Jews' throats, it foretells good to come for everyone. They've cut Jews' throats before, they're cutting Jews' throats now, they'll go on cutting Jews' throats in the future—just as if Jews were sheep. Whose throats are they cutting? Those of the Jews? Maybe you think they're doing it only to poor little fellows? No! Every Jew's! Then comes the question, what should the Jews do? We know. And what should someone like you, Cohan, or like you, Weitz, or like me, Leyzer, say? Well, what? What?"

"I know," responded Weitz.

"You all know," said Leyzer angrily. "Well, I'll tell you what. Well, then—ought to say I—Leyzer, with sick wife and little children, show me how you're going to run away from Russia."

"Excellent!" shouted Cohan.

"Well, just try and do as well as Leyzer!" cried Khova warmly. "You're a fool! Sit down! Why do you run up and down the room? And let that waistcoat of yours alone. Why, you've already torn off all the buttons. . . . And where do you intend going, Leyzer?"

"What do you mean, where?" There was astonishment in Leyzer's voice. "Are there two places to which one may run? Straight to America, of course! Perhaps not straight, but to America. Stop a moment, don't raise such a din. . . . The question arises: What am I, Leyzer, here? Answer: A dog! Two dogs! And what else? A scabby Jew. Whom everyone might beat, rob, and anything else you like, as you all know. And there? Do you know? Well, tell me if you do."

"I know," replied Weitz.

"Keep quiet, Weitz," whispered Khova.

"There," cried Leyzer triumphantly, "I am—a Yankee! Not Leyzer, but Yankee Eliezer. That's what I am. Yankee Eliezer! I stroll in the street with my wife and little ones. . . . There goes Yankee Eliezer in America with his wife and little ones and . . . he is afraid of nobody, of nobody!"

"If I had the money," shouted Cohan, "my feet would shed the dust of Russia tomorrow!"

"No, no!" cried Khova, distraught, for she was frightened of Cohan's outburst. "Let me think about it. Don't you go meddling in this business. You frighten one. Now you flame up, then you go out. Once you suddenly took it into your head to become a tailor. . . . Do you remember? Then suddenly you got the idea that you wanted to deal in horses."

She began to relate of the achievements of Cohan, and he listened as one listens to a fairy tale about someone else, and devoured her with his eyes, and shook his head and laughed, like an infant, especially when she recalled how once he had decided to become a cabby. . . . But in his head there were already floating alluring pictures of their departure from Russia.

"Just hold, there, just hold!" he shouted. "What's this being born in my head? What did Leyzer say? Yankee Eliezer? And how will I be called there? Yankee Cohan? I tell you, I'm going. . . . For the name of Yankee, I am ready to give my life. Tomorrow I am going to town. I shall find a purse full of money. I'll have to do a hundred things. Don't hinder me, Khova. . . . Listen to me."

His perturbation grew, and he raised his voice. So intensely did he desire the good, the human, that the whole truth of their terrible life vanished from him as by magic, and they all, captivated by his voice, his gestures, the sparkle of his eyes, yielded to him. . . . Yes, within a week, they would all be leaving!

"Well, well," Leyzer goaded him on, "don't stop! Go on, go on. . . ."

And Cohan went on creating his fairy tale, finding at his every call new astonishing words, and so passionate was the thirst for a quiet, tranquil life that even Khova yielded to him. . . . Within a week they would be leaving! . . .

Rabbi Leyb Saves the Jews of Prague from Evil Decrees (1927)

Shmuel Bastomski

RABBI LEYB, known as the Gut Aryeh, was on excellent terms with the ruler of Prague. The king held him in high esteem, and the rabbi served as his advisor. He visited the king every day, and the king would go strolling with him. He regarded the rabbi as a great sage and an honest man. He nicknamed him Leybl, Lion's Cub. And thanks to his dear friend, the king was favorable to Jews and greatly liked them. Indeed, the king told his guards that the rabbi could visit the king whenever he wanted.

One day, the rabbi appeared before the king, who had just finished his meal. The rabbi saw that the king was very sad, and he asked him: "Your Majesty, why are you so sad?"

The king replied: "Let me tell you the whole truth. My ministers have sent me documents for me to seal. And these documents contain very evil decrees against your Jews."

The rabbi said to the king: "Have you sealed them already?"

The king said: "No, but I have to seal them, for I've had to cope with them about Jews for some time now. They want to expel all Jews from our country, but I refuse to go along with that, and we've been arguing about it. But they've argued so vehemently that I've said I would seal the evil decrees against Jews."

The rabbi asked him: "Where are the documents?"

The king said: "They are in my small case together with my seal."

The rabbi begged the king to rip up the documents. But the ruler said: "I can't, I've already given my word."

However, the rabbi kept pleading until the ruler became very sad, and he said to the rabbi: "Let's stroll a bit in my garden."

And the two of them went strolling, and they kept discussing the evil decrees. But the king grew very tired and said: "Let's sit down a bit."

They sat down. And the king was so weary that he dozed off after saying "I'm going to lie down a bit. Wait until I get up again."

So, the rabbi sat there while the king slept. The king dreamed that a small king of a small country, which was under his control and paid him a tribute, now rebelled and refused to pay him. A letter arrived from the king of that country and the letter said: "You know that I now refuse to pay you a tribute, for I used to be afraid of you, but today I've become very strong, and I'm no longer afraid of you. And if you want to fight a war, then come here. I'm no longer afraid of you."

When the ruler read the letter, he hit the ceiling. He then ordered an aristocrat to lead two thousand men and to march to the small country and shatter the fortification and terrify the rebellious king so that he'd stop rebelling and that he'd know that he *should* be afraid of the king of Prague. He should humble himself and continue paying the tribute.

The aristocrat obeyed and led his army to the small country. But the small king defeated the aristocrat and wiped out his army. The shamed aristocrat appeared before the king of Prague and told him about the outcome of the battle. He said that the rebel's hand was very strong today and had wiped out the aristocrat's entire army and that he alone had escaped. The king was furious, and he said to the aristocrat:

"Take ten thousand men and attack him and wreak vengeance on him and his entire country. Kill the men and torture the women and children in prison and bring the ruler back to me alive."

The aristocrat marched off with his entire army, and he fought the small king for two years. Then the king of Prague received a letter from the aristocrat, and the letter said: "Your Majesty, I led the entire army to the rebellious country, and I attacked it with all our strength. But the king and his army outfought us and killed a lot of our men, and a lot of our men starved to death, for the enemy wouldn't let us get supplies. And they attacked us more and more powerfully. I was left with very few men. That is why I advise you to gather your own army and take your soldiers into battle yourself, for the enemy is very powerful today. When you arrive there, you will believe me, for you suspect that I am not loyal to you. Believe me when I say that I have fought loyally, but the enemy is very powerful."

When the king of Prague read the letter, he grew very angry. For not only had the enemy rebelled and refused to pay their tribute, but they had also killed a lot of his soldiers. So, the king gathered his entire army and furiously marched to the rebellious country and said: "I won't allow anyone to survive. I will burn all the towns, and all memory of that country will be wiped from the face of the earth. No one will know that that country ever existed."

And the king and his army arrived at the rebellious country, launched into a great battle, and the battle dragged on for two years. And the small king defeated the king of Prague, killing lots of men and then capturing him alive and imprisoning him. The small king brought the king of Prague back to his town and locked him in a room so tiny that the prisoner couldn't lie down or sit, he could only stand. High up there was a tiny window, through which he was given bread and water. And he spent eleven years there. Sometimes he would peer out through the tiny window, and one day he spotted Rabbi Leyb. He shouted at the rabbi: "Oh, Leybl! Save me and get me out of here! You used to help me in my troubles, and I've already been here for eleven years. I'm all skin and bones, and my hair and my nails have grown very long."

The rabbi went over to him and said: "What will happen if I get you out of there and take you home and set you on your throne again, so that you rule again?"

The king laughed and said: "You say something that I don't demand of you. All I ask is that you get me out of prison and bring me home. I will then be your servant, so long as I don't have to rot in this awful prison."

The rabbi said to him: "If I get you out of there, will you rip up the evil decrees that you issued against the Jews while you were in power?"

The king said to him: "You're a sage but you talk a lot of nonsense! I've been imprisoned any number of years. And where are the edicts? By now, there's a new ruler in Prague. I'll say it again: If you get me out of this prison, you can be my ruler, and I'll be your servant!"

The Gur Aryeh said to him: "You know that everything I tell you is the truth. I'll get you out of there and take you home and seat you on your royal throne, and you will be king again. But remember: When you sealed evil decrees against the Jews, I asked you to rip up those documents, but you said you couldn't, they were signed and sealed in your case. If you like, give me your seal, I'll go into your private study and tear up the seal and take out the edicts and rip them up and reseal them with your seal."

The king took out his seal, which he still had, and he gave it to Rabbi Gur Aryeh. And the rabbi went into the king's study and tore open the king's seal on his case and took out all the documents and ripped them up and resealed them with the king's seal. And even though the entire business was merely the king's dream, the king did give the rabbi his seal while he was still sleeping. And the rabbi had really taken out the documents and ripped them up and resealed the case.

The rabbi came back to the king in the vineyard, and the king was still asleep. And the rabbi handed back the royal seal. And the king took it and slipped it into his pocket. And the king dreamed that the rabbi took him from his prison through the tiny window and brought the king back to his vineyard. And the king awoke in a wonderful mood and he saw that he was sitting in his vineyard. He threw his arms around the Gur Aryeh and kissed him and said to him:

"I'm very thankful to you, Lebyl, because you got me out of a horrible prison and brought me to such a radiant place. And if you wish, you can be king, and I will be your servant."

The Gur Aryeh said: "Your Majesty, think where you have been. Remember when we went on a stroll."

The king said: "Yes, I remember. But a lot of years have passed."

The Gur Aryeh said: "No, it was today."

The king checked his watch. A mere hour had gone by. And now the king realized that it had all been a dream. And he said to the rabbi: "Good for you, Leybl! Now I see that I did good by not sealing the evil decrees against the Jews, and I see that Jews are very honest. From now on, I will no longer believe any libels against the Jews. For I see that my advisors are not loyal and that they act out of hatred for the Jews. That's why my advisors urge me to take such awful steps. And praised be God for preventing me from issuing the evil decrees."

And the king held the rabbi in a lot greater esteem, and he always asked his advice about everything. The rabbi was as dear to him as his own life, and he never did anything without first consulting the rabbi. And the king always did what the rabbi advised him to do. And it was very good for the king.

Pogrom (1930)

Arnold Zweig

THE RINGING OF shots awoke Eli Seamen. The double wings of his window thrown wide open with their curtains dangling in the wind like bodies of gallows' birds admitted the clear crack of the Browning pistols, which was carried over the roofs to his bedroom. He sat while the sky above the city was touched with the red either of a conflagration or of a multitude of lights; but directly overhead the legions of the stars worked through the infinite darkness. Against the faint, distant glimmer the window cut out a hard cross right in the center of the Great Bear. Seeing the arrangement of the stars, the boy thought it must be toward eleven o'clock; they are shooting. . . . The door to his father's room was flung wide open, and Inspector Sean strode over the threshold.

"Get up, Eli," he cried, his hard voice wild with excitement.

"Pogrom?" the son cried back, leaping with both legs onto the carpet; but no answer was needed.

He dressed himself with quick and trembling hands, while his father sealed a letter by the light of a candle stump. The chessboard still stood in the throes of the struggle, as they had left it the night before. The masterstroke had just been delivered; the figures loomed black in the candlelight, mustered with their stiff shadows on the divided board. Eli, filled with happy pride, threw one glance at it: his father, strong player that he was, had been compelled to yield in astonishment before that last triumphant move. . . . But in an instant he was pulled back into the present; while he laced his shoes hastily the thought occurred to him—and it gave him a sense of satisfaction—that things were going badly now for his enemies, those Jewish young boys who threw cakes of mud after him and shouted that he was desecrating the Sabbath and was eating uncleanliness; and he felt that it served them right, for they were many, yet never attacked him singly.

"Well, are you ready? Not yet."

The inspector, his fur cap on his head, raged up and down in the doorway, stamping in his high boots. He blew impatiently into his thick black beard: "Are you afraid?"

And suddenly—he had never thought of this before—Eli realized that he, too, might be assaulted, for the band could not know that he and his father lived in a state of enmity with the others. But he forgot it again on the spot. "No, no," he answered, angrily. "Here I am. Let's go."

The father locked the letter in the writing desk. "We must see. . . . *We* must help them out there. . . ."

Then he turned his face on his son and examined the sixteen-year-old boy closely, as if he were a piece of merchandise that had just been delivered; no, he was not afraid. "Listen, Eli. It's possible that something might happen over there . . . to me, too . . . you understand; and if I'm no longer here tomorrow—"

"Father!" the boy cried, and his eyes became two black holes.

"Anything can happen. In that case, listen—you return to Germany, at once. . . ."

"Father!"

"And then study something decent, see? Engineering."

"Oh, please, please, stop," the boy cried in a dying voice, and with both hands he seized his father's arm.

"In case you might need it—you're big enough—here!"

He thrust the flat pistol toward him. Eli seized the pistol in a strong grasp, though his hands shivered. "Will the police help us, father?"

But the inspector had already rushed through the door, in one hand his Browning, and in another a formidable stick, leather on the outside but iron within. His steps sounded down the corridor; hastily the boy snatched his mountain-climbing stick from the corner—a yellow oaken staff pointed with metal at the end. Beyond the outer door he found his father, clearly undetermined.

"As a matter of fact, I ought to leave you here. What should you be doing over there . . . ?"

"Without you? I won't let you go alone for a single instant."

"I want you to obey me," the father said.

"I'll break the door open, and follow you," the powerfully built boy cried. The inspector knew his oldest son. "Well, if you must. . . . It's probably for the best," and smiling weakly he turned the key strongly in the lock.

They stumbled down the three flights of steps and crossed the broad yard of the factory. In Eli the blood ran swiftly and joyfully: adventure! And what an adventure! A pogrom, right on the eve of Easter Sabbath! Tomorrow songs of praise in the churches. He was not at all frightened; his finger pressed happily against the trigger of the weapon. Would he have to shoot? And would he hit his man? Surely if only his hands wouldn't tremble too much. He promised himself to get Gabriel Butterman, the redhead, the thrower of stones. That man he wouldn't let escape . . . and he felt the advance happiness of envy that the whole class—and his brother Leos—would feel—when he would tell them about it. . . . He tightened his arm as though in exercise, so that the muscles rose quickly. The fifth-grade schoolboy lifted up his face, with its arched eyebrows, and its crown of black hair, to the night air. The gatekeeper was still awake; yellow light streamed from the windows of his lodge. The inspector gave him the keys of the house and said, in Polish: "Open the door for me. It isn't good to go out," the old man argued, while his mustaches, yellowed by smoking, wagged with his speech.

"It's true, Janek. But I'll be back at one o'clock. And look after the keys for me." The door shrieked on its hinges; in the distance was heard a faint sound of shots. The father was in such a hurry that Eli was nearly left behind. The streets lay black and deserted; only high up there were a few lighted windows. The two of them turned sharply to the right, went at a trot the whole length of the Petersburgerstrasse—blundering into pools of mud and water—straight across the Patjomkinplatz and right into the Schlusselstrasse. The noise became louder, became a wild tumult. They met people, more people, still more people.

"What's the matter?" the father asked in Russian of a figure hurrying by in the dark.

"They're beating the infidel Jews up, uncle, hurry up."

"And the police?"

"You won't find the soldiers lazy," the citizen answered, laughing contentedly and hurried on. Eli made up his mind to shoot the soldiers even if they had killed Gabriel.

The street grew brighter in the light of the lanterns and the lamps that streamed from the houses. Before long they found themselves in the midst of the crowds. They thrust their way through roughly, and when the father could not proceed fast enough, he seized his son by the shoulders and thrust him into the shelter of a high house.

"Where now?" the boy asked, excitedly.

"Come!"

They ran lightly, hastily, up two, three, four flights of steps. From the skylight, a small dirty opening, they peered out on the neighboring streets, for none of the neighboring houses were more than two or three stories high. The square frames of houses enclosed a clear picture, small in the distance, but marvelously sharp in outline. They saw flames flickering through the windows, and thickening smoke, streaked with red; they saw people running, limbs flying, men and women in knots and groups; they heard a deep roaring, the scream of high-pitched voices, single shots here and there, and through the fierce whisper and crack of conflagration dull thudding noises, as of falling beams and doors smashed open. For a single, hellish instant the horror of it beat up into his face.

Then suddenly the inspector pulled the son backward and thundered with him down the steps; instead of turning toward the door of the house, he went into the dark courtyard, and holding his stick in his teeth, square across his face, he climbed over the low wall into the neighboring house. Eli threw his cudgel over, leapt up, held on with his fingers, drew himself upward, lifted his legs over the obstacle, just as they did in the gymnasium, and landed on the other side almost on all fours.

And now they ran noisily through the back quarters across a second courtyard and by means of a low gate again reached the street. They went swiftly along the houses on the left, through two, three small streets, without seeing a single human being, and they stood again on the Katherinestrasse, which farther down was once more filled with noise, light, and smoke. They stood still for a moment, their beating hearts breathless; then they went some seventy steps slowly, easily, down to Metchnikoffstrasse, their Brownings in their hands. There they turned the corner—and something happened.

A woman came running toward them, in her underskirt; on the upper part of her body she wore a brown piece of cloth that covered her shoulders. She was out of breath, unable to utter a sound, her fleshy face distorted with the terror of death. She held her young daughter by the hand; the child had not even a cloth to cover her. Her hair hung loose around her face, and her bare feet, scarcely able to keep the pace up, seemed only to be falling forward. The woman's mouth was wide open, showing all the teeth, and her free hand was pressed against her left breast. Three young ones followed her—with just a short stretch of pavement between her and them. And on that short stretch a young boy, perhaps nine years old, stumbled horribly along, unable to catch up with his mother. . . . Eli thought he recognized Gabriel's younger brother; but at once he might be mistaken. The child reeled and fell, picked himself up, fell again, and as he rose to his feet for a second time, the first of the hooligans ran by; the second one, also running by, thrust a knife into his back.

"Ma-a—" he cried—the sound beginning high and shrill, then sinking downward and breaking.

The mother, hearing that piercing cry, turned her head, stiffened, sank on her knee, without loosening her hold on the girl. Then suddenly Eli was aware that his father, who had just been at his side, had leapt ten paces forward—and, a fiery tumult bursting out within him, he sprang after him. For a single, violent moment he was glad that his mother had long been dead, and then he saw how his father's horrible stick had whirled sideways at the skull of the first hooligan, smashing it as if it had been a clay pot, so that the man fell sideways on the stony ground. At the same instant he saw two others put themselves on the defensive. And then the fury broke loose. He heard one shot, two shots, and he shifted his Browning to his right hand. His father leapt to the attack of the man who was shooting, but the second man was behind him, his knife uplifted. Eli felt something cold at his heart; and then he stood still, shot, shot again, again; and the knife rang on the hard pavement. A terrific excitement cried out of him:

"He's hit!"

He heard the piercing cry of the women behind him, the sound of heavy footsteps, a shot thundered darkly behind him, another—no Browning this time, he knew—and then he saw the face of his father turned toward him, a vivid white, with far-off eyes blazing in terrific anger: and then nothing more. He fell forward.

"Father . . ." he thought, and at the same time something hammering down upon him flung him to the ground as with a lightning stroke. The police lieutenant wiped his saber and gave his command: "Forward!"

And as the policemen retreated swiftly the two women, dumb with horror, fixed a blank dead gaze on the figures lying on the ground: on the man, the youths, the boy, and the child.

The Fairy Tale about Technology (1935)

Alfred Döblin

THIS IS A TRUE STORY, and it shows that even in the most enlightened times miracles are possible.

There was once a small Jewish shtetl in the Ukraine, where a father was sitting with his family. The First World War had not occurred yet, and the tsar ruled in St. Petersburg. However, the "Black Hand" was a strong force in the Ukraine and reigned there. And people needed money again, and the Jews were there and had become prosperous through their various businesses. So, someone began to spread rumors, about Easter, about bad words that were said about the priests, and about a Jew who had laughed when someone had said something about the Holy Mother of God at Czestochowa, and other things were promulgated. Moreover, the Black Hand had arranged to provide the proper excuses later: the police were having a celebration, and the colonel was sitting at the banquet table right on the day that everything was to happen.

And what was to take place? They were going to band together. Their plans had already leaked out, but what good was it? —A pogrom is a pogrom. Blood flows. But the Jewish people are not children, and ultimately blood must be shed, for they won't let themselves be torn apart by vicious animals.

Now, there was a father who protected his home very, very well, and he also had an ax during the pogrom, and there were probably some who saw that he had an ax. Consequently, the father thought he had better not wait for the investigation and the trial, and he took off with his family, and since it was impossible to predict what might happen, he separated his two eldest sons and said "Lemberg!" and gave them money. But he saw only one of them later. The other, who could sing so beautifully, did not show up. They never heard a word from him. Their dear son had been swallowed up by the earth. Father and mother moved to a small city. The relatives did what they could for them, and they pulled themselves back up on their feet. Indeed, they also survived the First World War. But neither the father nor the mother was happy anymore. Their dear son was gone, and they talked about the whole affair a thousand times.

"You set an example for him," the mother complained. "He probably took an ax or a knife. A Jew should hide."

"Should I have let them kill me and all the rest of you as well?"

"Ah, there are still plenty of us living where we used to live."

And time passed. The mother died. The father was in poor condition. His surviving son supported him, and the relatives helped. Despite it all, the father still went wherever he could to hear voices singing, and he thought, "Oh, how my Izzie could sing! Such a beautiful, beautiful voice. Where can you find such beautiful voices today?"

The fact that he heard so much music and went to concerts was God's will. The mother had died, but the father was destined to learn that God lived and had not forgotten him. On his seventieth birthday, the head of the community gave him a gramophone as a present, and he had it played for him. In addition, his oldest son brought him the newest invention, a radio, and with that he could hear things from far, far away, wherever people sang in the entire world, no matter who it was. Not Izzie, though.

Day after day he listened to all the voices, so many, so resounding, and the pop hits they now made, the music that everyone danced to. And one day toward noon his radio was playing, and his daughter-in-law was cooking in the kitchen. The door swung open, and the old father, with his yarmulke slanted on the side of his bald head, came running into the kitchen with large, large eyes and screamed, “Rosalie, listen! Listen!”

“For God’s sake, what’s wrong with the man? I’m going to run and get Yankel.”

“Listen, Rosalie, he’s singing. It’s Izzie! Rosalie, my child, listen for a minute! I’m sure it’s Izzie!”

And she had to hold him tight and lead him to a kitchen chair, the old man. The music ended. It was a temple song. A pop song followed. She wanted to turn the radio off but didn’t. Perhaps it would come again.

What more is there to say? They believed the old man. The son traveled to Warsaw with him. There they found a record, and his name was on the record. He was an American cantor, a famous man. They found one more record by him in Warsaw.

And then the telegrams went back and forth, and it really was Izzie, who had made it to America with a push and a shove. He had searched for his parents in Russia, but then the war had come, and how could he have looked for them then? So finally, the radio had made everything possible, and that’s technology. It brought a son back to his father, and both know God’s alive, and whoever believes in him can count on him.

A Letter to God (ca. 1935)

Meri Balkon

ONCE UPON A TIME there was a king whose treasurer was one of the most honest men in the world. He managed the national budget, collected taxes, and accounted scrupulously for every penny. The king valued him highly, and this irritated one of the courtiers. "My lord king," the courtier said, "you have to expect a little larceny when your treasurer is a Jew."

"What are you talking about?" said the king. "He's an honest man."

The courtier said, "Put him to the test; dismiss him. I'll bet you that his standard of living doesn't change. Then you'll know that he's been stealing from you."

The king allowed himself to be persuaded. One day he said to his treasurer, "Yankl, I can't keep you in my service any longer."

The treasurer wondered what he had done wrong. "My lord, have I not served you faithfully?" he asked. "Is there even so much as a penny missing?" But the king wouldn't hear a word; he simply told him to pack up and go.

"Where will I go?" Yankl said. "I'll starve to death. Have pity on me and my family."

The king's heart was touched. But still he thought, "I have to test him." A peasant's wagon was sent for, and Yankl's furniture and everything else he owned was piled into it. Then the king gave his former treasurer five rubles and sent him away.

Yankl came to a village, where he moved his family into a hut. And now, his life turned dismal. It was just before Passover, and Passover, as everyone knows, is a serious matter. There's no end to the things one needs. Yet Yankl was penniless, with no job to be had anywhere.

His wife said, "It's almost Passover, and we have nothing for the holiday meals. Why don't you write a letter to God in Heaven to send us some wine and *manse* and meat and dishes—and everything else a Jewish home needs on Passover."

Yankl looked at his wife in surprise. "Listen," he said, "you can write a letter to anyone at all—even to the king. But you can't write a letter to the *reboyne shel oylem*, the Lord of the Universe."

But she wouldn't let the matter rest, and finally he thought, "What can I lose, after all?" And he sat down and wrote that he had been an official in the court of King So-and-So; and that he had served him faithfully and had been dismissed just the same; and that he and his family were hungry; and that here it was, nearly Passover; and would God please send wine and mead and meat and fish. Here Yankl listed everything that was needed. Then he tied the letter to the leg of a bird and the bird flew over cities and towns and from country to country. Flying thus one day, the exhausted bird saw a palace and lighted to rest on one of the window ledges.

Now this was the palace of a very great emperor, the greatest of the kings of the world. And the emperor happened to see the letter tied to the bird's leg. He commanded that the bird be caught and the letter brought to him, and then he read the tale of the man who had faithfully served his king but had been dismissed; and now he was poor and it was almost Passover time and therefore he begged God to send him wine and mead and meat and fish and utensils and everything else that was needed.

So, the great emperor commanded his servants to gather all the things listed in it and pack them into two big chests.

The emperor wrote a letter saying, "I am sending the things you asked for," and placed this and his ring in one of the chests. Then a guard delivered the two huge chests, setting them quietly in front of Yankl's door in the middle of the night, and went away.

In the morning when Yankl got up, he tried to open his door but could not and finally climbed out through a window. Seeing two such large chests, he was afraid that something dreadful was in them, that someone might be about to make a blood-libel accusation against him.

He went to call the village magistrate, who ordered the chests opened, found the letter, and read it. "God sends wine and mead and meat and fish and utensils to such-and-such a person."

What joy there was in Yankl's home! He was determined to make a Passover feast fit for a king. The envious courtier came just then to find how Yankl was celebrating Passover. He looked in the window and was stunned by what he saw: the best of everything. So, he ran off to the king to report: "The Jew is presiding over his Passover feast as if he were a king—and it's all at your expense."

The king got into his carriage and drove off to see for himself. And when he caught sight of Yankl at the head of his bountiful table, the king was outraged. "Now, there's a Jew for you. A shameless rogue! He complained to me that he was penniless, and look at him, stuffed with money."

The king ordered Yankl arrested. His house was searched and everything was taken away from him. The king personally took the ring from Yankl's hand and put him and his wife and children into prison. They were given only bread and water, and Yankl was beaten to make him confess where he had hidden "all the other things he had stolen." And when the poor man, weeping and wailing, said that he had never stolen so much as a penny from the king, and that it was God who had sent everything, he was beaten all the harder. "Don't invent tales," he was told.

It happened then that the great emperor was traveling through his domains to see whether he was being well served and justice was being done. His custom was to visit all the prisons and listen as the inmates told him why they were there.

When the emperor came to Yankl's country, Yankl's wife said, "Listen, dear husband: write a letter explaining why you were arrested. Tell the whole story." So, he wrote it all down, and when the emperor entered the prison, he stood to one side and handed him the letter. The great emperor read it and commanded that the king be brought to him. "Why did you arrest this man?" the emperor asked. "He was stealing me blind," the king said.

Just then the emperor saw his own ring on the king's finger. "Whose is that?" he asked.

"It's mine," the king said. "The Jew stole it from me."

Now the great emperor told the king the whole story. And the king bowed his head and said, "I am guilty, sire."

But the emperor was not satisfied. "Who knows," he said angrily, "how many innocent people you've arrested." He ordered all the jails emptied, and he imprisoned the king and the envious courtier and had them fed on bread and water. And he made a king of Yankl, who leads a happy life to this day.

A Shocking Tale of a Viceroy (ca. 1935)

Benyomin Pikover

THIS STORY TOOK PLACE IN Amsterdam a long, long time ago. That city belonged to an emperor who lived far away. It was ruled by a viceroy, in the same way that a district governor rules in Russia.

Nowadays taxes are paid by each person directly to the state. But long ago, things were different. A tax collector "farmed" the taxes and paid the king a certain amount. Later the collector got a commission from the state.

Now, this viceroy, one of the wickedest of the wicked and a big spender as well, was always in need of money. Where to get it?

Where else but from the Jews of Amsterdam? So, they endured a great deal from him.

There was a rabbi in that city, one of the great rabbis of the kingdom. He was as cherished and treasured as a precious stone. He lived to a ripe old age, then became ill and took to his bed. People knowing that his end was near mourned greatly. For who could possibly take his congregation when—may you live to a hundred and twenty—you pass on?

The rabbi said, "I've taken care of everything." Then he died and was buried.

When they read his will, this is what they found: "Let messengers be sent to such-and-such a town, where a rabbi by the name of Kashmen lives. Let him be made rabbi of the Jews of Amsterdam."

So, two messengers were chosen to find Reb Kashmen and bring him back to Amsterdam. They rode and rode, visiting towns and villages until, by the help of God, they arrived at their destination and put up at an inn. When they had eaten and rested, they approached the innkeeper. "Tell us, sir, where does the rabbi, Reb Kashmen, live?"

The innkeeper said, "I've lived here for I don't know how many years, and there's never been a rabbi with that name."

So, the messengers asked the same question of other people, who all said the same thing.

Concluding that their rabbi must have been mistaken, they returned home. Back in Amsterdam a special assembly was called, and the people decided that their rabbi would not have made a mistake about something in his will. So, two new messengers were dispatched to that town to examine the matter thoroughly. There they went from house to house and searched the village from one end to the other, but no one had ever heard the name of Reb Kashmen. They were on the point of returning home when one messenger said, "Maybe we ought to go to that settlement over there—those few houses in the open fields."

They went there and came to a small hut. An old woman and a girl sat there plucking feathers. The messengers said, "Good evening."

"Good evening and a good year," came the reply. "What do you want?"

One of the messengers asked whether Rabbi Kashmen lived there. The old woman nodded and the messengers were delighted.

"He'll be here soon, most likely," she said. They decided to wait. As they waited, the door opened and an old man came in. The woman went to the oven, from which she took out a dish of food. The old man washed his hands, recited a blessing and sat down to eat. He paid no attention to the messengers—as if they were not there.

When he had finished, they approached him. "Our rabbi of blessed memory," they said, "enjoined us in his will to bring to Amsterdam a certain Reb Kashmen so that he may take our rabbi's place."

Reb Kashmen said not a word, nor did he look at them. It was as if they were invisible, as if no one were speaking at all. He rose, walked into his room, and went to sleep.

The messengers, seeing that they would accomplish nothing, said good night and went away. They returned the next morning, but no matter what they said, he kept silent. Even when they nagged at him, he remained mute as a wall. Then they begged for his pity and said they would not leave without him.

He replied, "Why are you burdening me? I don't understand any of this. You want me to come? Very well, I'll come. Just stop tormenting me."

That was what they were waiting to hear. They put the old man and his wife and daughter into their wagon and drove off. When they arrived in Amsterdam, how happy everyone was! Reb Kashmen was welcomed with a parade. He was given a fine house with large rooms. Joy reigned, but the rabbi was silent even though people were dying to hear him say a few holy words. Finally, after much coaxing, he said, "Dear friends, I don't know anything."

This offended everyone. "What kind of a rabbi is this?" cried the synagogue officers. "He must be crazy."

So, the people began to put distance between themselves and Reb Kashmen. And finally, they moved him out of the fine house and installed him with his wife and daughter in a small room at the city's edge. And the community chose another rabbi.

Now, the viceroy was a great carouser and gambler, a man who danced all night at balls, who poured out money like sand. And now, on top of everything, he had acquired a mistress, so he needed even more money. Consequently, he went to the tax collector, Reb Azriel, and said, "Because of this and that, and such-and-such, I need a few rubles."

Reb Azriel handed him some money, and the viceroy went away. Not an hour later he came back again, and then again, and again. Finally, Reb Azriel said, "I can't give you any more."

The viceroy banged furiously at the collector's door, calling, "I'll rise against you the way Haman[1] rose against you." And he stormed off to the chief priest. Together they plotted to take a dreadful vengeance on

Reb Azriel and all the Jews. Just before Passover, they killed a Gentile boy and put his body, along with several bottles of blood, into Reb Azriel's house. Then they shouted, "The Jews have killed a boy!" So, they ordered a search of Jewish houses, and when the murdered child was found, the old tax collector was taken in chains to prison. Meanwhile the wicked viceroy wrote to the emperor: "The Jews have risen against the state; they are slaughtering our children."

The emperor replied, "Do what you like," which was all the viceroy wanted to hear. So, he issued a decree that on Yom Kippur, the Jewish Day of Atonement, the inhabitants of all the towns and villages must gather to see Reb Azriel hanged. The decree also said that anyone could do what he liked with the Jews.

As the day of the hanging approached, the cries and lamentations pouring from the Jewish homes would have restored hearing to the deaf. Feverish prayers to our Father in heaven rose from the synagogues. Finally, it occurred to someone to consult Reb Kashmen. A delegation was sent to his room, where they found him wearing his *tabs* and *kid*, his prayer shawl and robe, and intoning his prayers with so much grief that the group was afraid to move. Seeing them, he said, "Go quickly and command everyone to eat the meal that precedes our fast, as if tomorrow were Yom Kippur."

The Jews did as he commanded, and that evening everyone gathered in the synagogue. And when Reb Kashmen, standing at the podium, recited the *kolnidre* prayer, it is said that the walls quivered and the heavens shook. And each time he spoke, thunder roared, after which came the sounds of the congregation's weeping and lamentations.

When the *musef* prayers were finished, Reb Kashmen addressed the people. "My brothers, an evil decree hangs over us, but God's compassion is great. I am going to the emperor. Wait for my return." With that, he vanished.

Far away, the emperor had just eaten and was strolling in his garden. Growing weary, he sat down on a bench and fell asleep. He dreamed that he was drowning in a river of blood, and each time he struggled to the bank, the viceroy thrust him back. At last he was saved from drowning by a little old man, a Jew, who ran up and drove the viceroy off.

Now, the journey from Amsterdam to the emperor's palace ordinarily required some days, but Reb Kashmen accomplished it in an instant. The emperor was just waking. Seeing that Reb Kashmen looked like the Jew who had rescued him in the dream, the emperor said, "Holy man, I feel evil around me. Can you explain it?"

Reb Kashmen answered, "Great Emperor, it is clear that someone wishes you ill, and you know who it is: your viceroy. He and your generals have plotted your death. Command that his house be searched; papers that are in a drawer there will prove his guilt. And, Great Emperor, you should also know that the viceroy is tormenting the Jews of your kingdom. He has exacted tribute from us and has not given you a groshen. He squanders it all even as he skins us Jews alive. Recently, he has killed a Gentile boy and thrown the corpse into Reb Azriel's house, creating a blood-libel. Great Emperor, stand by us. Issue a proclamation to delay the execution while you determine whether I am telling the truth."

The emperor called in his general. "Take a regiment of soldiers," he said, "and go to Amsterdam. Delay the decree. Search the viceroy's house. If you find proof of wickedness, carry out whatever sentence he deserves."

Reb Kashmen returned miraculously to the synagogue. It was time for *rile*, the concluding Yom Kippur prayers. When the late-evening service was done, he said, "Brothers, go and break your fast. Let those of you who have food give it to those who have none. Things will be well. Reb Azriel will be saved."

In the morning after daybreak, crowds of Gentiles began to gather on all the roads from all corners of the land. Whole villages arrived bringing ladder-wagons to carry away Jewish property. They were armed with scythes and rakes and axes. But no Jews appeared anywhere. They had shut themselves up in cellars and attics.

The gallows had been erected in the market square, and there the Gentiles massed. At the time decreed, Reb Azriel was led in. The chains on his feet made it hard for him to walk, so he was driven along with blows from gun butts. He went quietly. So much goodness glowed in his face that the Gentiles fell silent and did not touch him.

As the guards were setting Reb Azriel under the gallows to throw the noose over his neck, the viceroy—that *Haman*—said, "Do you want to live? Then become a convert."

Reb Azriel raised his eyes to heaven and cried, "*Shma Yisroel,* Hear, O Israel." Then he was silent.

As the executioners were about to begin, shots were heard and the crowd saw riders approaching. The general arrived and handed the emperor's orders to the viceroy. The noose was removed from Reb Azriel's neck. The general quietly signaled his men to watch the viceroy, and his riders surrounded the viceroy's palace. When the soldiers began to search, they found papers describing a plot to kill the emperor and usurp his kingdom. So, the viceroy was hanged on the gallows that had been prepared for Reb Azriel.

The Gentiles scattered like mice, while the Jews left their hiding places and crowded into the streets, kissing and embracing each other for joy.

It was clear that the instrument of their happiness was Reb Kashmen, yet he was nowhere to be seen. They went to his room, but it was empty. Riders were sent out on all the roads, and they found him at last in a forest. Throwing themselves at his feet, they said, "Holy Rabbi, don't leave us."

In reply, Reb Kashmen said, "There is no further need for me here. I must go wherever Jews are troubled, wherever a Haman has risen."

Then he and his wife and daughter disappeared.

When the emperor returned to Amsterdam, he was very sorry to hear that Reb Kashmen was gone. "I didn't even get to thank him," he said.

From that time on, the emperor bestowed many favors on the Jews. He excused them from taxes, and there was prosperity and abundance on all sides. And they all thanked the Creator and lived happily.

This shocking tale has been told so that later generations may know and remember what once came to happen.

The Zaddik (1937)

Ilya Ehrenbourg

WITH DIFFICULTY I HAVE at last succeeded in finding a real Zaddik.[1] He is, perhaps, one of the last. His name is Reb Yosele from Skvernovic. He lives in Warsaw, in the neighborhood of the Jewish paupers. A tiny unheated room. I am reminded: "Do not forget to cover your head." This is his only request. The Zaddik is a tall, good-looking Jew of about fifty-five years of age, with a long traditional beard and the kind yet sad eyes of a village dreamer. He is dressed poorly, and everything around him is poor and shabby. The chairs are broken and the tapestry torn. This Zaddik resembles a great poet who is read only by ten or twenty people. His followers are poor workers from the Nalevki.

The Zaddik offers me a cigarette and lights one himself. By the awkward movement of his fingers, and his strenuous puffing, it is obvious that he is not a habitual smoker. Perhaps he only lit the cigarette so as to soften the tension of our strange meeting. However, he soon feels at ease and answers my questions. I ask him about the essence of Hasidism. He answers readily without stopping to think a moment, sometimes smiling ironically, sometimes inspired, like a real poet.

"The Misnagdim consider the 'Law' above all. But soldiers are trained differently in different countries. The English soldiers are taught differently from the Polish. However, soldiers of all the world are trained to obey the commands of 'one-two'; the good one forgets everything he has been taught."

The Zaddik caresses his long beard and looks at me questioningly. It seems that he is not certain whether I understood. He adds: "All life is war. . . .

"You ask what is 'Heaven' and 'Hell'? After death a man with strong will power lives his life all over again. The joy from the love and kindness he dispensed through his life is 'Heaven.' And 'Hell'? In order for a man to rise he must first fall. One cannot rise without having fallen. This is the law of life and the law of God. . . .

"Poverty is the path to God. In the book Zohar it is said that God has many attires, but he is always dressed in the prayers of the poor."

My last question: "What is more important, the relation between man to God or between man to man?"

The Zaddik smiles.

"At first it seems that his relation to God is the more important. For God is everything, and man—dust. But when you think about it, especially if you have lived and experienced, you will realize that man's relation to man is the most significant. If a man insults God, he has insulted God alone. But when a man insults a man, he has wronged both, God and man."

Reb Yosele has a score of followers. They always come to him for advice: "What's to be done, the daughter is sick?" or "Soloveichik will not return the ten zlotys he borrowed." His wisdom remains within the four walls, hidden under a faded cap, bent over an old book.

The Zaddik reminds one of an old master who remembers a secret of an ancient craft, but does not know where to apply it. Reb Yosele still remembers the words of the Besht, but his words nobody understands any more. He cures hearts not with his inherited wisdom but with his title of "Zaddik," and with a kind and generous smile.

The rich Jews go to the better-known Zaddikim. There, they too may expect some honor or benefits; the right to sit with the Zaddik, at one table, or with his influential assistants in some commercial scheme. These Hasidim wear silk *talletim* (prayer-shawls), their beards are neatly trimmed, and on Saturdays, they wear silk caps with borders of yellow fur. They call themselves Hasidim, but if you ask them about the teachings of Besht, they will not be able to answer. For them more important than the joy and ecstasy is: who will sit today next to the Zaddik, Aaron Shmulevich or Hayyim Rosenberg?

There are still other places where Hasidism is yet alive, not its philosophy but spirit—amid the poor of the synagogue of the so-called Brazlav Hasidim. They have no Zaddik at all. Their Zaddik died long ago—a century and a half ago. His name was "Reb Nachman from Brazlay." He was a great philosopher and poet. His sayings, legends, and poetry were recently published in a German translation. This first emergence of historical Hasidism from the borders of the ghetto was full of belated glory, to the classical astonishment of the descendants. "Whence such daring thought? Whence such poetry? From Brazlav? . . . Nobody ever knew about it. . . ."

Yes, only his Hasidim knew it. For them Reb Nachman was a great Zaddik. And when he died, they did not take another one in his place. They have chosen for their adviser the memory of this Zaddik-poet. Among the Brazlav Hasidim there are neither rich nor hypocrites. These have nothing to do here. Their place is at the table of the living Zaddik. And here? Here are only the paupers of the Nalevki: peddlers, tailors, cobblers.

I enter the synagogue. It is a small room in a worker's house, dimly lit by a tiny electric lamp. It is crowded to capacity, and with difficulty, I manage to elbow my way inside. At first it seems as though it were a trade union meeting. But no, here is a different century, a different chronology. Perhaps it is altogether beyond the concepts of our time. Bearded men in dirty caps who toil the whole week selling rags and herrings, pounding out a monotonous dreary existence. But now is Sabbath Eve. They came here to rejoice. And they are happy, not because it has been prescribed to be happy. No, in them is still alive the belief that is already dead outside of this tiny room. They are meeting the "Sabbath-Queen." They clasp their hands and sing. At first, they say words of prayer. But neither the tongue nor the mind can keep up with the gayness of the soul. Soon, the words are heard no more, only a gay, wide, soul-captivating melody. The feet will not stand in one place any longer, and they begin to jump. And they dance in this tiny and dimly lit room. Happiness! Life! I observe the faces and wonder. Who changed them? Who erased from their minds the memory of insults, hunger and "Zlotys"? One can speak here even about Catholicism, Freud, or "Mass Hypnotism." But is it worthwhile? These things can be read by everyone in solid books. Would it not be better now to accept the smile of the Brazlav Hasidim as an extraordinary happiness? Even though it is foreign, inaccessible, but human till the end. The joy of losing oneself in a greater joy, the joy of honesty and forgetfulness, the joy of simple and childish souls. Rejoice!!! . . .

Translated by Leon Dennen.

The Ba'al Shem Tov and the Sorcerer (ca. 1950–1960)

Told by a Yemenite Jew to Rachel Seri

FOR THREE DAYS, the Ba'al Shem Tov had been traveling with his disciples. On the evening of the third day, they reached a village. Entering the establishment of a Jewish tavern keeper, they asked if they could spend the night there. But the proprietor refused. They noticed that he seemed to be preoccupied and that, inexplicably, many candles were burning in the room.

The Ba'al Shem Tov asked the man what it all meant, but the villager did not want to answer. The Ba'al Shem Tov repeated his question.

"Even if your honor knew what my problem is," replied the tavern keeper, "how could you help me? Alas, no one has ever suffered a disaster like mine."

The Ba'al Shem Tov pressed him to know more, until finally the man agreed to tell his story.

"Tonight we are holding a vigil in the house, because tomorrow, with God's help, my newborn son will be circumcised. This is my fifth son. All his brothers died on the eve of their circumcisions, at midnight, without having been sick. So, I'm petrified that some disaster will happen to him tonight, as happened to his brothers."

"Fear not!" replied the Ba'al Shem Tov. "Go ahead and prepare for tomorrow's circumcision. I promise that the child will live. No harm will happen to him tonight."

The father was still afraid. But when he heard these words, he said, "If it turns out as my master says, I will give him half my wealth and will give thanks to the Holy One, Blessed he be, all the days of my life."

"I don't want wealth," the rabbi answered. "But you must not delay giving charity to ransom his soul. Now, call two strong men to stand next to the baby's cradle with an open sack in their hands. One man should mind on one side, holding the sack, with the second man holding the sack on the other side. But they have to be careful not to doze off for even a moment."

Turning to his disciples, he instructed them to sit at the table and learn Torah. Then, as he went to lie down on the bed and rest, he spoke to the men standing by the baby's cradle: "If you feel that something has fallen into the empty sack, close it up instantly, and tie it firmly with a cord. Then come wake me up, and I'll tell you what to do."

The men did as they were told. Then, just at midnight the candles started to flicker suddenly. The disciples did everything they could to block the draft that was extinguishing the candles. While they were doing this, the two men who were watching the child saw a weasel in the sack. Without delay, they closed it, and tied it firmly and went to wake the rabbi.

When he got up, he asked the men whether they had tied the mouth of the sack tightly. Then he said, "Each of you take a stick and beat the sack with all your might."

They did this until he gestured to them to stop. Then he told them to untie the sack and throw it outside with the weasel in the sack.

After doing this, they went to check whether the baby was all right and to get ready for the circumcision. When morning came, they prayed the *Shaharit* service. Then they brought out the baby and gave the Ba'al Shem Tov the great honor of being the *sandek*, holding the baby while the circumcision was performed exactly as prescribed.

After the ceremony, the father asked the Ba'al Shem Tov to stay for the feast. He added that first he had to bring sweetmeats from the circumcision festivities to the lord of the village, a very evil man of whom he was mortally afraid.

"Go in peace," said the rabbi.

The father went to the lord of the village. He found him indisposed, lying in his bed, the marks of a brutal beating visible on his face. The lord received him cordially, though, and asked, "Who is that man staying in your house?"

"He's a Jew from Poland who came to stay with me last night. He saved my son from death."

"Hurry home," said the lord, "and tell your guest to come see me today, without fail!"

The tavern keeper left the lord's house quite upset, terrified that he might be the cause of some disaster. When he got home, he begged the rabbi not to be angry with him and told him what had happened at this lord's house. He advised the rabbi not to go but to send his servant to say he had no time to accept the invitation, since he was leaving the village immediately.

"I'm not afraid of him," replied the Ba'al Shem Tov. "I will go see him."

After the feast, the rabbi went to the lord of the village, who said, "I knew you were the one who did this to me," the lord told him. "You got the better of me only because you caught me unaware, when I wasn't expecting it. If you want to match your sorcery with mine, to see who is greater in that art, wait until I recover. Then we'll see who's stronger."

"So be it," the rabbi replied. "But now I must hurry on my way. Let's set a day when you'll come with all your friends and I'll come with all my disciples to match our powers and see who's stronger. But there is one thing you should know: I'm not a sorcerer. I'm an ordinary God-fearing man and not afraid of sorcery."

So, they set a day. The rabbi agreed to come back then and continued his journey. When the appointed day came, the Ba'al Shem Tov traveled to the village with all his disciples. As soon as they arrived, they turned aside into a broad valley near the village. There the rabbi drew two circles, one inside the other. He stood in the inner circle; his disciples, in the outer circle. "Stand there and watch my face closely," he warned them. "If you see any change in it, set your thoughts on repentance and don't take your attention off me for even a moment."

The lord of the village came with all his fellow sorcerers. He too drew circle, and the two groups stood facing each other all day. The lord of the village called up hordes of snakes and lizards and beasts and wild animals who came bellowing toward the Ba'al Shem Tov and his disciples. But when the creatures reached the outer circle, they vanished as if they had never existed.

The sorcerer repeated the attack again and again, with variations. Once he sent wild animals; another time dogs; and yet another time snakes. But when they reached the boundary, they were unable to penetrate the circle. Seeing this, the sorcerer gathered all his remaining strength and sent a vast herd of wild boars against them, snorting fire from their nostrils. This time, the first circle was breached.

Seeing their master's face alter, the disciples concentrated on thoughts of repentance and called to God. And with God's help, the beasts disappeared before they could reach the second circle. Three times the sorcerer did this, before he faltered. Then he said to the rabbi, "My strength has failed. Take my soul. I knew that you would kill me and that none could save me from you."

"Didn't I tell you before," said the rabbi, "that I am not a sorcerer like you. I am only the Ba'al Shem Tov. If I had wanted to take your soul, you would have long since been a mutilated corpse. The night you came to kill the tavern keeper's son, I could have turned you into a pile of bones. But I spared your life so you would know that there is a living God in the world and that all who serve him truly and with a perfect heart need not fear sorcerers."

Suddenly the rabbi broke off his speech. He stood there thinking for a bit and then added: "But to show you the power and might of the Lord, look straight up into the vault of the Heaven now."

The sorcerer looked up into the sky and saw two crows flying down. Landing on his head, each one of them pecked out one of his eyes. Blind for the rest of his life and deprived of his sorcerer's powers, he could harm no one.

Thus may all your enemies perish, O Lord.

The City without Jews: A Novel about the Near Future (1924)

Hugo Bettauer

Part One

Chapter I. The Anti-Jewish Law

A solid human wall, extending from the University to the Bellaria, surrounded the beautiful and imposing Parliament Building. All Vienna seemed to have assembled on this June morning to witness a historic event of incalculable importance. Businessmen and laborers, fashionable ladies and women of the people, half-grown boys and old men, young girls, little children, invalids in rolling chairs—all were intermingled, shouting, debating, and perspiring. And every now and then someone suddenly felt the urge to deliver a speech before his neighbors, every now and then there burst forth the cry: "Throw out the Jews!"

Ordinarily it happened at such demonstrations that people with hooked noses or conspicuously black hair were given a thorough beating. But this time nothing of the sort occurred, for not a Jew was in sight; and the cafés and banking-houses of the Franzensring and Schottenring sagely considering all possibilities, had closed their doors and pulled down their shades.

Suddenly a deafening roar filled the air.

"Hail Dr. Karl Schwertfeger—Hail, hail, hail!
Hail the liberator of Austria!"

Slowly an open automobile rolled through the human mass as it receded to make way. In the car sat a powerful old man, his massive skull covered with unruly tufts of white hair. He took off his soft gray hat, nodded to the jubilant crowd, and twisted his face into a smile. But it was a sour smile, somehow belied by the two furrows that ran downward from the corners of his mouth. And the expression of his deep-set gray eyes seemed somber rather than joyful.

Laughing girls crowded forward, swung themselves on the running-board; one tossed flowers to the great man, another, bolder, threw her arms around Dr. Schwertfeger's neck and kissed him on the cheek. The chauffeur, apparently familiar with his master's reaction to such emotional outbursts, made the car give a lurch forward, so that the girls were suddenly thrown off backward. But they were not hurt, for a dozen arms stretched out to catch them as they fell.

Within the Parliament Building, however, the vociferous enthusiasm of the street did not prevail; in its place was feverish excitement, too intense to be expressed aloud. The deputies, not one of whom was missing, and the ministers and ushers went about in anxious silence; and even the overcrowded galleries did not make the slightest noise. Only whispers issued from the press tables, where careless ease had always been the rule. And a definite territorial division had been made. The compact Jewish majority of the reporters had crowded its chairs together, while the representatives of the Christian-Socialist and German-Nationalist papers formed a group of their own. Formerly the Jewish and Christian newspapermen had mingled freely. In their profession they were not partisans, but only colleagues. Furthermore, since the Jewish journalists generally had more news and were able to turn it to better account, their anti-Semitic brothers depended on them a good deal. Today, however, the Christians cast malevolent glances toward the Jews; and when little Karpeles of the *Weltpost*, who had just come in, greeted Dr. Wiesel of the *Wehr* with a friendly "Good morning," the latter turned his back without responding.

Newspapermen continued to pour in; among them were representatives of the foreign press, just arrived in Vienna for this occasion.

"Impossible to move," growled Herglotz, of the *Christian Tag*, whereupon a bearded little fellow with a tremendous waistline replied: "Only a few days more, then we'll have plenty of room here!"

Subdued coughs, laughter, and smiles on the one side, an exchange of significant glances on the other. A blond, pink-cheeked young man bowed slightly to the left and to the right.

"I'm Holborn, of the *London Telegraph*. Got here just an hour ago, and don't know where I am. Arrived in London day before yesterday after a six months' stay in Sydney and an hour later I was in the train again, on my way to Vienna. Our managing editor, the old fool, told me nothing, but only said: 'Plenty of excitement in Vienna these days—they're throwing out the Jews. Go there and cable me till the wires burn up!' So it would be very kind of you, I'd be eternally grateful, if you'd tell me what it's all about."

This speech had been delivered in so droll an Anglicized German that the tension was somewhat relieved. Gesticulating violently, Minkus of the *Tagesbote* took hold of his English colleague and began:

"Now, I'll explain everything to you. . . ." But Dr. Wiesel did not let him continue. "You will pardon me, but it would be more appropriate for this explanation to come from our side."

A menacing tone, ominous emphasis on the word "our."

And in a trice Holborn was in the Christian corner, where, in a few terse sentences, Wiesel sketched the situation:

"As to what is going to happen, you will hear that shortly from the lips of our Chancellor, Dr. Karl Schwertfeger, who will go into the details of the law for the expulsion of all non-Aryans from Austria. Briefly, the history is as follows: After our so-called financial recovery, which lasted for two years, Austrian money again fell into a disorganized state. And when the value of the krone had fallen to the two-hundredth part of a centime, chaos set in. Ministries fell one after the other, disturbances occurred every day there was looting of shops, to say nothing of pogroms—the populace, desperate, stopped at nothing, until finally new elections had to be called. The Social-Democrats entered the campaign with their old program, while the Christian-Socialists swarmed around their gifted leader, Dr. Karl Schwertfeger, whose rallying cry was: Throw out the Jews from Austria! Now, as you may be aware," Holborn nodded, though he knew nothing about it, "the result of the elections was a complete collapse of the Social-Democrats, Communists, and Liberals. Even the working masses voted for 'throwing out the Jews,' and the Socialist party, formerly the strongest, barely salvaged eleven seats. The Pan- Germans, however, who came out with flying colors, had also taken up the cry of 'Throw out the Jews.'

"So, with his genius, his fearless energy, his bold impetuosity and eloquence, Dr. Schwertfeger succeeded in obtaining the consent of the League of Nations for this great expulsion of the Jews; for he had placed before the League the alternative of the annexation of Austria to Germany or a free hand in this matter. And now Schwertfeger is to propose the law, which will certainly be passed. You are, therefore, witnessing a historic . . ."

Suddenly, calls of "Hush!" came from all sides. Wiesel could not continue, for the Presiding Officer of the House, a red-whiskered Tyrolese, flourished his gavel and gave the floor to the Chancellor.

Sepulchral silence, through which the humming of the ventilators sounded weirdly. A suppressed cough, the rustling of papers in the press gallery—everything was heard distinctly.

Inordinately tall although his head was thrust forward and his shoulders stooped, the Chancellor stood on the platform. His hands, clenched into fists, rested on the desk; from under the bushy gray brows his keen, glittering eyes sped over the auditorium. He stood thus, motionless, until suddenly, throwing back his head, he began with the powerful voice that had always commanded attention at even the most turbulent meetings:

"Ladies and gentlemen, I am about to propose the law and the amendments to our constitution that purpose nothing less than the expulsion of the non-Aryan—to be precise, of the Jewish—elements from Austria. Before I proceed to this, however, I wish to make some purely personal remarks.

"For five years I have been the leader of the Christian-Socialist party; and for a year I have been Chancellor, having been chosen for this position by an overwhelming majority of this House. During these five years the so-called liberal papers and the Social-Democratic sheets—in short, all the papers edited by Jews—have depicted me as a sort of bugbear, a rabid Jew-hater, a fanatic enemy of the Jews and everything Jewish. Just today, when the power of this press is approaching its irrevocable end, I feel compelled to explain that all this is not true. Yes, I have the courage to state today, from this platform, that I am much more a friend than a foe of the Jews!"

The hall rustled with whispers like a field from which a flock of birds is rising.

"Yes, ladies and gentlemen, I like the Jews. Before I entered the seething arena of politics I had Jewish friends; in the lecture halls of our Alma Mater I sat at the feet of Jewish teachers whom I revered, and still revere. And I am always ready to recognize—yes, to admire—the native virtues of the Jews, their extraordinary intelligence, their strivings for higher things, their model family life, their internationalism, and their ability to adapt themselves to any environment!"

Cries of "Hear! Hear!" were audible, the deputies and visitors became tense with excitement. The English journalist, who had not understood everything, curiously asked Dr. Wiesel whether the man down there wasn't the spokesman of the Jews.

The Chancellor went on.

"In spite of this, or, rather, because of it, I became more and more convinced, as the years passed, that we non-Jews can no longer live together with the Jews, that we must either bend or break, that we must give up either our Christian ways, our own life and customs, or the Jews. Ladies and gentlemen, the trouble is simply that we Austrian Aryans are no match for the Jews, that we are ruled, oppressed, and violated by a small minority because this minority possesses qualities which we lack. The Latin peoples, the Anglo-Saxons, the Yankees, even the North Germans and the Swabians can digest the Jews because these nations are their equal, if they do not surpass them in agility, tenacity, energy, and business sense. We, however, cannot digest them. With us they always remain a foreign element that spreads over our entire body and finally enslaves us. The vast majority of our people comes from the mountain country; it is a simple and sincere people, dreamy, playful, given to impractical ideals, fond of music and calm contemplation of nature, upright and pious, thoughtful and good. These are marvelously beautiful qualities that can give rise to a splendid culture and a wonderful new life, if they are given free play and an opportunity to develop. But the Jews among us did not permit this quiet development. With their uncannily keen intelligence, their worldliness and freedom of tradition, their catlike versatility and their lightning comprehension—with all their faculties, accentuated by centuries of oppression, they overpowered us, became our masters, and gained the upper hand in all our economic, spiritual, and cultural life."

Shouts of "Bravo!" "Quite right!" "That's so." With his bony right hand, Dr. Schwertfeger raised the glass to his thin lips, as his half-ironic, half-satisfied gaze swept the hall.

"Let us look at our little Austria today. In whose hands is the press, and therefore public opinion? In the hands of the Jew! Who has piled billions upon billions since the ill-starred year 1914? The Jew! Who controls the tremendous circulation of our money, who sits at the director's desk in the great banks, who is the head of practically all industries? The Jew! Who owns our theaters? The Jew! Who writes the plays that are produced? The Jew! Who rides about in automobiles, who revels in the night resorts, who crowds the cafés and fashionable restaurants, who covers himself and his wife with pearls and precious stones? The Jew!

"Ladies and gentlemen! I have said, and still maintain, that essentially, when considered objectively, the Jew is an excellent individual. But is not the rose-beetle with its iridescent wings essentially also a beautiful, excellent creature? And notwithstanding this, is it not destroyed by the careful gardener who is more interested in the rose than in the beetle? Is not the tiger a splendid animal, strong, fearless, intelligent? And do we not hunt it down because the struggle for our own existence necessitates it? Only from this standpoint can we Austrians view the Jewish problem. Either we, or the Jew! Either we, who make up nine-tenths of the population, must perish, or the Jew must go! And now, when at last we have the power, we would be fools, nay, criminals—we would be sinning against ourselves and our children were we not to make use of this power to expel the small minority that is destroying us. Here we cannot consider high-sounding words like humanity, justice, and tolerance—for our existence, our very lives and the lives of future generations are at stake! The past few years have increased our wretchedness a thousand-fold; our state is completely bankrupt, and we are headed for disaster. In a couple of years our neighbors, under pretense of restoring order here, will pounce upon us and tear our little country to pieces. But the Jews, unaffected by all these events, will continue to thrive and flourish and to be the masters of the situation. And since they have never been Germans in their heart and soul, they will remain the masters when conditions will have changed and we are slaves!"

Fearful agitation prevailed throughout the house. Savage cries burst forth: "That must never be! Let us save ourselves and our children!" And from the street came the echo, from ten thousand throats: "Throw out the Jews!"

Dr. Schwertfeger let the excitement run its course, shook hands with his colleagues in the ministry, and then spoke on the enforcement of the law. For the sake of humanity, and in compliance with the conditions specified by the League of Nations, great consideration and absolute justice would be the rule. Everyone was to have the right to take along as much of his property as consisted of cash, valuable papers, and jewelry, as well as to sell his real estate and business as he pleased. Enterprises that could not be sold would be taken over by the state; the net profits for the past year, as entered in the tax report; being taken as five percent of the total value. Thus, if an enterprise had produced a net profit of half a million in the past year, it could be redeemed for ten million.

The Chancellor's lip curled in a malicious smile.

"In the calculation of these amounts, as well as in giving permission for the taking along of cash, we shall of course be guided by the tax returns only. Thus, a man who has claimed to have no money will not be permitted to take any with him; and if he nevertheless has some property, it will be confiscated. If a man has given the net profit of his business as half a million, he may take along ten million, even though it should develop that his actual income was ten times more. In this way many a sin will receive bitter retribution," observed the speaker, as the hall rocked with laughter. Then he continued: "Those who do intellectual work and men who receive a definite salary, who really own no property—like physicians—will, on their departure, receive from the state the amount they designated as their yearly income on their tax report. So, that if a physician has stated his income to be three hundred thousand kronen, he will receive this sum. To prevent any further evasion of taxes the law includes the draconian provision that any attempt to take out sums greater than those permitted is to be punished by death. Similarly, Jews or those of Jewish origin who attempt to continue staying in Austria secretly do so under pain of death.

"The law is to be enforced as follows: 'Unregistered merchants, retail-dealers, and so-called commission agents must leave Austrian territory within three months of the passage of the law; registered proprietors of firms, clerks, civil service employees, and manual laborers, within four months; artists, scholars, physicians, attorneys, and the like, within five months. Directors of corporations, banks, and industries that paid taxes on an income of more than two hundred million kronen in the past year are given six months' time.'

"And now I come to an important point, to which I will ask you to give close attention. As you know, the law of expulsion applies not only to Jews and converted Jews, but to those of Jewish origin as well. This term includes the children resulting from mixed marriages. If, for example, a Christian woman of pure Germanic-Aryan stock has married a Jew, he and the children of this marriage are to be expelled, while the wife is permitted to remain in Austria. After mature deliberation, however, the government has decided to consider the grandchildren of mixed marriages as being not of Jewish origin, but Aryan. Thus, if a Christian has married a Jewess, the children will be expelled, but the grandchildren may remain in the country, provided that their parents have not mixed again with Jewish blood. This, however, is absolutely the only concession made by the law; no other exceptions can be permitted.

We have received requests from many quarters to provide for certain exemptions—that, for example, the law should not apply to people who have passed a certain age, to invalids, and to Jews who have performed special services for the state.

"Ladies and gentlemen! Had I listened to such counsel the whole law would have become a farce. Jewish money and influence would have worked day and night, tens of thousands of exceptional cases would have been fabricated, and fifty years from now we would be in exactly the same position as today. No! There will be no preference, no exception, no pity, no passive collusion. The government will place splendid hospital trains at the disposal of the sick and infirm; and only those Jews whom a medico-judicial investigation finds absolutely incapable of transportation will be permitted to await their recovery or death here."

Dr. Schwertfeger bowed slightly and sank heavily into his chair. But his last pronouncement had had a peculiar effect. Only a few cheers came from the audience; a distinct, almost palpable cloud of uneasiness hung over the house; many faces reflected unmistakable terror and anxiety; there was some disturbance in the gallery, and a woman shrieking, "My children" fell in a swoon. And though thunderous applause followed the Chancellor's speech, yet the little group of Social-Democrats shouted in unison: "Shocking! Shameful! An outrage!"

And now the red-bearded Presiding Officer gave the floor to Professor Trumm, the Finance Minister. He was a small man, dry and shriveled as a prune, endowed with a treble voice; and his speech suffered occasional interruptions that served to free his tongue when it became caught between his gums and the upper edge of his dental plate. He discussed the financial aspects of the expulsion law before a deeply interested house. The redemption of Jewish concerns and real estate would make heavy gains not only on the private capital of the Christians but on the finances of the state as well. Thousands of billions of kronen would barely suffice; and it had to be recognized that one of the first results of the expulsion of the Jews would be all sorts of financial difficulties.

"But, heaven be praised," here the Finance Minister crossed himself, "we will not stand alone in the dark days to come. I bring to the House the joyful tidings that the true Christians of all the world have united to help us. Not only has the Austrian government conducted international negotiations for months, but the Pius Association has been making unobtrusive but effective propaganda that is bearing splendid fruit. The League of the Active Christians of the Scandinavian Countries, whose members include many powerful bankers and merchants, places at our disposal great credits in Danish, Swedish, and Norwegian money. The American industrial king, Jonathan Huxtable, one of the richest men of the world and a zealous champion of Christianity, has declared his readiness to invest twenty million dollars in Austria. The Christian League of France is mobilizing a hundred million francs. In short, billions of kronen will have to be sent out of the country to let in a flood of billions in gold!"

Tremendous enthusiasm throughout the house. Several dozen deputies, hurriedly leaving their seats, dashed to the telephones to give their banks orders to sell foreign money. The switchboard could hardly manage the rush of calls for "Karpeles & Co.," "Veilchenfeld & Son," "Rosenstrauch & Butterfrass," "Kohn, Cohn, & Kohen," and all the rest of the great banking houses. And while the Finance Minister, who had wasted an entire minute to free his imprisoned tongue, went on with his speech, Holborn, the Englishman, grinned as he told the other newspapermen:

"Jonathan Huxtable is a fine fellow! He's been raving and ranting against the Jews ever since his wife eloped with a Jewish prize fighter. He's a strict prohibitionist, but he gets drunk every day on a cordial he buys from his druggist. Drinking a whole bottle of Eau de Cologne in one breath is said to be nothing unusual for him. And if he's going to invest twenty million dollars here, he surely expects to make fifty."

Dr. Wiesel's face expressed disapproval, while the Jewish reporters quickly took down notes for some last malicious items. Speakers, pro and con, came forward. The Social-Democrats attacked the law; but when Weitherz, their leader, in calm and measured terms expressed his indignation and called the proposed measure a disgrace to humanity, a terrific uproar arose, the galleries threw keys and crumpled paper at the Social-Democrats, a fist fight ensued, and the small opposition left the hall under protest.

Pastor Zweibacher lauded Dr. Schwertfeger as a modern apostle, who deserved canonization; the Pan-German deputies Wondratschek and Jiratschek, however, discussed the law from the racial point of view only, and Jiratschek, who spoke with a pronounced Bohemian accent, wept with emotion and closed with the words: "Wotan is among us!" The last speaker, received with cries of "Hep! Hep!" and jeering "Ai-wai" calls, was the solitary Zionist deputy, the engineer Minkus Wassertrilling. With folded arms the tall, slender, handsome young man waited until order was restored, and then said: "My dear disciples of the Jew who, in order to save humanity, was foolish enough to let himself be crucified!" Vehement interjections of "Throw out the Jews!"

"Yes, gentlemen, I join your cry of 'Throw out the Jews!' And I will gladly cast my vote in favor of this law. We Zionists welcome it, for it falls in line with all our aims and tendencies. About half of the five hundred thousand Jews expelled by this law will unite under the Zionist standard, and I know that the others will be received with open arms in France and England, Italy and America, Spain and the Balkan countries. I am not worried about the fate of my people—what your spiteful malice and stupidity intend as a curse will become a blessing."

The hooting that again broke out drowned the rest of his speech, and finally the Zionist also was pushed out of the hall.

When the roll was called, therefore, the law was passed unanimously; and that same day it was rushed through the committee and the second and third readings. Late at night, when the deputies were at last able to leave the hall, they saw Vienna illuminated for a celebration. Red and white flags waved over the public buildings, fireworks were displayed, and until long after midnight processions marched past the Chancellor's palace to cheer Dr. Schwertfeger and extol him as the liberator of Austria.

Chapter II. Herr Schneuzel and His Son-in-Law

The next morning was a Sunday, and Antonius Schneuzel, member of the National Assembly, the Municipal Council, the Board of Overseers of the Poor, and the Board of Trade, appeared at the family breakfast table a good deal the worse for his zealous celebration of the victory; and immediately he sensed trouble in the air. His wife's nose seemed longer than ever, a signal of approaching storm; the eyes of his daughter, Frau Corroni, were swollen; her husband, the young business man Alois Corroni, greeted his father-in-law with an impudent and scornful smile; and when Herr Schneuzel, worried and confused, let his little eyes rove about the table, his two grandchildren, Lintschi and Hansl, burst into a fearful howl.

"Why, what in the world is the matter?" he asked.

Frau Schneuzel held her arms akimbo.

"What's the matter, you idiot? Nothing's the matter, except that you, you old fool, have helped drive your daughter and your grandchildren out of the country!"

"Why, how in the world—" stammered Herr Schneuzel.

But the horrible truth began to dawn upon him. Quite right, in the course of the years he had entirely forgotten that in his early youth his son-in-law, Herr Alois Corroni, had borne the name of Sarni Cohn, that he had been able to stand on his own feet when he was received into the arms of the Church. And now he would have to get out, and with him would go the children, who were of Jewish origin!

"It's a mean trick," Frau Corroni sobbed into her handkerchief. "What'll I do with the children now? Perhaps you want me to emigrate to Jerusalem, you beastly father, you?"

"It really is going a little too far," Herr Corroni now declared, emphasizing every word, "to chase a man of my sort out of the country like a mad dog. I dare say I am at least as good a Christian as a thousand others who spend all day in the barroom. What good is it to drive out a man like me, whose children are growing up in the Christian faith!"

Herr Schneuzel wanted to reply and muttered something about a great and sacred cause, about principles that could give no consideration to individual cases. But no sooner had he begun than he felt his spouse seizing him by his thin hair, nor did she relax her grip before she had pulled out a good handful of the scantier foliage.

"Imbeciles, that's what you are, all of you! You can go to hell, you and your Christianity! Hasn't Loisl always been good to our Annerl? Didn't he give her a muskrat coat, doesn't he raise the children like princes? You should thank God she got a Jew, and not a fellow like you, a drunkard and rowdy!"

"I'm not going to Jerusalem," Lintschi now wailed, while Hans grasped the opportunity to snatch the sugar roll from grandfather's plate. When the uproar was at its height Pepik, the cook, came in, resolutely cleared the table, and calmly announced: "I'm goin'! I'm goin' to marry my Isidor. He's a clerk in the co-op, and if he has to get out, I'll get out with him. I wouldn't care if the deputy and the Chancellor would all hang themselves."

After the excitement had died down, Herr Corroni gave a calm explanation of the situation.

"Of course, I'm not even dreaming of emigrating to Palestine, if for no other reason than they wouldn't let me in since I'm a converted Jew. Now, I have a brother in Hamburg—Uncle Eduard, you know; and though he is angry with me because of my conversion, he won't leave me in the lurch now. Jews don't forget family ties, thank God." (These words were punctuated by a cutting glance at Schneuzel.) "And there I will build a new future for myself and my family—unless Annerl would prefer to stay with you."

Whereupon Frau Anna, tired and faded as is usual after fifteen years of married life, suddenly recovered the pink cheeks of her youth, and, fondly throwing her arms about the neck of Alois Corroni (né Sarni Cohn), kissed him as a bride kisses her bridegroom, and really looked like a girl again. And finally, Herr Schneuzel, desperate and altogether upset, had to promise to give his son-in-law a million to take along to Hamburg as a sort of cornerstone for his new future.

In the afternoon Schneuzel, member of the National Assembly, the Municipal Council, and the Board of Overseers of the Poor, went alone to a Sievering bar, and began to fight with a crowd that was still shouting "Throw out the Jews!" And he broke his bottle over the head of one of the shouting celebrants. Consequently, he received a most terrible thrashing.

Chapter III. At Closing Time

A talk in a niche beside a window of the Café Wogerer, opposite the Stock Exchange, between Herr Strauss, proprietor of a banking house, and his nephew, Siegfried Steiner, a medical student. Similar conversations were taking place at every table; and on this day, far from being boisterous, they were carried on almost inaudibly, with much gesturing.

The young man was shaking his uncle's hand. "I thank you, dear Uncle, for promising to take me to London with you. That's a great consolation for me. Between ourselves, I'd never go to Jerusalem—never! Not for me! Nothing but Jews—I can't imagine it!"

The uncle smiled a slow smile. "I don't give a damn about Jerusalem myself. In London I'll go into partnership with my old friend Moe Seegward, who has a fine brokerage house there."

Siegfried Steiner leaned forward and whispered: "I'd like to know one thing, Uncle. You surely didn't enter the actual amount of your fortune and income in your tax report. So how are you going to get your money over there, considering that since yesterday all our letters are being censored?"

The uncle let the ashes of his cigar fall on his vest. "Chammer! Why does one have Christian friends? I went to see Schuster the manufacturer today, and confidentially I gave him a billion in securities and cash, for which he gave me a draft on a London bank. Of course, the *ganef* doesn't do it for nothing, but makes quite a bit on this transaction."

The nephew nodded with satisfaction; and at thirty other tables various other conversations also ended with nods of satisfaction. An old Jew in a caftan, and with corkscrew curls, came in and went from table to table, repeating his little speech: "Give alms to an old Jew who lost everything he had in the Lemberg pogrom!"

Someone called from one of the tables: "Tell me, old man, where'll you go now?"

The old fellow wagged his head. "Herrleben, if I could get out of the burning Lemberg Ghetto and reach Vienna, I guess I'll find some place to go to from Vienna. It's all the same to me whether I schnorr in Vienna, or Berlin, or Paris. Only I won't talk about the pogrom any more, but I'll tell them how they threw out an old Jew like me. —Tell me, Herrleben, do you think it's good to buy Siemens before the Exchange closes?"

Chapter IV. A Shot

A group of friends had gathered in the villa of Herbert Villoner, the author, in Alt-Aussee. Well-known men of letters, painters, sculptors, musicians, publishers. As a rule, they went to the country resorts only after the summer had reached its height; but this year they had fled from the city in June, to escape as much of the filthy spray of Viennese politics as possible.

The evening meal was over. They were sitting on the terrace, leaning back in their wicker chairs; the lovely lake lay below, mirroring the moon—into the motionless air curled wreaths of cigarette smoke. Everyone was absorbed with his own thoughts, until Villoner broke the profound silence.

"So there is no doubt that most of us are spending our last summer in Aussee, and will have to shake the dust from our feet and proceed into foreign lands like vagabonds. Odd, isn't it? My father, a famous physician who contributed not a little to the fame of the Viennese medical school, my grandfather, a merchant of Mariahilf, whose family had long been resident there, and myself. Well, they say that my dramas and novels express the essence of Viennese life, that no one has matched my knowledge and descriptions of Viennese youth and the gay young thing. But now all this counts for nothing. I am merely an alien Jew and must get out like some Galician refugee washed into Vienna on a tide of speculation."

"Still," Max Seider, a young poet, said in a low, quivering voice, "you will be able to feel at home even when you are far away from your ungrateful native land. Berlin will receive you with open arms. The intellectuals there are already planning to honor you. You are so strong and mature that you will be able to produce great works wherever you may be. But what can I do? I am only at the beginning, I can live and work only when I stroll through the green Wienerwald, when the graceful outline of the Kahlenberg shows me my way. An inexhaustible fountain of life flows forth from there. I must labor and struggle for every line, for every stanza. I can only do this in Vienna."

"Nonsense," Wallner, a composer, exclaimed angrily. "To hell with Vienna and all the blockheads in it! I'm going to the South of Germany, where I'll rent a little house in the Black Forest and live like a lord with my Lene. Won't we, darling?"

The fair-haired young woman laid her Madonna-like little head on her husband's shoulder, but the shadow of a malicious smile hovered on her voluptuous lips as she exchanged a significant glance with the playwright Walter Haberer. The breast of the latter swelled with triumph. He knew that the composer's wife would stay in Vienna. No one could force her to accompany her husband into exile. And they had agreed that when the husband would at last be out of the way she would become his. Not only she, but all Vienna, all Austria would be his! For all those who had pushed him into the background, all those whose plays were being produced while his grew moldy in the pigeon-holes of the directors' desks—all of them, Villoner and Seider, Hoff and Thal, Meier and Marich, all would have to go away and leave him to rule the realm of the Muses. Frau Lene nodded and smiled at him while her husband lovingly stroked her cheek.

With a thunderous roar of laughter Armin Horch, the great actor, burst forth: "Gentlemen, now it must be told! I, too, will have to leave Austria! For I, whom *The Wehr* and other papers have always extolled as the ideal of Aryan beauty, I must confess to my Jewish descent. My father came from Brody, and his name was not Horch, but Storch!"

Peals of laughter broke out, the mirth became boundless, appropriate anecdotes were told.

"And you, Herr Pinkus, where will you transfer your publishing house?" someone asked the stout little publisher with the bowed legs and the unmistakably Jewish features.

"Me? I'll stay here! Don't you know that I'm a genuine Christian?"

And when everybody laughed, he said, with a serene smile: "All jokes aside, I am an unadulterated goy! My grandfather, Amsel Pinkus, was a cloth dealer in Frankfurt am Main, and a good, pious Jew. But when he fell in love with my grandmother, Christine Haberle, a little singer of Stuttgart, he converted because she wouldn't marry him otherwise. Well, my father also married a Christian girl, so that I'm a third-generation Christian; and therefore, I won't be expelled, although I look and act exactly like my grandfather."

"Long live Pinkus, the Christian," merrily cried the host, and, laughing, they all raised their glasses. Just then, like the lash of a whip, a report sounded from the lake. And Villoner, filled with a strange premonition, cried: "Where is Seider?"

But people were already bringing up the body of the young poet. He had shot himself, down there beside the lake, so that his sensitive, weary soul would not have to starve in a foreign land.

Chapter V. Girls among Themselves

Panic prevailed in Lona's house, in the Gumpendorfer Strasse. Eight young ladies, all superlatively beautiful, had already gathered there, and still the stout housekeeper, Frau Kathi Schoberlechner, had to open the door again and again to let in new arrivals. The drawing room was permeated with a strong aroma of Houbigant, Ambre, Coty Rouge, and cigarettes; golden, red, chestnut, and dusky heads, diamonds and pearls shone and glittered. All were dressed in silks and laces, only Lona wore a fragrant negligée, open in front so that her snow-white bosom almost burst forth; and her stockingless feet were encased in little red mules. Black-haired Yvonne wept as if her heart would break, while red-headed Margit pounded on the table and cried angrily: "We've got to protest! If I ever get hold of one of them deputies, I'll scratch his eyes out!"

"What a dirty trick! What do they expect us to do when they throw out the Jews?"

Yvonne wept more passionately. "And just now, when Fredi Pollak just ordered a new car for me."

"I've been getting ten million a month from Reizes. I've been going with him for two weeks. I'd like to know if those Christian gents will be so free with their money?"

"Y'know, I got that Zwitterbauch from Mahrisch-Ostrau, and that keeps me altogether, and he comes to Vienna only for a week out of every month!"

A voluptuous golden-haired Juno crossed her beautiful though rather thick-set legs so that her blue silk garters peeped out, drank a little glass of Cointreau, and said in a resonant alto: "Children, I think I've had more experience than all the rest of you put together. And all I can say is that, after the Jews are gone, we'll either have to starve or look around for jobs as cloak-room maids in the cafés. Only the Jews leave money behind them, the rest of them all want a lot of loving and no expense! I went with Baron Stummerl, of the Foreign Office, for ten years, and in those ten years, he gave me a gold bracelet, a fur neckpiece, and a thousand gulden. I was lucky. I had Herschmann of the Anglobank at the same time, or I might actually have had to go to work. Since then I've gone in for Jews only!"

Nervously Claire toyed with the diamond-studded gold cross she wore on a platinum chain. "Wonder what Karl will say when I stop getting things from Dr. Baruch!"

New complaints arose while wails filled the air. In the excitement of recent events they had not thought of this: What would become of the friends they loved and supported, after the friends who paid would be gone?

Just then Frau Kathi ushered in one of these friends. Pepi represented the ideal of the well-dressed man, impeccable from his soft gray velvet hat and his hand-knit tie to his tan oxfords and the dark blue silk socks. Sobbing, the charming black-haired Yvonne fell into the arms of her beloved. All greeted him noisily. Indeed, he was pelted with a shower of calls and questions. Calmly Pepi sank back into an armchair, took Yvonne on his knee, pinched the naked calves of Lona (who sat beside him), and, after permitting the girls to put a cigarette into his mouth, observed: "There's nothing to do, my dears. You'll have to leave the country, too!"

"Yes," countered clever, golden-haired Carola, "but where'll you get your passport, and who'll let you in?"

"Very simple," laughed Pepi. "Tomorrow I'll go to the City Hall and renounce all religious affiliations. The day after, I'll go to the Jewish synagogue, assure the Hebrew race of my staunch support, and become a Jew—without the operation, I hope. Then we'll get married, take the money that's coming to us from the government, and settle down somewhere else, as provided by the League of Nations. We'll go to Paris, or Brussels, or some other place where things are lively."

Yvonne laughed through her tears. "Go on! What'll I do in Paris after I'm married?"

"Silly! Nobody will have to know we're married! You rent a flat, find a friend who'll keep you, and I'll take care of your heart as always."

During the next few days the liberal papers reported that hundreds of valiant Christian youths, indignant at the injustice done the Jews, had demonstratively determined that they would convert to the Jewish faith so that they might share the fate of the sorely tried people of Israel.

Chapter VI. Dr. Schwertfeger

On a warm September day the Chancellor, who was also the Minister for Foreign Affairs, was working in the Foreign Office, where he stood on his balcony and looked past the street and watched the doings in the public park. But the movement there seemed less animated than in past years—only a few white-enameled baby carriages rolled over the paths, and in spite of the mild weather, the chairs and benches were almost empty.

Someone knocked at the door, and the Chancellor cried out: "Come in!" Immediately, his departmental chief, Dr. Fronz, entered. At the end of June, shortly after the passage of the expulsion law, Schwertfeger had gone to the Tyrol region to recuperate after the nervous strain caused by the great responsibility and hard work of the previous weeks. For more than two months he lived incognito in a village near the Arlberg. Except for his departmental chief, no one knew his whereabouts, for he permitted no letters or reports to be sent to him, paid no attention to current events, and let Fronz write him only of unusually important occurrences. As a matter of fact, everything had been provided for him. The chief of the Viennese police and the captains of the various districts had received precise instructions, and Parliament had adjourned until autumn. Therefore, Dr. Schwertfeger felt that he wasn't needed at that time and considered it his duty to gather new strength and energy for the tasks to come. He had returned to Vienna this morning, and now Fronz was to give him a detailed report. After various departmental matters had been settled, Schwertfeger sat down before his desk with a thud, took pen and paper for stenographic notes, and seemed very calm and cool, though his every nerve was vibrating with excitement.

"Now, dear friend," he said, "tell me about the visible results of the new law so far. How is our financial situation? I'm entirely in the dark, you know."

Dr. Fronz cleared his throat, and began: "Financially, things aren't running as smoothly as we had hoped. At first the krone rose by leaps and bounds to the hundredth part of a centime in Zurich. Then there were some slight though insignificant fluctuations, and since the end of July the krone has not progressed, but is remaining stationary, in spite of the enormous influx of gold from the treasuries of the great Christian associations and of the banker Huxtable. Strangely enough, our hopes for large payments from the exiles have not materialized as yet. No considerable amounts in either kronen or foreign securities are gravitating toward the revenue offices. It seems that our Christian fellow-citizens include thousands of parasites who unscrupulously take over the excess property of the Jews, taxes on which had been withheld fraudulently; and in return they give the Jews cheques on foreign banks."

"That was only to be expected," said the Chancellor, a contemptuous smile playing on his compressed lips. "All of them, Jew and Christian, are selfish and greedy!"

"The Jew papers mustn't hear that," thought Fronz as he continued. "As I may conclude from the extremely pessimistic report of our Finance Minister, Professor Trumm, the expulsion of the Jews will burden us with enormous debts, payable in gold, while the circulation of our banknotes will not be diminished to any appreciable extent."

"Is everything going smoothly in the liquidation and taking over of the financial houses, banks, and corporations?"

"In this connection everything is in full swing; but unfortunately it seems that our native capitalists are either unwilling or unable to take over the large undertakings, so that the overwhelming majority of the new entrepreneurs are foreigners. Already the Landerbank, the Kreditanstalt, the Anglobank, the Escompte-Gesellschaft, and other great banks have fallen into the hands of Italians, Englishmen, Frenchmen, Czechoslovaks, and the like, as have also our great industrial enterprises.

Only today a Dutch syndicate has taken over the Simmering locomotive factory. Of course, we're devilishly careful that no foreign Jews worm themselves into the country in this way, and every sale contract emphasizes the clause that denies the privilege of either temporary or permanent sojourn in Austria to foreign Jews also. But there is no way of preventing Jews from being included among the stockholders and directors of the foreign companies that are buying up our corporations."

The Chancellor rested his massive round forehead on his bony hand; with a wave of his hand he dismissed all unpleasant thoughts and said evenly:

"Transitory manifestations, which will take care of themselves later. How is the expulsion going on?"

"Exactly as provided by the law. Both the police and the railway bureau are doing excellent work; an average of ten trains full of exiles leaves Austria every day, going in all directions; and so far about four hundred thousand Jews have left the country."

Schwertfeger looked up in amazement. "How can that be? We had intended to exile about half a million. And now, when only a third of the calculated time has passed, we are through with four-fifths of them?"

Dr. Fronz smiled feebly. "We underestimated the great number of converts and of people of Jewish extraction. Today the state police, having a better view of the situation, no longer count with half a million, but with eight hundred thousand, perhaps even a million people who are subject to the law. I might mention, incidentally, that the expulsion has had some unexpected consequences, frequently very unpleasant, sometimes merely grotesque. Ten Christian-Socialist deputies had to be expelled as being of Jewish origin; almost a third of the Christian newspapermen were affected either directly or through members of their families. Our best Christian citizens are steeped in Israel origins. Our oldest families are being torn apart. Indeed, something that has made us the laughingstock of not only the Jewish papers, which of course will badger us to the last minute, but of the foreign press as well. A sister of the princely Archbishop of Austria, Cardinal Rossi, is married to a Jew, and his brother to a Jewess, so that the law robs His Eminence of his closest relatives, including all his nieces and nephews! Perhaps it would be advisable, under these circumstances, to submit to the National Assembly an amendment to the law, providing that in certain cases persons of Jewish origin be permitted to stay."

The Chancellor sprang to his feet and brought down his fist on the desk with such violence that the ink spattered out from its container.

"Never! Never, while I am in office. The granting of any such exceptions would make the entire law a universal joke, international Jewry would celebrate an unprecedented triumph, and all doors would be opened wide to corruption and bribery. You know our regional and government clerks with their open hands and empty pockets. No, there can be no exceptions! The grief of individual families may not shake the foundations of the law! The war that we waged in the name of the Hapsburgs cost a million lives, and no one dared say a word. Compared to that, what is a little inconvenience or vexation for a few thousand, or a hundred thousand persons? I will ask you to instruct the Christian papers accordingly. Better still, let the political press bureau immediately send out a statement on this matter to the papers. And I beg you never again to let yourself become the vehicle for such suggestions!"

Dr. Fronz went pale and bowed.

"Then it would be superfluous for me to tell Your Excellency of the terribly pitiful scenes that occur every day at the departure of the evacuation trains. They are scenes that often become so heartrending that even the mob, gathered about the outgoing trains to abuse the exiles, is moved to silence and tears."

"Such scenes were foreseen and are inevitable! Let the police be instructed immediately to shut down the railroad stations, arrange that wherever possible the trains should leave at night, and see to it that the main stations are not used, but only the shunting stations outside the city. And now one more question: How do people in general view the execution of the law?"

"With tremendous enthusiasm, of course. The police are having a hundred clever plain-clothes men mingle in the crowds and make observations. And they are unanimous in reporting that the Christian population is actually delirious and joyful and is expecting an early change for the better in general conditions, a decrease in the price of food, and a more equalized distribution of wealth. Even among the workers, who are still organized as Social-Democrats, there is great satisfaction with the exodus of the Jews. On the other hand, however, it cannot be denied that the populace is excited and uncertain. No one knows what the future will bring. The masses live from hand to mouth, and there is amazing extravagance among the lower classes, and intoxication is increasing from day to day. An important factor in the prevalent high spirits is the sudden end of the housing shortage. Since the beginning of July, forty thousand apartments, hitherto occupied by Jews, have been vacated in Vienna alone. A direct result of this is a veritable flood of weddings, and the priests have to marry ten or twenty couples at a time."

Schwertfeger, who was a bachelor, nodded and smiled with satisfaction. "I think we've done enough for today. Now that I have a more or less complete view of the situation, I'll settle down with the reports of the various ministries."

A nod, and the departmental chief was dismissed. But Fronz remained in the room and, discreetly clearing his throat, regained the attention of the Chancellor, who had already opened one of his reports.

"I should like to inform Your Excellency that the Municipal Council of Vienna has decided, by a great majority, to change the name of the Schottenring to 'Dr. Karl Schwertfeger Ring,' and that a similar renaming of streets and squares has been decided by three hundred other Austrian municipalities. In Innsbruck they have even organized a monument committee that expects to erect a marble monument to Your Excellency next year."

The Chancellor rose, went over to the balcony, and again looked down at the park. Then he paced furiously twice through the large room before he said: "Put a stop to all such tributes! Let them be postponed until we celebrate the tenth anniversary of the liberation of Vienna from the Jews!"

Chapter VII. A Middle-Class Viennese Home

Christmas Eve in the home of Hofrat Franz Spineder. The little yellow brick house, which the Hofrat had inherited from his grandfather, lay far out in Grinzing, beyond the end of the tramway line. Viewed from the outside, the one-story house with a high gate of green-painted wood and the green shades looked almost primitive; but when one opened the gate and saw the courtyard with its old-fashioned pump, one stopped short, amazed and delighted. The courtyard gradually developed into a gently sloping garden that seemed almost endless. In the summer wallflowers, tulips, roses, and carnations shone in southern splendor; the ornamental garden was full of hundreds of trees bowed to the ground under their burden of apples, pears, apricots, plums, and cherries. But the orchard was not the end of the garden, which rose steeply through a vineyard to a little Old Viennese summerhouse with multicolored windows, perched on the crest of the hill.

Enchanting as the unsuspected garden were the furnishings of the living room. Ancient, comfortable, stiff, and graceful furniture of the Baroque, Congress, and Biedermeier periods, valuable etchings and paintings on the walls, two genuine Waldmüllers, a Schwind in the drawing room, beautiful glassware of many colors, Old Viennese porcelain, sparkling silver in glass cases, and on the sideboard, one only had to close one's eyes to see men and women in the costume of Maria Theresa's time and in the Biedermeier coat.

Franz Spineder was a government official, as his father and grandfather had been before him; however, he was not dependent on his salary from the Ministry of Education, but possessed considerable private means. Even the house with its enormous garden and its valuable furnishings represented millions at the current rate. Besides, his wife came of the Halbhuber family, whose remote ancestors had amassed great wealth as tanners and manufacturers of leather goods. And since the Spineders now had only one child, Lotte, who was just eighteen, they could live comfortably in spite of the high prices and the confusion of the times.

Silently Lotte and Frau Spineder decorated the Christmas tree, attached chocolate cookies, candies, glass balls, and candles to the fragrant boughs. Frau Spineder, a plump, still pretty woman, cast a sidelong glance toward her slender, blonde, strikingly beautiful and charming daughter.

"Lotte! Now you've tears in your eyes again! Think of Papa tonight. He wants to see cheerful faces! And don't make poor Leo's heart any heavier!"

Lotte dropped a little chocolate chimney-sweep so that his head broke off; covering her face with her hands, she leaned on her mother's shoulder and began to sob bitterly.

"My heart's breaking, Mother! You'll see, I won't survive Leo's having to leave the country! Please, Mother—let me go with him!"

Frau Spineder, whose eyes also were moist, tenderly stroked the soft, shimmering golden hair of her daughter. "You can't do it, Lotte! Remember—Papa is sixty, and ever since that dreadful war took our son, he has only you. You can't expect him to let you go out into an uncertain future, however fond he is of Leo. Just think: Leo is going to Paris; because of the depreciation of the krone, we couldn't possibly support you with francs, and you might not afford Paris without Papa's being able to help you. But if he's alone, Leo will make his way, and you're both still so young that you can wait for better times. Now hush—father's coming! And the bell's ringing. I think that must be Leo."

Herr Spineder, who now came into the room to light the candles, was typical of the old Austrian Hofrat at his best. Fond of music and a skilled instrumentalist, highly cultured, well-groomed without and within, always seeking beauty, loving life and affirming it, just, conscientious, and tolerant, sometimes a little narrow-minded, cautious and hesitant. He still wore his beard in the antiquated fashion of Francis Joseph, for he considered it beneath his dignity to make any concession to the new conditions. Though he was a Democrat through and through, and a loyal servant to the Republic, Angeli's beautiful portrait of the emperor still hung over his desk. As he entered the room now, the old gentleman with his snow-white hair and his gentle grayish-blue eyes represented the genuine Old Austrian, whom we soon will know only from books.

"Leo is outside, scraping off the snow from his shoes," said Herr Spineder as he slowly lighted the candles. "Go out to him. I'll prepare the presents and ring when I'm ready."

Frau Spineder paid a brief visit to the kitchen to look after her carp, cake, and apple fritters; but Lotte, throwing her arms about Leo's neck, was weeping silently on his breast.

Leo Strakosch—slender, dark-haired, and smooth-shaven, with sparkling brown eyes that flashed wit and humor—was ten years older than

Lotte. During the last year of the war he had enrolled in the army for his obligatory years' service, and at the front he had met Rudolf Spineder, the Hofrat's son. Soon the young men, who were of the same age, became fast friends. In the last battle of the Piave, Rudolf had been wounded in the head and had spent his last day on this earth in the arms of his friend, but only after begging him to convey a last message to his parents and little sister. This is how Leo had come into the house of the Spineders, and the poor son of a petty commission-agent felt entirely at home in the cultured bourgeois atmosphere. When Lotte grew from childhood into a beautiful blooming girlhood, he determined: "This one, or none!" And Lotte returned the love of the bright, clever, talented young man with all her heart.

Herr Spineder had no objections as he watched the development of this love. Leo Strakosch was an artist, quite extraordinarily successful in spite of his youth; people were beginning to fight over his pictures, and a Leo Strakosch Album, which had appeared about a year before, was even being noticed abroad. Both the Hofrat and his wife rightly admitted to themselves that they could put their child in no better hands than Leo's, whom they gradually came to love as their own son. The fact that Leo was a Jew did not in the least perturb Herr Spineder. His house was a rendezvous for many musicians, authors, and painters, the majority of whom were Jews; and the late attorney Viktor Rosen had even been Spineder's closest friend. A year before, when political circles were just beginning to whisper about the plan of the Christian-Socialist leader to put through an anti-Jewish law, Herr Spineder was unwilling and unable to believe that such a thing could be done. And when events forced him to believe it, his indignation knew no bounds. Greater still was his sorrow over the blow that Leo's imminent expulsion would be for his daughter. But he rejected unconditionally the thought of permitting his Lotte to join Leo in his exile; for here his love for his only child and the egoism of age united to make him absolutely inflexible.

Christmas presents were plentiful; Lotte's parents had been generous, yet she scarcely glanced at the fur scarf, silk stockings, books, and music, but constantly pressed to her trembling lips the little picture of Leo, encased in a gold locket, that he had given her. Now they were all seated about the holiday table, but the mood was mournful rather than festive, and Herr Spineder's efforts to carry on a light conversation met with failure. When the homemade golden wine was poured out, Herr Spineder raised his glass and said, with deep feeling: "To your health, Leo! May good fortune be with you abroad, and may fate bring us all together again before long! I know that you are angry with me, children, but I can't do anything except suffer with you. You see, mother and I have the best part of our lives behind us. I'm on the threshold of old age. So, it's only natural for us to resist the departure of the last sunbeam that shines for us with every fiber of our bodies. But even if we were capable of such almost superhuman selflessness, my sense of duty would not permit it. Were we living in normal times, I would let you go and would say that after all we could spend a couple of months with you in Paris every year. But today, when the krone is almost worthless, that is impossible. Only speculators can indulge in such luxury today; and you know that, although we live well and comfortably, we nonetheless must keep close count of our finances. If Lotte were to go abroad with you now, she would lose her home forever. And not only she, but your children, too, would be homeless exiles, wouldn't know the soil in which their grandparents are buried. And—who knows? Perhaps the day will come when you, Lotte, would be seized with such homesickness that it would crowd out your love for your husband, and your entire being would become embittered with reproach of the man you followed into exile. You are young, both of you. You, Lotte, are almost a child, while you, Leo, are still youthful, and your whole life lies before you. Let a few years pass. Then, perhaps, you will have grown apart, or there will be new developments that will unite you again."

While Lotte and her mother wept inconsolably, Leo, too, raised his glass to Herr Spineder: "Father—I hope I may still call you by that name—I must respect your reasons for refusing to let Lotte go with me; I'd probably do the same if I were in your place. But there is one thing I must say to you, and to Lotte, whom I will always love: From now on my life will be one great struggle! My people, so it is said, possess great tenacity. I will unite all the faculties of my race in myself. With my brain and my heart, with all my power and all my will, I shall work to win

Lotte, by fair means or foul! They may drive me out like a mangy dog, but they cannot kill my will power! And I drink to your health and to our reunion, which will come sooner than any of us dares hope today."

The next day Leo Strakosch left the country on a train occupied mostly by intellectual workers and artists. The Hofrat, Frau Spineder, and Lotte saw him off. Except for them Leo left no dear ones behind him, for his parents had died long before.

Chapter VIII. My Dear Christians

For Vienna the last day of this year was a holiday unparalleled in the history of that gay and carefree city. By mobilizing all means of transportation, by borrowing locomotives from neighboring countries, and by interrupting all other traffic the authorities had succeeded on that day in sending out the last Jews, in thirty enormous trains. In the morning the directors and high officials of the great banks went away, at noon the Jewish journalists and their families. They had stayed to the last second, had composed and edited the evening papers, and had let the new masters take possession of the editorial rooms only after the damp sheets had begun to fly out from the whirling presses. Most of the Viennese journalists had found positions on papers in Germany proper, or on German papers in Czechoslovakia, and many were emigrating to America; and a few had decided to turn to other professions. However, the publisher of the great *Weltpresse*, together with a small staff of collaborators, was moving to London, where he intended to publish a German weekly, to be called *Im Exil*, which would concern itself primarily with Austria.

At one o'clock in the afternoon whistles proclaimed that the last trainload of Jews had left Vienna, and at six o'clock in the evening all the church bells rang to announce that there were no more Jews in all of Austria.

Then Vienna began to celebrate its great festival of emancipation. Red and white striped flags fluttered over a hundred thousand roofs. All the shops were decorated with these colors, and Japanese lanterns burned before every window. On this frosty starlit evening a million people walked over the creaking snow to form processions. Men, women, and children carried lanterns, the various district parades were headed by bands, loud rejoicing filled the air, and again and again one could hear the cry: "Long live Christian Vienna!"

All the parades met at the City Hall. Fairy-like in its splendor, Meister Schmidt's beautiful Gothic building shone as one enormous flame, fed by millions of electric lamps. On a platform the peerless Viennese Philharmonic Orchestra, purged of Jews, and therefore somewhat diminished in numbers, played popular airs, while the Male Choir of Vienna sang its best songs. The People's Hall, the large space before the City Hall, and the Ring from the Schottentor to the Bellaria formed a solid human wall. And at eight o'clock it was no longer a cry, but a howl that rose again and again from a million throats and shook the air.

At last the great moment came. Mayor Karl Maria Laberl with Chancellor Schwertfeger appeared on the balcony. With his powerful voice, audible even at the opposite end of the square, the Chancellor began to speak—briefly, coolly, but all the more effectively: "Fellow citizens, a gigantic task has been completed. Everyone who is not Austrian at heart has left the territory of our small but beautiful country. Now we are alone, a single family. Henceforth, we must depend on ourselves and our own peculiar qualities. With our own power and will, we can now reorganize our clean house, restore decaying walls, and build up falling foundations. Citizens of Vienna and of our entire country! Today we are celebrating a holiday the like of which has never been seen before. Tomorrow marks the beginning of a new year and of a new life for all of us. Tomorrow we may still lean back and meditate. But then we must work as we have never worked before. We must dedicate all our ability to our country—and must make the most of every hour. We must show all the world that Austria can live without the Jews. Nay, more, we must show that we will recover because we have removed the foreign element from our organism. In this solemn hour, fellow citizens, you must promise me faithfully that we will no longer live only for today and its pleasures, but that we will work, work, and do nothing but work until the fruits of our labors have matured."

"We promise!" roared the crowd. Strangers shook each other's hands, men and women wept and laughed in one another's arms, someone sounded the new national hymn and was joined by the entire chorus. And then, spontaneously, the cheer arose as if from one throat: "Hail our Dr. Schwertfeger, the liberator of Austria!"

When the joyful shouting had subsided a little, Mayor Karl Maria Laberl finally had an opportunity to say something. He began his speech with the words: "My dear Christians! . . ."

But the crowd did not hear much more, for the warm south wind that had been blowing through the previously ice-cold night was now followed by a shower. Screaming and shrieking, the mob dispersed, to hurry to the tramway lines through a sea of slush and melted snow.

Part Two

Chapter I. Lotte Spineder to Leo Strakosch, 22 rue Foch, Paris

"Just a year has passed, darling, since I stood in the West Station waving good-bye to you with my tear-soaked handkerchief. And the first Christmas that I have had to spend without you as your betrothed is over. It was very sad again, and Papa, quite worried, said that I would be sick and wretched if I continued giving way to my grief so much. I'm always very pale these days, sleep poorly, suffer much from headaches, and tire so easily. Our family physician thinks it's anemia, and prescribed Guber water for me, but I know that it's only my longing for you that makes me weak and ill. I can't tell you how happy I was over your wonderful album, which arrived just on Christmas Eve. As anyone can see from these marvelous etchings, you're a great artist now; Papa, who understands these things so well, says that you already are one of the great masters and railed against our government, which drives such men out of the country instead of honoring them. Of course, your letter in which you tell of your great success made me very happy, and Papa calculated that the thirty thousand francs that you got for this album amount to hundreds of millions of Austrian kronen. As you know, the krone has again fallen very low. But when I read that you attend so many social functions, and can hardly manage your innumerable invitations to the best houses, my heart missed a beat. Will you forget your poor little

Lotte, surrounded as you are by beautiful Parisian girls? Oh, what will become of us, Leo? When will I be able to put my head on your shoulder again? You know, Leo, the other day a big airplane flew westward over the Kahlenberg, and then I thought that if I only could, I'd fly straight to Paris to you, whether or not my parents would consent. If I knew how to get a passport without anyone's finding out about it, I'd let you send me the money and would run away to you. I know that would hurt Papa and Mama terribly, but my longing for you is so great that I've become very wicked and cruel.

"You ask me to outline for you the state of affairs since the Jews are gone, as the colorless and boring Viennese papers don't give you a real picture of conditions here. Well, I'll try to tell you everything I see myself or hear from others, but you mustn't laugh at me if it sounds silly.

"I suppose you read in the papers all about the great rejoicing and the many parades on last New Year's Eve, after all the Jews had left Vienna and Austria. Well, this mood continued throughout January. Everybody was cheerful, there was celebration after celebration, and again and again the people paraded before the City Hall or the Chancellor's palace, to pay homage to Mayor Laberl or Dr. Schwertfeger. I noticed myself that the people in the tramway were much more pleasant and courteous than before, and Hofrat Tumpel, who comes to see us, you know, the one with the blond beard, whom you never liked, said triumphantly: 'You see, the sunny Viennese temperament, which was so long overshadowed by all the foreign elements, is coming to the fore again.'

"'Fiddlesticks,' growled Papa. 'That's only because the whole thing is a big picnic for the Viennese, and because victuals are cheaper and it's possible to get apartments again.' But Tumpel retorted: 'Oh, no, my friend, that's not all—the Indo-Germanic naïveté of our people is venturing out in the open again!'

"Food really had become much cheaper, for at that time our krone was very high. I remember Mama coming home very happily one day last winter, and telling us that it was possible to cook again, as a pound of lard cost only about twenty kronen. And the apartments brought much joy to the Viennese. Just imagine, suddenly almost every house displayed a sign offering apartments or furnished rooms for rent. People used to go from house to house looking at apartments merely to pass the time. And moving vans were rolling through the streets all day long.

"This lasted till Lent, but then the high spirits subsided. Suddenly there was a good deal of unemployment. The clothing industry was at a standstill. We'd hear of a new failure every minute. The papers said that the honest Christian merchants who had taken over the old Jewish concerns were unable to cope with their task and should be subsidized by the state. But the unemployed raised a rumpus, paraded on the Ring, demolished a couple of stores, broke windows, and finally forced the state to pay them ten thousand kronen a day for the support of their families. Then the krone began to fall, for, as Papa explained, there was a tremendous increase in the circulation of banknotes. Say what they would, the krone soon was lower than ever, and victuals became as expensive as before, if not more so. Today Mama told me, with much agitation, that butter has gone up to a hundred and fifty kronen. Since spring people have been sulky again, and there is much grumbling on the tram. Especially about the profiteers, who are pushing up all the prices. Only, they don't talk about Jewish profiteers, but in general.

"You want to know whether I go to the theater often? Oh, no, dear Leo! Except for the opera there's nothing whatsoever going on in the theater. All the houses are continually playing Ganghofer and Anzengruber, for they're not allowed to produce anything written by a Jew, and the classics don't draw the crowds. For a while they played a good deal of Shaw; but since he declared in an English paper that Vienna has become an international exhibition of asininity, he is taboo. Especially because he also said that he prefers one intelligent Jew to ten stupid Christians. The musical comedy houses are all high and dry. (Do you remember how I laughed when I first heard you use that expression?) It developed, you see, that all of our musical comedies, old and new, were either written or composed by Jews, if not both. Besides, they are short of singers because practically all the tenors had to emigrate. Of course, a few one hundred percent Aryan musical comedies were quickly manufactured, but the audience hissed them, for they were fearful trash. Hofrat Tumpel declared that it was because Christian art is suited only for serious things, not for such frivolous stuff. When he heard this, Papa smiled and said that people would soon realize how well the Jews and Christians complemented each other in Austria.

"When I was in the Graben at noon the other day, it struck me that one does not see nearly as many well-dressed men and women this year as previously. People simply don't indulge in fashions anymore. I must admit, however, that I don't at all miss the repulsive faces of the Jewish profiteers, which used to make you so angry, too. Their place is taken by a great many young fops, who look like peasants and wear impossible clothes, and who infest the drive with their enormous watch-chains and fat diamond-ringed fingers. Altogether it seems to me that nowadays all our transient visitors are peasants. Recently the owner of the Hotel Imperial complained in one of the papers that the guests he has these days go to bed without removing their hobnailed shoes, and they wash their woolen underwear in the bathtubs. If you'd walk through the Kartnerstrasse you'd be amazed at the lack of elegance in the stores today!

"Now I must close, for it's one o'clock in the morning, and I have nothing more of importance to say. Good-bye, my beloved, and invent some way of bringing us together soon—for otherwise I can't live any more. Thousands and thousands of kisses from your disconsolate Lotte."

Chapter II. Rough Woolens—The Latest Style

Silent, morose, with wrinkled brow Herr Habietnik walked through the luxurious salesrooms of the great department store in the Kartnerstrasse, the store that had once been called Zwieback, but now bore the name of Wilhelm Habietnik. Herr Habietnik had been the head salesman in the ladies' tailoring department, and during the great expulsion of the Jews he had succeeded, with the assistance of the Central German Savings Bank, in acquiring the business. Now, as we have said, Herr Habietnik wandered from room to room, exchanging a few words with every aisle manager. His countenance became more and more gloomy, and angry snorts escaped him. He paced without stopping through the pink and white infants' clothes department; he threw a furious glance into the beautiful but entirely deserted pastry shop; and then, rushing into his private office, he summoned his manager, Smetana. "Look here,

Herr Smetana, things can't go on this way. Something has to be done! Easter's almost here, and this used to be our busiest season. The store used to be so crowded that it was impossible to walk through it, and on my rounds today I found three old women, two of whom were hunting together for a chenille scarf that died out long ago, and the third for a cotton petticoat. If this is the best we can do, we might as well shut up shop. Tell me, what's the amount of our deficit since I've taken over the firm?"

The manager smiled wryly: "Oh, I'd say about a billion—that should be fairly close to it."

Herr Habietnik walked about the room in great agitation. "I don't understand it! When the Jews were still here, we had a lot of Christian customers, too! What's become of them?"

Again Smetana, who had formerly occupied a desk in the bookkeeping department, where he had made out the bills, smiled. "Our Christian trade never was anything to brag about, Herr Habietnik; and there always was a catch to those of our customers who really were Christians. They were either the wives or the mistresses of Jews. Let me remind you of the beautiful Countess Wurmdorf, the one who, at the very end, ordered a masquerade costume from us for a million and a half. Very good; but who paid it? Her husband, perhaps? Nothing of the sort! It was the wealthy Eisler, of Eisler and Breislerl and Manoni of the Opera, who's the daughter of an honest-to-goodness Christian washerwoman, and who left a hundred million in cold cash with us every year. Why, the entire Hebrew community had to contribute there! Then there's . . ."

Herr Habietnik stopped him with a wave of his hand. "Nevertheless there were plenty of ladies who had no lovers and still bought quite a good deal. I know more about this because I was the head of the ladies' tailoring department."

"Yes. But you see, Herr Habietnik, even when they weren't Jewish, it was the competition of the Jewish women that helped us. When the Jewesses wore good, stylish clothes the Christian society women did not want to lag behind."

"You may be right there," the head admitted thoughtfully. "The other day I myself heard Frail Artander objecting to our prices and saying, as she left without placing an order: 'Oh, well—thank God we don't need to dress up so much anymore, or to take up every fashionable craze. I'll simply have my old things made over.'"

The memory made Herr Habietnik's blood boil so much that he brought down his fist on the table. "See here, I didn't call you in for a friendly chat, but for advice! That's what you get your high salary for!"

Smetana bowed. "I can give you an idea, Herr von Habietnik. People are going in for coarse woolens and other durable stuffs nowadays, as you saw yourself, there's even a demand for cotton goods. What do you say to filling up a few show-windows with woolens, rough wool skirts, cotton and flannel underwear? And a nice poster to go with it, and a lot of advertisements announcing: Rough Woolens, Cotton, Muslin, and Flannel—the Latest Paris Fashion!"

Seized with a hysterical fit of laughter, Herr Habietnik roared until the tears ran down his cheeks. "Flannels and woolens—the rage in Paris! See here, if Frau Ella Zwieback, who's now living in Brussels, ever hears of this, she'll think we've all gone crazy in Vienna! But all right, I'm sick of this business, and I get scared stiff when I walk through the empty house! Go ahead, make your wool displays! And don't forget the Alpine hats and hob-nailed shoes! As for the pastry shop, it will gradually be converted to a standing bar with hot frankfurters. It's all the same to me, whether we smash this way or that!"

Ten days later one show-window actually displayed red, blue, and printed flannel petticoats, drawers, and knitted vests, another showed cotton stockings and durable shoes, while a third revealed high piles of rough woolens in brown, gray, and black. And the salesrooms were filled until everybody's needs had been supplied, and the salesgirls again yawned or surreptitiously read Engelhorn's novels, which they carried in their black silk aprons.

Chapter III. The Old-Timer

Dr. Haberfeld, the lawyer, sat in the Café Imperial and angrily pushed aside the newspapers that Josef, the old headwaiter, had brought him.

"Tell me, Josef, why is it so empty here? A fellow could freeze next to the stove! In the old days, it was a hard job to find a seat, and now you could stage a derby race here. There's so much room!"

Josef stroked his grayish muttonchops, gazed sorrowfully at the other, wiped off the table with his napkin, and said with a worried air: "The Ring cafés are closing one after the other, and I guess we won't last much longer either. Y'know, Herr Doktor, what the Hebrew gentlemen, beg pardon, the Jews were, they always liked to go to the high-class places, where there's something doing and something to see. But the Christian gentlemen, they go to a coffee-house in the suburbs, and play tarot or billiards there, or else they go to a cheap room in a bar. Yes, sir, times have changed."

"A deaf, dumb, and blind man could see that," growled the lawyer. "Look here, Josef, we two have known each other long enough not to pretend that things are what they aren't. To tell you the truth, I don't like the whole business. Vienna's going to the dogs without the Jews!"

Josef started, and looked around with frightened air.

"Don't worry, nobody will hear us! Vienna's going to the dogs, I say; and when I, a veteran anti-Semite, say that, it's true, I tell you! And I'll tell you something more, Josef. You know, better than anyone else, that after I eat I always have to take some bicarbonate of soda to counteract the wretched acid in my stomach. But if I had no acid in my stomach, I wouldn't be able to eat anything anymore, and I'd kick the bucket. Now, you see, that anti-Semitism of ours was only the soda to counteract the Jews, to keep them from becoming a nuisance! Now we have no acid anymore, that is, no Jews—but only soda; and I'm afraid that'll be the end of us."

Josef, who had listened with breathless and reverential attention, dejectedly flicked a chair with his napkin as he whispered miserably: "Right you are, Herr Doktor, though a fellow doesn't dare say so out loud. I won't be able to work here much longer. In the last six months I've spent half my savings. Between ourselves, Herr Doktor, and because you yourself are a liberal gentleman, so the shoe doesn't fit you, the Hebrew gentlemen, beg your pardon, I mean the Jews, were really generous with their tips!"

Josef cleared away the papers that had been boring Dr. Haberfeld, and, on his request, brought him the Prague and Berlin papers. Then he attended to some other customers who had just come in, and who ordered a pint of wine each.

"Like in a saloon," Josef whispered as he passed the attorney. The latter nodded understandingly, lighted a cigar, and fell to dreaming of the days when he had sat there every evening with a group of Jewish colleagues and, political enmity notwithstanding, had exchanged with them many clever and original ideas.

Chapter IV. Something He Cannot Finish

This year the early spring, which always is marked by political disturbances, again brought some agitated days to Vienna. Unemployment spread to a terrifying extent, factory after factory closed down, and there were numerous failures among the retail establishments. Noisy demonstrations were held everywhere, not only by the laborers, who were partly provided for by the state, but by idle salesmen and salesgirls, bookkeepers and typists as well, until it was decided, at a stormy session of the cabinet, to stop these classes also during the time of their unemployment. The Minister of Finance fought against this measure with all his power, but finally the Chancellor, Dr. Schwertfeger, had his way. Dr. Schwertfeger, who had become even harder, stiffer, and bonier, declared that this additional burden would have to be borne. "We may not let things come to such a pass that the expulsion of the Jews should one day be blamed for misery and distress. So far, we have been able to persuade the *Arbeiter-Zeitung*, whose spirit is still Jewish, though its editors are Christians, to refrain from all criticism of the anti-Jewish law. But if we do not meet the demands of the unemployed businessmen and women, its patience will be at an end, and if only to draw these people into its camp, it will inaugurate a campaign that may prove ruinous; for we haven't yet passed the transitional stage between the reign of the Jews and our complete emancipation."

"And our krone?" sarcastically interjected Professor Trumm.

"We must turn to our Christian friends abroad and explain to them the straits in which we find ourselves. The best thing would be for you to leave immediately for Paris and London."

Trumm laughed harshly. "Quite futile! Even three months ago I returned empty-handed from my first begging tour. Those people will give no more. They haven't even adhered entirely to their solemn promises. You underestimate the influence of our former fellow-citizens, the Austrian Jews, some of whom hold positions in foreign banks today. Besides, the delirious enthusiasm of the Christians has passed, and people are again viewing things from a sober business standpoint. Even Mr. Huxtable has refused. But all right, let us grant the demands of the unemployed clerical workers! However, I wash my hands in innocence."

The next day the cabinet decision was published, and quiet was restored; but the day after the krone suffered a thirty percent fall on the Zurich exchange. And the *Neue Zuricher Zeitung* printed an article that proved statistically that slowly but surely Vienna was forfeiting all significance in Central European trade and losing in its competition with Prague and Budapest. The businessmen of Hungary were as crafty as those of Prague. They received with open arms certain classes of decent Viennese Jews, who brought trade with them. Besides, the buyers of the world, being mostly Jews, cannot go to Vienna anymore, and therefore go to Prague, Budapest, and, particularly, Berlin. The Christian buyers follow their example so that the Austrian manufacturers of finished products such as fancy leather goods, shoes, pottery, and the like must travel abroad with their sample trunks instead of receiving their customers at home. In short, no business worth mentioning carries on in Vienna, despite the unprecedented low status of the krone. This has, of course, put an end to foreign exchange speculation in Vienna, but, it seems, at the expense of the Austrian organism. Instead of accomplishing a great work with his law, the gifted Chancellor, Dr. Schwertfeger, seems to have started something he cannot finish.

As if in substantiation of the truth of this article, the banking world of Vienna became completely disorganized. The hopes of the foreign syndicates that had taken over the great Viennese banks met with bitter disappointment. Their turnover grew less and less, and the departure of the Jews had also caused a considerable decrease in activity on the stock exchange. To avoid a deficit, therefore, the banks were forced to give up one after the other of the thousands of branches with which Vienna was dotted. The organization of the bank clerks protested in vain against this deprivation of some of its members. Then the banks claimed the protection of their embassies, and there was some painful diplomatic intervention that resulted in the Austrian government being forced to take into its service the unemployed bank clerks, when it really needed to diminish its own staff. And the krone fell to the thousandth part of a centime.

Chapter V. Henry Dufresne

On a wonderfully warm, summer-like May morning an automobile, coming from the West Station, drove up before the Hotel Bristol, depositing there an elegant, slender, dark-haired man. With an experienced glance the hotel manager appraised first the heavy leather trunk and hand baggage and then the stranger, whose short imperial beard and turned-up mustache, twirled in a manner then unfashionable in Vienna, lent something exotic to his appearance. "From the south of France," was the manager's conclusion; by a rapid mental process he translated French francs into kronen, and determined the price of a room in accordance with the astonishing result. To the question, put in French, as to whether a room was to be had, he replied, with an effort to suppress an ironic smile:

"Surely, Monsieur—would you like a single room, or a suite with bath? Looking out on the Ring, or to the rear?"

Amazed, the newcomer dropped the monocle he had held in his eye.

"Why, how's this? It used to be impossible to get accommodations anywhere without previous reservation!"

"My dear sir," the manager heaved a profound and sincere sigh, "it must be a year and a half or more since you've been in Vienna. Much has changed since then!"

The stranger understood immediately, nodded sympathetically, asked for a room with a view of the Ringstrasse, and registered: "Henry Dufresne, artist, from Paris, 29 years of age, Catholic, unmarried."

M. Dufresne bathed, changed his clothes, merrily whistling the latest Parisian hit-song all the while, ordered an excellent breakfast to be served in his room, and, about ten o'clock in the morning, left the hotel, in a noticeably jovial mood.

The Frenchman with the little beard seemed to be quite familiar with Vienna, for he swung himself on a tramway car without asking his way; and he appeared to have an excellent command of the German language, for it was evident that he listened with interest to the conversation of those around him. When an old woman began to wail about the high prices, and to revile the authorities in no uncertain terms, M. Dufresne patted her shoulder and, in faultless German and with a Viennese accent, tried to pacify her:

"How can you say such things, granny? We must all feel glad and happy, now that we're rid of the Jews."

But granny now flared up in proper fashion. "The Jews never done me no harm! They could have stayed in Vienna as far as I was concerned. I had such good place with a Jewish gentleman. Whenever he brought home a girl and made a mess, he gave me an extra bill. Live and let live, he always said, and he was right!"

There was laughter on the platform, and a jolly chap with a nose that shone wine-red corroborated this testimony:

"Yeh, I guess a man could say that some of the Jews was real decent folks."

A peculiar smile played about the Frenchman's mouth as he left the car and strolled slowly along the Wahrinierstrasse, later turning into the Nussdorferstrasse. Occasionally he stopped before a show-window, shaking his head as he observed the prices marked on the goods displayed. Finally, he reached the Billrothstrasse, which eventually leads into the vineyard-studded suburbs Sievering and Grinzing. His attention was caught by a sign on the door of a modern apartment house in the Billrothstrasse.

"For rent: Small, elegantly furnished apartment with studio; immediate possession. Apply to janitor."

Quickly making up his mind, M. Dufresne entered the house and sought out the janitor, who, taking him up to the fifth floor by means of an elevator, showed him the apartment. It consisted of a bedroom, a parlor furnished as a den, and adjoining this, a large studio-like room with a skylight. A bathroom was also included.

"How does this apartment happen to be vacant?"

"For heaven's sake," cried the janitor, "why, there are about twenty thousand vacant apartments in Vienna today. An architect, a Herr Rosenbaum, used to live here, but he had to leave with all the rest of the Jews. The landlord bought his furniture, but hasn't been able to find a tenant because there's no kitchen."

Five minutes later a deposit in the shape of a five hundred thousand kronen bill was in the janitor's hand, and M. Dufresne had rented the apartment. Walking more rapidly, he proceeded on toward Grinzing, gaily swinging his cane and saying to himself: "A good beginning—I couldn't have had better luck with the apartment."

But the closer he came to Grinzing, the more excited he became. His cheek flushed, and his merry brown eyes grew feverishly bright. When he reached the Kobenzlgasse, his steps became slower and almost dragged. He seemed to be approaching a fateful moment. Drawing a deep breath, he stopped before the house of Hofrat Spineder and pulled his broad-brimmed gray hat down over his eyes so that only his moustache and beard remained visible. Apparently undecided, he walked back and forth, at times looking nervously at his wristwatch, whose hands pointed to half past eleven. Just as he stood before the green gate again, it opened to let out a maid. At this instant, while the gate was open, M. Dufresne saw a girl come out from the door of the house, to the left of the court—a young girl, dressed in white, her golden head uncovered, a book in her hand; she walked toward the back, through the court and up into the garden.

"Hurrah!" the man with the little beard said to himself, and his plan of action was complete. To the right of the Spineder grounds, separated from them by a wooden fence, lay a long empty lot that had temporarily, since the war, been transformed into a large kitchen garden. It extended upward as far as the summerhouse on the highest point of the Spineder garden. The other edge of the lot was separated by another wooden fence from a side street that opened on the Kobenzlgasse; but this fence was in a dilapidated state, and had broken down entirely in several places. The Frenchman crawled through one of the holes and dashed up through the kitchen garden, catching up with and soon passing the blonde girl walking on his right. Now M. Dufresne had reached the top;

he swung himself over the fence into the garden of Hofrat Spineder, and hid himself behind a massive linden tree that stood in the middle of the vineyard. A few minutes later the girl reached the tree; but she was not able to see the man hidden behind it. Not until, suddenly, something unexpected happened. M. Dufresne called, mezza voce: "Lotte!"

And when Lotte Spineder, startled and confused, stopped to look around, he called again: "It's me, Lotte! For heaven's sake, don't be frightened!"

The next moment the gentleman with the little beard had caught Lotte, who had become white as a sheet and had begun to sway, in his arms. Again and again he pressed his mouth to her cold lips, until the color returned to her cheeks and, trembling all over, she clung to him tightly, as if someone were trying to tear him away from her. And then they sat in the summerhouse, and Leo Strakosch held Lotte on his knee and told his story hurriedly: "Yes, Lotte darling, it's me, and it's for your sake that I grew this horrible beard and mustache. I longed for you so much, I simply couldn't stay away anymore; and when your father wrote me that he was really worried about your health and that he thought it wisest for us to stop writing to each other, since every letter opened the wounds in your heart, then my mind was made up. I confided in a dear and good friend, Henry Dufresne, who would go through fire for me; I grew a little imperial beard like the one he wears, and got all his papers from him: the certificates of his baptism, residence, and military service, and his passport, duly approved by the Austrian embassy in Paris. The beard made us look very much alike, so that he could take a chance on securing his passport with my photograph. And I did not forge his signature, but he imitated mine. Of course, this splendid fellow told all his friends and acquaintances that he was going to Vienna, while he actually went to his uncle's estate, in the south of France, where he will stay a year. And I can live in Vienna as Henry Dufresne just as long as he remains there."

Lotte wept and laughed in the same breath. "I'm so unspeakably happy, Leo! But I'm so afraid for you! You know there's a death penalty for returning here. Suppose they catch you?"

"Impossible, darling! The few friends I had are all Jews and had to leave the country when I did. Besides, the beard serves as an absolute disguise, especially when I wear a monocle. And even if someone were to come and declare that I'm Leo Strakosch, I'd simply deny it, and no one could convict me, for my passport is genuine, and if anyone should inquire of the Paris police he'd be told that Henry Dufresne has gone to Vienna with a regular traveler's passport."

"But what about Papa and Mama?" asked Lotte, after a number of whole-hearted kisses, which she found delightful, mustache and beard notwithstanding.

"Of course, they must not hear a single word about this, Lotte," was Leo's grave reply. "Not that they'd report me. But your father is too much of an official and a Hofrat not to be angry with me for this masquerade; and, besides, he would never permit us to meet, but would advise me to go away again. This way, however, we'll see each other every day, won't we, Lotte?"

And Leo told her of the cozy little apartment he had just rented, and described how they could spend a few hours together there every day, as much time as Lotte would be able to have to herself. At this Lotte blushed to the roots of her hair; but when she looked into the frank and sincere eyes of her lover, she knew that she would be safe with him even if they were all alone.

Leo had to go now, for someone might look for Lotte in the garden any minute. But before they bade each other farewell the girl's white forehead clouded again.

"But now you've given up your splendid career in Paris, Leo! And what will you do to support yourself here in Vienna, with this terribly high cost of living that even Papa is beginning to complain about?"

Leo laughed so merrily and boisterously that Lotte, frightened, put her hand over his mouth, which he construed as an invitation to kiss the rosy little fingers. He did this to his heart's content before he answered:

"What'll I do here, darling? Work, and work hard; and I'll save an enormous amount of money, for when they are reduced to francs, these high Viennese prices are ridiculously low. You see, I've been commissioned by the biggest publishing house of Paris to illustrate a new edition of the collected works of Zola. And the terms are marvelous, I'll tell you. Sixty thousand francs, half of which I got when I signed the contract. I'll get the other half when I deliver the two hundred drawings—and that must be in a year. So, you see again that we Jews are a wily race, and know on which side our bread is buttered."

Leo climbed back over the fence; and that very day M. Dufresne moved over to the Billrothstrasse. Hofrat Spineder and his wife, however, noted with great satisfaction that for the first time in more than a year, their little girl was in good spirits, and hummed a gay song to herself.

"You'll see," the Hofrat said to his wife, "by and by Lotte will forget all about this deplorable business. I feel sorry for the poor fellow, but it's better this way. Besides he wrote me quite a sensible letter in which he promised to give up corresponding with Lotte."

Frau Spineder shook her head in amazement, and thought: "How different girls are nowadays! If I had been in Lotte's place I'd never have overcome my love!"

Chapter VI. The End of the Tenants' Protective Law

The *Weltpresse*, once the liberal bourgeois paper, but now the principal organ of the Christian-Socialist party, received a communication from the owner of the house located at No. 19 Billrothstrasse, a communication containing a keen and logical argument against the continuance of the Tenants' Protective Law.

"This law," said the letter, "had reason and justification when there was a housing shortage and the populace had to be protected against being rendered homeless through the avarice of individual landlords. But today there is no more housing shortage; thanks to the beneficial anti-Jewish law of our revered Chancellor, normal conditions have been restored, and the necessary surplus of apartments exists. Therefore, this Tenants' Protective Law has become superfluous and, at the present time, constitutes only a brutal attack on the rights of the landlord. Furthermore, it conflicts with our Constitution. The repeal of the law would, of course, be followed by a rise in rents, but this would be entirely justified, and, in the long run, would prove salutary to the community, for the higher rents would raise the amount of taxes to be paid, as well as the value of the houses. It is characteristic that it was a cultured French artist, living in my house, who expressed to me his amazement at this Tenants' Protective Law. He declared that the capitalist circles of France find the law ridiculous, and that, among other things, it discourages foreigners from investing their money in Viennese real estate. Therefore, let us do away with the Tenants' Protective Law! The noble Christian spirit of the Viennese landlords, together with the automatic action of the law of supply and demand, will prevent an excessive rise in rents."

This letter appeared in a prominent position in the *Weltpresse*, accompanied by an editorial note that very cautiously approved the views of the esteemed correspondent, yet, at the same time, differed with him slightly. For neither the landlords nor the tenants were to be offended.

This marked the beginning of an animated public discussion. Letters poured into the editorial offices, and the landlords clamored more and more for the repeal of the Tenants' Protective Law, for the privilege of giving notice and of raising rents at their own discretion. Herr Windholz, the owner of the Billrothstrasse house, suddenly became an important personage. He was elected to the presidency of the landlords' association, and he came every day to his cultured French tenant, M. Dufresne, for advice. Gaily Herr Strakosch, alias Dufresne, egged him on, declaring emphatically one day: "If the landlords endure this slavery any longer, I'll consider them spineless fools one and all, and I'll leave the city where such conditions can continue to prevail."

"But what can we do?" Herr Windholz asked in despair. "What can we do when the government absolutely refuses to comply with our demands?"

"What can you do? I'll tell you: Get your association together today, and resolve to deliver a three days' ultimatum to the government. If by the end of that period, it has not restored the privilege of managing your houses in your own way, you, the landlords, will strike. You will pay no taxes, you will suspend the lighting and cleaning of your houses, you will refuse to pay interest on your mortgages. In short, you will commit sabotage against the state."

Herr Windholz waxed enthusiastic, embraced the Frenchman, and assured him that whatever may happen his rent would not be raised.

Subsequent events followed M. Dufresne's plan. The Viennese landlords' association accepted the ultimatum unanimously, and the government was defeated. In vain, did Dr. Schwertfeger realize that the repeal of the Tenants' Protective Law would have most disastrous results. His fellow ministers outvoted him. Primarily, as the *Arbeiter-Zeitung* maliciously pointed out, because the Ministers of Finance, Education, and Commerce each owned several houses.

Thus the Tenants' Protective Law fell. It had forbidden the landlords to dispossess their tenants or to raise rents at will; and twenty-four hours later there took place a stormy open meeting of the landlords, where it was decided to increase the current rents a thousand-fold, so that they would be somewhat more in keeping with the cost of living. A solemn pledge bound all to adhere to this decision.

The populace, only a small minority of which consisted of landlords, went mad. The working classes now had to pay millions in yearly rentals for their rooms, and a small middle-class apartment could not be had for less than fifty million. The housewives' organization, the unions, the association of steadily employed workers, the war invalids and war widows, the artisans' societies—all of them called mass meetings and staged demonstrations; for fully eight days no work of any sort was done in Vienna or the provincial towns, while demonstrations were held from morning to night. The number of broken windowpanes grew at a terrifying rate, and for the first time in a considerable number of years the streets resounded with the cry: "Down with the government!"

Both the Christian and the German-Nationalist papers lost many readers; but the *Arbeiter-Zeitung* again basked in the sunshine of fortune's smiles.

Chapter VII. Zwicker Goes into Bankruptcy

Herr Zwicker was in a bad humor, venting his wrath by furious pokes at the cherry strudel on the plate before him. Frau Zwicker anticipated the approaching storm:

"What's eating you now, Anton? Isn't business going well?"

This was too much for Herr Zwicker. He pushed away the cherry strudel, and his face grew redder than the cherries as he roared: "You bet business is going well! To the devil, that's where! I might as well tell you—I've got to declare bankruptcy!"

"Jesus Christ!" shrieked Frau Zwicker. "How can that be? The store's always been crowded, and everybody thinks you've got a gold-mine from that Jew Lessner!"

"Yah," sneered Zwicker, "a gold-mine full of mud! The more people buy, the more I lose. And you know what? It's all on account of that damnable hunchbacked Kohn of the Hermes Bank, where I had my account, and he says to me, 'Herr Zwicker,' he says, 'now you've got to store up marks, because the mark's going to go up'; or he says, 'the krone is going to be steadier now, so you should buy kronen.' And it always happened the way he said, and I made money, not only on my goods, but on the exchange, too. But now the monkeys who are in that bank now don't know nothin', and I don't know nothin' about it either, and everything's going to pieces, you mark my words!"

Herr Zwicker was one of the many petty businessmen whom the anti-Jewish law had raised to great heights. With the aid of the now thoroughly Christian Landerbank, he, the little small-scale merchant, had succeeded in acquiring the great dry goods store in the Mariahilferstrasse; and his first six months there had been a time of unalloyed happiness. When Herr Zwicker stood on the balcony of the store and looked down at the throng below, he felt like a petty monarch, becoming quite drunk with the ringing of the cash registers, the rustling of silk, and the confused hum of voices. Every evening, at supper, he drank to the health of Schwertfeger and repeated over and over again to his wife (who now wore her kid gloves even into the kitchen): "Now you see, old girl, now we can see how the Jews fleeced us! They had all the big stores, and we Christians had to worry and work our heads off in dingy little shops. Thank God, that's over now!"

But even the first semiannual accounting was a terrible disappointment for Herr Zwicker. In spite of the enormous turnover and the crowded store, there was not the shadow of a profit. Somehow or other some mistake had always been made in the speculation involved in purchases abroad. And more than once, Herr Zwicker sighed to himself: "If only I had a good Jew who could tell me what to do!"

Herr Zwicker actually had to declare himself bankrupt. Soon after, the store was closed, and was taken over by a realtor of the Gumpoldskirchen district, who made the great house over into a huge bar.

In the years that followed the war and revolution, Vienna had developed more and more into the hub of Central European extravagance, and the life of certain classes had grown so luxurious that it became the talk of all the world. The masses of Vienna, however, not only the laborers, but also the middle class, had gnashed their teeth as they watched the foreign elements, especially the Galician, Romanian, and Hungarian Jews, lord it over Vienna. Spending lavishly the practically worthless money of Austria, they drank champagne when the poor man could hardly pay for his glass of beer; they adorned their women with pearls and furs while the real aristocracy was forced to sell its family jewels one by one; they raced through the streets in their luxurious automobiles, they took away the homes of Viennese residents of long standing, and they filled the cultured old city with their noisy ostentation.

When the Jews had been exiled all this was changed entirely overnight. The dumbfounding extravagance disappeared; the Viennese rummage sales came to a stop. It no longer required superhuman effort to secure a seat for the opera, and life became calmer, simpler, and more substantial until it was apparent that Vienna could not exist without luxury. At the beginning, the Christian businessmen, who took over the Jewish shops, had also taken possession of the Jewish automobiles. The general prosperity seemed to be unchanged but merely to have been redistributed. The joy that the citizens of Vienna felt when they no longer had to bump into Jewish profiteers at every step was as genuine as it was easily comprehensible. But when the krone soon began to drop again toward the infinitesimal, and prices rose like a tidal wave—when every business that depended on unlimited luxury (like the exclusive stores, the cabarets, theaters, and princely restaurants and bars) failed, when unemployment became general and the export trade with foreign countries grew less and less, then high living also had its wings clipped.

The tens of thousands of automobiles that had gone over from Jewish into Christian hands were sold to foreign buyers for a handful of lire or francs, for business went so badly that it was impossible to buy gasoline. Art dealers complained of a complete standstill in their business, the deficit of the state-subventioned theaters grew by leaps and bounds, and eminent Christian artists and scholars, especially the great physicians, emigrated to other countries because their own people no longer were willing or able to pay them the fees to which they had become accustomed in the Jewish era.

And it was impossible to stop the constant growth of discontent, irritation, and the realization that the country was on the downward path.

Chapter VIII. The Sweet, Gay Young Things

Discontent was rampant among the happy young things of Vienna. Instinctively they felt in their subconscious minds that the lofty and exalted policy of the government was, to an appreciable extent, carried out at their expense. During the last half century, it had become a tradition that the pretty young girl of the Viennese middle class would have a Jewish sweetheart. Let the father be an enthusiastic Christian-Socialist, let the brother be just as enthusiastic a German nationalist-Poldi or Fini, Mitzi or Grete "went" with a Jew, who might be a salesman or a bank clerk, a businessman or a student. Those of their friends who had no Jews would often taunt and jeer at them—but they always secretly envied them. For to have a Jew as one's lover meant to be taken to the theater and to nice cafés, to be well treated and to receive generous gifts.

As for marriage with a Jew, that was considered the grand prize, a guarantee of comfort, fur coats, and pretty clothes. If one asked Poldi or Tini why she preferred a Jewish sweetheart, the answer was always the same. "A Jew's always liberal, and when he marries a Christian girl, he's her slave. Besides, they don't get drunk. I used to go with a Christian before, and on Sundays I was always scared to death that he'd get drunk and start a row. Now that I've got a Jewish friend, we always go to nice places. He hardly drinks anything. He's smart, always has a lot of things to talk about, and never gets rough."

But when the sweet young things were gathered together privately, in an intimate group, and began to tell one another their erotic experiences and exploits, then they spoke of the sensuousness of the Jews and of the manifoldness of their erotic inclinations as contrasted with their Aryan friends, good Christians and splendid fellows, but far less entertaining. . . .

It is possible, and even probable, that one cause for the profound and fanatic anti-Semitism among the male inhabitants of Vienna during the last few decades was the fact that the youth with the Hakenkreuz could not stomach the sight of his Jewish rivals snatching away all the pretty girls.

Now all this had been changed; no longer was it necessary to compete with the Jews, and the Viennese girl was wholly dependent on her fellow-Aryans. But comparison and reminiscence could be neither prevented nor prohibited.

The girls behind the counters and in the offices, in the sewing-rooms and factories, understood little of politics, but much of practical life. And they began to miss the young Jewish men very much. At first, they had been carried away by the general enthusiasm, but when the morning after dawned, they found their lives emptier and more poverty-stricken than before. They began to long for their exiled sweethearts, and the good qualities of the Jews as lovers were exaggerated. These good qualities were constantly thrown in the teeth of their Christian successors, and the two were compared continually, much to the disadvantage of those in power.

One day the *Arbeiter-Zeitung* described a characteristic scene, which a reporter had observed in the inn of an excursion resort. A beautiful young creature had, for some reason or other, quarreled with her companion, who exclaimed in the course of the argument: "Wish you'd gone away with your Jew!"

Whereupon the girl wiped the tears from her eyes and answered loudly: "Wish I had! I'm not the only girl who had a Jewish friend, and we're all sorry we don't have them anymore! What do we get from you? You drink and gamble away your money, and we've got to buy our rags with what we make ourselves. And none of you is so nice to us as my

Fritz was, or Trudi's Rudi, or his friend Karl, who went with Liesl. They never let us pick up or carry anything. They always bought us the prettiest and best things, and when we went out with them, they didn't take us to such cheap lunchrooms, but to Hopfner, or the Opera Restaurant, and later to a swell café where there was music and people in fine clothes. And as far as love is concerned you can't talk about such things, but those Jews knew how to treat a girl, and when they loved, they were never so selfish as you fellows are. You all just don't have an idea of what a woman needs!"

These resolute words called forth a storm of indignation among the young men. The young women, however, silently exchanged glances and nodded.

Chapter IX. The End of the Hakenkreuzler

At a political meeting held shortly after the expulsion of the Jews, Dr. Schwertfeger said that now, when the foes of the Aryan spirit no longer resided in Austria, there would be an automatic approximation of the various party groups, and a modification of political antagonism.

He seemed to have been right. Almost annihilated by the results of the last election, dumbfounded and staggered by recent events, robbed by the expulsion of their greatest minds, best journalists, and most spirited leaders, the Socialists remained silent and decided not to come out of their forced retirement for the time being. And the variance between the principles of the German Nationalists and the Christian-Socialists actually began to disappear.

After the expulsion, Vienna was totally transformed into an armed camp of Hakenkreuzler. Practically every man, woman, adolescent, and child wore the emblem that was displayed on all the posters, flags, and standards. But when things came to such a pass that every "drunk" and pickpocket was wearing it, when the police mentioned regularly that "the prisoner wore a Hakenkreuz," then the more intelligent people began to discard it, soon to be imitated by the middle class and the masses.

It was not long before it became evident that all the parties, the Christian-Socialist, as well as the Social-Nationalist, had as their common enemy the portrayal of the Jew as an evil spirit, a bogeyman, and a scapegoat. Now that there were no Jews or people of Jewish descent in Austria this no longer attracted the public, and party politics became even more stupid and boring than before.

Misery, unemployment, and the cost of living increased, and demagogues were at a loss to find someone to blame. For now, the rich were good Christians, as were also the exploiters and usurers (though the latter were not to be mentioned, for that would have been an admission that Christians, as well as Jews, could be profiteers and usurers). Formerly the Hakenkreuzler had attracted notice and aroused the masses with their posters. Bosel and other Jewish plutocrats had been called the rulers of Austria, had been reviled as vampires and oppressors. But now Bosel was living in London, and the Hakenkreuzler posters had become so colorless that no one bothered to read them anymore.

One after the other, the newspapers that displayed the Hakenkreuz suspended publication. Hakenkreuzler meetings no longer drew an audience. No more money poured into the party treasury, and the leaders found themselves in a pinch when they could no longer fleece rich Jews, and when there were no more Jewish banks to give them money. In fact, the Christianized banks did not need to contribute and could not have done so had they wished, for their situation became worse every day.

The leaders of the Hakenkreuzler made a last effort to save themselves and their slowly dying party. They informed the public on enormous posters and a million leaflets that it was again the Jews who were to blame for all the misery of Vienna. It was international Jewry, said they, that was shooting poisoned darts into Austria from foreign countries, that was hatching vengeance, that was forcing down the krone and, through the powerful organization of Freemasonry, was draining Austria and isolating her from international life.

For three or four days, these "revelations" served as topics of conversation, and for three or four days, the starving, desperate, jobless people stopped before the posters and shook their fists. Then they began to shrug their shoulders and to call the whole business nonsense, for the simple reason that even the most stupid of them could see that Austria was absolutely powerless against such a "plot" of international Jewry. In the old days they could have marched from a Hakenkreuzler meeting to Leopold Stadt, drunk with enthusiasm, and secretly hoping to plunder and burglarize a little on the way, to thrash a few Jews and break some windows. But now, when there were no more Jews in Leopold Stadt, such a demonstration would have been entirely senseless, and the formerly so tolerant and kindly police now would surely have cut down the looting demonstrators without much ado.

Thus, it happened that one day the principal organ of the Hakenkreuzler made the melancholy and yet defiant announcement that it would suspend publication. Incidentally, it revealed the heart-rending fact that at the last great assembly of the Hakenkreuzler, only twenty persons had gathered in addition to the officers and the waiters.

Dr. Schwertfeger had been right. Political opposition was becoming less vivid and was disappearing almost completely—but for an entirely different reason than he had believed. It was because of a total lack of motivation and because the Jews had taken all the dash and spirit of politics with them.

Chapter X. Cheap Summer Resorts

On a glorious June day, Leo Strakosch, alias Dufresne, went to the City Park to collect further impressions of the new Vienna. As a rule, he seldom left the Nineteenth District, where he was always either working in his studio or taking long walks in the Wienerwald with Lotte. Now, strolling about among the crowded tables of the inn, he felt so amused that he laughed aloud.

"For heaven's sake, what has become of my beautiful, elegant Vienna!"

There seemed to be a general craze for Alpine costume and tourist dress. As far as he could see, there were men, old and young, in rough wool coats, knickerbockers, and green Alpine hats. And most of the women wore peasant costumes, which, while it might have been very charming and graceful in the open country, looked more like a caricature or a bad joke. People had become very unassuming. Besides, now they were all one big family, and there were no strangers around for whom it might be necessary to "dress up." Occasionally one did see elegantly dressed men and women; but they were so few as to be conspicuous, and sneering remarks about them issued from the Alpine tables. Strakosch felt highly uncomfortable whenever he noticed a "peasant girl" staring at him through her lorgnette, probably only because his dark blue suit, patent leather shoes, and costly silk tie attracted attention.

An electric tramway line, municipal music, and peasant girls who wore lorgnettes—Leo pinched himself. He hurried out of the park into the Ringstrasse, where the cafés presented a sorry sight; he grinned as he noted that people were greeting one another with "Hail," and he had to search for quite some time before he found a taxicab. For even these public vehicles had become a luxury indulged in by so few that most of the drivers had given up their business. Late in the afternoon, around sunset, he met Lotte at the edge of the Kobenzlwald, just as they had arranged. They settled down on a bench, and, after a prologue of kisses, Lotte told him that her parents had decided to move to their little villa on Lake Wolfgang the next week.

"What'll become of us now?" she wailed. "How can I bear not to see you all summer?"

"Nothing of the sort is expected of you, darling. I'll take a vacation, too. When you're in St. Gilgen, I'll be in the village of Wolfgang, and you'll come over every day so that we'll be together at least an hour."

"M-m-m," Lotte replied happily, "that's something I like! But now I'll have to tell you about the argument Papa and I had yesterday. Just think, suddenly Papa looked me straight in the eye and said very seriously: 'What have you been doing all by yourself lately, for hours at a time? You know we give you as much freedom as possible—but there's a limit.'

"I felt myself getting red as a beet and thought the best thing would be for me to confess."

"What!" interrupted Leo, horrified. "You told your father?"

"Let me finish, silly," laughed Lotte, pinching his ear. "I confessed, but only what I wanted. I told Papa that I had met a very splendid young man at Erna's house, that I like him as well as he likes me, and that I often meet him for walks. He's a Frenchman, I said, by the name of Henry Dufresne, and he's putting through some big business deals here."

"At first Papa was absolutely speechless. Then he asked why I don't invite this Frenchman to the house. Whereupon I answered that I'm not entirely sure of my feelings, and therefore don't want to make the matter seem official. And finally, I cried, quite indignantly:

"'You know you can trust me, Papa! You can be sure I won't do anything wrong, and Henry will come to you as soon as I think it necessary and proper. But now let me go my own way!'

"After this Papa was very kind and nice to me, and so was Mama. But later I heard Papa telling Mama: 'I'd never have believed that Lotte would forget poor Leo so quickly and thoroughly. Still, I'm very glad she's found a new young man for her affections, and we won't put any obstacle in her way.'

"And Mama, who is so fond of you, shook her head and said: 'I don't understand that girl at all! Her cheeks have actually become pink again, and she sings all day as if she had never had a heartache.'

"You know, Leo, it surely isn't nice of us to fool my parents this way, but I'm so happy that you're here in Vienna!"

Leo pulled Lotte toward him, gave her a long kiss, and then said with an important air: "Now we'll go to the country, and when I come back, I'll fool the whole town, and I'll do it properly, too! I can't tell you anymore today—but you'll see some marvelous events."

This was the second summer to console the Viennese for the great inconvenience and bitter disappointments they had suffered. In former years the most beautiful towns and resorts of diminished Austria had become the playground of the Jews. All of the beautiful Salzkammer region, the Semmering district, and even the more modernized sections of the Tyrol had been flooded with Austrian, Czechoslovakian, and Hungarian Jews; the appearance of anyone who might be suspected of being a Gentile would actually create a sensation in Ischl, Gmunden, Wolfgang, Gilgen, Strobel, Aussee, or on the Attersee. Not without justification the Christians—partly because of lesser wealth, and partly because of greater conservatism in the matter of money-spending—felt that they were being pushed aside, and had to content themselves with the less expensive, but also much less beautiful resorts of Lower Austria, Steiermark, in Tyrolese villages. Since the expulsion of the Jews, all this had changed. The most beautiful summer resorts were no longer crowded; inquiries from city dwellers received immediate and very courteous replies, and in spite of the otherwise increased cost of living, the rents of rooms or summer homes were considerably lower than two years before. Consequently, all who had the time and the money flocked to the places that had formerly disgusted the genuine Viennese.

The owners of the great hotels, health resorts, and so-called sanatoria, however, were not so well pleased. They had always lived off international Jewry. Their entire business depended on people who do not calculate cost when their comfort is at stake, and now, since it was impossible for them to be cheap, they could not find enough patrons. The great Semmering hotels did not open at all, and many hostelries of the Salzkammer region and the Tyrol were forced to close and dismiss their employees in the middle of the season. This was gall in their cup of joy and caused ill will among the country people, who were accustomed to sell their products to the great hotels at enormous prices, and to let their sons and daughters make goodly sums of money as valets and chambermaids during the summer.

The mayor of Semmering had the courage to say openly, at a meeting of the Town Council: "Together with the Jews we drove prosperity out of the country. If this lasts a few years longer we may be good Christians, but we'll be as poor as church mice!"

Chapter XI. A Stormy Debate

When summer was over and autumn was tinting the leaves with its brilliant hues, the krone began to fall again (as was now its habit) and the cost of living to rise. Prices became preposterous, even the rich hesitated to buy new clothes; laborers, office workers, and even the unemployed made new demands. A ride on the tramway car cost ten thousand kronen and a pound of butter a hundred thousand.

In October, when bitterness, restlessness, and discontent were at their height, the National Assembly convened; the face of the Chancellor was careworn and deeply lined. When he spoke the awed silence of the old days did not prevail. Instead, there were calls and loud remarks, even the galleries hooted occasionally, and the small Social-Democratic opposition no longer let itself be intimidated, but constantly joined in the debate.

After surveying the hopeless financial condition of the country, Schwertfeger went on to say: "I must tell you frankly that the Christian people of Austria will be called upon to make many great sacrifices." (Call from the gallery: "Only the Christians, of course, since we threw out the Jews!") "Sacrifices that will require a stout heart and loyal patriotism! The government needs money to continue its administrative business, and since we are unable to obtain further credit abroad, we must resort to new taxes, direct and indirect, to bring in the enormous sums required for the administration, to cover the interest on our debt, and to pay for the support of the unemployed.

"I know, ladies and gentlemen, that the people are bitterly disappointed, and I assure you that I am also. The trouble is that we underestimated the difficulties of the transitory period, and thought that the Christian citizens would adapt themselves better to the control of our financial and business undertakings, which had been entirely in the hands of the Jews. But what are such disappointments in comparison with the lofty goal we have set ourselves—to return Austria to her Aryan people, to build up a country that will be free of the spirit of usury, free of Jewish skepticism, free of the corrupting properties and elements that represent Jewry!"

At the close of his speech the Chancellor, raising his voice, put the question of confidence. Dr. Wolters, representing the small Socialist fraction, spoke against the granting of credit, against approval of the government's plans, and against the vote of confidence. Vividly he portrayed the ever-growing misery, the imminent danger of national bankruptcy, the devastation of Austria's economic and intellectual life. Among other things he said: "More than two years ago, when he was arguing for his anti-Jewish law, the honorable Chancellor called our people honest, simple, and sincere, and declared that they are not fit to compete with that superior race, the Jews. But he overlooked one thing: even without Jews, we honest, sincere, and simple Austrians would be surrounded by nations that are all the more superior to us now that the Jews are no longer with us. What has become of Central European commerce since the Jews are gone? We have lost it, for the Jews have taken it along to Prague and Budapest. What has become of our flourishing clothing, jewelry, and millinery industries? They have disappeared almost entirely, for they cannot live on honesty and sincerity alone, but need the Jewish purchasers throughout the world, who make no bones about spending their easily acquired money. Today, it is evident that we cannot dispense with the Jews."

Wild shouts interrupted the Socialist leader. The Christian-Socialists and German Nationalists were furious, and cried, "Throw out the lackey of the Jews!"

The turmoil became so great that the Presiding Officer, the red-bearded Tyrolese, had to close the meeting temporarily. When he opened it again, he reprimanded Dr. Wolters severely, because his words had deeply wounded the Christian sentiment of the deputies, and because he had attempted to undermine the foundations of the new state. Finally, all the proposals of the government were accepted, over the opposition of the Socialists. But many deputies had left before the vote, and later Schwertfeger, smiling grimly, told his Presiding Officer:

"This time they ran away—but next time they'll vote against me, those opportunists, always looking for the winning side. Yesterday, they shouted 'Hosannah,' but tomorrow they'll cry 'Crucify him!'"

Chapter XII. The League of True Christians

Odd, mysterious things were happening. One morning hundreds of men and women stood before advertising kiosks at the Schotten Gate, before the Opera, in the Stubenring, and in other localities, where someone had attached, by means of a tack, small octavo leaflets bearing the following legend:

> Citizens of Vienna and Austria! Arise before you are destroyed altogether! With the Jews you drove out prosperity, hope and the possibility of future development! Accursed be the demagogues who misled you!
>
> —The League of True Christians

People read the impudent words aloud. Many were indignant and declared it was the work of Freemasons; others went away silently, and still others had the courage to voice their approval and to look defiantly at those who differed.

A few days later new posters appeared in various places, reading:

> Vienna is becoming provincialized! Citizens of Vienna, do you not see it? Another year or two, and the old metropolis, once the seat of emperors, will have become a shabby little hamlet, forgotten all over the world!

Since a good part of the poster was also being published in the *Arbeiter-Zeitung*, it began to affect the people's nerves, and to cause restlessness throughout the city. Was there not some truth in this last statement of the mysterious League of True Christians? It gave rise to heated discussions at meetings, in the barroom, and on the tramway. Somehow the remark about the provincialization of Vienna hovered in the air, and it seemed to acquire wings, for soon it was heard everywhere, and even the Christian *Weltpresse* quite unintentionally closed an editorial with: "We must do everything to avoid provincialization!"

The government, very much annoyed, exhorted the police to discover the malefactor who was putting up the posters. But their efforts were in vain. New leaflets appeared every day or two, always in different places—on the doors of the houses and churches, once even on the portals of the Chancellor's Palace, of Police Headquarters, and of the Parliament Building. Always they bore a terse but effective attack on the government, an inflammatory suggestion to the people. And each time the *Arbeiter-Zeitung* would receive a mailed copy the day before, and was able to publish in its early morning edition the contents of the leaflet that would be put up that day.

After a short while all Vienna was seething with excitement; almost all conversation centered about these leaflets, and everybody puzzled over who might be behind this mysterious League. From week to week the number of those who agreed with the message of the little proclamations increased, Social-Democratic meetings again drew large crowds, and the Chancellor's prestige fell to an appreciable extent.

One afternoon Lotte went over to Leo's earlier than he had expected. As she had her own key to the apartment, and since Leo was not waiting for her in the living room as he usually did, she went directly into the studio. Leo quickly threw a cloth over a little wooden table, and then greeted her with a somewhat embarrassed look.

Lotte pulled his little beard, looked straight into his eyes, and said: "Look here, Leo, you're trying to hide something from me! What have you got there under that cloth?"

Leo laughed heartily. "You've the eyes of a lynx, my darling! Well, I guess I'll have to tell you my secret now."

He pulled off the cloth, and Lotte saw, beside a box of type and a miniature hand-press, a pile of newly printed sheets. Amazed, she read:

> Citizens of Vienna! Are you better or worse off today than in the time of the Jews? Think it over calmly, and you will find the right answer! Years ago we all cried: "Throw out the Jews!" But today we cry: "Let the Jews return, for they really want to work loyally with us!"
>
> —The League of True Christians

Dumbfounded, uncomprehending, Lotte dropped the paper and picked up another sheet, on which was printed:

> We are not longing for the Jewish bankers. But if we want to escape hopeless misery, we must welcome back the intelligent, smart Jews who can be of value to us. Arise, and act, before it is too late!
>
> —The League of True Christians

Lotte looked inquiringly at her fiancée. He picked her up, kissed the tip of her nose, and again roared with laughter. "Don't you understand, you child? I created the League of True Christians all by myself, and it has been driving Vienna crazy for weeks! And I shan't stop before the great storm breaks. Mark my words, these two leaflets will do the work! They're my gas and stink bombs and flares, with which I kill, suffocate, and illuminate."

Lotte was trembling.

"If you're caught at it, Leo, it'll be all over with you!"

"If, if! But they won't get me! I have a marvelous technique for putting up the leaflets! As I stroll past a door or a wall in the morning without stopping for a second, I push in the tack to which the paper has already been attached. And even if the police tear down the leaflet a few minutes later there's no harm done, for the *Arbeiter-Zeitung* has already printed its contents. You can trust me, dear; it has to be done this way. I've mapped out my course to a 'T,' and I'm devilish careful anyway."

Swinging her slender legs as she sat perched on the broad drawing table, Lotte spoke thoughtfully: "You know, Leo, I think you've already accomplished a great deal. We had quite a crowd at our house yesterday, ten men and women, and mostly all the conversation was about the expulsion of the Jews and its consequences. Everybody, including Hofrat Tumpel, agreed that the expulsion should have been limited to some of the Eastern Jews—to those who could not prove that they had a decent occupation. And finally Hofrat Tumpel, who, a year ago, used to become furious if you dared to differ ever so slightly with the Chancellor, remarked: 'Yes, it seems that a very delicate mechanism has been interfered with too abruptly! There are some Jewish qualities that are not to be underestimated, and which we miss badly.'

"This may of course have something to do with the fact that the Hofrat's brother owns the bookshop in the Seilergasse where only deluxe and artistic editions are sold. Since the Jews are gone, his business amounts to practically nothing, and on two occasions his brother, the Hofrat, has had to give him large sums of money to save him from bankruptcy. Another thing, Leo: I always keep my eyes and ears open—in the morning when I do my shopping, and at concerts, at the opera, and on the tramway. And I always hear people recalling the past more and more wistfully, and speaking of it as if it had been very beautiful. They reminisce and say: 'In the old days, when the Jews were still here.' . . . —And they say this in every imaginable tone of voice, but never with hatred. You know, I think people are actually becoming lonesome for the Jews!"

Leo rewarded her keenness by pressing her to his breast. "And I'll do my share to make their longing irresistible."

"But be very careful, Leo! Don't forget that, if they kill you, I'll have to die, too!"

Chapter XIII. A Melancholy Christmas

Never had Vienna experienced a more melancholy Christmas. The enormous cost of living was supplemented by an absolute standstill of all activity. High prices alone would not have bothered the worthy Phreaceans. They had been accustomed to them for a decade; as a matter of fact, it did not make much difference whether a half-pint of wine cost five or ten thousand kronen, if people earned enough, if the laborer received high wages, and if the merchant had his safe full of money every evening. But this was no longer the case. The bulk of the currency lay dormant in the stockings of the peasants, and in the cities, no one wanted to buy anything. A large part of the working class was idle and dependent on government support; and the Christmas numbers of the papers published statistics that revealed that in two years about five thousand branch banks, cafés, restaurants, and shops had closed down in Vienna alone. Lately one big failure after the other had been occurring in industry. Corporations that to the last minute had been thought bomb-proof were now declaring themselves insolvent, and rumor predicted the collapse of two great banks.

Matters having reached such a state, what did it avail the Viennese that there was plenty of room everywhere, that the theaters were not sold out even on the Christmas holidays, and that one no longer had to meet those provoking Jewish noses? What did it avail them that they had returned to Christian simplicity and the full beard, when the barbers' assistants had to be discharged by the dozen because there was no more work for them?

The condition of the jewelers was the worst of all. Most of them had been Jews and had, therefore, been forced to leave; and now their business was being conducted by former petty watch-repairers and other doubtless very estimable individuals who, however, had no connections whatever with the Dutch precious stone market (which is almost exclusively in Jewish hands) and who, therefore, were thoroughly taken in at every purchase. Finally buying abroad stopped altogether, for the demand for jewelry disappeared entirely, while the number of those who were forced to sell increased constantly. Slowly but surely most of the jewelry belonging to Austrians traveled to neighboring countries, to England, France, and America; but even there the jewelers who were the agents for this export trade had to suffer. If a dealer bought a rope of pearls today from a private owner for ten billion kronen, and soon after deposited it on the neck of an American woman in exchange for thirty billion, he imagined that he had put through a splendid deal, celebrated the joyous occasion with wine, sang the praises of Dr. Schwertfeger, and bought a fat goose (which no longer was the special privilege of the Jews). But before he had digested the rich goose liver, his thirty billion were not worth as much as the ten he had spent, and he had no more money for further purchases. So it was not at all surprising that the Yuletide brought a wave of embitterment and discontent to Vienna, and that the customary noise and merriment of the New Year's Eve celebration was stifled under a blanket of ill temper and discouragement.

If the Chancellor had heard the conversation that occurred during Christmas week between Herr Habietnik, owner of the huge department store in the Kartnerstrasse, and Herr Mauler, proprietor of the large jewelry establishment on the Graben, his wrath would have waxed even greater. Sitting in the Grabencafe, Herr Habietnik and Herr Mauler were grumbling about the miserable Christmas business, which would surely seal the ruin of thousands of businessmen. Suddenly Herr Habietnik leaned over toward Herr Mauler and told him of a dream he had had the night before.

"Just think, Herr Mauler, I dreamed that all of a sudden only Jews and Jewesses start to come to my store. Every last one of them is dressed in the latest style, and carries piles of banknotes, and there's a big rush. The girls can't bring the furs and cloth and cloaks and suits fast enough for them, and all the ready-made clothing departments are filled with silks and velvets and laces and embroideries. But nothing's good enough for them, and one Jewish lady, dressed in very good and stylish clothes, keeps on crying: 'That's nothing! We're coming from Paris and Palestine, where everything's in the latest style. Show me the best you've got!' Then, without any warning, my head salesgirl brings out a pair of cotton bloomers and says: 'But my dear Jewish lady, this is the newest thing from Paris!' Then everybody laughs so terrible much that I wake up. Don't you think, Herr Mauler, that this dream means something?"

Herr Mauler grinned as he answered: "Yes—it means that pretty soon all the world will be laughing at us, and we'll be wrapping ourselves in flannel and cotton before we're buried for good. But one thing's sure, Herr Habietnik. If an automobile was to stop in front of my shop with a Jewish couple in it, I'd kiss them both, and I'd be happy again! You know, Herr Habietnik, in the old days, when I was still a clerk with Herr Zwirner, who used to have my store, I often thought it really was a shame that almost no one but the Jews had the money for diamonds and pearls. And once I even said so out loud. Then Herr Zwirner laughed in my face and said: 'Don't be a fool, Mauler, but be glad the Jews buy and put money in circulation. Or would you like it better if they were to hide and bury their money like the peasants? You'll see, if the anti-Semitism business keeps on, the rich Jews will leave the country, and then all the stores will have to close down!'

"Well—and now both the rich and poor Jews have left Austria, and we're all finished good and proper!"

Chapter XIV. An Inflammatory Speech

In the Spineder home, Christmas Eve had been celebrated in the usual patriarchal manner. But the atmosphere was not entirely cheerful. The Hofrat was beginning to have grave financial worries because of the depreciation of his fortune; Frau Spineder had not yet recovered from the shock of having had to pay a quarter million for her Christmas carp and three million for the Christmas goose; and Lotte was worried because she had received no news of Leo although she had hoped that he would at least remember her with a Christmas card.

As they were reverentially consuming the costly fish, the doorbell rang and the maid announced that a man had come to deliver something personally to the young lady. Lotte hurried out, and the fur-coated man who had something to deliver to her kissed her madly in the dark hall before he pressed a tiny package into her hand and hurried away. In the dining room Lotte unwrapped the little package and, from a leather case, drew out a ring set with a magnificent pearl the size of a hazelnut. "A Christmas present from Leo, I mean Henry," said Lotte, blushing furiously; and as she put the ring on her finger, her young heart was filled with infinite happiness.

The Hofrat, however, was quite taken aback and declared categorically: "But now, Lotte, this M. Dufresne must present himself at last, and ask for your hand. For if such a ring is given to a young woman, it's nothing less than an engagement ring."

Lotte laughed as she kissed her father.

"Only a little more patience. Henry says he'll come to see you very soon."

But the mother shook her head again and thought: "Strange times, strange children! She loves a man, forgets him, and then confuses his name with that of his successor!"

In January, a number of large consumers' organizations united to hold a mass meeting in the public auditorium of the City Hall with the slogan: "We cannot go on!" Tens of thousands of people attended the meeting, and in spite of the extraordinary cold weather, enormous crowds for whom there was no room within stood before the building. The assembly presented a remarkable appearance. Leo Strakosch, who had also come there, observed an unprecedented number of men with full beards, and of cries of "Hail!" With a slightly different background he could have supposed himself at an assembly of Tyrolese peasants in the days of Andreas Hofer. The gentle sex was also very well represented, but not by the most beautiful of its members in Vienna. Amid general cheering the druggist, Dr. Njedestjenski, opened the meeting with the declaration that things could go on thus no longer. He carefully avoided any connection of the widespread poverty and high cost of living with the expulsion of the Jews, but spoke in the most approved Pan-German manner, declaring that the cause of the pitiable ruin of Vienna lay solely in the fact that Austria could not be annexed to Germany. Whereupon a workingman interrupted, amid great hilarity: "We can't annex ourselves anymore! Or do you think the Germans are as silly as we, and will throw out their Jews?"

This wrecked the druggist's train of thought. So, he stammered a little more about German unity and national consciousness, shouted "Hail!"

and gave over the floor to the speakers of the evening. Then the Jews became almost the sole topic of discussion. And they were spoken of in such a way that an uninitiated auditor would have believed Vienna to be the most philo-Semitic city in the world. When a wine dealer began to speak in an anti-Jewish tone, he was actually howled off the stage, and when someone called: "We'd be better off if we'd learned from the Jews instead of driving them out!" there was much applause. Leo could control himself no longer. His heart beating wildly, he designated his wish to speak, saying to himself as he mounted the platform: "Impudence, stand by me!" He pretended to have an imperfect command of the German language, emphasized over and over again that, as a Frenchman, he was really not entitled to meddle in Austrian affairs; but, he said, his love for this incomparably beautiful and charming city, a close second to if not the peer of Paris, forced him to express his views. At this the bearded portion of the audience felt flattered, while the women were delighted by the slender young man, handsome in spite of his imperial beard; and everybody shouted: "Hail!" Consequently, Leo continued with his French accent:

"In Paris, too, we have very many Jews, good and bad, useful and noxious. In any case, many of them deserve all respect and are of great value to the country. But it would never occur to any of us to exile the Jews; instead, we all try to make use of their good merits. Since this is not my home, I don't know all the qualities of the Viennese Jews. But I can say that in Paris I met very many exiles from Vienna who made a splendid impression and who doubtless will be good Frenchmen very soon. It is possible that there is greater difference between the Austrian Christians and the Jews than between the latter and the more emotional and temperamental Frenchmen. But in that case, they should complement each other all the better. I hear that in this country the Jews were reproached with controlling capital and possessing more money, proportionately, than the Christian citizens. Very good, ladies and gentlemen. But this merely goes to prove that they think and act more quickly and from such qualities a wise government should be able to derive benefit for the community."

Loud interjections from all sides: "Yes, indeed, a wise government—but ours is stupid! He's right! Hail! Hail!"

"Ladies and gentlemen," continued Leo, smiling, "it really makes no difference whether one likes the Jews or not. The yeast that is used in the making of bread has a horrible taste, but bread cannot be made without it. We must look at the Jews in a similar light. Yeast, not very pleasant by itself, and harmful in excessive quantities, but indispensable, in the right proportion, for our daily bread. And I think your bread is refusing to rise for lack of yeast. However, now is not the time for arguments or for crying over spilled milk, but for seeing what can be done about it. I don't know what can be done in Austria. Were such a contingency to arise in France, the people would insist on new elections, to show whether the country is satisfied with conditions as they are, or whether they should be changed."

With these words Leo left the platform, and quickly became lost in the crowd. The assembly, however, became fearfully excited. The words "new elections" had struck the human mass as a spark might strike a keg of dynamite; the huge auditorium shook, as thirty thousand throats shouted these words, which found their way out on the street and became the catchword of the day.

In the editorial offices of the *Arbeiter-Zeitung* a conference of the chief editors and confidential agents of the party was held the next day; and for the first time in years they decided to inaugurate again an active, energetic political campaign, and to take this campaign out of the closed chamber and into the streets. The editor-in-chief of the *Arbeiter-Zeitung*, a former pen-cutter, Wunderlich by name, who managed the heritage of Viktor Adler as best he could, made the following pronouncement:

"We must adopt the slogan of this remarkable French painter, whose name cannot possibly be Diefress, as the idiotic chairman had it. Beginning right now we will voice incessantly a demand for new elections through our papers, assemblies, and councils. And now we will put to work our friends in France, Holland, Czechoslovakia, England, and America, and induce them to do their utmost to have large amounts of kronen thrown on the market. For if there is another appreciable fall of the krone, and another rise of the now stationary cost of living—then the time is ripe for us, and we will be able, if necessary, to use force to bring about the dissolution of the National Assembly."

Chapter XV. Herr Laberl Turns

The next few days were marked by another event that caused great consternation in uncompromisingly Christian-Socialist circles. The Mayor of Vienna, after Schwertfeger the most influential man of the country, Herr Karl Maria Laberl fell over, figuratively speaking. Not voluntarily, however, but because he was tripped up by the President of the Municipal Council, Herr Kallop. City Hall had long known that Herr Kallop's name should really be read from right to left, that is, "Pollak," as this had been his grandfather's name. When the Jews were still in Vienna, the story was told among them that the old Pollak had been an immigrant grain dealer from Galicia, who became converted on his marriage to a Christian. The name Kallop had been adopted by his son, who was a lawyer highly respected in Christian circles; he married a Christian also, so that, according to the Schwertfeger law, the grandchildren of the old Pollak were full-blooded Aryans. Josef Kallop, the lawyer's son, was a ne'er-do-well in his youth, unable to complete the studies required for admission to the bar; but he became a successful Municipal Councillor. Infinitely shrewder than most of his colleagues, he soon became the Presiding Officer, and for quite some time had been the right hand of Mayor Laberl.

It was Herr Kallop, therefore, who brought about the fall of the Mayor. He began by explaining that a great change was impending.

"As you can clearly see, Herr Laberl, things can't go on this way. The near future will bring disturbances that will be quite serious; and one of these days the government will go up in thin smoke, so to speak. If you don't want to go up with it, you'd better change your course before it's too late. Don't stick too closely to Schwertfeger. Admit that expulsion of all the Jews was going a little too far. And then, in the midst of the rumpus that is inevitable, all Vienna will suddenly stop and say to itself: 'Our Mayor is a smart fellow. He knows when we've had enough of a good thing, and he'll be able to help us out of this fix.'"

Herr Karl Maria Laberl nodded, stroked his fine white beard, and seemed entirely convinced by this superior reasoning; yet he asked, a little timorously: "What you say is quite right, my dear Kallop. It's just what I've been thinking for a long time. But how am I to go about it?"

"Very simple, Your Honor. We call a meeting of the Christian-Socialist citizens' league in the First District, for there the businessmen are actually in a panic. And then you'll make a speech that we'll work out together."

This was done; but it must be noted, however, that the "working out together" of the speech consisted in Herr Laberl's memorizing the oration composed by the President of the Municipal Council. At the meeting of the citizens' league Herr Laberl greeted the assembly with the utmost solemnity, spoke of the grave times and unbearable conditions, and finally said: "The demand for new elections is becoming more and more stormy; and I am the last man to refuse to heed that demand. On the contrary, I am, personally, in favor of doing what the people want, and of determining, by means of new elections, whether the voters of Austria still approve of what the government did more than two years ago or whether they want a radical change. I—and doubtless you also, gentlemen—see only one goal: To make possible the rehabilitation of our country, to bring back the light of day to our unfortunate nation, hurled into a labyrinth by the Entente, but, perhaps, by grave errors of its own also. Gentlemen, we may be guided by no dogma, no fanaticism, no personal likes or dislikes, but only by the thought of what is best for our country!"

Kallop saw to it that the Municipal Press Bureau gave the Mayor's speech to the papers word for word that very night; and the next day even the simplest among the Viennese knew that at the proper moment Karl Maria Laberl would leave the Chancellor in the lurch.

When Dr. Schwertfeger read the Mayor's speech in the morning papers—of which only the *Arbeiter-Zeitung* provided adequate comment—bitter gall rose in his mouth, and he spat it out. Then he looked long, forlornly, dully over the public park, covered with a white shroud.

However, in the City Hall, Herr Kallop gaily rubbed his hands. And after making sure that neither a colleague nor an inferior was in the room, he said loudly and distinctly, "Mazeltov!" knocking the underside of the table three times. Incidentally, it might be divulged that Herr

Kallop admired a voluptuous Jewess—twice divorced, to be sure, but blessed with many millions by way of compensation—who now lived in exile in Prague. And he longed for nothing so much as for the return of her person and her millions to his beloved country if for no other reason than because he could not possibly cope any longer with the rising cost of living on his salary as President of the Municipal Council, and because, furthermore, he had made a mistake in his speculations on the Polish mark.

Chapter XVI. Down with the Government!

The Mardi Gras season of this year was powerless to improve the humor of the Viennese. Bitter cold, much snow, rooms unheated because a hundred-weight of coal cost a hundred thousand kronen, failure after failure, and the closing of a great bank in which many had deposited their money.

Dances and fancy-dress balls were held in the sign of the peasant costume exclusively. As extravagant dress was not indulged, necessity was made into a virtue, and only country dances were given, and Vienna looked more like a country fair than a metropolis.

The city's theatrical life had come to an absolute standstill. The best members of the National Opera were constantly playing abroad. The Philharmonic Orchestra was just finishing a tour in South America, the private theaters had degenerated into provincial troupes with inadequate direction, inferior actors, and antiquated scenery; and visiting artists from abroad had long ago stopped coming because Vienna could not pay the great sums they demanded. Besides, some papers had lately had to suspend publication because the number of their readers was constantly diminishing; and suddenly the alarm was sounded again: "The krone is falling!"

Enormous quantities of kronen were being sold on the foreign exchanges, so that Zurich soon rated them at the thirty-thousandth part of a centime. Prices rose in proportion, and the populace began to grow desperate. When a pound of fat cost a half million kronen, the mysterious little leaflet of the League of True Christians appeared again with the question:

> How long, Citizens of Vienna, will you bear this government? When will you at last make the National Assembly dissolve, and force new elections to be called?

The morning of the next day was marked by looting in the markets; the embittered housewives stormed the stands, beat their owners, and took possession of the foodstuffs. In Favoriten the riot developed a revolutionary character; but the National Guard, which was called out, refused to proceed against the women.

In the National Assembly, which was in session just then, not only the Social-Democrats, but some Christian-Socialists and Pan-Germans as well, put the question to the government as to what it proposed to do to help the desperate people. The Social-Democrats made a declaration of urgency and moved that the government immediately call new elections, so that the voters could decide themselves whether they were prepared to bear present conditions any longer.

Deathly pale, the Chancellor rose to rejoin: "To call new elections at this moment of general confusion would be to deliver the fate of our country into the hands of the radical elements, and to open our gates wide to the Jews! The proudest and greatest work ever created by the Austrian legislature would collapse because we are not patient enough, because we are not capable of sufficient self-denial to endure present conditions and overcome our difficulties. I know that international Jewry is mixed up in this, and doubtless agitators, bought with Jewish money, are working to. . . ."

The rest of the Chancellor's words were lost in the terrific hullabaloo that now filled the house. The Social-Democrats knocked on their desks, the galleries shouted wildly, and even from the benches of his partisans came calls like "Have you proof for your statements?"

At six o'clock in the evening the Social-Democrats' declaration of urgency was still being discussed; and its proponents were very evidently doing their utmost to prolong the session. Every speaker talked for hours. As soon as one had finished another took the floor. Most of the deputies had stopped listening long ago and were refreshing themselves at the buffet, and even the ministers' bench was empty. Only Schwertfeger, rigidly sullen, his arms folded, was still in his seat.

Suddenly new life came into the house. The rumor spread that masses of workers were advancing. Immediately after, the sound of the workers' song was heard from afar, the cheering and shouting of the excited mob became louder and louder, until finally a single howl penetrated the closed windows: "Down with the government! Down with the National Assembly! We demand new elections!"

Great crowds with their flags and standards were surrounding the Parliament Building, new processions were constantly arriving; all the workers of Greater Vienna, clerks and office employees, all had marched out in closed groups from the factories and shops, stores and offices.

Now powerful blows thundered on the doors of the building, which had been locked hurriedly. Then a hailstorm of stones rattled against the windows, and a deputation of workers had forced an entry. Their leader—an ironworker by the name of Stirmer, a powerful fellow with bright eyes and an enormous head—took up his position in the midst of the deputies, who, panic-struck, were huddled together like sheep during a storm; and he declared briefly:

"The army is with us, and so are the younger men on the police force. Either the government dissolves Parliament within ten minutes and orders new elections to be called immediately, or the masses will proceed with violence. The bitterness of the people is boundless; this time the middle classes stand behind the workers, and the question is not political, but one of actual desperation. The women are the most furious. Listen to them shrieking. They want to set the building on fire. If the government does not give in, we will not answer for the consequences!"

And the inevitable happened. After a brief consultation with the Christian-Socialist and Pan-German party leaders, the government announced that it would submit to the terror, would dissolve the Assembly, and would call new elections immediately. The Chancellor handed in his resignation then and there, but his colleagues and the party chiefs convinced him not to desert them at this critical moment. So, he consented to keep the reins of government in his hands until after the elections.

When the excited mob was informed of the dissolution of the National Assembly the tension was transformed into wild joy; and in the evening that followed the wine supply of Vienna suffered considerable diminution.

Even the Frenchman, Henry Dufresne, who had witnessed the memorable meeting from the gallery, drank a great deal too much, all alone in his studio. The next morning, however, he was in perfect condition again; he made an excellent sketch for the title page of one of Zola's novels, and when Lotte came to him, snow-covered and with cold red cheeks, he picked her up and swung her around.

Lotte was in as high spirits as he was, for after reading the morning papers, her father had said to her very gravely: "I see a great conflict in store for you, my child! Everything indicates that Leo Strakosch will soon be able to return to Vienna. And then you'll have to choose between him, whom you loved so much and whom I would welcome as a son, and this mysterious Frenchman, whom we have never met!"

When Lotte smilingly replied that she would like to have both Leo and the Frenchman, Hofrat Spineder became really angry, called her frivolous and immoral, and required much coaxing before he could be placated again. Afterward, Lotte sat on her lover's knee and kissed Henry Dufresne and Leo Strakosch, combined in one person, with great enthusiasm.

Chapter XVII. Preparations

Leo, who had almost no chance to speak with anyone except Lotte and his cleaning woman, had lately made the acquaintance of two men whom he considered important. One was the Deputy Wenzel Krotzl, the other the proprietor of the great department store in the Kartnerstrasse, Herr Habietnik.

Leo had met Krotz in the following manner: Returning home late one night from the coffeehouse where he used to read his papers and magazines, he found a man lying on the bottom step, very much the worse for liquor, weeping bitterly and making vain efforts to get on his feet. Leo helped him to his apartment, which was located under his own studio, and discovered, by the way, that he had before him the honorable Deputy Wenzel Krotzl, whose avocation was that of real estate profiteer. Not only was this advertised on the door, but as he reeled forward and back Herr Krotzl persisted in proclaiming at the top of his voice:

"If anyone says I'm drunk, he's a crook and a Jew besides! I'm a duly elected deputy and member of the National Assembly and I've got fifty houses to sell that used to belong to those Jewish pigs."

In the course of time Leo had opportunity to learn that Herr Krotz was not only a rabid anti-Semite but also a notorious drunkard, who usually had a drop too much even at breakfast at the Parliament buffet. However, he had considerable gifts of persuasion and was quite popular among his constituents for his homely way of putting things. He was a widower, and from time to time harbored in his home a presumable housekeeper, occasionally one who had barely passed the legal limit of fourteen years.

It was in a much more conventional manner that Leo met Herr Habietnik. M. Dufresne was accustomed to supply his wants in the line of ties and underwear in the Kartnerstrasse department store, which in spite of its epidemic of woolens still carried the best wares; and on one such occasion he had entered into conversation with Herr Habietnik. The latter was delighted to wait personally on this Frenchman of distinction who bore himself impeccably and knew that a blue cheviot suit required a pearl-gray silk tie. There ensued an animated talk in the course of which Leo saw how deeply the intelligent merchant suffered from prevailing conditions. Thereafter the two frequently met in the store, and finally he made occasional appointments to meet in the Grabencafe.

After the National Assembly had been dissolved Leo hastened to get in touch with Herr Habietnik again, and in the course of the conversation asked him for his opinion on future developments.

"Well, the Socialists are working full steam again, and will win back the votes they lost the last time. The Christian-Socialists and Pan-Germans have lost their heads and haven't come out with their platform as yet; but of course, everyone who is not a Social-Democrat will have to vote for one of the two."

"So that the Jewish law may remain in force?"

"Maybe, if the Socialists don't get the two-thirds majority necessary for every constitutional amendment. I'm afraid that the Christian-Socialists and Pan-Germans won't have the courage to repeal the special legislation against the Jews. I mean—I should say I hope, for if the Jews come back they may eventually even take away the store from me."

"Nonsense," Leo declared energetically. "No one can take from you what you have. Perhaps they'll buy it from you, or the former owner will content himself with a partnership with you. But the most important thing is that you'll be able to throw out the Alpine hats and woolen skirts, and will be able to arrange your displays as you used to."

Habietnik's eyes shone as he replied with genuine warmth:

"Yes, indeed! That's the most important thing! When I think that there might be life and luxury here again, as in the old days—no, that dream is too beautiful to come true."

"Listen here, Herr Habietnik," said Leo, laying his hand on the merchant's arm, "you're the man to make this dream come true. We are still weeks away from the elections. That's long enough for the formation of a Citizens' Party, consisting of the liberal elements, the solid merchants, scholars, lawyers, artists, and industrialists, with the frank and open motto: 'The repeal of the special legislation against the Jews!' Take it up today, form a committee of twelve, to include three merchants, three industrialists, three steadily employed office workers, and three men of the free academic professions. Since you have no newspaper at your disposal as yet, print ten thousand posters, organize district committees, make propaganda from street to street and from house to house, and you cannot fail to be successful. I am a stranger and therefore not as familiar with conditions as you; but this enables me to judge more objectively, and I am quite sure that a considerable section of the public will greet the new party with great enthusiasm."

Herr Habietnik was all enthusiasm. That very evening he gathered about fifty downtown merchants, manufacturers, and lawyers, and at one o'clock in the morning a committee was organized that had at its disposal a fund amounting to millions, pledged by the members of the group.

The new party was called the "Party of the Active Citizens of Austria," stood on a wholly liberal-bourgeois platform, and began its work with an animated and thorough campaign of agitation. No one except Herr Habietnik knew that it was the Frenchman Dufresne who composed the leaflets and proclamations.

Their success surpassed their wildest expectations. Formerly the people had been highly suspicious of every attempt to found a democratic bourgeois party, because the Jews would always push themselves to the fore. But this time it was a purely Christian matter—the names of the leaders were sufficient guarantee that this was no conspiracy hatched by exiled Jews, and all the people who had been harmed by the Jewish law crowded the committee headquarters to join the new party. They came in swarms, the merchants, the jewelers, the assistants of the great tailors, the unemployed chauffeurs—they brought their wives, and the rush became ever greater, in spite of the hue and cry raised by the Christian-Socialist papers. The *Arbeiter-Zeitung* kept quiet, refraining from all aggression. Its chiefs knew that while the Party of Active Citizens would doubtless take many votes from the Social-Democrats, it would, on the other hand, attract all the votes that usually remained uncast, and some of those that would have gone to the Christian-Socialists and Pan-Germans. So it limited itself to an occasional polemic against some plank of the Citizens' platform; but in doubtful districts there even were some secret combines of the two parties.

As April third, the date that had been set for the election, approached, the entire world began to show interest in the outcome. The foreign exchanges, adopting an attitude of waiting, permitted the krone to rest peacefully in the depths; in Vienna the excitement grew hourly, and gave rise to repeated excesses and malignant riots. For all the parties worked with every means at their disposal: The anti-Semites shouted treason and told hair-raising stories of the international conspiracy of the Jews; the Social-Democrats agitated against the peasants—who, they said, were robbing the workers of the city—and against the Christian demagogues who had only wanted to enrich themselves through the expulsions of the Jews; the new Citizens' Party, however, continually put out enormous posters that demonstrated with figures the terrible misery prevailing in Vienna since the expulsion, and showed how the city had actually degenerated into a gigantic village, how all the spirit and enterprise had vanished from its life. Over and over again, in every key and variation, they asserted:

"The special legislation against the Jews must be repealed. But at the same time it will be the business of a wise and conscientious government to keep out those elements that did not reside in Vienna before the world war, unless they can prove before a competent court, composed of members of the middle and working classes, that they were willing and able to do useful, productive, valuable work that is essential for the common good of Austria."

In the Chancellor's office there were daily sessions that lasted far into the night, where consultations were held as to the best way of counteracting the new party and the reinvigorated Socialist group. Schwertfeger had had the right instinct. An enormous new loan had to be floated, the krone had to rise, so that the people would see how solidly all Christendom stood behind them—then the government would be victorious. Immediately after the dissolution of the Parliament, Professor Trumm, the Minister of Finance, had hurried to Berlin, Paris, and London to beg and to plead. In vain, the great Christian leagues abroad, the French anti-Semites, the Dutch Christians—all expressed their sympathy and friendship, inquired eagerly after the fate of the many millions they had already sacrificed to the cause, and refused to unseal their pockets again. Most disappointing of all was the reaction of the American billionaire Mr. Huxtable, on whom they had counted with absolute certainty. He answered none of their telegrams or pleas; and ten days before the election a cable came from the Austrian government's confidential agent in New York, with this crushing message:

"Huxtable unapproachable. Secretly married to Jewish girl from Chicago. Intends to sell loan given Austria three years ago to Kuhn and Loeb Banking Company for quarter of value."

Schwertfeger began to freeze into his now habitual gloom, the anti-Semitic chiefs lost their heads entirely; but Mayor Laberl did something that created a tremendous sensation. Three days before the election he resigned from the Christian-Socialist Citizens' Club, and joined the

Party of Active Citizens. And more than half of the Municipal Council followed his example.

On this day a warm wind blew away the last traces of snow from the hills around Vienna. And in the Billrothstrasse studio two young people were clasped in an ardent and yearning embrace. He whispered:

"Oh, when will you be mine?" And she replied dreamily:

"If you could only take off that little beard! It tickles me so!"

Chapter XVIII. The Election

The election called forth an interest unprecedented in all the world. Old men, invalids, and cripples went to the ballot boxes; and in the afternoon, when the polls were closed, it was known that ninety-nine percent of the enfranchised citizens of Vienna had performed their duty to their country. Then the counting of the votes began throughout the country, lasting till early in the morning; and in the forenoon extra editions of the *Arbeiter-Zeitung* and the *Weltpresse* announced the amazing result.

Only the rural districts had remained faithful to the Christian-Socialists and Pan-Germans. Vienna had elected the candidates of the Socialists and the Citizens' Party almost exclusively, as had also the smaller towns and the industrial region of Austria. The new Parliament, therefore, was composed as follows: seventy Social-Democrats, thirty-six members of the Active Citizens' Party, thirty Christian-Socialists, and twenty-four Pan-Germans. This gave 106 votes for the repeal of the special anti-Jewish legislation, and 54 for its continuance. Leo's beautiful dream—and that of the liberal Citizens and Socialists—therefore seemed destroyed, for they lacked exactly one vote for the two-thirds majority without which the Constitution could not be amended. In spite of their overwhelming defeat, in spite of the fact that the government had to resign immediately to make room for a Social-Democratic ministry, the anti-Semites were rejoicing, and paraded about the town with banners inscribed with the slogan: "The Jews are staying out!"

Just one thing did the vanquished victors fear. The majority had announced that it would wait only for the second session of the newly elected House, which would take place in a week, before it would put forward a declaration of urgency for the repeal of the Jewish law and for the restoration of freedom of movement for everyone without discrimination. But what would happen if a Christian-Socialist or Pan-German deputy were to fail to appear at the session? Voluntary absence was beyond the imagination. But, after all, one of the deputies from the rural districts might fall ill or meet with an accident, and this one would assure the enemy of his two-thirds majority. To prevent such a calamity the minority parties, on the day before the assembly of the House, ordered special trains with attendant physicians for all their deputies. In this way they believed themselves secured against any disastrous incident. For Vienna itself precautions were unnecessary because their one and only representative was the realtor Herr Wenzel Krotzl, elected by the vine-growers and innkeepers of the Nineteenth District, who were very prosperous in Jew-purged Vienna. They were sure of him in every respect, and he enjoyed excellent health.

Now this Herr Krotzl was Leo's last hope, while Lotte almost broke down under the terrible disappointment. She wept all day long, and scarcely could muster the energy to race every day to Leo, who vainly endeavored to inspire her with courage and faith in the outcome. Hofrat Spineder, himself deeply hurt and disappointed by the continuance of the anti-Jewish law, could understand his daughter no longer, and began to harbor grave doubts as to her sanity. He showed that he was very worried as he discussed her remarkable behavior with his wife. "What in the world does it mean? She's forgotten Leo, spends half the day with a new lover, this Frenchman, whom I'm beginning to hate without ever having seen him. Suddenly she declares that she'd like to have both Leo and Dufresne, and now, when Leo can't come back, she sits there and cries her eyes out. I think the girl's out of her head!"

Frau Spineder sighed deeply. "I can't understand it myself, dear. I don't know my own child anymore, and I've no idea as to what's going on in her heart. But in any case, if it develops that the Jewish law remains in force, we must insist on meeting this M. Dufresne."

Herr Spineder nodded.

"Yes, indeed! And if Lotte refuses again, or tries to postpone the matter, we'll send her to Klagenfurt, to her Aunt Minna! . . ."

After days and nights of strenuous thought, Leo finally conceived a plan that would decide whether he could remain in Vienna openly or would have to go back to France. If the law were not repealed, his departure would become a matter of urgent necessity, for his friend Henry Dufresne, whose name he bore, himself wanted to return to Paris from southern France, and thenceforth Leo's reckless game would be in danger of discovery.

Chapter XIX. A Disastrous Drink

On the day of the opening of the National Assembly, that is, the day before the first vital session, Leo Strakosch, equipped with a valise, made various purchases. At Sachet's he bought, for an outrageous sum that once would have paid for an entire building on the Ringstrasse, a Strasbourg pâté de foie gras in the original dish, and in the Hotel Imperial he acquired three bottles of a delicious white Burgundy, three bottles of the heaviest and most costly Bordeaux wines, and a bottle of ancient French cognac. In the evening he waited before the entrance of his house until he saw Herr Krotzl, about to go to a bar after the solemn opening session of the Assembly. Leo congratulated him heartily on his reelection, and said:

"My dear sir, I should also like to attend the historic session of the House tomorrow. The meeting begins at eleven, so I'll order my car for ten o'clock; and if you've nothing against it, I'll drive you over."

Herr Krotzl felt highly flattered at the cordiality of the aristocratic and apparently very wealthy young Frenchman. Thanking him profusely, he accepted the invitation, adding:

"I'd be much obliged to you if you'd come to me at ten o'clock, because then I won't be taking no chances of sleeping too late. My housekeeper, the poor fool, might forget to wake me, and I sleep so sound that the alarm can't get me up. And that would be a fine howdy-do, if I was to oversleep tomorrow. Twenty-four hours later we'd have them damned Jewish pigs back in Vienna!"

Henry Dufresne seemed to take his self-assumed task of saving Austria from the Jews very seriously, for he rang Herr Krotzl's doorbell at only half-past nine. A slovenly, unwashed, but still rouged and powdered young thing opened the door, and without further ado let in the handsome Frenchman, whom she knew well and who was carrying a large box. She was a little disappointed that he did not pay the slightest attention to her, and her considerably exposed body, but merely gave her a banknote and asked her please to fetch the morning papers immediately from the store.

In the anteroom Leo made a great to-do about unpacking his box until the girl had gone out on her errand; then he went quickly into the kitchen, set the cuckoo clock back a full hour, tiptoed out into the living room and did the same to the grandfather clock there, and finally, without knocking, noiselessly entered the door of the Deputy's bedroom, where the honorable gentleman lay under the covers, thunderous snores issuing from his open mouth. Leo immediately discovered the gold watch on the night table, pointing to a quarter of ten. In a flash it was set to a quarter of nine, and then the Frenchman entered on the unpleasant task of waking Herr Krotzl, the Viennese pillar of the Christian-Socialist party. It took quite some time before Krotzl at last opened his swollen little eyes and grasped the situation.

"Oh, Lord, it's Herr Dufresne. Is it as late as all that?" Then, glancing at his watch, he growled: "It ain't even nine yet! I could have slept another hour!"

"Yes," laughed Leo, "but I know a better way of entertaining you and myself. Just think, when I came home last night I found a package from Paris, and in it the best wines of France. Well, since I'm really happy about your success, I thought we could celebrate our victory a little, just us two, before we go on to the Parliament. For you, my dear sir, being a connoisseur, will soon admit that never in all your life have you tasted a wine to compare with the one I'll pour out for you now."

Electrified, Herr Krotzl leaped out of his bed, got partly dressed, and admiringly stroked one after the other the six wine bottles that stood before him with all the earmarks of venerable age. There was white bread, and the Strasbourg patty drew from Herr Krotzl a half-belch, half-grunt that became a hymn of joy as the first glass of the golden Burgundy trickled down his throat.

"What a wine! If I could have that all the time I'd be a different guy! No wonder you Frenchies know how to live, if you got wine like this!"

The second glass was drained to the victory of Herr Krotzl, the third to "Down with the Jews," the fourth to "Long live beautiful Vienna, free of Jews." Then the neck of a bottle of blood-red Bordeaux was broken, and when only the dregs were left in it, and Leo was uncorking the third bottle, Krotzl declared he loved him like a brother. At the fourth bottle he acquainted the Frenchman with the secrets of his sexual life, and proclaimed that skirts over fourteen was nothing more nor less than old women. When they reached the sixth bottle, Leo, unobserved by the half-dazed and quite dizzy Krotzl, mixed the wine with an equal amount of cognac; but now they had to stop, for else it would have been impossible ever to bring the worthy Deputy downstairs. Besides, the correct time was twelve o'clock, so that there was danger of Krotzl's colleagues coming in at any moment to look for him. Leo's own sobriety after this drinking party was due solely to the circumstance that he had each time emptied the contents of his glass under the table, on the beautiful Persian rug.

With hard work Leo finished dressing the Deputy, practically carried him down several flights of stairs, and, with the assistance of the chauffeur, put him in the interior of the closed car. The chauffeur had grinned as he nodded to the Frenchman, whom he often drove about the town. Leo entered, sat down beside Krotzl, who was lying in the corner dead drunk, and the car rolled forward at moderate speed.

The day before, Leo had had an important conference with the chauffeur, beginning with the question:

"How'd you like to make a hundred French francs?"

The chauffeur's eyes had grown to the size of saucers, his face had flushed and he had gasped: "Sir, I'll take you to the moon for a hundred francs!"

But the Frenchman's demands proved much more modest. He said that he wanted to settle a wager, and that the chauffeur would merely have to wait before the house in the Billrothstrasse until he, M. Dufresne, would enter the car with a presumably very tipsy gentleman. Thereafter the automobile was to go toward the Opera, where the Frenchman would get out. Then the ride was to continue to the large insane asylum in Steinhof, far out in the extreme southwestern section of the city. There the chauffeur was to wait until his inebriated fare would give a sign of life. This was followed by further detailed instructions for the quick-witted chauffeur.

Everything went off as had been planned. Even before the car reached the Opera, Herr Krotzl had a violent attack of sickness and then was enjoying the sleep of the just tippler, so that his companion could leave him without any difficulty. While Leo hastened to the Parliament the chauffeur continued on his half-hour's ride to Steinhof. Once there he calmly stopped in the middle of the road and smoked one of Leo's good cigarettes after the other. It was nearly two o'clock when Herr Krotzl finally woke up, his head throbbing. Minutes passed before he remembered where he was and realized that he was all alone in an automobile, and covered with filth from head to foot. Finally, after some more minutes, he saw that he was not in front of the Parliament Building at all, but in the immediate vicinity of the insane asylum in Steinhof. Confused he consulted his watch, which, being an hour slow, pointed to one o'clock. Horrified, Krotzl flung open the door and vented a furious flood of abuse on the chauffeur, who declared with equanimity that he had understood Steinhof to be indicated as the goal, and that the other gentleman had got out on the way. Thereupon, Krotzl tore his hair, wept and shouted, almost went raving mad, called the chauffeur a traitor, hinted at a fearful conspiracy and revenge, and finally pleaded with the driver, who was fast losing his polite attitude, to drive to the Parliament Building at full speed.

The car actually went back about a thousand yards; then, however, it stopped, far away from any human habitation, and the chauffeur, shrugging his shoulders, announced that he could not go on, as the motor was out of order. Entirely sober by this time, Krotzl now sprinted the thousand yards back to the insane asylum. There he confronted the doorman with so much vehemence that the good fellow took him for an escaped inmate, and summoned some keepers. Another half-hour passed before Krotzl was taken to a telephone; he could not, of course, be connected with the Parliament Building immediately, as all its lines were busy; and when he finally did get his connection, and the secretary of his party came to the other end of the wire, a voice shouted in his ear that he was a drunken swine, a crook, bought and paid for by the Jews, and that all was over long ago. "The Jewish law has been repealed!" With these words ringing in his ears the wretched Deputy fell in a profound and beneficent swoon.

Chapter XX. The Repeal of the Anti-Jewish Law

When Leo entered the Parliament Building the newly elected Presiding Officer had just greeted the ministers he had chosen the day before to replace the old cabinet and had informed the Assembly that two declarations of urgency had been presented to the effect that Paragraph Eleven of the Constitution, prohibiting sojourn in Austria to Jews or persons of Jewish origin, should be repealed.

A Social-Democratic deputy rose to move that the declarations of urgency be taken up immediately. In spite of the noisy objection of the Christian-Socialists and Pan-Germans, the majority voted for the motion, whereupon the Presiding Officer gave the floor to Dr. Wolters, the leader of the Social-Democrats, as the first speaker in favor of the proposal.

Wolters pointed out that he and the other members of his party had opposed the law even three years ago as a direct blow to the most sacred rights of man, and as indicative of retrogression into the darkest of the Dark Ages. At that time the opposition had been hooted down, abused, and crowded out of the hall; today, however, the once misled and deluded people had brought them back in such numbers that the power now lay in their hands and in those of other liberal-minded men. Continuing, Wolters sketched the events of the past few years, pointed to the terrible collapse of Austria, cited striking statistics, and closed with these words:

"The audacious, too audacious, work of the man who once assumed divine powers and now could not even obtain a seat in this House, has gone to pieces; outside a hundred thousand unemployed citizens, together with all our working but desperate people, are waiting for the new House to open our gates to a new future, and to give our Jewish fellow-citizens the opportunity to work again side by side with us—not against us—to employ their intelligence, their industry, and their creative force in the interests of our sorely tried and almost ruined country."

After the applause, to which the galleries contributed their share, had died down, the second majority speaker, Herr Habietnik, who had been elected by the downtown businessmen, was given the floor. In a whimsical speech, frequently interrupted by loud laughter, he described the poverty-stricken, provincialized Vienna of the day, regaled his audience with tales of his experiences in his line of business, and declared: "The tiniest hamlet is a metropolis compared with Vienna today. Vienna has become a huge village with a million and a half inhabitants, and if we don't let the Jews in now, we'll soon see country fair booths in the Kartnerstrasse instead of exclusive shops, and livestock markets being conducted on the Stephansplatz. This retrogression, against which they are powerless to do anything, has brought profound despair into the hearts of the citizens of Vienna. By deserting the Christian-Socialist party the Viennese women and girls have not been the last to indicate that they want to have a flourishing and sparkling Vienna, a city of luxurious life, even though it may have a slight Oriental tinge."

Herr Habietnik's further remarks were lost in an odd restlessness that was spreading over the house. What had happened? The Right had at last discovered that Deputy Krotzl was absent, and the Christian-Socialists and Pan-Germans were in a panic. They did not even listen to their own speaker, but sent out ushers with automobiles to fetch Krotzl from his downtown office or from his house in the Billrothstrasse.

The situation might have been saved if someone had had the presence of mind to prompt the minority speaker to continue his speech for hours, until Krotzl should put in his appearance. But they had lost their heads entirely; the Christian-Socialist speaker, Herr Wurm, even curtailed his speech when he noticed the disturbance and saw his colleagues going out. And in a few minutes a Citizens' motion to close the debate and set a five-minute limit for all further speeches was passed by the required two-thirds majority.

In vain did the surprised anti-Semites make a loud outcry; the Socialist Presiding Officer ruled with an iron hand, and permitted none of the previously announced speakers to talk for more than five minutes. Laboring under terrific tension, and greatly agitated, the deputies poured back into the hall in order to be present at the forthcoming roll call. Herr Krotzl had not yet arrived; the ushers could report only that he had not been in his office at all, and had left his home in the morning in a noticeably flushed state, accompanied by another gentleman.

A Pan-German made the last attempt to save the day. Requesting his right to speak on the floor, he said: "Deputy Krotzl is not present, and we have indications that he is being detained by force; indeed, we have cause to fear that he is the victim of foul play. This being the case, the House cannot possibly vote on a law that will determine the fate of our country. If the new majority of this House possesses the slightest sense of decency, it will agree with me that we must immediately adjourn for two hours. During that time we shall probably learn whether our esteemed colleague, Deputy Krotzl, is still among the living."

The import of these words could not be ignored. They were followed by a dead silence.

If Krotzl had really been prevented by force from attending the session, they would have to wait. At this most critical moment a gentleman with a little beard came on the floor furtively and unobserved; he beckoned Herr Habietnik to him, and, breathing hard with agitation, whispered something in his ear, whereupon Herr Habietnik asked for permission to speak.

"I can give the honorable House my word as a gentleman that Herr Krotzl has not been murdered; nor has he been prevented by force from attending this exceedingly important session. At the present moment Herr Krotzl is somewhere in our city, in an automobile, so soundly asleep as the result of indulging in the flowing bowl that the chauffeur is unable to rouse him. For the estimable Herr Krotzl, this sole Viennese ornament of the Christian-Socialist party, undertook in a small way, to celebrate his victory early this morning, in the company of a jolly neighbor; and he drank decidedly more than he could stand. His neighbor, who has given me this information, and whom I know personally as a reliable man of honor, then entered a taxicab together with Krotzl to come here. But he had to get out before they reached their destination, as he could no longer endure the stench in the car. For Herr Krotzl belongs to the old guard that would rather give up than die. I don't know where the thoroughly alive corpse of Herr Krotzl happens to be just now; but this doesn't concern us, and surely no one will demand that we adjourn until Herr Krotzl has sobered up."

The House rocked with laughter; and now the Presiding Officer called the roll. One hundred six deputies voted for the elimination of the special anti-Jewish legislation, 53 against—and the law was repealed!

This time the hundred thousand men and women who were waiting on the street before the building cried "Hurrah!" instead of "Hail!" They were not as enthusiastic as three years before, but seemed a little ashamed of themselves. However, they had recovered their sense of humor, and jests began to fly through the air again.

Immediately after the vote Leo rushed out of the Parliament Building, jumped into a taxicab, and sped to the Linke Wienzeile, to the *Arbeiter-Zeitung*. There, pleading urgent business, he obtained an audience with the editor-in-chief, conversing with him privately for half an hour. As he was about to depart, the editor warmly shook both his hands, laughing: "You've accomplished something extraordinary, and I rejoice with you with all my heart. I can't help admiring your impudence! Really, it's impossible not to. . . ."

"Call it Jewish impudence," Leo supplemented cheerfully, as he hurried down the stairs.

The extra editions of the newspapers, announcing the end of the exclusion of the Jews, had barely appeared before a second extra edition of the *Arbeiter-Zeitung* printed an article with the title:

> The Krone Is Rising
>
> Zurich: The telegraphed and telephoned reports of the decisive session of the Viennese National Assembly were watched with feverish interest on the stock exchange here. The definite news of the repeal of the anti-Jewish law was immediately followed by large purchases of kronen, the buyers including groups of American and English financiers. The stamped Austrian krone doubled its value by leaps and bounds and had tripled it by closing time.

At six o'clock in the evening there appeared a third extra edition that attracted attention throughout Vienna and called forth great merriment mixed with slightly off-color jokes. The announcement was as follows:

> FIRST JEW ARRIVES IN VIENNA
>
> We have the honor to inform the public that the first Jew has just returned to Vienna from his exile. He is the young but already a world-famous painter and etcher Leo Strakosch, who, longing for his own country, spent the period of banishment in Paris, leaving that city the day before yesterday to proceed to Lundenburg, on the Austro-Moravian border. When the news of the nullification of the expulsion law was telephoned to him, he immediately went on by automobile to his native Vienna. At the present time he is staying at the home of his future father-in-law.
>
> —Repeal of the Anti-Jewish Law

This extra edition represented a well-meant bit of mischievous pleasantry on the part of the editor-in-chief of the *Arbeiter-Zeitung*. It was followed by an extra edition of the *Weltpresse*, containing two sensational news items. One was to the effect that the former Chancellor, Dr. Schwertfeger, despondent over the wreck of his nobly and sincerely conceived work, had committed suicide by means of a bullet. The other was an announcement by the *Weltpresse* that, submitting to the will of the overwhelming majority of the inhabitants of Vienna, it would thenceforth appear as the organ of the new Party of Active Citizens.

Chapter XXI. My Beloved Jew!

From the office of the *Arbeiter-Zeitung*, Leo had of course gone directly to Grinzing. Lotte, who, together with her parents, was already aware of the results of the Parliamentary session, was waiting for her lover at an open window on the ground floor. And when the automobile drove up and Leo saw her, the passage through the hall seemed too long for him. So, he swung himself through the window, and an instant later the two young people were in each other's arms, laughing and weeping at once. In spite of his athletic skill, however, Leo had broken a windowpane when he made his shortcut into the house; and as this caused an audible crash, the Hofrat and his wife, alarmed, hurried in from the neighboring living room, only to stop in amazement at the sight of their daughter being covered with kisses by a strange bearded man. Until the Hofrat began to cough so energetically that Lotte heard him and, flushing deeply, extricated herself from her lover's arms to present him to her parents:

"Papa, Mama—this is my fiancé, Henry Dufresne!"

"Leo Strakosch by rights," he added as he threw himself in the arms of the Hofrat and of his future mother-in-law.

After the joy and confusion of the surprise had abated a little, Herr Spineder did what a Hofrat should do in such a case. He added: "Now, children, tell me everything just as it happened."

And Frau Spineder did what any good housewife would have done in her place. She cried, declared that she was so excited she couldn't see straight, and hurried into the kitchen to prepare a dinner to fit the occasion.

In the meanwhile, the Hofrat, Lotte, and Leo conversed in the bathroom, where Leo cut off his beard with a pair of scissors before he shaved and told his story simultaneously. And it was fortunate he did so, for just as he finished shaving and again was a handsome, smooth-faced young man, something quite unexpected happened.

An automobile containing Herr Habietnik, a Socialist Deputy, and a converted Municipal Councillor, arrived, and these men informed Leo that he absolutely had to go to the City Hall with them in order to appear before the crowds gathered there, and to endure an address by the Mayor.

It was useless to resist. Leo was forced to go along, but Lotte, who assumed the responsibility of bringing him back in time for the evening meal, went with him. They rode on undisturbed until they reached the Schottentor, where their course was obstructed. For here the crowd was so dense that the car could not go on. Consequently, the Municipal Councillor leaned out, and with excellent intentions, though not very tactfully, shouted to the people:

"Hey, let's get through! Herr Leo Strakosch, the first Jew to come back to Vienna, has to go to the City Hall!"

These words called forth a thunderous shout of joy. The car was not permitted to pass, but had to wait there with Lotte; Leo, however, now found himself on the shoulders of two sturdy men, and was carried to the City Hall amid the exultant cheers and yells of the masses.

The beautiful building was illuminated again and looked once more like a flaming torch. The men who carried Leo on their shoulders had difficulty in making their way there. And as the trumpets blared, the Mayor of Vienna, Herr Karl Maria Laberl, stepped out on the balcony. He stretched out his arms in a gesture of benediction, and pronounced an impassioned speech that began with the words: "My beloved Jew!

Essays

The Jewish Question (1896)

Theodor Herzl

NO ONE CAN DENY the gravity of the Jewish situation. Wherever they live in perceptible numbers, Jews are more or less persecuted. Their equality before the law, granted by statute, has become practically a dead letter. They are debarred from filling even moderately high positions, either in the army, or in any public or private capacity. And attempts are made to crowd them out of business. Also, "No dealing with Jews!"

Attacks in Parliaments, in assemblies, in the press, in the pulpit, in the streets, on journeys—for example, their exclusion from certain hotels—even in places of recreation, become daily more numerous, the forms of persecution varying according to the countries in which they occur. In Russia, impositions are levied on Jewish villages. In Romania, a few human beings are put to death. In Germany, they get a good beating when the occasion serves. In Austria, anti-Semites exercise terrorism over all public life. In Paris, they are shut out of the so-called best social circles and excluded from clubs. Shades of anti-Jewish feeling are innumerable. But this is not to be an attempt to make out a doleful category of Jewish hardships. It is futile to linger over details, however painful they may be.

I do not intend to awaken sympathetic emotions on our behalf. That would be a foolish, futile, and undignified proceeding. I shall content myself with putting the following questions to the Jews: Is it true that, in countries where we live in perceptible numbers, the position of Jewish lawyers, doctors, men of science, teachers, and officials of all descriptions, becomes daily more intolerable? True, that the Jewish middle classes are seriously threatened? True, that the passions of the mob are incited against our wealthy representatives? True, that our poor endure greater sufferings than any other proletariat?

I think that this external pressure makes itself felt everywhere. In our upper classes it causes unpleasantness, in our middle classes continual and grave anxieties, in our lower classes absolute despair. Everything tends, in fact, to one and the same conclusion, which is clearly enunciated in that classic Berlin phrase: "Juden raus!" (Out with the Jews!)

I shall now put the Jewish Question in the curtest possible form: Are we to "get out" now? And if so, to what place? Or, may we yet remain? And if so, how long?

Let us first settle the point of staying where we are. Can we hope for better days, can we possess our souls in patience, can we wait in pious resignation till the princes and peoples of this earth are more mercifully disposed toward us? I say that we cannot hope for a change in the current of feeling. And why not? Were we as near to the hearts of princes as are their other subjects, even so they could not protect us. They would only feed popular hatred of Jews by showing us too much favor. By "too much," I really mean less than is claimed as a right by every ordinary citizen, and by every tribe.

Every nation in whose midst Jews live is, either covertly or openly, anti-Semitic.

The common people have not, and indeed cannot have, any historic comprehension. They do not know that the sins of the Middle Ages are now being visited on the nations of Europe. We are what the ghetto made us. We have doubtless attained preeminence in finance, because medieval conditions drove us to it. The same process is now being repeated. Modern conditions force us again into finance, now the stock exchange, by keeping us out of all other branches of industry. Being on the stock exchange, we are therefore again considered contemptible. At the same time, we continue to produce an abundance of mediocre intellects that finds no outlet, and this endangers our social position as much as does our increasing wealth. Educated Jews without means are now fast becoming socialists. Hence, we are certain to suffer very severely in the struggle between classes, because we stand in the most exposed position in the camps of both socialists and capitalists.

The artificial means heretofore employed to overcome the troubles of Jews have been either too petty, such as attempts at colonization, or mistaken in principle, such as attempts to convert the Jews to peasants in their present homes.

What is the result of transporting a few thousand Jews to another country? Either they come to grief at once, or prosper, and then their prosperity creates anti-Semitism. We have already discussed these attempts to divert poor Jews to fresh districts. This diversion is clearly inadequate and futile, if it does not actually defeat its own ends; for it merely protracts and postpones a solution, and perhaps even aggravates difficulties.

Whoever were to attempt a conversion of the Jews into a husbandman would be making an extraordinary mistake. For a peasant is a historical category, as is proved by his costume, which in some countries he has worn for centuries; and by his tools, which are identical with those used by his earliest forefathers. His plow is unchanged; he carries the seed in his apron; mows with the historical scythe and threshes with the time-honored flail. But we know that all this can be done by machinery. The agrarian question is only a question of machinery. America must conquer Europe, in the same way as large landed possessions absorb small ones.

The peasant is consequently a type that is in course of extinction. Whenever he is artificially preserved, it is done on account of the political interests that he is intended to serve. It is absurd, and indeed impossible, to make modern peasants on the old pattern. No one is wealthy or powerful enough to make civilization take a single retrograde step. The mere preservation of obsolete institutions is a task severe enough to require the enforcement of all the despotic measures of an autocratically governed state.

Are we therefore to credit Jews, who are intelligent, with a desire to become peasants of the old type? One might just as well say to them:

"Here is a crossbow; now go to war." What? with a crossbow, while the others have rifles and Maxim guns? Under these circumstances the Jews are perfectly justified in refusing to stir when people try to agrarianize them. A crossbow is a beautiful weapon, it inspires me with mournful feelings when I have time to give way. But it belongs rightly in a museum.

Now, there certainly are districts where desperate Jews go out, or at any rate are willing to go out, and till the soil. And a little observation shows that these districts—such as portions of Hessen in Germany, and some provinces in Russia—these very districts are the principal seats of anti-Semitism.

For the world's reformers, who send the Jews to the plow, forget a very important person, who has a decided objection to seeing them there. This person is the agriculturist. And the agriculturist is also perfectly justified in his objections. For the tax on land, the risks attached to crops, the pressure of large proprietors who cheapen labor, and American competition in particular, combine to make his life hard enough. The duties on corn cannot go on increasing indefinitely. Nor can the manufacturer be allowed to starve; his political influence is, in fact, in the ascendant, and he must therefore be treated with additional consideration.

All these difficulties are well known. Therefore, I only referred to them cursorily. I merely wanted to indicate clearly how futile had been past attempts—most of them well intentioned—to solve the Jewish Question. Neither a diversion of the stream, nor an artificial depression of the intellectual level of our proletariat, will overcome the difficulty. The supposed infallible expedient of assimilation has already been dealt with.

We cannot get the better of anti-Semitism by any of these methods. It cannot die out so long as its causes are not removed. Are they removable?

We shall not again touch on those causes that are a result of temperament, prejudice, and limited views, but shall here restrict ourselves to political and economic causes alone. Modern anti-Semitism is not to be confounded with the religious persecution of the Jews of former times.

It does occasionally take a somewhat religious bias, but the main current of the aggressive movement has now changed. In the principal countries where anti-Semitism prevails, it does so as a result of the emancipation of the Jews. When civilized nations awoke to the inhumanity of exclusive legislation and enfranchised us, our enfranchisement came too late. It was no longer possible legally to remove our disabilities in our old homes. For we had, curiously enough, developed while in the ghetto into a bourgeois people, and we stepped out of it only to enter into fierce competition with the middle classes. Hence, our emancipation set us suddenly within this middle-class circle, where we have a double pressure to sustain, from within and from without. The Christian bourgeoisie would not be unwilling to cast us as a sacrifice to socialism, though that would not greatly improve matters. At the same time, the equal rights of Jews before the law cannot be withdrawn where they have once been conceded. Not only because their withdrawal would be opposed to the spirit of our age, but also because it would immediately drive all Jews, rich and poor alike, into the ranks of the revolutionary army.

Nothing effectual can really be done to our injury. In old days our jewels were seized. How is our movable property to be got hold of now? It is comprised in printed papers that are scattered over the world, locked up maybe in the coffers of Christians. It is, of course, possible to get at shares and debentures in railways, banks, and industrial concerns of all descriptions, by taxation, and where the progressive income tax is in force, all our realized property can eventually be laid hold of. But all these efforts cannot be directed against Jews alone, and where they have nevertheless been made, severe economic crises with far-reaching effects have been their immediate consequence. The very impossibility of getting at the Jews nourishes and embitters hatred of them. Anti-Semitism increases day by day and hour by hour among the nations; indeed, it is bound to increase, because the causes of its growth continue to exist, and cannot be removed. Its remote cause is our loss of the power of assimilation during the Middle Ages; its immediate cause is our excessive production of mediocre intellects, who cannot find an outlet downward or upward—that is to say, no wholesome outlet in either direction. When we sink, we become a revolutionary proletariat, the subordinate officers of the revolutionary party; when we rise, there rises also our terrible power of the purse.

The oppression we endure does not improve us, for we are not a whit better than ordinary people. It is true that we do not love our enemies; but he alone who can conquer himself dare reproach us with that fault. Oppression naturally creates hostility against oppressors, and our hostility aggravates the pressure. It is impossible to escape from this eternal round.

"No!" some soft-hearted visionaries will say; "no, it is possible! Possible by means of the ultimate perfection of humanity."

Is it worthwhile pointing out the sentimental folly of this view? He who would found his hope for improved conditions on the ultimate perfection of humanity, would indeed be painting a utopia!

I referred previously to our "assimilation"; I do not for a moment wish to imply that I desire such an end. Our national character is too historically famous, and, in spite of every degradation, too fine, to make its annihilation desirable. We might perhaps be able to merge ourselves entirely into surrounding races, if these were to leave us in peace for a space of two generations. But they will not leave us in peace. For a little period they manage to tolerate us, and then their hostility breaks out again and again. The world is provoked by our prosperity because it has for many centuries been accustomed to consider us as the most contemptible among the poverty-stricken. It forgets, in its ignorance and narrowness of heart, that prosperity weakens our Judaism and extinguishes our peculiarities. It is only pressure that forces us back to the parent stem; it is only hatred encompassing us that makes us strangers once more.

Thus, whether we like it or not, we are now, and shall henceforth remain, a historic group with unmistakable characteristics common to us all.

We are one people—our enemies have made us one in our despite, as repeatedly happens in history. Distress binds us together, and, thus united, we suddenly discover our strength. Yes, we are strong enough to form a state, and a model state. We possess all human and material resources necessary for the purpose.

This is the strictly appropriate place for an account of what has been somewhat roughly termed our "human material." But it would not be appreciated till the broad lines of the plan, on which everything depends, had first been marked out.

The Plan

The whole plan is in its essence perfectly simple, as it must necessarily be if it is to come within the comprehension of all. Let the sovereignty be granted us over a portion of the globe large enough to satisfy the rightful requirements of a nation; the rest we shall manage for ourselves.

The creation of a new state is neither ridiculous nor impossible. We have in our day witnessed the process in connection with nations that were not largely members of the middle class, but poorer, less educated, and consequently weaker than ourselves. The governments of all countries scourged by anti-Semitism will be keenly interested in assisting us to obtain the sovereignty we want. The plan, simple in design, but complicated in execution, will be carried out by two agencies: the Society of Jews and the Jewish Company. The Society of Jews will do the preparatory work in the domains of science and politics, which the Jewish Company will afterward apply practically. The Jewish Company will be the liquidating agent of the business interests of departing Jews, and will organize commerce and trade in the new country. We must not imagine the departure of the Jews to be a sudden one. It will be gradual, continuous, and will cover many decades. The poorest will go first to cultivate the soil. In accordance with a preconceived plan, they will construct roads, bridges, railways, and telegraph installations; regulate rivers; and build their own dwellings; their labor will create trade, trade will create markets, and markets will attract new settlers, for every man will go voluntarily, at his own expense and his own risk.

The labor expended on the land will enhance its value, and the Jews will soon perceive that a new and permanent sphere of operation is opening here for that spirit of enterprise that has heretofore met only with hatred and obloquy.

If we wish to found a state today, we shall not do it in the way that would have been the only possible one a thousand years ago. It is foolish to revert to old stages of civilization, as many Zionists would like to do. Supposing, for example, we were obliged to clear a country of wild beasts, we should not set about the task in the fashion of Europeans of the fifth century. We should not take spear and lance and go out singly in pursuit of bears; we would organize a large and active hunting party, drive the animals together, and throw a bomb into their midst.

If we wish to conduct building operations, we shall not plant a mass of stakes and piles on the shore of a lake, but we shall build as men build now. Indeed, we shall build in a bolder and more stately style than was ever adopted before, for we now possess means that men never yet possessed. The emigrants standing lowest in the economic scale will be slowly followed by those of a higher grade. Those who at this moment are living in despair will go first. They will be led by the mediocre intellects that we produce so superabundantly and that are persecuted everywhere. This pamphlet will open a general discussion on the Jewish Question, but that does not mean that there will be any voting on it. Such a result would ruin the cause from the outset, and dissidents must remember that allegiance or opposition is entirely voluntary. He who will not come with us should remain behind.

Let all who are willing to join us fall in behind our banner and fight for our cause with voice and pen and deed. Those Jews who agree with our idea of a state will attach themselves to the Society, which will thereby be authorized to confer and treat with governments in the name of our people. The Society will thus be acknowledged in its relations with governments as a state-creating power. This acknowledgment will practically create the state. Should the powers declare themselves willing to admit our sovereignty over a neutral piece of land, then the Society will enter into negotiations for the possession of this land. Here two territories come under consideration, Palestine and Argentine. In both countries important experiments in colonization have been made, though on the mistaken principle of a gradual infiltration of Jews. An infiltration is bound to end badly. It continues till the inevitable moment when the native population feels itself threatened, and forces the government to stop a further influx of Jews.

Immigration is consequently futile unless we have the sovereign right to continue such immigration. The Society of Jews will treat with the present masters of the land, putting itself under the protectorate of the European Powers, if they prove friendly to the plan. We could offer the present possessors of the land enormous advantages, assume part of the public debt, build new roads for traffic, which our presence in the country would render necessary, and do many other things. The creation of our state would be beneficial to adjacent countries, because the cultivation of a strip of land increases the value of its surrounding districts.

The Essence of Survival (1935)

Leo W. Schwarz

"IT WOULD HAVE BEEN ABSURD AND PETTY," remarked Heine in a conversation with Alfred Meissner, "if, as I am accused, I had been ashamed of being a Jew; yet, it would be equally ludicrous for me to call myself a Jew."

In this sentence the sagacious poet hit upon one of the central paradoxes of the modern Jew.[1] Thrust with incredible suddenness into the arena of industrialism and accepting avidly the slogans and promise of liberalism and democracy, he completely identified himself with western culture and statehood. He attempted, in a spirit of noblesse oblige, to merge himself in the new world by means of assimilation, conversion, and intermarriage. Nationalism, however, and its lusty handmaiden, anti-Semitism, quickly dissipated the "new springtide of humanity": it was made clear to the Jew that he was at the same time part of and apart from the land in which he dwelt. Even within his own lifetime, Heine discovered his fate: "I am no longer the freest man since Goethe. I am no longer a fat Hellenist with a contemptuous smile for the lean Jews. I am only a poor, sick Jew, a picture of grim misery, an unhappy being."

This tragic cycle of release, exaltation, and disillusionment has become an individual and collective social pattern of the modern, emancipated Jew. In our own day it is grotesquely exhibited in the catastrophe of German Jewry in the Third Reich, but its symptoms—inner conflict and moral defeatism—are discernible everywhere. The philosopher Asher Ginzberg (Ahad Haam) coined the phrase "slavery in freedom" to describe an external emancipation accompanied by moral and intellectual slavery to western civilization. So deep did the conflict strike at the roots of Jewish life that by the end of the nineteenth century thinkers and leaders began to wonder whether the Jewish people could survive[2] at all in the modern world, whether the ancestral culture had any relevancy to modern life. And what of Judaism?

"As the ways of thinking and ways of behaving based on science and conditioned by industry enter into the texture of the daily life of Jews," writes a contemporary social philosopher, "Judaism and its institutions fall more and more into an innocuous desuetude." The first gleam of this social conflict is already discernible in the charming ghetto tales of the writers of the early and middle of the nineteenth century—Auerbach, Kompert, Bernstein, Franzos, Goldschmidt, Mosenthal, and others. To Be or Not to Be?—it pervades the enormous literary output of the Jews during the last fifty years.

But it would be misleading to regard this conflict as an isolated phenomenon. One has to consider it as the result of the impact of the changing modern world upon essentially ghettoized Jewish communities. They felt the pull, first, of economic change. At the beginning of the nineteenth century, the majority of Jews were engaged in petty commercial pursuits as land-tenants, innkeepers, brokers, and tradesmen, and were living in indescribable poverty; less than two percent were engaged in agriculture and a numerically insignificant minority played a prominent role as international bankers. Today more than seventy percent of the Jewish people are engaged in trade and industry, almost seven percent in professional and governmental occupations, and about five percent in agriculture. This extraordinary economic restratification brought in its train a greater interdependence of Jews and non-Jews and a closer knitting together of middle class and proletarian Jews with those who had similar economic interests. The effect upon Jewish life was a progressive weakening of Jewish institutions and mores and, in many instances (for example, education), their replacement by general institutions and habits of living. Moreover, it resulted, as it did in the case of all the European peoples, in a series of migrations toward western Europe and the Americas, and the increasing urbanization of the Jewish population. Since the Jews were a minority with the baggage of medievalism not entirely cast off, both of these factors affected them more drastically than it did the surrounding populations.

The Industrial Revolution paved the way, but it was civil and political emancipation that opened the portals of western civilization to the Jews. A number of social and intellectual currents, symbolized in the persons of Voltaire, Rousseau, and Paine, culminated in the two major political revolutions of the eighteenth century. These brought about complete equality for the Jews in the United States in 1787, in France in 1791, and in Holland in 1796. The struggle for political freedom continued throughout the nineteenth century, when we find Jews among the prominent leaders in the struggles of both the masses (Marx and Lassalle) and the bourgeoisie (Riesser and Cremieux). It was not, however, until the establishment of the Soviet Union and the granting of minority rights to the central European Jews by the Versailles Treaty that eastern and central European Jews were emancipated; there are, however, several countries, like Romania and Morocco, where they still live under medieval conditions. Thus the Jewish people became part and parcel of the economic, social, and intellectual life of western nations. They became identified with the countries (Bergson the "French" philosopher, Einstein the "German" scientist, and so on) of which they were citizens. They became more and more divorced from Jewish life and institutions.

Conceivably the Jewish people might have been assimilated into the western nations, but they were not. Some historians and controversialists ascribe this to the rise of modern anti-Semitism. For anti-Semitism in its modern garb was the very antithesis of the social and political objectives of liberalism. It represented the pseudo-scientific conviction that the Jews were different in character, in culture, in ethics, that they were "demonstrably" alien and inferior. It penetrated every class and bred intense hostility and contempt. That anti-Semitism quickened the Jewish people's national consciousness, threw the people upon their own resources, and stimulated auto-emancipatory movements within

Jewish life is unquestionable. That it demonstrated the illogic of the preachment of liberalism and the technique of democracy is also true. But another factor, the people's will to survive and to express itself, played as direct a role in stemming the tide of assimilation. The inner compulsion to express the folk spirit was especially potent in the masses so that it is among them that the severest struggles for adjustment and rehabilitation took root. But Jews of every economic and social grouping were compelled to weather the storms of this period of transition and thus to make some kind of adjustment. Caught between the anvil of the Machine Age and the hammer of anti-Semitism, they inevitably turned to their reservoir of historical experience and tradition as well as to nondiscriminatory social movements to escape dissolution and disintegration. Concretely, they turned to two chief types of self-expression: (1) A number of religious movements arose to preserve intact traditional Judaism (Neo-Orthodoxy); to adjust Judaism to modern life by the introduction of western forms of worship and customs and by denying the validity of Jewish law and Jewish nationality (Reform Judaism), by utilizing the method and spirit of scientific method; to establish Judaism in the modern world as a humanistic culture (The New Learning); and finally to reevaluate Jewish life in terms of the spirituality and the romanticism of Jewish mysticism (Neo-Hasidism). (2) With the dominance of nationalism during the nineteenth and twentieth centuries it was natural that national movements should have played a prominent role in Jewish life. While some Jews, particularly those resident in western lands, surrendered themselves to the national culture of their country, others advocated the assimilation of western culture into Jewish life by fostering Jewish nationalism. This set into motion two powerful and productive movements that stimulated both economic and social adjustments and cultural creativeness. One is distinctly secular in character, insisting upon the cultivation of the Yiddish vernacular as the national language and viewing the establishment of autonomous Jewish communities with minority rights as the solution of the Jewish problem. The second, the Zionist movement, is a union of the traditional national idea with the territorial element in modern nationalism. Zionism advocates the establishment of a Jewish state (or "homeland") in Palestine and the use of Hebrew as the vehicle of cultural expression.

Thus a people singularly uniform and unified for almost fifteen centuries[3] was torn in many directions. "A people," observes Van Wyck Brooks, "is like a ciphered parchment that has to be held up to the fire before its hidden significances come out." The modern world cost the Jewish people its social and political autonomy; it created sharp and conflicting divisions, and revealed, above all, the potential strength that centuries of suffering and discipline had stored up.

The World War marks a decisive turning point in contemporary history. For the Jewish people it was a catastrophic event. A fantastic loss of lives, the resurgence of brutal pogroms in central Europe, the collapse of the economic structure of Polish and Russian Jewries, the helplessness of the newly created minorities, and a score of postwar social evils converge to build a tragic picture of human distress. The war also set the pendulum of Jewish history in motion again: the hegemony of Jewish life shifts westward to America, and in the East two new social frontiers appear on the horizon in Palestine and in the Soviet Union.

In North and South America, where Jewish history runs back to 1492, about one-third of world Jewry lives. The largest percentage—about four and one-half million—are concentrated in the United States, but the social origins, character and problems of the Jewish communities of Montreal, New York, Chicago, Mexico City, and Buenos Aires are, with minor differences, identical. The Jews have participated enormously in building up the American countries; they have made unique contributions to the cultural development of the "new world." In doing so they have emasculated the European traditions that they transplanted so that the vast network of Jewish institutions in the United States, for example, lacking Jewish content, are in search of new wine to pour into old bottles. But this has been the fate of other minorities in America. It is admirably summarized in the shrewd observation of a literary critic: "In America we have an incongruity, perhaps even a very shambles, of cultures, with a fusion of racial strains, an interruption, thinning out and borrowing of traditions, a continual shifting of literary fashions, a vast and diversified heritage of exemplary European casts of thought." The extraordinary interplay of social and intellectual conflicts that are present in the American Jew of every walk of life are vividly pictured in a huge body of Anglo-Jewish and Yiddish literature that has poured out of America during the twentieth century (America).

To effect a complete social and economic transformation of the Jews has been the policy of the Soviet Union since its inception. The process has been slow and painful since the bulk of the Jewish population were of the lower middle class, without experience in industry or agriculture. But within the last decade the map of Soviet Jewry has been considerably altered: Jews have thronged to urban centers from which they were once excluded; they have drifted into collective agricultural colonies in the Ukraine and Crimea; and they are now laying the foundations of an autonomous Jewish state in Asiatic Biro-Bidjan. The virtual replacement, however, of traditional customs and religion by communist doctrine and institutions has given rise to numerous social and intellectual conflicts, chiefly between the passing generation and the youth. Intermarriage and Russification are on the increase, and those who see no incompatibility between a collectivist economic order and the preservation of Hebraic ideals are deeply concerned with the future of Soviet Jewry. Whatever the outcome may be, the transformation and the tensions and torsions of Soviet Jewry constitute a social upheaval of the first magnitude (Soviet Russia).

More inspiriting to those concerned with the preservation of the Jewish tradition and its values is the development of Palestinian Jewry during the past fifty years. Here the Zionist movement established agricultural colonies and Jewish institutions that have grown remarkably. The most spectacular growth has occurred during the postwar years, during which more than two hundred thousand Jews from every continent and of every variety settled in the country: Kurdish porters, Yemenite silversmiths, Polish storekeepers, German physicians, American manufacturers, and, above all, splendid agricultural pioneers from Europe and America. Hebrew has become the language of the farm, the factory, the bank, the theater, and the University on Mt. Scopus. But Palestinian Jewry, too, is beset with challenging issues: the Arab problem, political relations with Great Britain, the mandatory, the struggle of an admirably organized labor movement and a growing capitalist class, and the economic and social reorientation of an increasing immigration. On the hills and in the valleys of this historic land one feels, despite the complexity of its conflicts, a sense of stability and one cannot fail to be impressed by a new generation stirred by the ideal of reconstituting its people on its ancestral soil (Palestine).

Everywhere, like all peoples today, the Jew is concerned with his future. The theologian declares: "The Jewish people, like its God, is eternal!" "No," observes the social philosopher, "the Jews are an ailing people, perhaps beyond recovery." "True," asserts the social revolutionary, "but the Jew really has nothing to lose but the chains of tradition and discrimination; he has a world of freedom and health to gain." A Christian sociologist proposes a remedy in the form of a new mission: "The achievement—let me state it boldly—is the salvaging of Western civilization. That is the challenge to Israel." The mystic sings: "I believe that Judaism has truly not yet arrived at its real task, and that the great forces that live in this most tragic and incomprehensible of all peoples have not yet spoken their most significant utterance in world history."

Which of these is the true prophet? Only Clio knows, but she won't reveal her secret to our generation.

NOTES

Introduction: Never-Ending Jewish Tales and the Jewish Question

1. See Ritchie Robertson, *The "Jewish Question" in German Literature, 1749–1939: Emancipation and Its Discontents* (1999), 1.

2. Irving Howe and Eliezer Greenberg, eds., *A Treasury of Yiddish Stories* (1989), 31.

3. Élisabeth Roudinesco, *Revisiting the Jewish Question* (2013), 35.

4. Franklin Foer, "The End of the Golden Age," *Atlantic Monthly* (April 2024): 25–35.

5. *Week* (November 4, 2022): 16.

6. See Alexander Cockburn and Jeffrey St. Clair, eds., *The Politics of Anti-Semitism* (2003); Steven Baum, *When Fairy Tales Kill: The Origins and Transmission of Antisemitic Beliefs* (2008); Lisa Silverman, *Becoming Austrians: Jews and Culture between the World Wars* (2012); Caspar Battegay, *Geschichte der Möglichkeit: Utopie, Diaspora, und die "jüdische Frage"* (2018); David Sorkin, *Jewish Emancipation: A History across Five Centuries* (2019); David Edmonds, *The Murder of Professor Schlick: The Rise and Fall of the Vienna Circle* (2020); Adam Sutcliffe, *What Are Jews For? History, Peoplehood, and Purpose* (2020); Jeffrey Veidlinger, *In the Midst of Civilized Europe: The Pogroms of 1918–1921 and the Onset of the Holocaust* (2021); and David Baddiel, *Jews Don't Count: How Identity Politics Failed One Particular Identity* (2021).

7. See Ian Lustick, *Paradigm Lost: From Two-State Solution to One-State Reality* (2019). Lustick's thorough analysis of the conflict between the Israeli Jews and the Palestinians reveals that Jewish Zionism has led to a transformation of Jewish sensibility so that the Jews in Israel have oppressed the Palestinians.

8. Jack Zipes, *The Operated Jew: Two Tales of Anti-Semitisim* (1991), 87–88.

9. Battegay, *Geschichte der Möglichkeit*, 3.

The Story about the Sorcerer

1. Editor's note: "Di Majnse vin dem Pojps," *Mitteilungen der Gesellschaft für jüdische Volkskunde* 9.2 (1902): 104–107. Translated as "The Sorcerer's Apprentice" in *Yiddish Folktales*, ed. Beatrice Silverman Weinreich, trans. Leonard Wolf (New York: Pantheon, 1988).

Two Anti-Semites

1. Editor's note: On April 6, 1903, and April 19, 1905, there were two major pogroms in Kishinev. Jews were accused of various crimes, including the ritual murder of a Christian child. Pavolachi Krushevan, the editor of the newspaper *Bessarabets*, published numerous anti-Semitic articles, and more than a hundred Jews were killed and more than a thousand Jewish shops and stores were destroyed during these pogroms. These events became known as the Kishinev Massacre and led to massive emigrations of Jews.

A Shocking Tale of a Viceroy

1. Editor's note: Haman is the anti-Semitic viceroy at the court of King Ahasuerus in the Book of Esther, which is read every Purim.

The Zaddik

1. Editor's note: "The Zaddik" was published in 1937 in a New York magazine called *Opinion*.

The Essence of Survival

1. The following books will open the main avenues of modern Jewish life to the reader: *The Jews in the Modern World* by Arthur Ruppin (New York, 1934); *Hebrew Reborn* by Shalom Spiegel (New York, 1930); *Yisroel*, edited by Joseph Leftwich (London, 1933); *The ICWI and Other Minorities under the Soviets* by Avrahm Yarmolinsky (New York, 1928); *Modern Palestine*, edited by Jessie Sampter (New York, 1933).

2. It is not a question of physical survival. The Jewish population has increased fivefold since the French Revolution.

3. For a detailed exposition and critique of these movements, see *Judaism as a Civilization* by Mordecai M. Kaplan (New York, 1934).

BIBLIOGRAPHY

Literature

Abramovitsch, S. Y. *Tales of Mendele the Book Peddler*. Eds. Dan Miron and Ken Frieden. New York: Schocken Books, 1996.

Aleichem, Sholem. *The Best of Sholom Aleichem*. Eds. Irving Howe and Ruth Wisse. Washington, DC: New Republic Books, 1979.

———. *Old Country Tales*. Trans. Curt Leviant. New York: Paragon Books, 1966.

———. *Tevye the Dairyman and the Railroad Stories*. Ed. and trans. Hillel Halkin. New York: Schocken, 1987.

Batchinisky, Julian, Arnold Margolin, Mark Vishnitzer, and Israel Zangwill. *The Jewish Pogroms in Ukraine: Authoritative Statements on the Question of Responsibility for Recent Outbreaks against the Jews in Ukraine*. Washington, DC: The Friends of Ukraine, 1919.

Ben-Amos, Dan. *Folktales of the Jews, Volume 1: Tales from the Sephardic Dispersion*. Philadelphia: The Jewish Publication Society, 2006.

———. *Folktales of the Jews, Volume 2: Tales from Eastern Europe*. Philadelphia: The Jewish Publication Society, 2007.

Berg, Liz, ed. *Jewish Folk Tales in Britain and Ireland*. Cheltenham: History Press, 1920.

Bettauer, Hugo. *Die Stadt ohne Juden: Ein Roman von Übermorgen*. Vienna: R. Löwit Verlag, 1924.

Cahan, Abraham. *Yekel and the Imported Bridegroom and Other Stories of Yiddish New York*. Salt Lake City, UT: Stonewell Press, 2013.

Der Nister. *Contes Fantastiques et Symboliques*. Trans. Delphine Bechtel. Paris: Les Editions du Cerf, 1997.

———. *Regrowth: Seven Tales of Jewish Life before, during, and after Nazi Occupation*. Evanston, IL: Northwestern University Press, 2011.

———. *Unterm Zaun: Jiddische Erzählungen*. Frankfurt am Main: Insel Verlag, 1988.

Frank, Helen, trans. *Yiddish Tales*. Philadelphia: Jewish Publication Society of America, 1912.

Franzos, Karl Emil. *Der Bart des Abraham Weinkäfer under andere Novellen aus Osteuropa*. Berlin: Holzinger, 2017.

———. *Die Juden von Barnov, Geschichten*. Leipzig: Duncker & Humblot, 1880.

———. *The Jews of Barnow: Stories (The Modern Jewish Experience)*. New York: Arno Press, 1975.

Gaster, Moses. *Ma'aseh Book: Book of Jewish Tales and Legends*. Facsimile of original 1934 edition. Philadelphia: Jewish Publication Society of America, 1981.

Hautzig, Esther, ed. and trans. *The Seven Good Years and Other Stories of I. L. Peretz*. Philadelphia: Jewish Publication Society, 1984.

Hermand, Jost. *Geschichten aus dem Ghetto*. Frankfurt am Main: Hain, 1990.

Howe, Irving, and Eliezer Greenberg, eds. *A Treasury of Yiddish Stories*. 2nd rev. ed. New York: Viking, 1989.

Landsberger, Artur. *The City without Jews; A Novel of Our Time*. Trans. Salomea Brainin. New York: Bloch Publishing Company, 1926.

———. *Das Ghettobuch: Die schönsten Geschichten aus dem Ghetto*. Munich: Verlag Georg Müller, 1914.

Neugroschel, Joachim, ed. *The Golem*. New York: W. W. Norton. 2006.

———, ed. *Great Tales of Jewish Occult and Fantasy: The Dybbuk and 30 Other Classic Stories*. New York: Wings Books, 1976.

———, ed. *Radiant Days, Haunted Nights: Great Tales from the Treasury of Yiddish Folk Literature*. New York: Overlook Duckworth, 2005.

Peretz, I. L. *The. I. L. Peretz Reader*. Ed. Ruth Wisse. New York: Schocken Books, 1990.

Roskies, David. *The Literature of Destruction: Jewish Responses to Catastrophe*. Philadelphia: Jewish Publication Society, 1989.

Schwartz, Howard. *A Palace of Pearls: The Stories of Rabbi Nachman of Bratslav*. New York: Oxford University Press, 2018.

Schwarz, Leo. *A Golden Treasury of Jewish Literature*. New York: Farrar & Rinehart, 1937.

———. *The Jewish Caravan: Great Stories of Twenty-Five Centuries*. New York: Farrar & Rinehart, 1935.

Singer, Irma. *Das verschlossene Buch. Jüdische Märchen*. Vienna and Berlin: R. Löwit Verlag, 1918.

Stavans, Ilan, ed. *The Oxford Book of Jewish Stories*. New York: Oxford University Press, 1998.

Stromberg, David, ed. *In the Land of Happy Tears: Yiddish Tales for Modern Times*. New York: Delacorte Press, 2018.

Zangvill, Israel. *Dreamers of the Ghetto*. New York: Harper & Brothers, 1898.

Zipes, Jack. *The Operated Jew: Two Tales of Anti-Semitism*. New York: Routledge, 1991.

Nonfiction

Ackerman, Spencer, and Eric Orner. "Meet the 'Winners' of the War on Gaza." *Nation* (July 2024): 4–45.

Antin, Mary. *The Promised Land*. Ed. Werner Sollors. New York: Penguin, 1997.

Arendt, Hannah. *The Jew as Pariah: Jewish Identity and Politics in the Modern Age*. Ed. Ron Feldman. New York: Grove Press, 1978.

Avrutin, Eugene, and Elissa Bemporad, eds. *Pogroms: A Documentary History*. Oxford: Oxford University Press, 2021.

Baddiel, David. *Jews Don't Count: How Identity Politics Failed One Particular Identity*. London: TLS Books, 2021.

Bartov, Omer. "Antisemitism: A Guide for the Perplexed." *Nation* (July 2024): 35–39.

Battegay, Caspar. *Geschichte der Möglichkeit: Utopie, Diaspora und die jüdische Frage*. Göttingen: Wallstein Verlag, 2018.

Bauer, Michael. *Oskar Panizza: Ein literarisches Portrait*. Munich: Carl Hanser Verlag, 1984.

Baum, Steven. *When Fairy Tales Kill: The Origins and Transmission of Antisemitic Beliefs*. New York: iUniverse, 2008.

Bemporad, Elissa. *Legacy of Blood: Jews, Pogroms, and Ritual Murder in the Lands of the Soviets.* Oxford: Oxford University Press, 2019.

Birnbaum, Pierre, and Ira Katznelson, eds. *Paths of Emancipation: Jews, States, and Citizenship.* Princeton, NJ: Princeton University Press, 1995.

Braun, Robert. "Borderlands and Antisemitism in Weimar Germany: Evidence from Children's Stories." July 9, 2021. https://broadstreet.blog/2021/07/09/borderlands-and-antisemitism-in-Weimar-Germany.

Brown, Peter. *Oscar Panizza: His Life and His Works.* New York: Peter Lang, 1983.

Bruner, Andreas. *Die Stadt ohne: Juden, Muslime, Flüchtline, Ausländer.* Vienna: Verlag Fimarchiv Austria, 2018.

Cockburn, Alexander, and Jeffrey St. Clair, eds. *The Politics of Anti-Semitism.* Oakland, CA: Counter Punch and AK Press, 2003.

Dawidowicz, Lucy. *The War against the Jews, 1933–1945.* New York: Bantam Books, 1986.

Diner, Dan. *Beyond the Conceivable: Studies on Germany, Nazism, and the Holocaust.* Berkeley: University of California Press, 2000.

Edmonds, David. *The Murder of Professor Schlick: The Rise and Fall of the Vienna Circle.* Princeton, NJ: Princeton University Press, 2020.

Foer, Franklin. "The End of the Golden Age." *Atlantic Monthly* (April 2024): 20–35.

Frankel, Jonathan, and Steven Zipperstein, eds. *Assimilation and Community: The Jews in Nineteenth Century Europe.* Cambridge: Cambridge University Press, 1992.

Gaster, Moses, ed. and trans. *Ma'aseh Book: Book of Jewish Tales and Legends.* 2 vols. Philadelphia: Jewish Publication Society of America, 1934.

Gonzales, Matt. "Stories of Antisemitism." May 14, 2022. https://www.shrm.org/hr-today-news/all-things-work/pages/antisemitism.

Gottstein, Michael. *Felix Salten (1869–1945): Ein Schriftsteller der Wiener Moderne.* Würzburg: Ergon Verlag, 2007.

Götz, Aly. *Europe against the Jews, 1880–1945.* New York: Metropolitan Books, 2020.

———. *Why the Germans? Why the Jews? Envy, Race, Hatred, and the Prehistory of the Holocaust.* Trans. Jefferson Chase. New York: Metropolitan/Holt, 2014.

Granick, Jaclyn. *International Jewish Humanitarianism in the Age of the Great War.* Cambridge: Cambridge University Press, 2021.

Hall, Murray. *Der Fall Bettauer.* Vienna: Löcker Verlag, 1978.

Horn, Dara. *People Love Dead Jews: Reports from a Haunted Present.* New York: W. W. Norton, 2021.

Jelen, Sheila. *Salvage Poetics: Post-Holocaust American Jewish Folk Ethnographies.* Detroit: Wayne State University Press, 2020.

Jospe, Alred, ed. *Tradition and Contemporary Experience: Essays on Jewish Thought and Life.* New York: Schocken, 1970.

Lehnemann, Widar. "'Judelnde Hasen.' Felix Saltens Roman *Funfzehn Hasen.*" In Ekehard Czucka, ed., *Die in dem alten Hause der Sprache wohnen,* 453–484. Münster: Aschendorff, 1991.

Levinson, Julian. "Jewish Storytelling as Counterethnography." *Prooftexts* 36.3 (2018): 286–306.

Lustick, Ian. "Must Every Golem Die?" *Palestine/Israel Review* 1 (2024): 237–241.

Lustick, Ian. *Paradigm Lost: From Two-State Solution to One-State Reality*. Philadelphia: University of Pennsylvania Press, 2024.

Niewyk, Donald. *The Jews in Weimar Germany*. Baton Rouge: Louisiana State University Press, 1980.

Oisteanu, Andrei. *Inventing the Jew: Antisemitic Stereotypes in Romanian and Other Central-East European Cultures*. Lincoln: University of Nebraska Press, 2009.

Roback, A. A. *The Story of Yiddish Literature*. New York: Gordon Press, 1974.

Robertson, Ritchie. *The German-Jewish Dialogue: An Anthology of Literary Texts*. Oxford: Oxford University Press, 1919.

———. *The "Jewish Question" in German Literature, 1749–1939: Emancipation and Its Discontents*. Oxford: Oxford University Press, 1999.

Rokies, David. "Catastrophe in Jewish Literature." *Prooftexts* 2.1 (January 1982): 53–77.

Roudinesco, Élisabeth. *Revisiting the Jewish Question*. Trans. Andrew Brown. London: Polity Press, 2013.

Schama, Simon. *Belonging: The Story of the Jews, 1492–1900*. New York: Vintage, 2017.

Schwarz, Leo, ed. *The Great Ages and Ideas of the Jewish People*. New York: Random House, 1956.

———. *The Redeemers: A Saga of the Years 1945–1952*. New York: Farrar, Straus and Young, 1953.

Shohat, Ella. *Taboo Memories, Diasporic Voices*. Durham, NC: Duke University Press, 2006.

Shulman, David. "Israel: The Way Out." *New York Review of Books*, April 11, 2024, 10–12.

Silverman, Lisa. *Becoming Austrians: Jews and Culture between the World Wars*. New York: Oxford University Press, 2012.

Simon, Carsta, and William Baum. "Expelling the Meme-Ghost from the Machine: An Evolutionary Explanation for the Spread of Cultural Practices." *Behavior and Philosophy* 39.40 (2011): 127–144.

Sorkin, David. "Between Messianism and Survival: Secularization and Sacralization in Modern Judaism." *Journal of Modern Jewish Studies* 3.1 (2004): 73–86.

———. "Emancipation and Assimilation: Two Concepts and Their Application to German-Jewish History." *Leo Baeck Institute Yearbook* 35 (1990): 17–33.

———. *Jewish Emancipation: A History across Five Centuries*. Princeton, NJ: Princeton University Press, 2019.

———. *The Transformation of German Jewry: 1780–1840*. New York and Oxford: Oxford University Press, 1987.

Sutcliffe, Adam. *What Are Jews For? History, Peoplehood, and Purpose*. Princeton, NJ: Princeton University Press, 2020.

Teter, Magda. *Blood Libel: On the Trail of an Antisemitic Myth*. Cambridge, MA: Harvard University Press, 2020.

———. "Rehearsal for Genocide." *New York Review of Books*, June 9, 2022, 8–10.

Veidlinger, Jeffrey. *In the Midst of Civilized Europe: The Pogroms of 1918–1921 and the Onset of the Holocaust*. New York: Metropolitan Books, 2021.

Voss, Rebekka. "Entangled Stories: The Red Jews in Premodern Yiddish and German Apocalyptic Lore." *Association for Jewish Studies Review* 36.1 (April 2012): 1–41.

Wiener, Leo. *The History of Yiddish Literature in the Nineteenth Century*. 2nd ed. Intro. Elias Schulman. New York: Hermon Press, 1972.

Yassif, Eli. *The Hebrew Folk Tale: History, Genre, Meaning*. Trans. Jacqueline Teitelbaum. Indianapolis: Indiana University Press, 1999.

Zipes, Jack. *Yale Companion of Jewish Writing and Thought in German Culture, 1066–1966*. Ed. with Sander Gilman. New Haven, CT: Yale University Press, 1997.

Žižek, Slavoj. *Living in the End of Times*. Shanghai: Expo, 2010.

BIOGRAPHIES OF AUTHORS AND EDITORS

SHOLEM ALEICHEM (SOLOMON NAUMOVICH RABINOVICH) (1859–1916) was a Yiddish writer and dramatist. Born in a Russian shtetl in what is now Ukraine, Aleichem began writing stories as a teenager, and adopted the pseudonym "Sholem Aleichem," which means "peace be with you." One of the foremost champions of Yiddish literature and culture, Aleichem lectured in Europe and the United States about the necessity of making Yiddish a national language. Some of his best works have been gathered in *Tevye's Daughters: Collected Stories of Sholem Aleichem* (1949), *Some Laughter, Some Tears* (1969), and *The Best of Sholem Aleichem* (1991). The 1964 musical *Fiddler on the Roof* was based on his stories about Tevye the Dairyman.

MERI BALKON, a storyteller, was born in Grodne, Poland.

SHMUEL BASTOMSKI (1891–1942), a prominent secular educator and editor, was born in Vilna, Poland. He was orphaned at a young age, and after graduating from Vilna Teaching Institute in 1912, he worked at various schools in the region. In 1914 he was hired to teach at the Society for the Promotion of Culture among the Jews of Russia, where he worked until the late 1930s. He established one of the first Yiddish publishing houses in Poland, edited important children's literature journals, and had a great interest in all kinds of Yiddish folklore. As a socialist and Zionist, he sought to use Yiddish riddles, legends, songs, and tales to educate children. Bastomski also published small chapbooks and pamphlets in Yiddish to distribute among Jewish people. These often consisted of short tales and legends that he had personally collected and edited to further the growth of literacy in Poland.

DAN BEN-AMOS (1934–2023), a Jewish folklorist, was born in Tel Aviv. After immigrating to the United States, he received his PhD from Indiana University in 1966 and became one of the "Young Turks," a group of scholars who developed new perspectives for the study of folklore. A longtime professor of folklore and folk life at the University of Pennsylvania, he published numerous theoretical studies of folklore and three major anthologies: *Folktales of the Jews: Tales from the Sephardic*, Volume I (2006); *In Praise of the Baal Shem Tov: Tales from Eastern Europe*, Volume II (1970); and *Tales from Arab Lands*, Volume III (2011).

DOVID BERGELSON (1884–1952) was born in a shtetl of Kiev and became one of the foremost Yiddish modernist writers of the twentieth century, beginning with his novel *At the Depot* (*Arum Vokzal*, 1909). He focused on the conflict of secular protagonists who rebelled against the strict Hasidic laws and provincial shtetl life. In 1921 he moved from Kiev to Berlin, where he wrote notable stories and traveled throughout Europe and the United States. He also wrote for the Yiddish-language New York newspaper *The Forward*. At one point he became convinced that the Soviet Union enabled greater assimilation for Jews, and he began writing for two communist Yiddish newspapers in New York and Russia. In 1933, with the rise of the Nazis, Bergelson fled to Russia, where he joined the Jewish Anti-Fascist Committee during World War II. His faith in the Soviet Union was betrayed, however, when he was arrested during an anti-Semitic campaign in 1949 on false pretenses and executed in 1952.

HUGO BETTAUER (1872–1925) was an Austrian-Jewish political journalist and prolific writer. Born into a Jewish family in the city of Baden near Vienna, he ran away from home at sixteen and converted to Lutheranism. After serving in the Austrian mountain infantry for one year, he moved to Zurich, inherited a large sum of money, and soon moved to New York, where he made a living as a journalist and novelist. Upon returning to Europe in 1910, he settled in Vienna, where he worked for the *Neue Freie Presse*. During World War I he worked as a correspondent for several New York papers and magazines. At the same time, he founded an aid program for the people of Vienna. During and after the war he established himself as one of the most popular writers of mysteries and erotic novels in the German language. Almost all his works contained social messages critical of the reigning forces in Austria and Germany. His major work, *Die Stadt ohne Juden* (*The City without Jews*, 1924), a satire of the Viennese, sold 250,000 copies when it was published, and enraged the fascists in Austria and Germany. The Nazis declared him a "Red Poet," dangerous to youth, and the threats to his life were realized by his assassin, a dental technician with close ties to the Nazis, who was never punished for his heinous deed.

ALFRED DÖBLIN (1878–1957) was a doctor, essayist, and novelist. Born in Stettin, Germany, and raised in Berlin, he studied at the Humboldt University of Berlin from 1900 to 1904 and earned a medical degree from the University of Freiburg in 1905. But his real love was literature, and he began writing novels and novellas. He had a great interest in modernism and expressionism, and his third historical novel, *The Three Leaps of Wang-Lung* (*Die drei Sprünge des Wang-Lun*, 1913), which dealt with a political revolt in the eighteenth century, brought him recognition from the artists and writers of the Weimar Period. In 1929 he made a name for himself with his experimental and controversial masterpiece *Berlin Alexanderplatz*, which depicted a brutal but vigorous side of life in the city. With the rise of Nazism, Döblin fled to Paris in 1933 and remained there until 1940, when again he had to flee, this time to the United States. He returned to Berlin in 1945, but it was no longer the city he had experienced during the Weimar Period, and consequently he spent his later years in France. An assimilated Jew, Döblin converted to Catholicism in Los Angeles, but he fought anti-Semitism throughout his life.

ILYA EHRENBOURG (1891–1967), a writer, poet, and journalist, was born in Kiev (Ukraine), and moved to Moscow when he was four years old. Drawn to the Communist Party during his teenage years, he was arrested for his antigovernment activities in 1908 and then sent to France, where he abandoned political activism and took an interest in art and literature. He also began writing for magazines and newspapers.

In 1917 he returned to Moscow. At first he supported the Bolshevik takeover, but opposed the anti-Semitism in Soviet Russia and exposed the pogroms that the Jews suffered. In 1921 he returned to western Europe and often wrote about Jewish suffering. At the same time, he resolved some of the problems that he had with the Kremlin and began writing for different Russian publications as well as writing his own novels. His major concern while living in Paris during the 1930s was fascism, and in 1940 he returned to Moscow, where he became a war correspondent for the Red Army and was considered one of the prominent journalists in the Soviet Union. After World War II, Ehrenbourg focused on exposing Nazi atrocities during the Holocaust. In 1948, when Stalin began his anti-Semitic campaign that led to the execution of Russian Jews, Ehrenbourg managed to evade arrest. After Stalin's death in 1953, he was accused of supporting Stalinism. However, these accusations have proved to be false, and he continued to write and critique the anti-Semitism that was still alive and dangerous in the Soviet Union.

HELENA FRANK (1872–1954), a British translator, was not Jewish, but she learned Hebrew and Yiddish and became one of the major translators of such writers as I. L. Peretz, Hayim Nahman Bialik, and Shaul Tchernichovsky. Her translations of Peretz include *Stories and Pictures* (1906) and *Yiddish Tales* (1912).

KARL EMIL FRANZOS (1848–1894), an Austrian novelist, focused his attention on diverse regions of the Pale Settlement, which included parts of Ukraine, Galicia, Poland, Bukovina, and other Central European regions. Franzos was born in the Austrian Kingdom of Galicia. His family descended from Sephardic Jews who had fled the Spanish Inquisition in the eighteenth century. Franzos himself was raised in a liberal and educated family in the Bukovina capital Czernowitz. Later he studied law at the universities of Graz and Vienna, but he was unable to practice law because of the rigid laws of the Austrians and Germans. Consequently, he turned to journalism and prose writing. All of his writing was in German, and he idolized German culture. After moving to Berlin in 1886, he was considered

novels and plays together. She wrote a children's column in the *Jewish Chronicle* and published *Jewish Fairy Tales and Legends* in 1919, which included fables and other new stories in the editions that followed.

ARTUR LANDSBERGER (1876–1933), a German-Jewish novelist and screenwriter, received his law degree in 1908, but he never practiced law. Instead he began writing for different magazines and newspapers, and in 1910 published his first novel, *Wie Hilde Simon mit Gott und dem Teufel kämpfte* (How Hilde Simon Fought with God and Satan), which ignited his career as a writer of potboilers. He was not very much attached to his Jewish origins and converted to Protestantism in 1922. Nevertheless, he produced two significant collections of Jewish tales, *Das Ghettobuch, die schönsten Geschichten aus dem Ghetto* (The Ghettobuch, the Most Beautiful Stories from the Ghetto) in 1914 and *Das Volk des Ghetto* (The People of the Ghetto) in 1916. In addition, he published a satirical German version of Hugo Bettauer's *The City without Jews*, called *Berlin ohne Juden* (Berlin without Jews), in 1925. Haunted and hunted by the Nazis, Landsberger died by suicide in 1933 when the Nazis came to power.

JOACHIM NEUGROSCHEL (1938–2011), an American translator, editor, and art critic, was born in Vienna. His family fled the Nazis in 1939, and, after a brief stay in Rio de Janeiro, landed in New York City in 1941. Neugroschel studied English and comparative literature at Columbia University. After spending six years in Europe following his graduation, he returned to New York in 1964 to become one of the most gifted and prolific translators of Yiddish, German, and French literature. He was the winner of multiple awards and was made a Chevalier in the Ordre des Arts et des Lettres in 1996.

HERSH DOVID NOMBERG (1876–1927), a writer of essays and stories and a political activist, was born in a small town near Warsaw and grew up in a strict Hasidic community. At the age of twenty-one, he moved to Warsaw, where he received a more secular education and was strongly influenced by I. L. Peretz and socialist organizations. Aside from writing in Yiddish and Hebrew, he also taught himself to read and write Russian, Polish, and German. Nomberg wrote numerous short stories, novellas, and plays during his life. He traveled extensively to promote what he called Yiddishism, a recognition of the significance of Yiddish culture. Not only did he visit and lecture in different parts of Central Europe, but he also journeyed to the United States, Argentina, and Palestine. Writing for various Yiddish newspapers and journals, Nomberg was recognized as one of the foremost political journalists of his time.

OSKAR PANIZZA (1853–1921) was a controversial writer, essayist, novelist, psychiatrist, poet, and publisher. Born in Badkissingen in northern Bavaria, Panizza began rebelling against all organized religions and all institutions at an early age. In addition, he struggled against his mother, Mathilde, who owned a prestigious hotel in Badkissingen that catered to the upper classes. When Panizza turned seventeen he moved to Munich and eventually completed his medical studies in 1880 with a specialty in psychiatry. During this time he turned to writing poetry. By 1883 he convinced his mother to establish a trust for him after she sold her hotel. Thanks to this financial support, he was able to abandon medicine and became known as an experimental poet. In 1890 he was also considered one of the most interesting writers among the avant-garde Munich Moderns and wrote numerous articles for their journal *Die Gesellschaft für modernes Leben* (The Society for Modern Life). By 1893, Panizza became notorious with the publication of two anti-Catholic works: *Die unbefleckte Empfängnis der Päpste* (The Immaculate Conception of the Popes) followed by *Der teutsche Michel und der römische Papst* (The German Fool and the Roman Pope). At the same time, he published his anti-Semitic story "The Operated Jew," which parodied and caricatured Jewish endeavors to assimilate themselves and become ethnic Germans. Largely accepted by German readers, this was not the case with Panizza's *Das Liebeskonzil* (The Love Council, 1894), which was a devastating critique of traditional Catholicism. Due to the publication of this work, he was sentenced to twelve months in a Munich prison. From this point on, Panizza continued to write unusual satires while living in Switzerland and Paris. By 1905 he had developed a progressive case of paranoia and had himself admitted to an asylum in Bayreuth, where he spent the last sixteen years of his life.

ISAAC LEIB PERETZ (known as I. L. Peretz; 1852–1915) was born in Poland and is considered one of the great Yiddish writers of his time. He was sympathetic to the labor movement and wrote folk tales and plays in Hebrew and Yiddish. Unlike many great writers of the Jewish Enlightenment, Peretz, who was raised in an orthodox Jewish home in Zamosé, received a traditional education and could read several European languages. In 1878 he passed the law examination. About ten years later, however, he had to abandon this profession because the Russian authorities accused him of supporting socialists and Polish nationalists. From this time onward he supported himself through odd jobs and his writing. His career developed quickly after the publication of the ballad *Monish* and *Bilder fun a Provints Rayze* (Pictures from a Country Journey). After he settled in Warsaw in 1888, he collaborated with other Jewish writers to promote Yiddish works. In addition, he formed a drama group in 1907, and many of his significant Yiddish dramas of socialist realism had an influence on the rise of the American Jewish theaters as well as other European Yiddish theaters until 1933. A political activist until he died in 1915, he founded an orphanage and schools during World War I for displaced Jewish children.

BENYOMIN PIKOVER, a storyteller, was born in Grodne, Poland.

ALEXANDER SISKIND RABINOVITZ (also known by his pseudonym Azar; 1854–1945) was born in Liady, part of the Russian Empire, to a poor family. During his youth, he received a Talmudic education and learned Hebrew and Russian. After marrying at the age of eighteen, he tried to earn a living as a peddler but failed. By the time he turned twenty-one, he traveled throughout Lithuania and earned a living through teaching. Eventually he went to Moscow in the 1880s and tried to work as a journalist. His major accomplishment at that time was the publication of his first novel, *Al ha-perek* (On the Agenda). After moving to Poltava, the capital city of Lithuania, he taught and became known as a pioneer of Hebrew socialist literature. In 1906,

Rabinovitz emigrated to Palestine, where he worked as a translator, editor, and writer of popular historical novels. He is considered to have written more than 100 books for children and adults. In addition, he inspired younger members of the Second Aliyah (1904–1914), which consisted of young Jews who fled Russia and Eastern Europe in the wake of pogroms in Tsarist Russia and the eruption of anti-Semitism. The Hebrew language was revived as a spoken tongue, and Hebrew literature and Hebrew newspapers contributed to the formation of a new independent state. Rabinovitz played a special role as surrogate father for many of the young Jews who settled in Palestine.

SHLOYME-ZANVL RAPOPORT (pseudonym S. Ansky; 1863–1920) was an extraordinary Yiddish writer and activist who consistently opposed the oppressive laws of the Russian Empire. He is most famous for his Yiddish play *Der dibek: Tsvishn tsvey veltn* (The Dybbuk: Between Two Worlds, 1912–1913), and he demonstrated his commitment to the Russian Jewish Labor Bund by creating its anthem, "Di Shvue" (The Oath). Born in Chashniki, Russia, near Vitebsk, his family was very poor and supported by his mother. Fluent in Russian and Yiddish, Rapoport left his family after finishing elementary school when he was in his teens. Aside from finding various jobs as a tutor and contributing his services to the labor movement, Rapoport published his first novel, *Istoriia odnogosemeiistva* (History of a Family), in 1884, when he was only twenty-one. During his travels in the 1880s and 1890s he lived among the Russian peasants and did all he could to counter their exploitation. At the same time he collected folk songs and tales and gave political talks that led to his arrest by the political authorities. Once released, he continued to demonstrate his dedication to the working class and peasants through organizing and writing until his death.

PAUL SCHLESINGER (1878–1928), considered one of the most famous news reporters and writers during the Weimar Republic, was born in Berlin. He first began working in the textile industry and performed in a cabaret in Munich. It was during this time that he took a great interest in the German courts and became a key reporter for the Ullstein

Publishing House. After working in Paris and Switzerland as a reporter, Schlesinger returned to Berlin in 1921 and became a news reporter for the *Vossische Zeitung*. He also wrote children's books, short stories, and reviews of theater and music. Schlesinger wrote under the nickname Sling and was co-editor of *An den Wassern von Babylon: Ein fast Heiteres Judenbüchlein* (On the Waters of Babylon: An Almost Cheerful Little Book, 1920). He died unexpectedly of a heart attack in 1928.

LEO W. SCHWARZ (1906–1967) was an American essayist and author of two important anthologies of Jewish literature, *The Jewish Caravan* (1935) and *A Golden Treasury of Jewish Literature* (1937). After serving in the U.S. Army during World War II, he became director of operations of the American Jewish Joint Distribution Committee in the U.S. zone in Germany. This committee helped displaced persons and was the subject of Schwarz's novel *The Redeemers* (1953). In 1960, Schwarz became a professor of Judaic studies at the University of Iowa, a position he held until his death.

RACHEL SERI (b. 1944), a storyteller, is featured in *Folktales of the Jews, Volume 1: Tales from the Sephardic Dispersion*, edited by Dan Ben-Amos (2006).

ITSHE MEYER VAYSENBERG (I. M. Vaysenberg; 1881–1938) was born in Zelechow, Poland, into a working-class family. He was recognized early in his life by I. L. Peretz, who published Vaysenberg's first two Yiddish stories in his journal *Di yudische bibliotek* (The Jewish Library) in 1904. These stories already indicated the prime place that Vaysenberg was to occupy in the development of Yiddish literature in the Pale. Peretz was a major influence on Vaysenberg, and in particular on his novella *A Shtetl* (1906), which dealt with social struggles in a traditional hierarchical community. Vaysenberg was a master of naturalism and realism in most of the stories that followed *A Shtehtl* during the 1920s and 1930s, and after Peretz's death in 1915, he mentored many of the younger Yiddish writers by publishing their stories in a literary magazine he edited while he continued to be active in causes related to the labor movement in Poland.

BEATRICE SILVERMAN WEINREICH (1927–2008) was a Jewish writer, folklorist, and editor of *Yiddish Folktales* (1988).

LEO WIENER (1862–1939) was a Russian Jew and later an American historian and linguist. Born in Bialystok, he studied first at the University of Warsaw and then at the Friedrich Wilhelm University in Berlin before emigrating to the United States in 1880. After teaching at the University of Kansas, he returned to Europe to do research on his major work, *The History of Yiddish Literature in the Nineteenth Century* (1899). Upon his return to America in 1896, he was offered a position as professor of Slavic cultures at Harvard University and later translated twenty-four volumes of Leo Tolstoy's works into English.

RUTH WISSE (b. 1936), a distinguished Canadian professor of Yiddish and comparative literature, was born in Czernowitz, which is part of Ukraine. She grew up in Montreal, and later, while teaching at McGill University, she developed an unusual and informative program of Jewish studies. She has done notable work on such books as *If I Am Not for Myself: The Liberal Betrayal of Jews* (1992) and *Jews and Power* (2008), and she has also collaborated with Irving Howe to produce two anthologies of Jewish tales, *The Best of Sholem Aleichem* (1979) and *The Penguin Book of Modern Yiddish Verse* (1988).

ISRAEL ZANGWILL (1864–1926), a British author and Jewish activist, strongly supported Theodor Herzl's Zionist program and, later, a territorial movement for Jews. He was born in London and educated at the Jews' Free School and the University of London, where he received his BA in 1884. He began his writing career early in life and became noticed when he published *Children of the Ghetto: A Study of a Peculiar People* (1892). Moreover, his play *The Melting Pot* (1909) attracted great attention in America. Zangwill believed that racial and religious differences could be respected and overcome. From this point on, Zangwill wrote numerous plays and became involved in Jewish politics, advocating for any territory in which Jews could make their homeland. He also was known for his support of feminism and pacificism, and he continued to support progressive causes until his death.

ARNOLD ZWEIG (1887–1968), a German writer and socialist, was born in Prussian Silesia. After graduating from high school in Kattowitz, Zweig studied the humanities at universities in Berlin, Munich, Tübingen, and Breslau. In 1914 he joined the German army and experienced the anti-Semitism of the Germans when they administered the Jewish census (Judenzählung) to make sure that enough Jews were patriotic. The war led him to become both a pacifist and socialist. During the 1920s, Zweig devoted himself to opposing war and anti-Semitism, and he was influenced by Sigmund Freud's theories. In 1933, when the Nazis gained power in Germany, Zweig fled first to Czechoslovakia, then to France and Switzerland. By 1935 he moved to Palestine, where he helped found a German-language newspaper, the *Orient*, and wrote numerous stories and novels that depicted the negative side of anti-Semitism and war. In 1948, he received a formal invitation from the newly founded East Germany, where he played a major role in the cultural development of the German Democratic Republic until his death in 1968.

CREDITS

"The Ba'al Shem Tov and the Sorcerer" by Rachel Seri, reproduced from *Folktales of the Jews, Volume 1: Tales from the Sephardic Dispersion,* edited by Dan Ben-Amos by permission of the University of Nebraska Press. Copyright © 2006 by The Jewish Publication Society.

The City without Jews: A Novel about the Near Future (1924) by Hugo Bettauer, translated by Salomea Newmark Brainin. New York: Bloch Publishing Company, 1936.

"The Convert" by Dovid Bergelson, in *The Shtetl,* edited and translated by Joachim Neugroschel. Woodstock, NY: Overlook Press, 1989, 269–272.

"The Golem" by I. L. Peretz, translated by Irving Howe, from *A Treasury of Yiddish Stories: Revised and Updated Edition,* edited by Irving Howe and Eliezer Greenberg. Copyright 1953, 1954, © 1989 by Penguin Random House LLC; copyright renewed © 1981, 1982 by Irving Howe and Eva Greenberg. Used by permission of Viking Books, an imprint of Penguin Publishing Group, a division of Penguin Random House LLC. All rights reserved.

"Happiness" by Hersh Dovid Nomberg, from *Radiant Days, Haunted Nights,* translated, compiled, and introduced by Joachim Neugroschel. Copyright © 2005 by Joachim Neugroschel. Used by permission of Overlook Press/Abrams, an imprint of Harry N. Abrams, Inc., New York. All rights reserved.

"A Letter to God" by Meri Balkon, from *Yiddish Folktales* by Beatrice Weinreich, translation. Copyright © 1988 by YIVO Institute for Jewish Research. Used by permission of Pantheon Books, an imprint of the Knopf Doubleday Publishing Group, a division of Penguin Random House LLC. All rights reserved.

"The Penitent: A Tale" (1912) by S. Ansky (Shloyme-Zanvl Rapoport), in *Great Tales of Jewish Fantasy and the Occult,* edited and translated by Joachim Neugroschel. New York: Overlook Press, 1976, 107–113.

"Rabbi Leyb Saves the Jews of Prague from Evil Decrees" by Shmuel Bastomski, from *Radiant Days, Haunted Nights,* translated, compiled, and introduced by Joachim Neugroschel. Copyright © 2005 by Joachim Neugroschel. Used by permission of Overlook Press/Abrams, an imprint of Harry N. Abrams, Inc., New York. All rights reserved.

"The Rebbe of Apte and Tsar Nicholas" by S. Ansky (Shloyme-Zanvl Rapoport), from *Radiant Days, Haunted Nights,* translated, compiled, and introduced by Joachim Neugroschel. Copyright © 2005 by Joachim Neugroschel. Used by permission of Overlook Press/Abrams, an imprint of Harry N. Abrams, Inc., New York. All rights reserved.

"Two Anti-Semites" (1909–1910) by Sholem Aleichem, in *The Best of Sholem Aleichem,* edited and translated by Irving Howe and Ruth Wisse. Washington, DC: New Republic Books, 1979: 115–121.

"The Wedding That Came without Its Band" by Sholem Aleichem, from *Tevye the Dairyman and the Railroad Stories* by Sholem Aleichem, translated by Hillel Halkin, edited by Ruth Wisse. Translation copyright © 1987 by Penguin Random House LLC. Used by permission of Schocken Books, an imprint of the Knopf Doubleday Publishing Group, a division of Penguin Random House LLC. All rights reserved.

Despite diligent efforts, some rightsholders could not be determined or located. We encourage any party claiming licensing authority to contact us.

INDEX

A NOTE ON THE TYPE

This book has been composed in Arno, an Old-style serif typeface in the classic Venetian tradition, designed by Robert Slimbach at Adobe.